ABDUCTED

The private investigator hired by Sally peeked into the living room. But Anna headed toward the dining room and kitchen. One of the dining room chairs was tipped over. It was the chair closest to the kitchen entrance. "Hey!" Anna called to the man.

She turned around and realized he was right behind her.

"Don't touch anything," he said. Brushing past her, he moved around the corner into the kitchen. The sharp, burning smell came from there. Anna was almost afraid to follow him. She thought the worst. She imagined finding Taylor dead on the kitchen floor.

Covering her nose and mouth from the stench, she stepped around the corner. It was a modern kitchen with stainless steel appliances, granite countertops, and a subway-tile backsplash. After the smoke, the next thing Anna noticed was the dark red puddle on the black-and-white tiled floor.

"I'll go check the bathroom and bedroom," Anna said.

Sally's man put his hand out to stop her. "No, don't go anywhere, and don't touch anything. Let me speak to Sally first, and then the police."

Anna was obedient. A hand still over her nose and mouth, she stood there and waited while the private investigator phoned Taylor's mother.

All Anna could think was that "Bud" had found himself another deaf girl . . .

Books by Kevin O'Brien

ONLY SON

THE NEXT TO DIE

MAKE THEM CRY

WATCH THEM DIE

LEFT FOR DEAD

THE LAST VICTIM

KILLING SPREE

ONE LAST SCREAM

FINAL BREATH

VICIOUS

DISTURBED

TERRIFIED

UNSPEAKABLE

TELL ME YOU'RE
SORRY

NO ONE NEEDS
TO KNOW

YOU'LL MISS ME
WHEN I'M GONE

HIDE YOUR FEAR

THEY WON'T BE
HURT

THE BETRAYED WIFE

THE BAD SISTER

THE NIGHT SHE
DISAPPEARED

Published by Kensington Publishing Corp.

THE NIGHT SHE DISAPPEARED

KEVIN O'BRIEN

PINNACLE BOOKS
Kensington Publishing Corp.
www.kensingtonbooks.com

PINNACLE BOOKS are published by

Kensington Publishing Corp.
119 West 40th Street
New York, NY 10018

All Kensington titles, imprints, and distributed lines are available at special quantity discounts for bulk purchases for sales promotions, premiums, fund-raising, educational, or institutional use. Special book excerpts or customized printings can also be created to fit specific needs. For details, write or phone the office of the Kensington sales manager: Kensington Publishing Corp., 119 West 40th Street, New York, NY 10018, attn: Sales Department; phone 1-800-221-2647.

PINNACLE BOOKS and the Pinnacle logo are Reg. U.S. Pat. & TM Off.

First Pinnacle printing: August 2021

10 9 8 7 6 5 4 3 2 1

ISBN-13: 978-0-7860-4509-9
ISBN-10: 0-7860-4509-4

Printed in the United States of America

Electronic edition: August 2021

ISBN-13: 978-0-7860-4512-9 (e-book)
ISBN-10: 0-7860-4512-4 (e-book)

This book is for my dear friend,
Marlys Bourm.

ACKNOWLEDGMENTS

Here's a huge Thank-You to my brilliant editor and good friend, John Scognamiglio, and the remarkably talented team of pros at Kensington Books. Without you, I'm nothing!

Thanks also to my agents, Meg Ruley, Christina Hogrebe, and everyone at Jane Rotrosen Agency.

I'm in debt to my Writers Group for helping me get this book off the ground: David Massengill, Garth Stein, Colin McArthur, and Sasha Im. And speaking of writers, my old Seattle 7 Writers pals have always had my back, especially Garth, Dave Boling, Erica Bauermeister, Terry Brooks, Lynn Brunelle, Carol Cassella, Bridget Foley, Laurie Frankel, Elizabeth George, Suzanne Selfors, Jennie Shortridge, Stephen Susco, and Susan Wiggs. Thanks, you guys!

Another great big thank-you goes to my fellow Kensington author, Carlene O'Connor, for helping me with my research on hearing loss and sign language. Thanks also to John Flick for answering so many pesky questions about TV news reporting. And thanks to my wonderful proofreader/editor, Cathy Johnson, who always does an amazing job of correcting my typos, bad grammar, inconsistencies, and inaccuracies before anyone else sees them.

A special thank-you goes to Jim Munchel and the late Jennifer Musser (1971–2020) for hand-selling so many of my books.

And a special shout-out to the terrific team at Reader-Link Distribution Services.

I'd also like to thank the following friends and groups, who have been incredibly supportive: Dan Annear and Chuck Rank, Jeff Ayers, Ben Bauermeister, Dante and Pattie Bellini, A Book for All Seasons, The Book Stall, Amanda Brooks, Judine Brooks, George Camper and Shane White, Barb and John Cegielski, Barb and Jim Church, Marti Converse, Anna Cottle and Mary Alice Kier, Paul Dwoskin, Eagle Harbor Books, Elliott Bay Book Company, Margaret Freeman, Matt Gani, The Girls Gone Wild Reading Books, Cate Goethals and Tom Goodwin, Bob and Dana Gold, Island Books, Elizabeth Kinsella, David Korabik, Stafford Lombard, Susan London, Paul Mariz, John and Tammy and Lucas Millsap, Roberta Miner, Dan Monda, Debbie Monda, Deborah Neff, my wonderful friends from Sacred Heart School, Mike Sack and John Saul, Eva Marie Saint, Michael Schuler, the cool gang at Shelf Awareness, John Simmons and Scott Hulet, Roseann Stella, Dan Stutesman, George and Sheila Stydahar, Marc Von Borstel, and Ruth Young.

Finally, thanks to my marvelous sibs and their families. Adele, Mary Lou, Cathy, Bill, and Joan . . . I love you to smithereens.

"For a moment, I couldn't move. My heart was racing. I couldn't believe what I'd just done. But then something clicked, and I suddenly realized I had to clean up all the blood. I grabbed a towel out of the bathroom and wrapped it around her head."

—Excerpt: Session 3, audio recording
with Dr. G. Tolman, July 23

CHAPTER ONE

Friday, July 10—9:13 A.M.
Seattle

Anna Malone woke up to her phone ringing. But for a few seconds, she didn't move.

Her head ached and throbbed. It hurt just to roll over—away from the phone. She didn't even want to open her eyes.

Thankfully, the phone went to voice mail.

Her mouth was pasty, and she felt dehydrated. Where the hell was her night guard?

She'd had *way* too much to drink last night.

Now it was coming back to her: feeling so tense and uncomfortable, sitting in that elegant restaurant with Russ and Courtney, and wishing the entire time that a hole would open up in the floor so she could just slide under the table and disappear. What was the name of the drink Courtney had ordered for her again and again? *Lemon Drop*. Anna wondered how many she'd put away. She'd lost track after three.

She barely recalled anything else. She must have blacked out.

It took Anna another few moments to realize she wasn't in her own bed. That was why the room was so hot and bright. The shade wasn't down, and the sun streamed through the window. She could feel it against her face.

Grimacing, she opened her eyes. "Oh shit," she muttered.

She was in her mother's bedroom.

She still called it that sometimes—even though her mom had been dead for twelve years. The compact little room was now Anna's office, with a daybed for guests—though she rarely had any.

Back when she'd been in high school, when she and her mother had first moved into the Lake Union floating home, this had been Anna's bedroom. Her mom had had the bigger bedroom upstairs. But then, after only a few months, the steep, narrow stairs that led up to those quarters became too much of a challenge for her mom. She was only fifty but claimed her balance was failing her, so she wanted to be on the main level, closer to the bathroom.

The truth was, in the course of those few months, her mother had become an alcoholic. That was why they'd switched rooms and Anna had gotten the master bedroom upstairs. Her mother was usually too drunk or hungover to make it up and down those steep steps.

She used to stay sober long enough to punch in and out at Macy's, where she was a clerk in Kitchenware. Then she'd come back to their charming little floating home and get quietly smashed on bourbon and water while watching TV. Anna's mother wasn't a mean drunk. She'd merely become sleepy, sloppy, and out of it by the fourth drink. But she always stayed sweet.

Looking back, Anna knew she was pretty pissy and impatient with her poor mother, who, after all, had been through hell. Anna regretted how bratty she'd been back then—always rolling her eyes at her mother. But at the time, she felt that, if her mother could stay sober at work, couldn't she stay sober for her at least one or two nights during the week? Anna used to do all the cooking, and she remembered some evenings acting as if it was a major burden to fix their dinner and clean up afterward. Occasionally, her mother would insist on washing the dinner dishes. But Anna would only have to wash them over again, because her well-meaning, inebriated mom did such a crappy job of it.

Anna still didn't have a dishwasher, and sometimes, when she noticed a spot of food she'd missed on a dish in the drying rack, she would think she was becoming just like her mother.

That was why Anna rarely drank more than one glass of wine a night.

And that was why she hated waking up in her mother's old bedroom, barely remembering anything from the night before. This was a first for Anna, and a wave of panic went through her. What the hell had happened? How did she get here?

She rolled over again, sending a jolt to her aching head. She grabbed the phone off the end table and squinted at the time. She should have been at work an hour ago.

Throwing back the bedsheet, Anna realized she was wearing—along with her panties—a semidressy, striped tee from J.Crew. She usually wore a large, old T-shirt to bed. It made no sense that she'd decided to sleep in this seventy-nine-dollar top.

She staggered into the bathroom, turned on the cold water at the sink, and slurped from the faucet. She was dying of thirst. After splashing some water on her face, she winced at her reflection in the mirror. She was thirty-one, but this morning, she looked more like fifty. *Rode hard and put away wet*, as her mother used to say. Her face was pale and droopy, her green eyes bloodshot, and her shoulder-length, cinnamon-colored hair was a hopeless mess.

A major part of Anna's job was appearing presentable. She was a reporter for KIXI-TV News. Fortunately, she didn't have to be in front of the cameras until six o'clock tonight. But she'd missed this morning's editorial meeting. She also needed to edit a feature story for the evening's telecast, a piece she'd been working on for most of the week. She and her cameraman, George, had an editing room reserved for nine this morning. And they still had to record her voice-over.

The story was about Courtney Knoll, her dinner companion from last night—the Lemon Drop pusher. Anna had known Courtney for about a month—a miserable, confusing, conflicted month. She'd known *about* Courtney for over a year before that.

Anna took two aspirins and slurped them down with more water from the faucet. While brushing her teeth, she staggered into the kitchen and turned on the coffeemaker.

The phone rang again. Anna spit out the toothpaste in the kitchen sink, rinsed out her mouth, and hurried into the office to answer the phone. She figured it was probably George at work. They had the editing room only until noon.

She snatched the phone from the end table and saw

Russ was calling. She clicked on the phone. "Hey . . ." she murmured.

"How are you feeling?"

"Like I should get the license plate number of the truck that hit me," Anna replied, rubbing her eyes. "My head's about to explode. I overslept. I'm still home. Did you try calling me earlier?"

"Yeah, about ten minutes ago. So—I'm guessing you haven't heard from Courtney this morning."

"Let me see. Give me a sec." Anna checked her missed texts and e-mails. Her hands were trembling. Was this what people called *the shakes*? She took a deep breath, tried to steady herself, and got back on the line. "Um, looks like you're the only one who called. Listen, what—what happened last night? I don't remember anything after the restaurant . . ." Her voice started to crack. "It's really scaring me . . ."

"I'm sorry," he said, sighing. "It's Courtney's fault. She kept reordering drinks, and you kept telling her that you'd had enough. By the time we left Canlis, you were pretty wasted. Courtney insisted you come by our place for coffee—"

"I had coffee at your place?"

"You were at our place, but the coffee never got brewed. Once we returned from the restaurant, Courtney headed straight for the liquor cabinet, and the last thing she needed was a nightcap. She started to get nasty—to me and especially to you . . ."

"Were there accusations?" Anna asked warily.

"She didn't come out and actually say anything, but

she made a few insinuations. I couldn't take any more. So I drove you home—"

"You drove me?" she asked. Russ and Courtney's $2 million floating home was two docks down on Lake Union from her place, only a ten-minute walk away.

"Well, you could barely stand," Russ said. "By the time we reached your place, you got sick. You just made it to the head. I cleaned you up, gave you an aspirin, and put you to bed."

Anna didn't remember any of it. She still had the shakes. She hadn't felt this awful since she'd had the flu two years ago. She glanced down at her J.Crew tee again and realized Russ must have put it on her, thinking it was a pajama top. "So you tucked me in. Well, thanks . . ." She headed into the kitchen. "What time was that?"

"Around midnight. I wasn't ready to go back for more abuse. So I drove around for a couple of hours. When I finally came home, Courtney was gone . . ."

Anna poured her coffee. A few drops spilled on the countertop. "What do you mean 'gone'?"

"Just what I said, *gone*. No note, no message, nothing. Looks like she took her overnight bag. She must have Ubered. Her car is still in the lot. I guess she was smart enough not to drive while drunk. Anyway, I thought she might have texted you this morning to apologize. After all, you're airing that promo piece on her tonight . . ."

Anna sipped her coffee. "Well, like I say, I haven't heard from her. Has Courtney ever done this before?"

"You mean, packed a bag and disappeared? No, this is something new, and I'm going nuts here . . ."

"I'm sure that's exactly what she wants you to do." Anna sighed. "Are you at work?"

"Yeah," he said. "Anyway, I have a feeling that, before she contacts me, Courtney will get in touch with you—if for no other reason than to make sure you don't yank her story off the news tonight. She's been counting on it to boost her book sales. Could you do me a big favor and let me know as soon as you hear from her? Maybe find out where she is, too . . ."

"Sure, no problem." Anna was getting impatient with him. She glanced at the clock on the microwave. "Listen, I need to go. I'll call you as soon as I hear from her, okay?"

"Okay, I'll—"

"Bye," she said, cutting him off.

Then she hung up before he could say anything else.

She hated how upset he sounded—as if his wife packing a bag and leaving was the worst thing that could happen. Hell, wasn't something along those lines just what Russ had been hoping for these past several months? Weren't they planning to split up anyway?

That was what Russ had told her. Or was that just something married men said to their gullible girlfriends?

No, Russ wasn't like that.

He'd mentioned that Courtney's car was still there in the boat slip's private lot. For a moment, Anna imagined a drunken Courtney with her suitcase, stumbling off the dock, falling into the water, and hitting her head on one of the pilings.

That would be one solution, she thought.

She immediately felt awful for even letting such an idea enter her head. For the last year, her number one concern had been that no one got hurt. And here she was imagining how convenient it would be if Courtney were dead.

She didn't mean it.

Anna told herself that her thinking was muddled because of this horrible hangover.

She wished she could remember what had happened last night after the restaurant. She'd never blacked out or "lost time" before in her life.

Did Courtney know about Russ and her? Russ had said she'd "made a few insinuations." But he didn't elaborate. Whatever was said, for Anna, it felt like there was no going back to the way things had been for her and Russ this past year. Either the two of them would move forward, or he'd reconcile with Courtney. It was why Anna hated to hear him sound so worried. It was the sound of a husband ready to reconcile with his spouse.

Anna kept going back to last night, wishing she could remember exactly what had happened and what had been said. But it was all muddled.

For now, she'd just have to take Russ's word about everything that had occurred.

Still a bit shaky, Anna took another gulp of coffee and started to get ready for work.

CHAPTER TWO

The woman on the computer screen was strikingly beautiful with long, chestnut-colored hair, big brown eyes, and full lips. She wore a simple, elegant, sleeveless white blouse that showed off her tan. She looked smart, sexy, and sophisticated. But when she opened her mouth, out came a halting voice that seemed to belong to a breathy, young Southern girl.

Anna knew it would jar TV viewers when they first heard Courtney Knoll speak. They'd expect her voice to sound as refined as she looked. But then they'd see her gesturing and using sign language, and they'd finally realize that Courtney Knoll was deaf.

Courtney had grown up in Florida, and lost her hearing because of a bout with measles when she was eight. Anna made sure that fact came up early in the segment so that viewers would understand why Courtney spoke the way she did. It was as if her voice was locked in the time before she'd lost her hearing.

Anna sat in front of the computer with George Danziger, a lean, still boyishly cute thirty-eight-year-old. Anna thought he looked like Sam Rockwell, a comparison he frequently got from others, too. George had been the videographer on nearly all her stories. Anna always asked for him.

She'd been working at KIXI-TV for two years. At the start, she'd had a little crush on George. But he was married with two kids. So Anna had managed to suppress those romantic notions. Still, she picked up an occasional vibe that he was attracted to her. Fortunately, neither one of them ever acted on their unspoken feelings. Anna didn't want to jeopardize their working relationship or screw up yet another marriage.

She and George knew each other so well. Most of the time, they talked in shorthand and finished each other's sentences. She rarely had to tell him how to shoot a subject. George automatically knew how she wanted things to look.

Anna could usually read his moods—and vice versa. George seemed kind of off today—subdued and serious. Anna had figured he wasn't happy with her for being late this morning. She'd apologized as soon as she'd staggered in. They were in Editing Bay B, one of four small offices with a sliding glass door off the main newsroom. George had waved away her apology with a "Don't sweat the small stuff." He'd already edited some of the piece without her— from the script she'd written late yesterday afternoon.

Anna was on her third cup of coffee and second round of aspirin. Her head still ached—a dull pain that echoed the insufferable throbbing from two hours ago.

It was impossible for her to look at the sound bites of Courtney without wondering what had happened to her. A part of Anna still clung to the idea that Courtney had deliberately disappeared just to screw with Russ's head and teach him a lesson. But during the last couple of hours, she'd begun to think maybe something far more serious had happened.

"I just had a weird thought," George said. Slouched in his chair, he popped a couple of pieces of Trident into his mouth. "Do you think we ought to have someone double-check the sign language—just to make sure it all makes sense? I mean, we have no idea what she's signing, or if it matches what she's saying."

Clicking the mouse, Anna paused the video on the computer screen. She squinted at him. "Why wouldn't it match what's coming out of her mouth?"

He shrugged. "I don't know. There are a lot of variations in sign language. Do you know what she's signing here?"

"I get some of it—or enough," Anna said. But that was a stretch. She'd picked up a bit of sign language from her interactions with Courtney during the past month. And for the last three days, Anna and George had been closely working with her—shooting segments on Courtney and Russ's beautiful houseboat, at Courtney's book signing, and at some of the Seattle locales in her latest book: Gas Works Park, the Fremont neighborhood, and the University of Washington campus. Anna figured she understood about 20 percent of what Courtney was signing. Then again, she wondered how well she'd comprehend Courtney if they turned off the audio right now.

She pinched the bridge of her nose. "I ask you again, why would she be signing something different from what's coming out of her mouth?"

"Well, for instance, I had a buddy who shot a story once about a charter boat capsizing, and the captain only spoke Swedish. The captain was a real son of a bitch. This guy on the crew interpreted for him, and what he said was all bullshit. He went on and on about how grateful the captain was to the Coast Guard for their help. Meanwhile, the asshole captain—in Swedish—was calling the Coast Guard guys imbeciles and throwing around the Swedish equivalent of a lot of four-letter words. No one bothered to double-check what the interpreter said. The piece ran on the news, and the station got flooded with calls from people who knew Swedish."

Anna shook her head in disbelief. "Okay, well, that's a real cute story. But why in the world would Courtney deliberately sabotage her own segment?"

"It's not her segment," George replied. "It's yours. You're the one responsible for it."

Anna looked at Courtney on the computer screen— frozen in midsentence, her eyes closed, her mouth open, and her expressive hands perfectly still.

Courtney's first two books, a romance and a thriller, published by a tiny press, didn't earn her a dime. But four years ago, her first young adult novel—*The Defective Squad*—was picked up by a major publisher. The edgy, fast-paced thriller featured a band of four disabled American teens—sort of *X-Men* meets *Stranger Things*. Each teen had a gift: the blind seventeen-year-old white kid had the ability to tune in and listen to conversations miles away, while his Black sixteen-year-old deaf girl-friend could see through walls; the mute Native American girl, also sixteen, took on the shapes and capabilities of her animal spirit totems, and the fifteen-year-old Samoan American paraplegic used his wheelchair to fly at jet speed.

Anna had read *The Defective Squad* in two days and found it exciting, but silly and cringeworthy at times. Some of the online reviews—including ones from readers with disabilities—called the book "insulting," "laugh-out-loud ignorant," "condescending," and "pandering, with something to offend everyone." Still, *The Defective Squad* was a modest success. So Courtney followed it up with a sequel, *Blind Fury*, which did an even better business. Her new book in the series, *Silent Rage*, was just released last week. At the same time, a major Hollywood production company announced its intention to film the whole series—on location, in Seattle.

This seemed to make Courtney's book release newsworthy. At least that was what the station head and the news director thought. After all, *Twilight* had put Forks, Washington, on the map. And after one look at Courtney's photo, nearly all the men in the newsroom wanted to work with her or know more about her. But Courtney had specifically asked for her *friend* Anna to cover the story. It was one of those assignments Anna couldn't wriggle out of.

She couldn't very well tell the station head or the news director that she and Courtney were hardly friends—or that she was sleeping with Courtney's husband.

When Anna and George had prepared the shooting schedule, he'd pointed out that the story about Courtney seemed like little more than a promotional piece. He didn't think it was newsworthy at all.

But then, Anna rarely covered hard-hitting news items. Most of her segments were offbeat, human-interest stories—sometimes funny, sometimes heartwarming or inspirational. Back before KIXI, when she'd been working at a station in Spokane, they'd gotten word about a local farmer who had amassed a collection of potatoes that resembled famous people, and everyone in the newsroom had said without hesitation: "Well, here's one Anna can cover."

Lightweight as her segments seemed, they were always the stories that garnered the most viewer feedback, the segments people were talking about around the water-cooler at work the next day. Her segments were often picked up by affiliate stations—and sometimes by the network. Her stories had heart, and she did them well.

Anna wondered if Russ's wife was truly interested in her TV-reporting skills. Or had Courtney picked her with an ulterior motive in mind? At times, Anna was absolutely certain that Courtney knew about her and Russ and sadistically relished this whole setup. It was so perverse, employing her husband's mistress to produce a promotional piece about her. Anna wondered how far Courtney planned to push her and manipulate her into getting what she wanted. And what exactly did Courtney hope to gain from this uneasy alliance?

To Anna's total surprise, Courtney was warm and friendly to her during the shoot. She'd studied Anna's work and often brought up different news stories she'd done: "Maybe we could have a shot of me in my favorite coffee place, you know—like you did in your profile of that teacher from a couple of months ago."

Anna found that she liked pleasing Courtney and lapped up her compliments. It was a hazard of the job, becoming a fan of her subjects. She wouldn't have admitted it to anyone, but Anna also got immediate satisfaction from helping someone with a disability. Seeing Courtney sign *thank you* to her filled her with pride. And after some studying online, she got a kick out of being able to sign certain words and phrases back to Courtney.

Anna started to hate herself for what she and Russ were doing behind Courtney's back. But if Courtney knew about them, she didn't let on at all.

Then, after a couple of days, Anna realized she'd handed most of the control on the project over to Courtney. It irritated the hell out of George. For example, Anna found it fascinating that, at age nineteen, Courtney had had cochlear implants that had marginally increased her hearing capacity. She kept the required external hardware hidden under her thick chestnut brown hair. Anna never caught a glimpse of the microphone behind Courtney's ear and a recharger near the back of her skull. Anna could have done a whole series on how these implants helped different hearing-impaired people. But Courtney didn't want it mentioned at all, because some members of the deaf community thought the procedure negated deaf culture and its own communication system of signing. Courtney didn't want to risk alienating any potential fans by mentioning that she'd had the controversial operation. So the topic was verboten.

Courtney also told Anna that she could show only preselected photos of her with her husband. She also didn't want them to interview Russ or her mother. And she wouldn't talk about the two unsuccessful books before the *Defectives* series, written under her maiden name.

Anna and George had spent the better part of Wednesday afternoon at Courtney's floating home, where they filmed her tutoring sign language to an eleven-year-old deaf boy. She'd supported herself as an American Sign Language tutor before the book sales took off.

"To find clients," she explained in the sound bite, signing as she spoke, "I used to go around to doctors' and pediatricians' offices and leave my card and my résumé. That's how I met my husband, Russ. He was a pediatrician at one of those offices."

The eleven-year-old was adorable, and they got some cute scenes with Courtney and him interacting at her kitchen counter. But the following day, Courtney let it slip that she hadn't actually tutored in three years, and the kid had been a former student.

George was livid. He wanted to toss out the entire tutoring scene because it was merely an act. Rather than scrap the whole thing, Anna reduced the scene to a twelve-second sound bite. It was a compromise to please Courtney. Anna and George fought over it. In fact, it was one of the worst fights they'd ever had.

Anna had figured Courtney would have tried harder to make friends with the cameraman. After all, George was the one who made her look good. She remembered Courtney once telling her how annoying it was when she used an interpreter and people speaking to her would look at the interpreter instead of her. So it seemed kind of strange that Courtney always addressed Anna as if she interpreted for George. *"Tell the cameraman I don't want that side of the living room in the shot, because you can see out the window and someone might figure out where I live."* She'd said this with George seven feet away from her, right there in the room. Maybe because she couldn't see his face behind the camera, Courtney felt she couldn't talk directly to him. Still, it was odd. Even when George wasn't holding the camera in front of him, Courtney often treated him like he was invisible.

"Listen, I don't blame you for not being a fan," Anna said, sipping her coffee. On the computer screen in front of them, Courtney was still frozen in midsentence. "If she wasn't very friendly to you, I think you can chalk it up to her being nervous and on edge about the shoot."

"I can't believe you're making excuses for her." George shook his head. "The reason I'm not a fan is because it was pretty clear to me—and obviously not to you—that she doesn't like you at all. God knows why."

Anna glanced at the computer screen—and the still image of Courtney holding her hands in front of her as she signed. The engagement and wedding rings gleamed on the third finger of her left hand.

"I see you bending over backward to please her," George continued. "I've seen you do that before with different people we've profiled, but not to this extent. I know you want to make allowances for her because she's deaf. But what baffles me is why you're even friends with her. The entire time we've worked with her, I've had this feeling she has something on you—as if you *owed* her. Do you actually even like her?"

Anna just shrugged uneasily.

"That's what I thought. This whole puff piece was motivated by guilt."

She gave him a narrow look. "Why would you say that?"

"Because you can hear," he replied. "And ever since she was eight, she hasn't been able to hear anything. No Beatles, no Ella Fitzgerald, no Springsteen, no waves splashing on the shore, no sounds of children laughing. So you're motivated by guilt."

That wasn't why Anna felt guilty in regard to Courtney. But obviously, in just three days, George had picked up on something she hadn't about Russ's wife: Courtney had been manipulating her all this time.

Anna let out a long sigh. "Well, even if she's a total bitch and hates my guts, I sincerely doubt Courtney would purposely screw up a promotional piece that benefits her more than anyone else. I mean, why would she shoot herself in the foot like that?"

"Just what I said, maybe to bring you down," George explained.

Anna realized he might be right. What if—while she verbalized about something else in her little-girl voice—Courtney was signing and trashing the reporter responsible for this piece? Was that even possible? Could someone do that, sign and speak two different messages at the same time? Wasn't it like simultaneously rubbing your belly and patting your head?

If Courtney was out to destroy her, Anna wondered just how far she was willing to go.

She glanced at her wristwatch. "Well, I guess it wouldn't hurt to get someone to check her signing before this goes on the air tonight."

George nodded. "Good." He clicked on the video, and it resumed playing. Courtney broke out of her frozen pose and began talking and gesturing once more.

"So—you'll contact an American Sign Language interpreter to double-check that what Courtney's signing matches what she's saying." He pointed to the screen. "I think after this bit, we could insert the first book cover and then dissolve to that sweeping shot of Gas Works Park."

Two hours later, a sign language expert confirmed that everything Courtney had signed matched what she'd said.

Anna left Courtney two text messages, letting her know that thirteen affiliates had already picked up the story. It was a major publicity coup for her book release. Anna figured that ought to get a response out of her.

But she never heard back.

She did, however, receive a text from Russ at 4:52 P.M.:

Just spoke to C's agent. C has been texting/talking to her every day since book release last week. And today, nothing. Am really worried now. Call if you hear from her. Sorry about this. xxx

Anna's segment ran on the six o'clock news—right after the weather. It made Courtney out to be warm, friendly, smart, and down-to-earth—a poster girl for the deaf community, as well as the talented author of a series of books that inspired teenagers everywhere.

As the piece wrapped, Anna felt like such a hypocrite, live, on camera, sitting at the news desk, singing Courtney's praises and pushing her stupid books.

And all the while, Anna couldn't help wondering if Courtney was putting the screws to Russ and her with this disappearing act.

Then again, maybe it wasn't an act at all.

CHAPTER THREE

Friday, July 10— 7:11 P.M.

As she turned left off Eastlake Avenue, Anna had a feeling she'd find some jerk's car in her parking spot. It hadn't happened in a while, but considering her awful day so far, she figured the shitty streak hadn't quite ended yet.

She never understood how people rationalized parking in a spot clearly marked PRIVATE PARKING —VIOLATORS WILL BE TOWED. Maybe they thought if they got away with it, then they didn't really do anything wrong. Perhaps they told themselves, *It will only be for a few minutes* or *Everybody does it*. Nice people always had rationalizations for their bad behavior. Or maybe they were just assholes.

A breeze off the lake swept through the open car window. Anna told herself to perk up. She didn't have to go back to the station for tonight's eleven o'clock newscast. They were repeating her segment without her live intro and wrap-up. Before leaving the studio, she'd washed off her HDTV makeup and changed into a pink sleeveless top and khakis. Unless they called her during the weekend with an emergency assignment, she didn't have to work until Monday morning.

And her headache was gone.

It was a gorgeous evening. She planned to order some cashew chicken from the local Thai place. She'd walk over to the restaurant, pick up dinner, and bring it back to eat in front of a movie on Netflix.

And she'd try not to obsess over Courtney.

Cruising down the narrow street that ran parallel to Lake Union, Anna looked at the long, slightly dilapidated carport in the distance. Under its moss-covered, corrugated tin roof, the carport sheltered a dozen vehicles— all of them belonging to residents of the floating homes off the two nearby docks.

One of the drawbacks to owning a floating home was that parking wasn't nearby. Anna had to walk about two blocks from the car to her front door. It wasn't too bad, unless she had a ton of groceries or it was raining. When it was dark, she sometimes got spooked walking by herself down that shadowy, tree-lined road close to the water's edge.

That had been particularly true last fall, when she'd had a stalker. Somebody had attempted to break into her house; then her Mini Cooper had been keyed in the carport. She'd also had countless calls and hang-ups at all sorts of hours. For two weeks, she'd endured other little acts of sabotage, and she'd called the police on several occasions. Then, the harassment had stopped just as abruptly as it had begun. The police never found out who had been responsible.

For a while, she'd suspected Courtney. She'd figured Russ's wife had found out about them, and this was her revenge. But Anna had told herself she was just feeling guilty and paranoid. Her stalker was probably someone who had seen her on TV. Maybe he—or she—didn't like one of her news stories. She was a public figure. It came with the job sometimes.

Yet, occasionally, Anna got a feeling that the culprit was still out there watching her, ready to start up again and make her life miserable.

Right now, it was still light out. People were walking or jogging along the side of the road, and boats were out on Lake Union. Anna heard laughter and music in the distance.

As she pulled closer to the carport, she saw her spot was empty. Maybe her night would be okay after all.

She backed her blue four-year-old Mini Cooper into the spot. She was just climbing out of the car when her phone rang.

Stepping out from under the cool shade of the carport, she checked the name on the caller ID: *Russell Knoll, MD*. Anna clicked on the phone. "So, have you heard from Courtney?"

"No, I was hoping she'd watched your segment and called you."

"Nope, sorry," Anna muttered. "After the broadcast, I left her another text message. That makes three unanswered texts I've left for her today."

The voice mail greeting on Courtney's phone hadn't been her usual recording. Instead, each time Anna had called, she'd gotten an automated message from the provider. It made her wonder if Courtney's phone was out of commission. Was the battery dead? Anna figured Russ had gotten the same impersonal greeting when he'd called his wife. So she didn't say anything. But it was troubling.

"Well, your segment was terrific," Russ said. "I figured, for sure, Courtney would text you after seeing that."

"Thanks," Anna said. She started walking toward her dock. "Anyway, she didn't get in touch with me. You sure she didn't go to your cabin on Whidbey Island?"

"Positive. I checked with the neighbors. They have a key. They said the place is empty." He paused. "God, I'm so torn. Part of me is like, *good riddance*. But I'm terrified something bad has happened to her. And I miss you. I really want to be with you right now, even if it's just for a walk."

Anna hesitated. "I don't think that's a good idea, Russ."

"Are you mad at me or something?"

She sighed. "No, I'm just tired . . ."

"Boy, do I feel like an idiot."

"Why?"

"Because I thought you'd be happy to see me. Turn around."

Anna stopped. "What do you mean?"

A woman jogger ran past her.

"Turn around," Russ repeated.

Anna obeyed and saw him about a hundred feet behind her. Russ had the phone close to his ear. He stood six feet four inches tall and had a swimmer's build. He was handsome with thick, wavy black hair and brown eyes. In his sage-colored polo shirt, khaki shorts, and sandals, he looked like a J.Crew model, the summer catalog.

As the woman jogger passed him, she slowed down to check him out. Then she moved on. Women—and quite a few men—were constantly checking him out, and he was oblivious.

Anna gave him a tentative wave. "Hi," she said into the phone.

"Can I walk you home at least?"

"Sure," she said, working up a smile, which quickly faded. "So, is Courtney's car still in the parking lot?"

She saw him nod as he walked toward her. "Yeah," he answered on the phone. "I checked the house, and it doesn't look like she's been back. I even left a voice mail with her mother on the off chance Courtney's been in touch with her. I haven't heard back yet. It's really driving me crazy."

"I'm sure that's her intention!" Anna called to him as she put away her phone.

She watched him slip the phone into his pants pocket as he approached her. He shook his head. "I'm sorry to go on about this, honey," he said. Russ cautiously glanced around and then drew her close and briefly kissed her on the lips. "How are you doing? Feeling any better?"

She nodded. "Better than this morning. It'll be a cold day in hell before I ever drink another Lemon Drop."

He put his arm around her as they started walking. "I think I'm starting to get your headache. I've been a wreck all day. I can't help thinking that something's happened to her."

"You said she packed a bag," Anna pointed out. "That's usually an indication someone has gone away of their own volition."

"I know, that's what I keep telling myself. At the same time, I wonder if I should call the police. I keep going back and forth about it. I don't want to jump the gun. She hasn't been missing twenty-four hours yet. And like you say, the packed bag's an indication . . ."

Anna squirmed away from him.

"I'm sorry, I'm sorry," Russ said. "I'll shut up. I know you don't want to hear it. But you can't expect me not to worry about her."

"Of course you're going to worry about her." Anna sighed. "And I really don't mind you talking about it. I just feel a little ridiculous hearing it while you have your arm around me."

Russ shoved his hand in his pocket. "I was right earlier. You're mad at me, aren't you?"

Anna shook her head. "No, I'm just disappointed in how this is all—evolving. For a while, the last thing I wanted to do was break up your marriage. I never thought of myself as a homewrecker. But then, I knew you were miserable. I kept hoping you'd pack a bag and walk out on her. Instead, last night, Courtney did the packing and walking. And now you're worried about her. She's not here, and yet she's still making you jump through hoops. The kicker is, I can't really blame you for letting her do that to you, Russ. I mean, I don't even like her. Yet, an hour ago, on the news, I sang her praises to half of Seattle. I don't even like her writing, for God's sake. So Courtney's been controlling me, too. And like you, I'm worried. If something serious has happened to her, we'll never forgive ourselves. And if she's purposely disappeared just to screw with our heads, I'm worried you and she are going to reconcile."

Anna turned down a short path to the chain-link gate to the dock. A wood placard was attached to the gate: PRIVATE PROPERTY—NO TRESPASSING. Russ opened the gate for her, and they both stepped down onto the wooden dock. Seagulls squawked overhead. A gentle breeze drifted off the lake. Anna could smell someone barbecuing dinner on an outdoor grill.

"I promise you, Courtney and I are finished," Russ said, shutting the gate behind them. "I'm sorry she beat me to the punch and left first. But the point is—she and I aren't getting back together after this. We're done."

"Meanwhile, she's putting us through the wringer, isn't she?" Anna said.

They passed the other floating homes off the dock. Anna noticed her neighbors out on their deck—with the grill smoking. Ordinarily, she would have held on to Russ's hand, but not now. She waved and nodded at the older couple and kept walking toward her place at the end of the dock.

Anna often referred to her home as a houseboat, but it didn't sail out on the water, so technically her place was a floating home. The cedar shake–style bungalow had a fresh coat of white trim. There was a deck in the back, and a second deck off the boxy-looking master bedroom loft upstairs. The front door was painted red, with a port-hole window beside it. The potted azaleas by the entrance were in full bloom.

"Anyway, Courtney's gone," Anna whispered, reaching into her purse for her keys. "But we can't exactly kick up our heels about it, not until one of us hears from her—or her lawyer."

"I'll know more by tomorrow afternoon," Russ said. "Courtney has a book signing at noon on Bainbridge Island, Eagle Harbor Books. If she doesn't show up for that, well, then I'll know for sure something's wrong. She wouldn't miss one of her author events. Courtney could have triple pneumonia, and she'd still drag herself to a book signing."

"In the meantime, you and I can't afford to be seen together," Anna said. She unlocked the door and turned to face him. "What if something really did happen to Courtney, and you end up calling the police tomorrow to report her missing? I can just hear it now. *So what did you do on that first night after your wife went missing, Dr. Knoll?—Why, I took a nice, little stroll with my mistress and hung out with her for a while. Is there anything wrong with that?*"

She collected her mail from the box. "Anyway, in answer to your question ages ago, no, I'm not really mad at you. It's the whole situation I'm mad at."

Russ nodded sheepishly. "I understand. And I agree. It's just there's a part of me that feels like we're finally free, and I want to start my life with you right now."

He leaned in close. His mouth brushed against hers.

Anna pulled away. She glanced out at all the boats on the water. She couldn't help wondering if Courtney was very much alive and on one of those vessels right now, spying on them through a pair of binoculars, maybe even reading their lips.

"Russ, we can't," she whispered.

He nodded again.

In their silence, Anna heard a knocking noise.

"What is that?" Russ asked, obviously hearing it, too.

They followed the noise down to the end of the dock, near where Anna had her dinghy tied to the lower deck of her floating home. In the gentle breeze, ripples ran across the water, and the dinghy kept tapping against the deck. The boat was a good size—with room enough for four passengers. A power motor was attached to the stern. The shiny, dark blue tarp covering the boat was slightly askew. Anna hadn't taken the dinghy out on the water in two months. It didn't make sense that the lines had suddenly gotten loose. It hadn't stormed or anything last night.

"How did that happen?" Anna heard herself ask.

"Weird," Russ murmured. "I didn't notice any tapping noise when I brought you home last night. At least, let me secure the boat for you before I go. You don't want it drifting away."

The dinghy couldn't be reached from the dock, only from the water or from Anna's deck.

She had some weatherproof patio furniture from Costco on the deck—along with a few potted plants. There was also a cheap, portable outdoor grill. A metal railing surrounded the outdoor space, except for a gap that left access to the dinghy. A gate was supposed to slide across the breach, but it had been stuck in the open position for years.

Anna noticed one of the patio chairs was tipped over. As she started back to the front door with Russ, she wondered if somebody had broken into her houseboat—or at least, had tried to break in.

Russ must have been thinking the same thing. "Better let me go in first," he said, reaching the front door. He stepped inside, and Anna followed him into the house.

On the wall in the front hallway, Anna had a huge, framed poster for the Seattle World's Fair from 1962, with the Space Needle prominently featured. To her left were the bathroom, linen closet, and the study that had been her mother's old bedroom. The steep stairway led to the master bedroom in the loft. Anna headed in that direction and took a quick glance around. Nothing seemed out of place. Her laptop was still on the desk in the study. The built-in bookcase still had her TV journalism awards on one shelf. Some of them were silver- or gold-plated, and the rest at least looked expensive. But nothing was missing.

Meanwhile, Russ headed in the other direction—past the front hall closet and into the living room. It was only a few moments before Anna caught up with him. Nothing seemed to have been disturbed in there, either. One wall had another built-in bookcase; and the various family antiques her mother had managed to hold on to were still on the shelves, untouched. On the other side of the book-case was the kitchen entrance. Anna poked her head in. Everything was as she'd left it this morning. The kitchen was small, lacking in counter space. Her empty coffee cup was still on the slightly banged-up table of the built-in breakfast booth, the same table where she'd often done her homework while in high school. The appliances were all new, stainless steel and "apartment size." A Tiffany-style lamp hung above the breakfast table. The lamp always swayed a bit during windstorms.

The door connecting to her mom's old bedroom was open—just as Anna had left it this morning.

Russ headed for the sliding glass doors at the far end of the living room. The spectacular view included the lake, the Space Needle, and Queen Anne Hill with all the lights twinkling. The dusk sky was beautiful, almost surreal against the gleaming water. A big picture window—with a built-in love seat—provided a view to the north with Gas

Works Park and the Aurora Bridge. On the other side of the room was a stand-alone cone-shaped midcentury modern gas fireplace and, behind that, another picture window that looked out at Lake Union Park and the downtown skyscrapers.

She watched Russ move the sawed-off broom handle she always kept lodged in the grooves to the sliding glass door for extra security. Then he unlocked the door. It squeaked as he slid it open.

She told herself that if someone had broken in and gone out on the deck, they'd certainly done a damn good job of covering their tracks. Nothing was out of place or missing.

Anna wandered out to the deck. She watched Russ climb down to the lower tier and retie the lines to secure the boat. He peeled back the off-centered tarp. "Have you used this at all recently?" he asked.

"Not since we took it out on that warm Saturday in May," she said. She remembered Courtney had taken a weekend alone to write at their place on Whidbey Island. So Anna and Russ had spent that Saturday aimlessly motoring around Lake Union in the boat together. Then they'd had a cozy dinner at her place, where he'd spent the night, quite the rarity.

"I remember," he said with a brief, wistful smile. But then he looked down toward the floor of the boat and sighed. "Anyway, there's some water in here, just a couple of puddles. You sure no one has taken this out in the last day or two?"

"Not that I know of." From where she stood at the edge of the deck, Anna craned her neck to have a look. "Are the paddles still in there?" she asked.

"Yeah," he said. Russ checked the outboard motor. "You still have half a tank of gas. The motor looks okay." Balanced on the ledge, he started to tug the tarp back in place over the top of the dinghy. "Maybe I'm making too big a deal out of this. Some rain might have gotten in here or something. But it's weird that the lines suddenly came loose for no reason."

Biting her lip, Anna watched him for a moment. Then she looked at all the boats out on the water—at least twenty of them cruising around this part of the lake.

Once again, she wondered if Courtney was aboard one of those vessels, watching their every move.

CHAPTER FOUR

Friday, July 10—11:28 P.M.

On TV, Courtney was addressing an audience in a bookstore. It was the final sound bite from Anna's news segment. Courtney signed as she spoke in her slightly faltering, childlike voice. When she finished her speech, the crowd gave her a standing ovation.

"Courtney told me," Anna said in voice-over, "that she might not hear the applause, but she can see it and feel it. This is Anna Malone reporting for KIXI News at Elliott Bay Book Company in Seattle."

"Okay, that was a bit much," Anna muttered to herself. She rarely watched her own segments once they aired because she was so self-critical. And even though she could have easily pulled it up on her phone or computer, Anna watched her segment on Courtney again as it ran on the eleven o'clock news. She needed to make sure the segment wasn't just a sappy puff piece.

For the most part, it wasn't—though she could have done without that last line.

Curled up on the sofa in her living room, Anna reached for the remote and switched off the TV.

Russ had left nearly four hours ago, shortly after securing the dinghy. Once alone, Anna had ordered dinner over the phone and walked to the Thai place to pick it up. Returning home, she'd gone upstairs to change into her "grubby clothes"—a T-shirt and her well-worn, comfy jeans. But she couldn't find her jeans. They usually hung on a hook just inside her closet door. The jeans weren't in her hamper, either, nor were they in the wash. She realized her knockabout canvas sneakers were also missing.

She wondered if, maybe last night when she'd been so drunk and out of it, she'd changed out of her dress after Russ had taken her home. Putting on her grubby clothes was always one of the first things she automatically did whenever she returned home from work or an event. Russ had said she'd gotten sick. Had she thrown up all over her clothes or something? Maybe Russ had tossed them out.

Anna decided to ask him later. Her Thai dinner was getting cold.

She changed into some shorts and a pullover, and then ate in front of an old Barbara Stanwyck movie on Prime. It was a warm night, and she had the sliding glass door open. The screen door was shut to keep the mosquitoes out. The floodlight for the deck was on. She could see moths and other insects swirling around the bulb over the screen door.

Every once in a while during the movie and the newscast, Anna would hear a splash, and she'd go to the screen door to investigate. This mysterious business with the dinghy had her on edge. And of course, it was no help that Russ's wife had been missing for nearly twenty hours.

Now, with the television off, Anna was aware of every little sound. She could hear water lapping against the pilings. She went to look out at the dinghy again. It teetered slightly in the dark water. The slick blue tarp cover caught the moonlight. She hadn't noticed anything wrong with the dinghy yesterday.

Anna wondered if some homeless person had taken a catnap in there today. It was a perfect place to stow away. For all she knew, someone could be hiding under that tarp right now.

But it wasn't very likely. The Gettles, who lived at the other end of the dock, always locked the gate after nine o'clock. Anyone attempting to climb into the boat would have had to swim to it, and Anna would have heard them.

Still, she pulled the sliding glass door shut, locked it, and then secured the sawed-off broom handle in place. Back on the sofa, Anna grabbed the remote again and switched on the TV. She was tired, but too wound up to sleep and too distracted to read. She settled for a *Golden Girls* rerun, riddled with commercials, on cable.

Though it had been the right and sensible thing to do, she wished she hadn't sent Russ on his way earlier tonight. She would have liked him to be there with her now. Maybe then she could have relaxed. She wanted to phone him, but for all she knew, Courtney had returned home tonight. Or perhaps he was asleep already. He hadn't gotten much sleep last night, either. If he really needed to talk to her, he'd call. She'd wait for him.

That was the whole story of their relationship.

Anna handed all the control over to him. He was a

married man. So, she settled for being a small part of Russ's life. It was strange, the compromises she made because she was in love. Anna told herself she wouldn't make any demands or threats, and she wouldn't complain. If she didn't like the arrangement, if she didn't like the sneaking around, she should just walk. She didn't want to be responsible for ruining a marriage, not even a bad one. So she left everything up to him.

It was how she lived with herself in this role as "the other woman." If she remained passive and selfless for the duration, she could think of herself as a nice person in a desperate situation—just like some of those "nice people" who sometimes used her parking spot for a little while.

Who was she trying to kid?

No matter how one rationalized it, a jerk was still a jerk, and a homewrecker was still a homewrecker.

But for a while, Anna had truly been blameless. She'd had no idea Russ was married when she'd first met him. That had been a year and a half ago.

At the time, Anna didn't think she'd ever be in a relationship. She'd never had much luck in love. She didn't need an analyst to help her figure out why, either. She was pretty sure it had something to do with her dad and her older brother, Stuart.

She adored her brother. Everyone did, but no one more than Anna. Stu called her *Anna Banana* and made her feel like the most important person in the world. He was the first one Anna ran to whenever she needed consoling. Somehow, he always managed to cheer her up and make her laugh. Stu was three years older than her. By the time he was in high school, he'd gained a reputation as a bit of a wild man. He was also handsome with wavy brown hair—a real charmer, too. Even the teachers he drove crazy with his clowning around in class begrudgingly liked him because he was sweet. He always rushed to the defense of kids who were being picked on. There wasn't a mean bone in his body. He was just crazy and impulsive. The Bainbridge Island Police who hauled him in for his various offenses—speeding, skinny-dipping, being drunk and disorderly—seemed amused by his antics and almost always cut him some slack.

Anna could imagine him at the police station, trying to talk his way out of whatever trouble he'd gotten into. Stu had a charming little nervous tic. When he got anxious, he'd squint and scratch the top of his head. As he winced like that, his dimples showed. It was hard not to forgive Stu for whatever he did.

But Martin Malone didn't find his son's behavior the least bit funny. Stu's nervous tic didn't melt their father's heart. Martin Malone was a hugely successful corporate lawyer. His VIP status on the island meant that the cops were willing to drop the charges whenever Stu's escapades got him into trouble. Their dad often reminded Stu of that fact: "You'd be in some kind of reform school by now if it weren't for me and the fact that people in this town are willing to bend the law out of respect to me. It's only because of me that they look the other way."

Anna used to duck into her bedroom whenever the two of them came to blows. She'd hear them downstairs in her father's study yelling at each other. The study was where all the serious talks occurred—a paneled room with a fireplace, a big mahogany desk, and their dad's framed diplomas and awards on the wall mixed in with his framed coin collections.

Whenever the two of them started going at it, Anna's mom would stand outside the study door, wringing her hands and crying. The sun rose and set on Stu as far as she was concerned. Anna's mom rarely stood up to their dad and she was always so ladylike. But Anna remembered one argument that resulted in Stu storming out of the house. "You know, it's true, Martin," she heard her mom tell their father. "A lot of people in this town kiss your ass. But that's not the only reason they give Stuart a break when he's in a jam. They give him a break, because they *like* him, goddamn it. Maybe if you tried to like him, too, he wouldn't act out all the time."

Stu ran away that weekend. He forged their dad's name on a check, made out to himself for $897.96. No one in the bank questioned it. He also stole over two thousand dollars' worth of rare coins from their father's collection.

It killed Anna that he'd run away without saying good-bye to her or leaving a note. It killed her mother, too.

Anna's parents hired a private detective, who was able to trace Stuart as far as Spokane before he lost track of him.

Stu's absence left such a void. There was no more laughter in that big, stately brick house. Anna would cry and then sneak into Stu's bedroom—only he wouldn't be there to console her or say something to make her giggle. So she'd just curl up on his bed and keep crying. She knew her mother often did the same thing. She could hear her in there some nights.

The following year, on a beautiful Friday evening in April, when Anna was a sophomore, she came home late from school. She'd had a video club meeting. It was close to dinnertime and already dark out. But from the end of her block, she could see the red lights swirling from the roofs of police cars parked in front of the house.

Anna immediately thought of Stu.

She started running. At the end of the long driveway, a husky, young cop with a buzz cut stopped her. "Wait a minute," he said, all authoritative. "Where do you think you're going? Who are you?"

"I'm Anna Malone," she answered, out of breath. "I live here. Did something happen to my brother? Did something happen to Stuart?"

Past the policeman's shoulder, she saw two unmarked cars parked in the driveway, and someone walking through the front door of the house. He had FBI written on the back of his jacket.

Wide-eyed, she turned to the young cop. "Did something happen to my brother?" she asked again, the panic rising in her voice.

"No, it's your father," the cop said. "Do you know what insider trading is? The feds are arresting him for it."

Anna remembered how the smug son of a bitch had seemed to get a perverse kick out of telling her. She figured he must not have been a fan of her father's. Or maybe he was just an asshole.

Her father pled guilty. The authorities confiscated everything—including the house. Her mom was able to save a few heirlooms and antiques from her side of the family. The houseboat on Lake Union in Seattle had been a gift from Anna's grandparents a few years before, and it was in her mom's name. The monthly mooring fee had been paid through 2015. Her parents had used it as a pied-à-terre for trips to Seattle. Anna had spent the night on the floating home only a handful of times.

Suddenly, it was her new home.

Two weeks after they'd moved in, the police came to their door with the news that Anna's father had hanged himself in his prison cell. He'd used a jump rope he smuggled from the exercise room. There was some loose talk that he'd managed to persuade the prison guards to look the other way.

"Your father always did have a certain clout with the authorities," Anna's mom pointed out—on the way home from the meager funeral.

Along with her mom, Anna had hoped that Stu would somehow hear about his father's death and then return to them. But it never happened.

She started at a new high school in Seattle. Her mother started a new job at Macy's, and she also started drinking.

Though they'd been dead for years, Anna's grandparents came through again when it came time for her to go to college. They'd put aside an annuity for her tuition and her room and board—with the stipulation that she attend a Catholic university. Anna picked Gonzaga because Spokane was only a five-hour bus ride away from her mother. She also remembered it was the last place anyone had seen her brother. Somehow, she thought she might find Stu there.

What she found instead was a passion for broadcasting, reporting, and making short films. She had friends at school, but no steady boyfriend. A love life just wasn't a priority for her. Anna told herself there just wasn't time. She took a bus or got a ride to Seattle every other weekend—to check on her mom. She had the occasional date, but always came up with a reason why the guy wasn't right for her: this one wore sandals and had ugly, dirty toes; that one was too much of a sports fanatic; and another chewed gum in an annoying way.

"Now, let me get this straight," her mother said. "You met him for a walk by the river and it was ninety degrees. And even though he was very nice and seemed to like you, you didn't want to go out with him again because he wore a sleeveless T-shirt."

"I don't like sleeveless T-shirts on men," Anna said, shrugging, "unless they're in a gym, and even then, that's pushing it." She was sitting in the passenger seat of her mother's Camry.

It was late September of Anna's junior year, during a weekend home from school. They were on their way to a rare fancy dinner out at Luc in Madison Valley. Her mom was at the wheel. Wind from the half-open window blew through her auburn-colored hair. Though she was still pretty, the last couple of years had made her careworn. Anna figured after a few cocktails, her mom would be too drunk to drive home. She made a mental note not to get all disapproving and snotty later, taking over as designated driver on the way back.

"Honey, that's a terrible reason to write off another potentially nice guy," her mother said, watching the road ahead. "Don't you want to have a regular, steady fella?"

"Most of the guys I'm attracted to are unattainable—or they're just good-looking jerks," Anna admitted. "I had a crush on this teacher's assistant. He was so handsome and charming. Nearly all the girls in class were crazy for him. And—big surprise—he ended up screwing most of them, but not me. Anyway, maybe I'm just not meant to be in a relationship."

"You know, sweetie," her mother said, sighing, "not every man in your life is going to end up abandoning you."

She wanted to ask: *How can you say that when the two most important men in your life abandoned you?*

Instead, Anna just smiled wistfully. "Do you think we'll ever see Stu again?"

"Oh, I—I—think—I think—he . . ." Her mother fell silent.

Anna glanced over and saw her mother trying to talk. Blinking, she repeatedly opened and closed her mouth.

"Mom? Mom, are you okay?" Anna felt the car lunge forward and speed up. A panic swept through her as they started to careen downhill, out of control.

A woman in running shorts and a tank top darted out in front of them. She had her blond hair in a ponytail and wore headphones.

Anna's mother slumped in the driver's seat and her head rolled back.

Horrified, Anna went to grab the wheel, but she was too late.

The car smashed into the jogger with an awful thud. The woman's thin body tumbled over the front hood and hit the windshield. Blood splattered over the splintering glass. The jogger's broken body spun off the passenger side of the hood.

Anna helplessly watched the car veer to the left and scrape against a row of parked cars on the side of the steep road. Car alarms blared, but Anna could barely hear them past the din of shattering glass and twisting metal. It seemed like a thousand pebbles of glass were bursting inside the vehicle.

The last thing Anna remembered was trying to pull her mother's body toward her as the runaway car crumpled in on both of them. There was a deafening crash and then, just blackness.

The jogger, Sarah Adamson, was twenty-nine and engaged to be married in October. She died on the way to the hospital.

The emergency responders had to cut Anna and her mother out of the wreckage. Her mom was dead before they could get to her. Later, they determined that she'd had a massive stroke at the wheel.

Anna was in the hospital for five days. She had whiplash, a broken arm, a shattered wrist, and several sprains and fractures. Her face was battered. Her whole body was covered with bruises, cuts, and lacerations. She'd lost so much blood, the doctors needed to give her a transfusion. She had a total of forty-two stitches.

While recovering, she hoped against hope that Stu might have heard about the accident and would come visit her at the hospital. But that didn't happen.

Most of her visitors were lawyers, eager to represent her. The airbags in the car had never deployed, and she had a cut-and-dried lawsuit that could be settled out of court. Anna had to pay the hospital and funeral bills. She picked an attorney who had been an associate of her dad's. He handled the whole thing. He also handled Sarah Adamson's family, who tried to sue Anna's mother's meager estate. Though the coroner had found no trace of alcohol in her mother's blood, Anna still had to sign a statement that her mom wasn't inebriated at the time of the accident. No help to the Adamsons' case was the fact that their daughter had been in the street, jogging with headphones on when she was hit. They didn't get any money.

Last year, when Anna had had her stalker and endured all those little acts of sabotage, she'd wondered for a while if perhaps the culprit was someone who had been close to Sarah Adamson.

Anna returned to school as soon as she'd recovered. She rented out the houseboat. There had been no reason to keep coming back to Seattle for weekends and vacations. At Gonzaga, she dated and slept with a few men. None of them ever noticed her scars, and none of them ever really got to know her.

She recalled one of the nicer guys asking her what he'd done wrong, why they'd broken up. Anna hadn't been able to explain it to him.

She'd become so cautious about relationships. She couldn't allow herself to depend on anyone. For her college graduation ceremony, she'd had nobody there in the audience for her. She'd convinced herself that it didn't matter, she didn't mind.

Looking back now, Anna realized how she'd set herself up. No wonder the big love of her life would turn out to be someone who could never be all hers.

She heard a muted thump outside.

Anna sat up. Then she grabbed the remote and muted *The Golden Girls.* She froze at the sound of another thump. It seemed to come from the deck outside. She reached over and turned off the light on the end table. In the darkened living room, she had a clear view outside—

and she figured whoever was out there could no longer see her.

Getting to her feet, she padded toward the glass door and peered out. Beyond the glare of the overhead light on the deck—and all the insects swirling around it—she could see the dinghy gently swaying on the dark water. Nothing had been disturbed. Nothing looked suspicious.

She glanced out the picture windows on her left and right. She didn't see anybody out there. And yet, she still felt someone watching.

There were a couple of things she'd never completely gotten used to in all her years living on the lake. First, every little noise carried on the water. Worse, she felt so exposed—particularly in that living room with its huge windows. There were no bushes or trees between her and the outside world. All it took were a good pair of binoculars, and anyone could have watched her—from a boat, a neighboring dock, or even the other side of Lake Union. Anna rarely closed her curtains in the living room except in her most private moments. The main point to living on a floating home was the incredible view. The trade-off was her privacy—and feeling vulnerable on nights like this when she was scared.

It was quiet now.

The ringing phone startled her. A hand over her heart, Anna hurried back to the sofa and swiped the phone off the cushion. The caller ID read: *Unknown Caller.*

She immediately thought of Courtney. Every time Anna had called her today, it had gone directly to the provider's impersonal voice mail greeting, leading her to believe that Courtney's phone was damaged or disabled.

Was this Courtney, calling from a pay phone or some kind of burner phone?

Anna tapped the phone screen to pick up. "Hello?"

A strange groan came from the other end. It sounded almost inhuman.

Anna winced.

Somewhere nearby, a car alarm went off. It competed with the raspy voice murmuring something on the other end. It came across as gibberish.

Anna covered her left ear to hear whoever was on the phone. "Hello?" she repeated.

"You're . . . not . . . fooling . . . anyone," the unknown caller said in a strange, singsong tone.

"What? Who is this?"

Anna listened. The person hadn't hung up yet. But she could clearly hear an echo in the background. It was the car alarm that had gone off.

The caller was close by.

"Who's there?" Anna asked, her voice turning shrill. "Who is this?"

Then she heard a click.

"I remember hitting her in the head with that thing. It's so clear to me now. I can almost hear the crack—and the strange, sickly warble that came out of her mouth. I was splattered with blood . . . It was all down the front of me—on my clothes and my sneakers. I felt the droplets on my face . . . A drop must have gotten in my mouth. It tasted like copper. When I went into the bathroom to get the towels to wrap around her head, I stopped and rinsed out my mouth at the sink. But I could still taste that little bit of blood—like an old penny."

—Excerpt: Session 3, audio recording
with Dr. G. Tolman, July 23

CHAPTER FIVE

Saturday, July 11—12:47 A.M.

On *Golden Girls*, Blanche said something funny in her Southern accent, and it sent the studio audience into hysterics. But Anna barely cracked a smile.

She was too damn nervous to find anything amusing right now.

Curled up on the sofa, she had the phone and a steak knife on the cushion beside her. The living room lights were on. The curtains were drawn. And she'd double-checked that the windows and doors were locked. With everything closed up, she had the fan on to keep from sweltering.

Anna desperately wanted to call Russ, but figured he was asleep.

She kept reminding herself that what the caller had said wasn't exactly threatening. In fact, it hadn't made much sense—unless it had been Courtney, saying she knew all about her affair with Russ: *"You're . . . not . . . fooling . . . anyone."*

But it couldn't have been Courtney. She couldn't hear and talk on a regular pay phone or a burner phone. She usually texted.

Anna couldn't help thinking about her stalker back in October. The unnerving late-night calls and hang-ups had been her tormentor's specialty. But the creep had never actually said anything to her. Whenever she answered the phone, she'd hear background noise, and maybe an occasional sigh. She could feel the person listening— as if he or she just wanted to hear her voice. One night, she'd gotten nine calls at various intervals until she'd finally switched off her phone at two in the morning.

Was her tormentor back?

The car alarm from somewhere nearby had stopped blaring moments after she'd hung up. It hadn't started up again. Anna knew the sound of her Mini Cooper's alarm, and that hadn't been it. So she knew her car was okay. No one had keyed it again. She figured the car alarm probably had nothing to do with the call.

Glancing at the clock on her cable box, Anna realized the call had been nearly forty-five minutes ago. If the caller had planned to phone again or pay her a visit, it would have happened by now. At least, that was what she told herself.

She would keep watching *Golden Girls* until she started to nod off. Even if she ended up falling asleep on the sofa, that was better than fretting over every little sound and tossing and turning until dawn in her bed upstairs.

Once again, the TV was her substitute for a boyfriend,

keeping her company through the lonely hours and scary nights.

It was all she could do to keep from calling Russ. Sometimes, she wished she'd never met him. Maybe she would have been better off staying in Spokane.

She'd gotten her first job after college there, working as an associate producer for a Spokane station's evening news. After a couple of years, she began to work with some of the news reporters, and on occasion, she put together little feature stories. Eventually, one of those stories came to the attention of the station head of KIXI-TV in Seattle, and Anna got the offer to work there.

Anna had been renting out the houseboat all that time. She gave her tenants their notice, cleaned up and remodeled the place, and moved back in. She focused on her career. KIXI-TV felt like a stepping-stone to a job with one of the networks. In fact, Anna could more clearly see herself on a prime-time network news show or a popular podcast than she could see herself in a steady relationship. She dated, but never really clicked with anyone. She remembered one guy asking on their first date about her previous relationships. When Anna admitted she'd never really had a long-term relationship, he said he felt sorry for her.

Last year, turning thirty had been damned depressing. Anna suddenly realized just how lonely she was. The milestone birthday had her suddenly aware of other women her age with husbands and families. Her clock was ticking, and she couldn't help wondering if she was going to be alone for the rest of her life.

Anna remembered when she had a story assignment at Children's Hospital, looking at all the sick kids and their families. She knew the parents were going through hell, and yet, she almost envied them, because they had someone to love and care about.

Anna was at the hospital because her program manager wanted coverage of a special visit there from Olympic gold medal figure skater Margaret Schramm. Anna hated doing stories like this because she knew it would feel exploitative, what with all the heart-tugging shots of the sick kids, some of them bald. But Margaret Schramm turned out to be a good sport and so much fun. Plus the kids and hospital staff were ecstatic to see her.

While Anna and George got coverage of Margaret chatting with some kids in the physical therapy room, Anna noticed a tall doctor among the parents and staff watching off camera. He wore a white coat with a visitor's badge. He was so handsome that Anna thought he looked more like a soap opera actor playing a doctor than a real MD.

Everyone was watching Margaret Schramm, but the handsome doctor was looking at Anna— —and smiling.

During a break in filming, he approached her. "You're Anna Malone, aren't you?" he said. "I can't believe I'm actually meeting you. I'm Russ Knoll, and I'm a huge fan of your work."

He was so charming, Anna might have been tongue-tied if she hadn't managed to slide into her professional reporter mode. "Well, thank you," she said, smiling cordially. She stole a glance at his left hand: no wedding ring.

She learned that he was a pediatrician in private practice. He was visiting one of his regular patients who was recovering from surgery there. She and Russ didn't talk long, and no phone numbers were exchanged. But later, she couldn't take her eyes off him as he talked to a little boy in a wheelchair and then conferred with the child's parents.

The following afternoon, he called the station and left a message on her voice mail, asking her to dinner. By then, Anna had already Googled him and learned that Russell Knoll was thirty-three, and for the last six years, he'd been at First Hill Medicine, chalking up glowing reviews and recommendations online. Anna also came across a gorgeous photo of him in *Seattle Magazine* from a silly article entitled "Seattle's Sexiest Doctors." It was a strange, double standard because the article didn't include any women doctors; and yet, if women doctors had been included, labeling them as sexy would have been viewed as incredibly chauvinistic. The feature was five years old, and there was no mention of a wife or girlfriend, just that he was a Mariners fan and loved swimming and rock climbing.

Anna was cautious during their first date—dinner at the Tin Table, a chic, semi-bohemian eatery in Seattle's trendy Pike/Pine neighborhood. Working in TV, she'd encountered her share of glamour boys and been burned the few times she'd allowed herself to be vulnerable. She'd made up her mind that she wouldn't let this gorgeous doctor sweep her off her feet.

But then, at dinner, he admitted he'd seen her on TV three years before, when she'd been at the station in Spokane. He'd been at a medical convention there. He even remembered the feature she'd done—about a decorated Vietnam vet, who was a mailman, ready to retire. "It was so well done," Russ told her. "In just a couple of minutes, you made me feel like I really knew the guy. And when I saw you after the segment, talking about him, I have to admit, I was instantly smitten."

Anna couldn't believe a man nowadays actually used the word *smitten*, and she liked him for it. "Anyway, about a year ago, I caught you on the news here in Seattle," he said. "I realized you'd moved. And I've had KIXI News programmed on my DVR ever since."

He held her hand as they walked back to his car together. Then Russ kissed her good night at her door. By then, she was pretty damn smitten herself. It took all the willpower Anna could muster not to invite him in and take him to bed. That didn't happen until the end of their third date. But a part of her still held back. She was wary about falling in love and getting her heart broken.

But she fell in love with him anyway. And the more Anna found out about Russ, the deeper she fell. He was a good man. He spent three weeks every year working nonstop and sleeping in a tent wherever Doctors Without Borders happened to need him.

Like her, he'd lost both his parents. He was the only child of a wealthy couple from Colorado Springs. During his third year in the University of Washington's medical program, his parents were traveling with friends whose private plane crashed thirty minutes after takeoff from Phoenix.

Anna's friend in Spokane, Christie, summed it up for her: "So —in addition to being gorgeous, he's also sweet and altruistic, and rich. Plus, if you marry him, you won't have to deal with any in-laws. Honey, hold on to him."

Though she'd told her friend in Spokane all about Russ, Anna didn't say anything to George—except that she was seeing someone. She claimed: "I'm afraid I'll jinx it by talking too much about him." But that was only half-true. She didn't want to rub George's nose in her happiness. She knew he and his drippy wife, Beebe, were having problems. Telling him about some guy who had her walking on air—that just seemed cruel.

Still, Anna figured the two men in her life had to meet sometime. A Humanities Washington fund-raiser dinner seemed like the perfect occasion. Anna and George had done a ten-minute promotional film for the nonprofit. It would be shown at the dinner, to which they'd both been invited. George was bringing Beebe. So Anna invited Russ. But he said he had to attend a medical convention in Tacoma that evening.

So Anna was dateless for the swanky dinner in the Spanish Ballroom of the Olympic Hotel. Still, she looked pretty sensational in a black Calvin Klein spaghetti-strap sheath. In fact, she seemed wildly overdressed next to Beebe, who wore a brown jumper over a black leotard. Her mousy brown hair was swept up in a messy bun with a couple of sticks in it. And around her neck, she sported a clunky piece of jewelry she'd made herself. Beebe considered herself an artist. She eyed Anna's cocktail dress and put on a puzzled look. "Aren't you afraid people won't take you seriously when you're wearing something so provocative?"

Beebe was always trying to put her down one way or another. She was such a sourpuss. Everybody at the station loved George, but no one could stand his wife.

"I don't think this dress looks particularly *provocative*, Beebe," she answered. "I think it's pretty. That's why I wore it. Excuse me . . ."

Anna glanced around for an escape route. That was when she noticed a tall man over near the bar.

It was Russ, looking handsome in a dark blue suit.

Anna figured he must have gotten out of the medical convention early or something. She couldn't believe he'd decided to surprise her. It was the kind of thing a boyfriend or a husband did. She felt as if he was taking their relationship to another level by showing up like this. They weren't just dating; they were a *couple*.

Anna eagerly headed through the crowd, toward Russ. She could see he was checking out the room. Obviously, he hadn't spotted her yet.

She was just a few feet away when his eyes met hers.

"Well, this is sure pretty wonderful!" she called to him, beaming.

But he just stared back at her with a stunned, almost horrified look on his face.

Anna hesitated. She watched him turn away—toward another woman, a strikingly beautiful brunette in a blue sequined sleeveless dress. She planted a kiss on Russ's cheek and set her drink in his hand. Then she turned to someone else and started talking in sign language.

Anna stood there frozen. Russ glanced her way for a second. He looked sick.

She was close enough to notice he was wearing something she'd never seen on him before: his wedding ring. It was there on his left hand, the same hand that held his wife's drink for her.

Backing away, Anna bumped into another guest and knocked the woman's wineglass out of her hand. The glass shattered on the floor. Utterly demoralized, Anna felt tears sting her eyes as she apologized to the woman. Everyone in the general vicinity was staring at her—except Russ's wife. Had she not heard the glass break? She was still talking in sign language to someone. Was Russ's wife deaf?

Anna managed to find George and told him she wasn't feeling well. Then she got the hell out of there. She kept thinking Russ might try to meet up with her before she left the hotel, but he didn't.

He probably never left his wife's side.

During the taxi ride home, Anna felt sick to her stomach.

He called her an hour later, but she didn't pick up. She listened to his message. "Hey, it's me. God, Anna, I'm so sorry. I—I'm still at the hotel, in the lobby. I had no idea this was the same dinner you invited me to. Anyway, okay, yeah, that was my wife with me. Anna, please, I don't expect you to forgive me. But just let me explain. I feel terrible. I'll try to get away in a little while and come over."

Ninety minutes later, he left two more voice mails and a text for her. He said he was at the locked gate at the end of her dock. He really needed to talk with her. Could she please let him in?

Anna didn't respond to any of his messages, nor did she reply to the countless others that followed in the ensuing days. He even sent a long, rambling e-mail explaining his situation. He and Courtney had been married for five years, the last three of which had been bad. They were both married to their careers. It was Courtney's goal to become a bestselling author, and she'd decided to create a public image of herself as a strong, independent deaf woman. So she'd practically cut him out of her social life. Just weeks ago, they were on the brink of separating, and that was when he met Anna at Children's Hospital. *So I took off my wedding ring and introduced myself to a woman I'd had a crush on for years,* he explained in his e-mail. *I figured Courtney and I were separating soon, and then I could tell you. But around that same time, she got this new publicist who thought she should promote herself as half of a "high-profile Seattle power couple," whatever the hell that means.*

What it meant was that Russ had agreed to make several public appearances with Courtney if she agreed to a friendly divorce settlement in a year—sometime after her next book came out. Their marriage was just a facade.

He wrote to Anna that he hated deceiving her: *I should have told you at the start that I was married, but I didn't want to lose you. You're the best thing that's ever happened to me.*

Anna didn't answer the e-mail.

She Googled *Courtney Knoll* and found several links: mostly book reviews and author interviews. Russ wasn't mentioned in any of the articles, not until a lengthy interview with Courtney from two weeks before, which included a photo of her and Russ together. No wonder her publicist wanted to exploit them: the beautiful, promising young author and her handsome pediatrician husband — they looked so glamorous. That was one reason seeing them at the Humanities Washington dinner had blindsided her. Anna had felt like such a fool—not just because she hadn't known he was married, but because Russ and his wife seemed so perfect together.

There were more photos of them on Courtney's Face-book fan page and on her Instagram page, all recent. There was even one of them at the Humanities Washington dinner.

After five days, Russ showed up at the TV station. Anna was furious when, an hour before she was going on the air to introduce her latest segment, the receptionist buzzed her and said that a Dr. Knoll was waiting in the lobby for her.

"Could you please tell him to wait, Roseann?" Anna said. "I'll be right there."

Marching into the lobby, she barely broke stride and wouldn't even look at him. "Come outside with me, will you?" she said, heading toward the exit.

Once they were outside, Russ started pleading for her forgiveness. Anna kept walking a step ahead of him—toward the sidewalk. The roar of rush hour traffic on Westlake Avenue almost drowned him out. Russ apolo-gized for bothering her at work. "But you wouldn't see me at your place," he said. "And you won't return my calls or texts. I'm sorry, Anna, but you left me no choice. You have to hear me out—"

Anna swiveled around. "I don't have to do anything!" she said, cutting him off. "I haven't answered your mes-sages because I don't want anything more to do with you. Is that clear enough? Or do I have to bone up on my sign language and explain it to your wife?"

Russ stared back at her, looking wounded.

Anna swallowed hard and marched back inside the building.

From behind her desk in the lobby, the sixty-year-old receptionist, Roseann, gave her a smile. "Honey, whatever that fine-looking doctor's selling, I'll buy it!" she chirped.

Anna couldn't look the receptionist in the eye; she focused on the desktop instead. "If he ever comes back, I'm not in," she said under her breath. Heading back into the newsroom, she went straight through to the women's lavatory, where she ducked into a stall and cried.

Russ didn't try to contact her again.

Of course, she wanted him to. She wanted him to call and tell her that his beautiful, deaf, author wife had left him, and if Anna could just forgive him, he'd spend the rest of his life trying to make it up to her.

Looking back, Anna remembered how she'd been with him for only three weeks. Yet, she'd been miserable for months after they split. Was it love or was she just a masochist? She couldn't stop thinking about him.

She often wondered, if she hadn't gotten back together with Russ, would she have eventually forgotten him? Or would she have compared every man she dated from then on to him?

Her phone rang.

Anna gasped. For a moment, she couldn't move. Finally, she grabbed the remote and muted *The Golden Girls*. Then she snatched up the phone and checked the caller ID: *Russell Knoll, MD*. She tapped the phone screen. "You're still awake," she said, getting to her feet. "Have you heard anything?"

"No, nothing," he answered. "I can't sleep. I took a chance you hadn't gone to bed yet. I hope I didn't wake you."

Anna switched off the lamp by the sofa and then the other light in the corner of the room. "No, I couldn't sleep, either," she said. Opening the curtain to the north-facing window, she gazed out at the lake—in the general direction of his floating home. She did that sometimes when she talked with Russ on the phone. It was silly, because she couldn't actually see his place from there. But somehow looking across the silvery rippled dark water toward his house made her feel more connected to him.

Anna had turned off the lights because she was still worried that the anonymous caller might be looking in on her. The only light in the living room was the flickering, muted TV.

"I got a weird phone call a little over an hour ago," she admitted.

"What did they say?"

"It was just a bunch of moaning, and then they said in this bizarre cartoonish voice, *'You're . . . not . . . fooling . . . anyone.'* Just like that, like a chant. I wouldn't be so creeped out if I hadn't realized from the background noise over the phone that they were calling from some-where close by."

"My God, do you want me to come over and check around? I can be there in five minutes—"

"No, I'm okay," Anna said. She felt better just hearing the concern in his voice—and being reminded that he was so close. She stared out at the water and at the head-lights from the traffic on the Aurora Bridge. "Like I said, it was over an hour ago. I think they would have called back or done something else by now if it was really worth worrying about."

"You don't think it's that creep from last fall, do you?"

"I hope not. I thought about that, too. But it doesn't fit the MO. That one never said a word to me on the phone."

"Listen, I'd feel better if I came over and took a look around."

"No, really, I'm fine. But I may take you up on that later if I get really scared."

"Well, I'm here. Keep the phone beside you."

Anna's eyes had adjusted to the shadowy living room, and she glanced down at her bare feet. "Before I forget, I'm missing a pair of sneakers and some jeans—my comfort clothes. Did I change into them after you took me home last night?"

"No."

"Are you sure?"

"Positive. After you got sick, I helped you out of your dress and hung it in your bedroom closet. Then I gave you a Tylenol, put a T-shirt on you, and got you into bed."

"And you didn't touch the jeans that were on a hook in the closet—or the canvas sneakers on the floor?"

"No. You still don't remember anything from last night, do you?"

"I vaguely recall leaving the restaurant, and the next thing I knew I was waking up with the hangover from hell in my mom's old bedroom." Anna sighed. "I wish I knew what I did with my jeans and my sneakers. Was I asleep when you left here last night?"

"You were in bed, and you said good night to me. But you were definitely down for the count." He paused.

"Anna, we have to figure out what we're going to do. I searched around here earlier. The night cream Courtney uses, the book she was reading, her prescriptions—they're all still here. It's clear she took a suitcase and packed some clothes, jewelry, makeup, and things. But she wouldn't have left behind this other stuff, not even for just one night."

"Well, you said she was drunk," Anna pointed out. "Maybe she just forgot."

"She would have come back for them today. I can't help thinking something happened to her after she left here. Courtney likes to think of herself as independent, but her being deaf puts her at risk . . ."

"What do you want to do? Do you think you should call the police?"

"Courtney has that book signing at noon tomorrow— or today, rather—on Bainbridge Island. I'm going there. If she doesn't show up, then I'll call the police and report her missing. I'm not sure what they'll do—if they'll just file a missing person report or investigate the hell out of it. But should the police want to talk to you, you can't tell them you don't remember anything."

"But that's the truth, Russ."

"Yeah, but it'll seem like you're hiding something."

"Well, yeah, I'll be hiding the fact that you and I have been having an affair for the past year."

Anna wondered if this was what Courtney's disappearance was all about. Was it part of a plan to expose and humiliate the two of them? Sure, Courtney would have to endure some humiliation, too. But once she reappeared, she'd emerge as the victim in this scenario. Meanwhile, her cheating husband and his TV news reporter mistress would look like pond scum. It was a win-win for Courtney: payback for her wandering spouse, and she'd also generate a ton of publicity that would translate to book sales.

Anna hated being so cynical. After all, what if Courtney really was hurt—or dead?

"You know, if Courtney stays missing," she said, "once this gets out, it won't take long for people to connect the dots. They'll know about us."

"I thought of that," he said glumly. "The whole thing looks suspicious as hell: The three of us at a restaurant, where people have seen her picking fights with you and me. Then we leave, and within hours, she vanishes without a trace. Not another soul has seen her in that time. And you're going to tell the police that you don't remember anything?"

Still standing at the window, Anna could see her worried expression in the darkened glass. "Well, what do you expect me to tell them?"

"I just think it'll help if you and I gave them the same story."

"You mean, *Let's get our alibis straight*? That's how you make it sound—like we're covering up a crime."

She heard him sigh on the other end of the line. "For all we know, the police might not even want to talk to you. But, Anna, if they do, I'd like you to back me up on what I tell them."

"You're basically asking me to lie."

"No, I'm not. I plan on telling the police the truth. I'm not volunteering any information about you and me. But

I'll be honest about what happened last night. I'm merely asking you to back me up, that's all."

"But, Russ, what if they ask me for details I can't provide? I have no idea what was discussed at your place before you took me home. What if they ask when you drove me home and how long you stayed? I won't be able to answer honestly. I'm just not comfortable with this tactic, Russ. It feels like some kind of cover-up. I know it isn't, but still . . ."

"Okay, okay, listen, do me a favor." He sounded exasperated. "Try to remember what happened last night. If you can't recall, well, maybe it's no big deal. Maybe Courtney will show up at the signing tomorrow, and all our worries will be over. If I report her missing, maybe the police won't feel the need to talk with you. I'm probably overthinking this whole thing. Right now, we're both exhausted. I'm sorry. I didn't mean to upset you."

"I'm not upset," Anna said, staring out at the dark water. "I'm just baffled by this strategy you're proposing."

"Well, let's just skip it for now, okay?" he said. "Can you forget I even brought it up?"

"Fine," she replied. But she knew it would bother her all night.

"Maybe things will look better in the morning. Are you going to be okay tonight? You sure you don't want me to come over and check around?"

"Positive," she murmured.

"Well, I'll call you in the morning before I head out for Bainbridge. I love you."

"I love you, too," Anna replied.

She listened to the click on the other end of the line. Then she pressed the hang-up icon on her phone. After a moment, the screen went dark.

CHAPTER SIX

Saturday, July 11—2:11 A.M.

Sometimes, when she couldn't sleep, Anna would climb out of bed, go down to the kitchen, and have a few spoonfuls of ice cream. It didn't make her sleepy as much as it pacified and relaxed her.

She sat in the breakfast booth of her darkened kitchen, eating from the Breyers Vanilla Caramel Swirl Gelato container. She'd raised the blinds and cracked open the window. To hell with her weirdo anonymous caller; if he was still around trying to get a peek at her, he could look all he wanted.

She stared out at the water and the city lights in the distance. She was wearing one of her oversized KIXI-TV News T-shirts.

For the last ninety minutes, she'd been lying in bed, trying to recall some details from Thursday night— specifically, after they'd left the restaurant. Anna remembered sitting in the backseat of Russ's BMW—with Russ driving and Courtney in the passenger seat. Courtney was talking. Anna couldn't quite hear her because the window was open, but she sounded angry. Russ didn't talk at all.

Anna wondered if it was because he had nothing to say—or if he couldn't speak because that meant taking his eyes off the road and turning to face Courtney so she could read his lips.

Anna couldn't recall anything else. In addition to having been dead drunk, Anna figured she must have also had some kind of mental block about what had happened. Maybe on some subconscious level, she didn't want to remember.

Had she seen or done something horrible?

Maybe she'd watched too many melodramas in which someone had amnesia after a traumatic event. Still, it was alarming to lose a big chunk of time like that.

Something else bothered her tonight. It was Russ, asking her to lie to the police. She understood his intentions. Telling the police she didn't remember anything from Thursday night would make it seem like she was hiding something. It would help if they had their stories lined up. And everything he'd told her about Thursday night made sense. She was sure it had all happened just as he'd said. But Russ was asking her to blindly trust him, stick her neck out with the police, and give them whatever story he fed her.

She wanted to believe him, but he'd lied to her before.

After finding out that he was married, it had taken her three months to forgive him, three awful months. Anna remembered torturing herself by frequently checking Courtney's Facebook fan page, her Instagrams, and her interviews online. Every few days, Anna found a new photo of Courtney and Russ together at one high-society function or another. They looked so right together. It was hard to believe they were as unhappy as Russ made them out to be. In the articles about Courtney, she came across as remarkable, someone Anna couldn't help admiring.

"I grew up in a poor section of Saint Petersburg, Florida," Courtney told the interviewer for *Fantastic Fiction Magazine*. "My mom was a waitress. How she managed to keep us clothed and fed is beyond me. My dad ran out on us when I was four. He died in a motorcycle accident later on. I barely remember him. I learned most of what I knew about him from my sister, Cassie, four years older than me. What I didn't know about my father, I invented. I guess that's how I started to develop my love for storytelling."

Then came Courtney's bout with the measles when she was eight: "There were complications. I ended up completely deaf in one ear, and lost over ninety-five percent of my hearing in the other ear. I was luckier than kids who are born deaf, because I could already talk. I can't imagine how hard it must be to learn to speak when you've never heard people talk. I'm told that I've held on to my Southern accent, but I wouldn't know. I learned sign language and how to read lips. But I was incredibly lonely because I didn't know any other deaf kids. Neither my mother nor my sister ever learned how to sign very well. I spent so much time alone, reading and making up my own stories. I decided early on that I wanted to be a writer. In fact, I was just a teenager when I first got the idea for *The Defective Squad*."

The older sister died from a drug overdose when Courtney was in high school. Then Courtney got into the University of Washington on a scholarship.

The more Anna read about Courtney, the more certain she was that she'd done the right thing breaking it off with Russ. She couldn't have lived with herself if she'd knowingly ruined this woman's marriage.

Last September, Anna spotted a copy of the recently released *Blind Fury* at University Bookstore. Picking up the book, she opened it to the title page, which had been autographed by Courtney.

"She signed that like, five minutes ago," the petite young clerk with long, corkscrew brown hair told Anna. "You just missed her. She's super nice. She has two books out. That one's a sequel. They both take place in Seattle. I hear they're really good."

Anna noticed, several feet away, another employee of the store—a tall, gray-haired, bearded man. He was watching them and smiling.

Putting Courtney's book back on the shelf, Anna nodded at the young clerk. "Thanks, I'll think about it." She backed away and wandered around the corner to another section. She caught a glimpse of the gray-haired man heading toward his coworker.

"Did you recognize who you were talking to?" she heard the man whisper. "That was Anna Malone. She's a TV reporter—on KIXI. Now, *she's* nice. But believe me, Courtney Knoll isn't."

"What do you mean?" the girl asked. "Courtney seemed really sweet when I talked to her."

"Well, wait until you have to work with her on an event. Why do you think I was hiding the entire time she was here? Did she say where she was going?"

"You mean Courtney?" the salesgirl asked. "She went

downstairs to talk to Beth. I really can't believe she's so bad."

"She's a total diva. I know you want to cut her some slack because she's deaf and she's got that deaf-speak thing going on. But wait until you've been bitched at in deaf-speak. You're not going to like it. Did you meet the husband?"

"No."

"They came in together. He was here just a couple of minutes ago. Anyway, the husband's nice enough. I feel sorry for the poor guy."

Anna stepped out from behind the other corner of the bookshelf to look around for Russ. She spotted him near some stairs, by the Pacific Northwest section. He was alone, paging through a picture book. She felt a sweet, sad ache in her stomach just seeing him again.

It was another minute before he looked up and his eyes met hers.

Neither one of them moved. Anna sighed, and she started to smile.

But he quickly looked away, turned, and walked into another section of the store. Anna lost sight of him. She was crestfallen.

"Anna Malone?" she heard a woman ask in a strange voice.

She glanced over to her right and saw Courtney. Anna's first reaction was to back away. But she just nodded.

Courtney signed as she spoke. "My husband and I are big fans of yours," she said. "My name's Courtney Knoll. I'm an author."

"Hi, nice to meet you," Anna said, smiling and trying to keep her cool.

"Maybe you've heard of me. I write a popular young adult series, *The Defective Squad*."

Anna just nodded again.

"You know, I think we could help each other out, Anna. I've heard from so many people that my books and the work I do with disabled kids would make a perfect news story for you. We should meet for coffee sometime."

Within five minutes, Courtney had given her a combination bookmark/business card, led her over to her books on the shelf, and talked her into buying one. "If you do a story on me, you can write off the cost of the book," Courtney suggested. "This copy's already signed, but I can personalize it for you."

"Thanks, that—that's great," Anna said. But Courtney had her head down as she signed the book, and Anna realized that Russ's deaf wife couldn't have picked up on what she'd just said.

Courtney peered up from the book to glance around the vast bookstore. "My husband's here somewhere, and I know he'd love to meet you."

Anna quickly took the book from her. "Maybe some other time. I just realized I'm going to be late for something. But I'm really glad to have met you, Courtney. I can't wait to read this." She started to edge toward the cashier.

"Well, text me, okay? We'll make that coffee date. I really mean it about us getting together."

Anna nodded and waved. She had her credit card out

before she even reached the cashier. She couldn't get out of the store fast enough.

That night, she kept thinking Russ might call or text her, but he didn't. She didn't hear from him the following day, either. By the time she crawled into bed the following night, Anna realized she *wanted* to hear from him.

After three days, she phoned Russ, got his voice mail, and hung up—twice in a row. He called her back within an hour.

"Anna? I'm sorry, but I got two hang-ups from you," he said. "Is everything all right?"

"I was going to ask you the same thing—after running into your wife at the bookstore the other day. She gave me her card. She wants to meet for coffee. I'm not sure what to do . . ."

"Don't do anything. It has nothing to do with us. I'm certain she doesn't know. She just wants you to do a story about her. She can get really pushy. She's that way with reporters. Just throw her card away and forget about it. She'll forget about it, too—eventually. I'm sorry she bothered you, Anna."

"That's all right," Anna said. Then she hesitated. "So—how are you?"

There was a long pause. "I've missed you," he whispered.

That was how they got back together, and Anna let herself become the other woman.

Anna realized she only needed to see Russ again and overhear some disinterested third party mention that Courtney was a pill. That was all it took for her to cave—

that, and the fact that she'd never really fallen out of love with him.

She remembered Russ saying that he and Courtney had agreed they would initiate friendly divorce proceedings once Courtney's new book came out. Since they'd gotten back together, he'd mentioned it again only twice and not recently. Anna was tempted to bring it up, but didn't—even though Courtney's new book had been out for a week now. Anna told herself she was in no position to make demands.

Her girlfriend in Spokane, Christie, was still the only one who knew about them. "You're shortchanging yourself, Anna, but you already know that," she told her over the phone. "You deserve better."

Her work friend George knew nothing about her relationship with Russ. George could be pretty judgmental at times. She didn't want him thinking that she was sleazy or that Russ was sleazy. She had a tough enough time justifying to herself what she was doing.

Except for all the secrecy and some bouts with guilt, their illicit relationship worked surprisingly well. She and Russ managed to see each other at least once a week. Sometimes, he was even able to spend the night. They texted or talked every day. They had their fights and rough patches, like everyone else.

It might have been nice if she'd had a regular boyfriend staying with her during that scary period last October when someone had been stalking her and making her life miserable. In addition to the countless hang-ups at all hours and her car being keyed in the carport, the Mini Cooper was vandalized again in the lot at work. Her trash cans and recycling bins kept getting knocked over, someone threw a rock through one of the big windows in the living room; and obviously the same someone scrawled CUNT in black paint on her front door. When she returned home from work one evening, she found a dead seagull in the middle of her living room; and most frightening of all, someone attempted to break into the house in the middle of the night. Those were just the incidents she reported to the police. She didn't dare call Russ when she was scared. She called him only during work hours—or when she knew Courtney was out of town.

It was such an awful time. Anna was a wreck through most of it. She was tempted to move to a hotel. If she'd been in a normal relationship, she could have temporarily stayed with her boyfriend—or had him stay with her. But she and Russ weren't in a normal relationship.

Though Anna had told herself the perpetrator of all her miseries was someone who didn't like one of her stories on TV, she could never completely dismiss the idea that Courtney had been behind it all.

Then, in February, they'd hit another rough patch. Anna was almost ready to break up with him. Russ and Courtney had decided to move from their apartment in Queen Anne into a $2 million floating home just five blocks away from her. That wasn't exactly what a couple did when contemplating an amicable split. Russ said it had been Courtney's idea. His image-conscious wife had insisted on the place because it seemed like an ideal home for the Perfect Seattle Couple. She figured their new house on Lake Union would remind everyone of Tom Hanks and his floating home in *Sleepless in Seattle*.

Anna couldn't help wondering if there was more to it than that. Had Courtney found out about them? Maybe she'd figured they wouldn't have the nerve to carry on their affair right under her nose. If that was Courtney's strategy, it kind of worked. Anna hated knowing she might run into Courtney in her own neighborhood.

And of course, that was exactly what had happened six weeks ago—in the wine section of Pete's Supermarket, the neighborhood grocery store near the lake.

Anna didn't recognize Courtney until it was too late. They were face-to-face at the end of the aisle. Their grocery baskets even accidentally touched. "Hello, Anna!" Courtney said, signing with her free hand. "I'm Courtney Knoll. Remember, University Bookstore?"

"Well, hi," Anna managed to say—even though her heart seemed to stop for a moment. "How are you? It's been a long time . . ."

"I should be so mad at you!" Courtney gave her a side-long glance, but she was smiling. "You were supposed to text me! But I forgive you. I know you're super busy. Do you live around here?"

Anna nodded. "Yes, in the general neighborhood."

"What did you say?" Courtney asked. "You had your hand in front of your mouth for a second."

"Oh, I'm sorry." Anna felt awful. She dropped her free hand to her side. "I said, yes, I live near here—in the general neighborhood."

"My husband and I have a floating home just a couple of blocks away," Courtney said. "Now that I know we're neighbors, Russ and I will have you over for drinks. Russ is my husband."

Anna noticed her rapidly spell out his name with her fingers.

"He's a big fan of your work," Courtney continued.

Anna tried to keep smiling, but she hated every minute of this. She thought about how she needed to split up with Russ. She couldn't do this anymore.

Courtney squinted at her. "Anna? I'm sorry, but do I make you uncomfortable?"

She quickly shook her head. "No, not at all."

"Are you sure? Over the years, I've gotten pretty good at reading people. I can pick up when they're uncomfortable around me because I'm deaf. They feel guilty or awkward or whatever. I've learned not to take it personally. Anyway, I was sort of getting that vibe from you."

Anna shook her head again. "No, no, I—I just feel bad that I didn't text you," she lied. "I really meant to. I enjoyed your book very much." She felt as if she was digging herself in deeper and deeper—when all she wanted to do was get out of there. She'd read the book and thought it was kind of stupid, but then she'd wanted it to be bad. "I read it in just a couple of days," she said.

Courtney smiled. "Well, if that's the case, I'm going to ask again if we can have coffee sometime. Better yet, maybe you can come over to the house for dinner—"

"No, coffee works better for me," Anna interrupted. "I've got such strange hours with my job."

"All right then. But I won't let you go until we actually make a date." Courtney put her basket down, then reached into her purse and pulled out her phone. "How's next week looking for you?"

They made a date to meet for coffee at Top Pot Doughnuts on Capitol Hill the following Wednesday afternoon. Though Anna still had some items to buy at Pete's, she headed directly to the checkout line. She was about to make a clean getaway and duck out when Courtney called to her: "Anna, do you need a ride?"

With the bag of groceries in one hand, she waved and shook her head. "I'm fine, thanks!" she called. It took her a moment to realize she didn't need to raise her voice. It didn't make any difference. "See you on Wednesday!" she said, making sure Courtney saw her. Then she hurried out of there.

A half block from the store, she had Russ on the phone.

"Wait until Tuesday night, and then cancel," he told her. "Send an e-mail and say you're sick or something. She just wants you to do a spot about her on the evening news. I can guarantee this is all about promoting her new book."

"God, I hate this," Anna muttered, hurriedly walking along the narrow road at the lake's edge. The grocery bag she carried felt heavy. "With you two in the neighborhood, I knew it was only a matter of time before I ran into Courtney. Now that she knows I live here, too, I'll be afraid to even leave the house. And she has my contact information. I'm going to have to keep dodging her."

Anna ended up going with Russ's strategy. She sent Courtney an e-mail late Tuesday night, explaining that she was coming down with a cold and couldn't make it to Top Pot the following afternoon.

Courtney texted back:

So sorry 2 hear UR not feeling well. Let me know if I can pick up anything 4 U at the store or if U need a ride 2 the doctor. Russ or I will B happy 2 drive U. Let's reschedule. Get well soon!

Anna almost wished Courtney wasn't so sweet about it.

One of the things she admired about Russ was that he didn't bad-mouth his wife to her all the time. He'd told Anna just enough so she automatically believed the gray-haired bookseller's remarks about Courtney's nastiness. But from the two times Anna had met her—and all those interviews—Courtney seemed perfectly decent. Anna felt horrible that she was sleeping with this nice, deaf woman's husband.

Courtney sent her a follow-up text a few days later:

Hi, Anna. I loved UR story on the news 2nite. U looked tabulous. I hope that means UR fooling a lot better. I low about coffee this week? I have a little gift 2 give U. I'm free in the afternoons. I think U said afternoons R best 4 U. Hope 2 hear from U soon!

"Just don't respond," Russ told her. "She'll get the picture and back off."

Anna didn't respond, but Courtney didn't back off.

Courtney talked to the station head at KIXI-TV, then he talked to Anna's boss, and Anna got the assignment to cover Courtney's book event at Elliott Bay Book Company the second Wednesday in July.

So Anna had to make—and actually keep—a coffee date with Courtney, who bought her a box of salted caramels. She said she remembered Anna mentioning on TV several weeks before that she loved salted caramels. Anna had expected her to be pushy and manipulative, but she was very pleasant. Courtney seemed genuinely interested in her.

"You certainly have the looks for TV," Courtney told

her, signing as she spoke. They shared a café table at Top Pot Doughnuts. "You're so pretty. In fact, my husband has a little crush on you. I should be jealous."

"Well, I—I'm flattered, thank you." Anna managed to smile, but she couldn't help squirming a bit in her chair.

"Do you have a partner?" Courtney asked. "Do you mind me asking?"

"No, I don't mind you asking," Anna lied. "And no, I don't have a partner. I—I'm not seeing anyone at the moment."

"I'll have to get to work on that," Courtney said. "I know a lot of handsome, eligible men—if you like men, that is. Just say the word, and I'll set you up."

"Well, I'm not in any hurry to get paired up with anyone just yet," Anna replied, the smile still plastered on her face. "But thanks anyway."

"You're smart," Courtney said with an exaggerated sigh. "Sometimes, I wish I were single. I find myself constantly compromising my career for my husband . . ." She continued to sign as she spoke. Anna wondered why she did that when talking to a non-deaf person who clearly didn't understand sign language. She figured maybe it was out of habit, or maybe it was to help educate people, albeit subliminally.

"Russ is a doctor," Courtney said. "And sometimes, I think, he expects me to put my writing second to meeting his needs, because, after all, he's out there saving lives. He works hard. I understand. He was an only child, and his parents were very wealthy, so he's pretty accustomed to getting everything he wants. It's not that he's demanding. He's just used to having things his way and being the center of attention."

Anna took a sip of coffee and said nothing. She hadn't noticed that about Russ.

"He's very attractive," Courtney went on. "You'll see that when you meet him. That's kind of a problem, too—women."

"Women?" Anna murmured, staring at her and blinking.

"They flock to him." Courtney frowned. "And like I said, Russ is accustomed to getting everything he wants. I had to break up something between him and this yoga instructor a couple of years ago. It was going on for a few months, and I finally told him, *'It's either me or her.'* I figured he would drop her, and he did. She moved to Pittsburgh, thank God. One thing I take comfort in—I know he's never going to leave me."

Anna just kept staring at her. All she could think was: *What about their agreement to divorce? Had Russ simply made that up?*

"I get the feeling he's recently started up with someone else," Courtney went on. "I have no idea who the woman is—or if there really is another woman. It's just that whenever I'm busy promoting a new book or working on a deadline, he starts to get restless."

"So—this happens a lot with him?" Anna heard herself ask.

Courtney took a bite out of her maple-glazed doughnut and shrugged.

"Why—why would you want to stay with him?" Anna asked. She suddenly felt sick.

"Once you get married, you find yourself making allowances you never thought you'd make." She laughed and quickly shook her head. "I can't believe I told you all this—and on our first coffee date! TMI, right? I know it's hard to believe, but Russ is really a very good man. I want you to like him when you meet him. Please, forget I said anything. We should be talking about the news story we're putting together."

After leaving Top Pot, once Anna climbed into her car, she phoned Russ. She was too upset to drive. So she just sat at the wheel and told him what had transpired over coffee with his wife.

"That's such a crock of shit!" he angrily whispered on the other end of the line. He was at work. "There haven't been any women. You're the only 'other woman,' Anna. I've never been involved with an aerobics instructor. I don't know why she'd tell you that—"

"*Yoga* instructor," Anna corrected him.

"See? I don't know what the hell she's talking about."

"Was this why you didn't want me getting together with Courtney?" Anna pressed. "Were you afraid she'd tell me about the other women?"

"I didn't want you to get together with Courtney for the same reason you didn't want to get together with her—because I knew it would just lead to trouble. Anna, she's lying. All I can think is that she's trying to get some sympathy from you. Maybe she figures you'll want to help promote her more if you feel sorry for her. God knows what her thinking is."

"She said she's pretty sure you're seeing someone right now, which just about gave me a heart attack. She also claims you're never going to leave her. That doesn't sound to me like someone who's about to have an amicable split with her husband."

"Oh God," he muttered. "I don't know where she came up with that, Anna. I didn't think she knew about us. But maybe she does—if she told you something like that. She's screwing with your head. This is classic Courtney. I shouldn't be surprised. She's been stalling on the lawyer talks, but I thought that was just because she's busy promoting the new book."

"I don't know which one of you I'm supposed to believe, Russ," she said into the phone. A few drops of rain hit the parked car's windshield. "But I have to say, I'm really getting fed up with both of you. I'm sorry, but I can't do this anymore."

"Please, Anna, just hang in there. Don't give up. Do her stupid promo piece for the news, and I guarantee she won't bother you again. That's all she wants from you. Once that segment goes on the air, you won't have her in your life anymore. And I'm going to end it with her. I promise, soon, neither one of us will have to deal with her."

Anna and Courtney met again to discuss the shooting schedule and locales for the profile segment. Then there were three long days of working closely together. All the time, she kept thinking: *This is Russ's wife.* It seemed so surreal.

Though Courtney was very friendly, Anna felt tense around her much of the time, and the sense of dread had her stomach in knots. She kept giving up a bit more control to Courtney at every turn—just to keep her happy. She was certain Courtney knew about her and Russ. And Anna desperately wanted to avoid any kind of confrontation.

But it seemed that all her fears were for naught. During those three days, Courtney mentioned Russ only in passing. There was no more talk about his alleged infidelities.

However, twice, she invited Anna to dinner so she could meet him. Anna politely wiggled out of both invitations. She couldn't imagine suffering through a sit-down dinner with the two of them.

Russ was supposed to attend Courtney's book signing, which Anna was covering on Wednesday night. But Anna's nerves couldn't take it, and she talked him out of coming to the bookstore. At the last minute, he pretended to have an emergency with one of his patients.

Anna could hardly wait for the assignment to wrap up—so she could breathe easily again. Though Courtney acted as if the two of them were fast friends, Anna believed what Russ had said was true. She and Courtney probably wouldn't see each other after the program aired. That was pretty much standard operating procedure with Anna's job anyway. She got extremely close to her subjects for a few days, but rarely saw them again. There were exceptions, of course; but Courtney wouldn't be one of them—not if Anna could help it.

She also believed what Russ had said about her being the only "other woman." But that didn't make the situation any less unseemly. She hated the idea of giving him up. It broke her heart. But she didn't want to live like this anymore.

Anna started to check out houses and condos in other parts of Seattle. If they didn't move out of her neighborhood, she'd be the one to relocate. She even thought about leaving Seattle. Maybe this was just the incentive she needed to apply for a job with one of the networks. Anna thought she might be able to make a clean getaway from this situation—no one besides her hurt, no confrontations, no mess. Dealing with the heartbreak of splitting up with Russ would be bad enough.

But then, on Thursday afternoon, as the shoot was wrapping up, Courtney insisted on treating her to a celebratory dinner at Canlis. She said that Russ was busy, and she didn't want to be alone.

Except for her call begging Russ to skip Courtney's book signing, Anna had purposely not talked with Russ. She had no idea what his plans were for the evening. She figured she could handle one last date with Courtney. She'd use editing the story as her excuse for leaving early.

Canlis was expensive and chic, so Anna donned a smart, red sleeveless cocktail dress for the dinner. The restaurant was on the other side of what Anna called "Amazon Hell," because of the insane traffic around the Amazon campus. So she took an Uber there. The restaurant was a big, midcentury modern edifice of stone, steel, and glass on the side of a cliff by the Aurora Bridge. The huge windows provided a spectacular view of North Seattle. Anna had eaten there a few times. It was quite posh.

Stepping inside the restaurant, Anna told the pretty young hostess that she was meeting Courtney Knoll: "She made reservations, but she might not have arrived yet."

The hostess smiled brightly. "Actually, they're here! Come this way."

They? Anna wanted to ask. With sudden trepidation, she followed the woman through the restaurant—with its wood paneling, white tablecloths, and diners dressed to the nines. The hostess led her to a booth with a crescent-shaped sofa and table.

Courtney looked beautiful in a simple brown sleeveless dress.

Russ sat next to her, wearing a blue blazer and a white shirt with the collar open.

Anna locked eyes with him and stopped dead. The stunned look on his face probably mirrored her own expression. Obviously, like her, he wasn't expecting a third for dinner.

Courtney smirked at her, and then she turned to Russ. Obviously, she enjoyed having set this up.

She knows, Anna thought.

The confrontation she'd been dreading suddenly seemed unavoidable.

Russ looked a bit unsteady as he politely stood.

Courtney turned to her again. "There you are!" She signed as she spoke. She patted the seat cushion. "Sit down. I've already ordered you a Lemon Drop."

Looking back on it, Anna wished she'd turned and walked out of the restaurant the moment she'd heard the hostess say "they." Maybe then, Courtney wouldn't be missing right now.

Within ninety minutes of sitting down in that semicircular booth with them, Anna would be too drunk to remember anything.

And now Russ wanted her to tell the police his version of what had happened after that. Anna had been determined to break up with Russ. But Courtney's sudden disappearance had instead made them coconspirators.

Staring out her kitchen window, Anna thought she saw movement out there in the darkness. But it was just shadows playing tricks on the indigo water. Still, she shuddered.

She remembered something Russ had told her earlier when he'd claimed she wouldn't see anything of Courtney once her story aired on the news. "I promise," he'd said, "soon, neither one of us will have to deal with her."

Anna shuddered again

She took one more spoonful of gelato before getting up from the breakfast table and returning the container to her freezer. She glanced at the clock on the microwave: 3:03 A.M.

Tired as she was, she probably wouldn't fall asleep tonight. And all the ice cream in the world wasn't going to help.

CHAPTER SEVEN

Saturday, July 11—12:42 P.M.

When her phone rang, Anna didn't have to wonder who it might be. She'd been anxiously waiting for Russ's call for the last forty-five minutes.

He'd phoned two hours earlier from the Bainbridge Island ferry. He'd said he would try to text her the minute Courtney showed up for the noon book signing—if she showed up.

The morning was gray and rainy. Anna had kept busy searching the house for her blue jeans and sneakers. It had become an obsession, so perturbing she'd almost forgotten about Courtney for a few minutes. It made absolutely no sense that these two items, which she wore practically every night, had suddenly, inexplicably vanished.

Just like Courtney, Anna thought.

The jeans and sneakers couldn't have been stolen. Who would want them? Besides, nothing else in the house was missing.

All she could think was that something had happened

to them late Thursday evening when she'd been so drunk. Had she woken up, put them on, and then, for some reason, thrown them away? Had all this happened during the time she'd lost?

Anna had looked inside her closet and under her bed—as well as under the daybed in the study. She'd gone through the garbage in the kitchen, her rag bin, and her storage closet. She would have even checked the dumpster by the dock access gate—if the city hadn't already collected it Friday morning. She'd practically turned the house upside down in her search. The place was a shambles.

She'd just started to clean up the mess when her phone rang.

Anna snatched it off the kitchen table on the third ring. She answered without looking at the caller ID: "What's happened?"

"She didn't show," Russ whispered glumly. "There were at least a hundred people here to see her, but no Courtney. They had to send everyone home. I talked to the store owner, which was awkward—a husband asking a total stranger if his wife had texted to cancel her book signing. I concocted some excuse about Courtney spending the night at a friend's on the island. Anyway, the store owner said she e-mailed Courtney last night to check in, and she never heard back."

Anna sat down at the kitchen table. "So, are you going to call the police?"

"I have to." He sighed. "Damn. I kept hoping Courtney had vanished just to screw with me. But she wouldn't miss this book signing. Something happened to her. God, I should've reported this earlier."

"You didn't know."

"Yeah, but then I think of all the crucial time I've wasted. And I just missed the ferry. There won't be another boat for an hour. Now I can't get home and call the police until three at the earliest."

"Why don't you just call them now—from the ferry terminal?" Anna asked.

"What if I get home and she's there? Or maybe I'll find she's packed another couple of bags and disappeared, or her car's gone. I'd have called the police for nothing."

"You just said something about all the valuable time you've wasted. Do you really want to put off calling the police for another couple of hours? Listen, if you want, I'll go over to your place and check to see if Courtney's car is in the parking lot. It's a silver Mazda CX-3, right? I can also check your house, ring the bell and see if she's home."

"I couldn't ask you to do that."

"You don't have to. I volunteered. So you're parked in the ferry terminal, waiting for the next boat?"

"Yeah, I'm not going anywhere," Russ said.

"Well, if there's no sign that Courtney's come home, I'll let you know. Then you can call the police from there. That will give them a couple of extra hours to start looking for her." Anna got to her feet. "I'll phone you in about a half hour—or less."

The small, fenced-in parking lot was close to Russ and Courtney's dock. The gate was locked, but Anna didn't need to get in. She could see Courtney's Mazda, parked just on the other side of the chain-link fence.

Holding an umbrella over her head, Anna stared at the car and the beads of rain on the windshield. Earlier in the week, she'd ridden in the Mazda a couple of times during the shoot with Courtney. While in the passenger seat, she'd noticed the custom oversize rearview mirror and the wide-angle side mirrors. They were supposed to give the deaf driver a visual advantage. Now, as she got a look at the driver's side, Anna noticed a blue and white sticker near the top of the door. It had a blue Star of Life sticker and the words DRIVER IS HEARING-IMPAIRED.

She had hoped the car would be gone. But, no, it was Courtney who was gone.

Anna shivered.

The rain had brought a slight chill to the air. Anna wished she'd worn something heavier than her shorts, a long-sleeve tee, and sandals. Her feet were getting wet. She'd left the house in a hurry to get here and hadn't been thinking.

Russ had given her the dock access code. Anna punched in the numbers, opened the metal gate, and stepped down to the dock. The floating homes were all upscale and pristine—in much better shape than the quaint houses on her dock. What a difference a few blocks made.

It was a short walk from Russ and Courtney's front door to the parking lot. Anna wondered if Courtney had been heading toward her car on Thursday night when something had happened to her. The dock was sturdy and wide enough, but the so-called railing bordered only one side: a cable—not even waist-high—ran from post to post. It was more decorative than practical. Someone who had had too much to drink easily could have tripped and fallen over the flimsy barrier.

Anna imagined Courtney hitting her head on one of the pilings or on the edge of the dock. She could have been knocked unconscious and then drowned. There would have been no scream to wake the neighbors, just a splash. Maybe the suitcase had fallen in with her.

Approaching Russ and Courtney's place, Anna paused and glanced down at the rain-dotted grayish water. She couldn't help wondering if Courtney's body was beneath the surface somewhere, snagged on a piling or trapped underneath one of these luxurious homes—like an old piece of rubbish.

She turned toward Russ and Courtney's two-story floating house near the end of the dock. The modern construction gave the place a boxy, sleek, almost charmless look. But it also smacked of money. The dark wood, metal, and glass house was surrounded by pots with perfectly trimmed small trees and shrubs. Russ said a gardener tended to them every week. The inside of their house was like something out of *Architectural Digest*. The views from the huge windows were magnificent—when the remote-controlled shades were up.

An arty-looking metal-and-glass piece above the front door served as a canopy. Anna collapsed her umbrella as she stepped under it, and then she rang the doorbell. It was a special bell that flashed the lights on inside the house—so Courtney would know someone was at the door.

Past the rain patter, Anna didn't hear a sound from inside the house. She really didn't expect Courtney to be home. But like Russ, she needed to make certain before he called the police to report her missing.

Anna knocked and waited again. Finally, she walked

around one of the potted shrubs and peered through the rain-beaded window. The living room was impressive and elegantly furnished, but not exactly cozy.

Right now, it was empty.

Russ said that the three of them had been in there Thursday night. He said Courtney had gotten abusive, but Anna couldn't remember any of it. She didn't even recall leaving Canlis with them.

What she remembered was the stricken look on Russ's face as she'd sat down at their table in the posh restaurant. He'd moved down toward one end of the semicircular cushioned seat to make room for her in the booth.

Courtney was between them. "At last, the three of us together!" she declared, signing as she spoke. She looked smug—or maybe she was already a little drunk, Anna couldn't be sure. Raising her glass as if to toast her, Courtney sipped her Lemon Drop.

Anna politely nodded at Russ, pretending he was a stranger. She couldn't help thinking that Courtney probably saw right through the facade. "I've heard a lot about you," Anna said.

"Same here," Russ replied with a tight smile.

"I've never seen him act so shy with a woman before," Courtney said. She patted Russ's arm. "Anna already knows you have a little crush on her. I told her so the first time I met her. The cat's out of the bag, Russ. She knows you DVR her news program every night." She turned to Anna, still signing—and smirking. "He's a big fan. He casually mentioned it to me years ago, and I teased him about it for the longest time after. You've never been married, Anna, so you might not get this. But it became one of those little jokes with us, the kind married people share. That's what you were to us—a joke."

Russ touched Courtney's arm, and she turned to him. He signed as he spoke: "I'm sure you didn't mean that the way it sounded."

The hell she didn't, Anna thought.

The young, pretty blond waitress arrived with Anna's drink—a slightly cloudy, pale-yellow concoction in a martini glass with a wafer-thin slice of lemon perched on the rim.

Courtney finished hers and pointed to the empty glass to let the waitress know that she was ready for another. Russ's pilsner beer glass was still three-quarters full. Courtney waited until the waitress left. She nodded at Anna's cocktail. "Drink up. We're celebrating."

Anna sipped the sweet-and-sour vodka mixture. It had a kick. She worked up a smile. "Very nice," she murmured.

"Funny thing," Courtney said. "But about a year or so ago, I noticed Russ no longer wanted to talk about you. I'd say something to him like, *Your girlfriend was on the news tonight,* and he'd act indifferent. I knew he was still watching you. I knew he was still a fan, but obviously, he didn't want to talk about it. I wondered what happened. Maybe he got tired of my teasing."

In her previous discussions with Courtney, Anna hadn't been able to distinguish inflections in her tone. It was hard to pick up when Courtney was being sarcastic. But tonight, practically everything she said dripped with irony. She was mocking the two of them, and relishing it. Clearly, she was aware of what had been going on. It had been a little over a year since Anna had first met Russ. Had Courtney known all this time?

Russ touched Courtney's arm once again to get her attention. "I don't really remember that far back, but maybe you're right," he said—and signed. His expression was deadpan. "I probably got tired of your teasing."

It was strange for Anna to see him using sign language with his wife. They had this connection she knew nothing about. She sat there, watching them bicker in sign language—and it was all about her. Anna just wanted to get out of there.

The waitress arrived with Courtney's second cocktail. Courtney turned to Anna: "You're not going to let me drink alone, are you?"

Anna reluctantly took another swallow of the potent concoction.

"We're lucky Russ could join us tonight," Courtney said. "One thing you can always be sure about when you're a doctor's wife, and that is, you can't count on them for anything—dinners, birthdays, anniversaries"—she shot Russ a look—"or book signings. He's constantly missing special occasions. Some emergency always comes up. Somebody always gets sick. You can't plan anything because, inevitably, some little bastard is going to get the croup."

As she spoke, Courtney's voice became a bit louder and her gestures a bit wilder. "Everyone thinks it must be so wonderful to be married to a doctor. I suppose that's true, if you don't care about having a career of your own—if you like being a sidekick, always in the background. I've had years of that. People think Russ is a saint, because he's a doctor and because he married a 'handicapped' woman . . ."

Russ tapped her arm again. "That's bullshit," he whispered, frowning at her.

Courtney sipped her cocktail and waved away his comment. Her eyes narrowed at Anna. "Drink up! Don't you like it?"

Shifting on the seat cushion, Anna took another swallow of the drink.

"I'm just telling Anna what it's like to be married to a doctor," Courtney continued, "just in case she has any plans along those lines. It's not what it's cracked up to be. No one ever thinks about lawsuits. The possibility is always hanging over your head. It's not a matter of *if* you might get sued. It's more like *when* your husband will eventually be sued—especially if he's a pediatrician. Can you imagine what it's like living with someone who has that hanging over his head all the time? He gets so moody and depressed."

Anna knew what she was talking about. She'd comforted Russ when certain patients of his had died or gotten a grim diagnosis, and when he'd had to give a speech to the devastated parents. The fact that he cared so much was one of the things she loved about him. But, of course, she couldn't say anything. Anna took another gulp of her cocktail, which was starting to taste smoother.

"Courtney," Russ said, getting her attention again. "I don't think Anna necessarily wants to hear all this."

"Nonsense, I'm sure she finds it fascinating—and very educational." Courtney turned to Anna. "For example, did you know that every year in the United States, over four hundred doctors commit suicide?"

Russ gently took hold of his wife's arm. "And if you don't change the subject soon, as of tonight, it's going to be four hundred and one."

Laughing, Courtney took another hit of her drink, and then turned to Anna. "Do I sound like a disgruntled wife? If I do, let me assure you, I'm never going to leave my husband. You know, everyone thinks doctors make a ton of money. Well, not really, not when they're starting out. Thanks to Russ's parents, we've never been poor, but we also had his medical school student loans to pay off, which was like the national debt. With my movie deal, now I'm the real moneymaker between the two of us. And I'm not giving any of that up. As long as we're living in Washington State—with its community property laws— we're staying married."

"Isn't that sweet?" Russ said. He tapped Courtney's shoulder, and then signed as he spoke. "You're embarrassing me with all this romantic talk, sweetheart."

Anna was silent. Courtney had just confirmed for her what Russ had said about his wife suddenly changing her mind about separating. The movie deal was recent. It made sense now. And it was reassuring to realize Russ hadn't merely been stringing her along. At the same time, Courtney was spelling it out for her: the possibility of a divorce was next to nil.

"Let's change the subject," Russ announced. He looked at Anna. "So, have you put together the story on Courtney yet? Or are you doing that tomorrow?"

"Tomorrow," Anna answered. "I have a bunch of notes on how it's going to be edited. We got some great material." She reached for her glass and saw it was empty. Anna hadn't realized how much she'd been drinking.

"Waitress!" Courtney called. It seemed like most everyone in the restaurant had heard her—including their young waitress, who hastened to their table. Courtney pointed to Anna's empty glass—and then to her own, which was half-full.

"I'll get those for you," the waitress said with a cordial smile. "Meanwhile, would you like to hear about our dinner specials?"

"I can't *hear* anything!" Courtney snapped, signing wildly. "I'm deaf! Just the drinks, okay?"

"Yes, ma'am, right away," the young woman murmured. Then she withdrew.

"Jesus," Russ grumbled. The way he signed—so close to his chest—it almost seemed like a visual whisper. "You know I can't stand it when you're rude to waitpeople."

Courtney belted down the rest of her drink. "She knew I was kidding."

"She wasn't laughing. Anna's not laughing, and neither am I."

"Sorry," Courtney muttered, glancing at Anna. Then she rolled her eyes at Russ. "I forget—you're trying to impress your newslady crush. But I don't have to. Anna and I have been hanging together for most of the week. We're friends, aren't we?"

Anna nodded. "Of course."

"Anna knows all about me. But she has no idea that I've done my research on her, too. When I found out a few tidbits about Anna's past, it suddenly made sense to me why you have a thing for her, Russ. She and I are a lot alike. You must have a thing for successful women who come from trash—me with my trailer park slut mother and my sister dying of a drug overdose . . ." She turned toward Anna. "And you, your father ended up hanging himself in jail, and your mother killed someone and herself driving while drunk. I'll bet you had no idea I knew about that."

"All right, that's enough," Russ growled.

"My mother wasn't drunk when she had that car accident," Anna said. But Courtney's head was turned slightly, so it was lost on her.

The waitress arrived with their drinks.

"Thank you!" Courtney said—and signed. "You know, earlier, I was just kidding. I didn't mean to make you uncomfortable. If I did, I'm so sorry."

The young blonde smiled. "It's perfectly fine."

"By the way, you've been so great. It's easy to read your lips, and you don't talk down to me. You wouldn't believe how many people speak to me like I'm a child just because I'm deaf. But you don't do that at all. Could you tell us about the dinner specials? I think we're ready to order."

The waitress nodded. "Sure, I'd love to tell you about our specials. Tonight, we have a salmon . . ."

Anna saw how Courtney worked the waitress, getting her sympathy so quickly after being rude to her. It was how, in part, Courtney had been manipulating her, too. Anna had spent the better part of the week trying to please her. Now she was sorely tempted to get up and leave. She wanted to tell Courtney that Russ already knew about her family —and by bringing it up, she was only coming across as a first-class bitch.

But Anna continued to sit there while the waitress described the specials. Anna reached for her second Lemon Drop.

She still couldn't remember how many of those lethal cocktails she'd had. But she recalled, once they'd ordered dinner, she'd felt trapped at that table with the two of them. And she'd been utterly miserable.

Courtney's cattiness had come in waves. She'd be nice one minute, then nasty the next. Most of her snipes had been aimed at Russ. She'd never come out and accused the two of them of having an affair, but she'd sure as hell danced around the subject.

Looking back at it now, Anna figured Russ's wife must have been very drunk. Sober, Courtney wouldn't have allowed her to see that awful side of her, not the night before the promo spot was going to air.

Anna had never seen Russ so tense and exasperated. But he'd kept his cool. And from what she could remember, he'd had only the one beer.

Anna shivered.

She realized she'd been standing in the rain for several minutes now. Russ and Courtney's living room was still unoccupied. No one was home.

Opening her umbrella, she retreated down the dock and took out her phone. She called Russ.

"Hey," he answered.

"The car's still here, and the house is empty," she told him.

"Thanks for checking, honey. I'll call the police and report her missing. Listen, I'm not going to tell them about us. But if they ask, I won't lie. So—keep that in mind if they end up talking to you before we get a chance to connect again."

"Okay," she said, taking a deep breath. "Now that the police are getting involved, I guess it's official."

"Looks that way," he murmured.

Anna shut the dock gate behind her. Then she glanced back at the rain on the silver-gray water. She knew nothing was going to be the same again.

"I love you," Russ said. It sounded so final.

"I love you, too," she said.

Then Anna hung up.

CHAPTER EIGHT

Saturday, July 11—5:07 P.M.

Heading down the tree-lined road at the lake's edge, Anna glanced over her shoulder.

The black Jetta was still behind her. It had been following her since she'd left her dock—four blocks back.

Anna had been going stir-crazy, waiting around the house for a call from Russ—or from the police. She'd thought Russ would have at least texted to update her on what was happening. He should have returned home two hours ago. Had he been talking with the police all this time?

She'd kept busy cleaning up the mess she'd created earlier looking for her sneakers and jeans. Then she'd noticed a break in the rain and decided to walk down to Pete's Supermarket for some groceries. She'd been so stressed, she'd figured, fight or flight, the exercise would do her some good—even if it was just five blocks each way.

Anna had brought along her phone, of course. She also had her umbrella, figuring it might start raining again.

What she hadn't counted on was someone tailing her.

For the last ten minutes, the black Jetta had been crawling behind her. With the treetops and the overcast sky reflecting on the dark windshield, Anna couldn't see the driver. And she couldn't tell if anyone was in the passenger seat. So far, the Jetta had pulled over and stopped three times to let other cars pass. Then, each time, after a few moments, it would resume creeping behind her. At first, Anna had figured someone was merely looking for a parking spot. But she'd already walked past three open spots. The ever-lurking vehicle passed them, too.

She glanced over her shoulder again. Right now, she was more annoyed than scared. If it were nighttime, she'd be freaking out.

She told herself it could be a tourist. Maybe they were looking for the *Sleepless in Seattle* houseboat. She got that on occasion while walking to Pete's. Someone would pull over and ask where Tom Hanks's floating home was. They didn't realize it was on the other side of the lake. But wouldn't the driver of the black Jetta have pulled up and asked her by now?

It was driving her crazy. She couldn't help thinking this person following her might be Courtney. Or maybe it was someone involved in Courtney's disappearance.

She finally reached Pete's. The supermarket was in a '70s-era tan brick structure with big windows. It had a wood-sided, two-story apartment building tacked on above it—one of those places that look like they were put up in a hurry. There was a pay phone on the wall by the market entrance. The shell around the pay phone was kind of beat-up and marred with graffiti, but the phone was intact. Despite a new illuminated sign above the entry, the store—like that relic of a phone—seemed happily stuck in the '70s.

Anna wondered if the Jetta might pull into one of the diagonal parking spaces beside the market. What then? Would someone get out of the car and follow her into the store?

With uncertainty, Anna headed toward the entrance. But then she stopped and swiveled around. She glared at the black Jetta. The pay phone had given her an idea.

Eyes still glued on that darkened windshield, she reached into her purse and took out her phone. She was about to take a photo of the car—and its license plate.

The Jetta suddenly lurched forward.

For a horrible moment, Anna thought the car was going to plow into her. But, with tires screeching, the vehicle spun into a right turn and sped up a side road.

Her heart beating wildly, Anna stood there for a moment, paralyzed.

When she could move again, she ducked into the store. It took a few moments for Anna to catch her breath. She wished she'd gotten a photo of the car's license plate.

Grabbing a grocery basket, she started down the first aisle. She felt a little shaky. She had a weird thought: *What if the driver of that car had been a cop?* Now that Russ had called them, maybe the police had assigned someone to follow her around.

She quickly dismissed the notion. It was ridiculous. It just showed how paranoid she'd become. She already had herself pegged as a suspect in Courtney's disappearance— and the police hadn't even talked to her yet.

Still, they would almost automatically have their

doubts about Russ. Wasn't the husband always the first suspect? Plus he had an awfully weak alibi for his whereabouts when Courtney had vanished: aimlessly driving around from midnight until two in the morning. Maybe the police had already figured out he was hiding something—specifically, something about the other woman who had dined with him and Courtney on Thursday night.

But it made no sense that the cops were following her already. And the crazy way that black Jetta had peeled up the side street, no cop would drive that way—not unless they were chasing somebody.

Now that Courtney's disappearance was an official police matter, Anna couldn't help feeling nervous—doomed even. Russ's and her past would be held under public scrutiny. And any hopes for a future together were impossible.

Despite accumulating evidence to the contrary, Anna still hoped that Courtney's vanishing act was just that—an *act* to screw with Russ's head. Anna didn't even want to think that Courtney might be dead.

Either way, she had to brace herself for a scandal. She'd probably lose her job. Her likability quotient was bound to plunge once it got out that she'd been sleeping with someone's husband—and not just *someone*, but the popular author of young adult books, a deaf woman who had overcome her deafness to inspire others.

What was wrong with her? Here she was, worrying about her job when Courtney could be dead.

Anna was leaving the checkout stand with a bag of groceries when her phone rang.

Russ, at last, she thought, *thank God.* She almost dropped the bag as she frantically dug into her purse for the phone. She stepped over to one side, by an ATM, and set down her groceries. She didn't even glance at the caller ID before answering: "Yes? Hello?"

"You bitch," someone whispered in a raspy voice.

Anna couldn't tell if it was a man or a woman. And she wasn't sure if she'd correctly heard what the caller had said. "What?" she asked. "Who is this?"

"I saw you fucking kill her. I saw it."

There was a click on the other end—then a clatter, as if the phone had been dropped.

Anna stood there. Once again, she couldn't get a breath.

What the hell?

She checked her phone screen: *Caller Unknown.* She immediately thought about her unknown caller last night: *"You're . . . not . . . fooling . . . anyone."* And she also thought about the black Jetta that had been tailing her ten minutes ago.

The phone still clutched in her hand, she grabbed the grocery bag and hurried outside. She glanced up and down the narrow street. There was no sign of the black car anywhere. Hurrying to the corner, Anna looked up the side street: nothing. She turned toward the market entrance.

The pay phone dangled in the air, gently swaying at the end of the cord—like a corpse at the end of a hangman's noose.

Anna's phone rang in her hand, and she almost jumped. This time, she immediately checked the caller ID: *Russell Knoll, MD.*

"Russ?" she said anxiously.

"I'm so sorry I haven't called," he whispered, sounding hurried. "My phone battery died twenty minutes into my conversation with the police. And I didn't have my charger with me—"

"That's okay," she interrupted. "Listen, somebody just called me—"

"The police were waiting for me here when I got home," he said, talking over her. "They've been grilling me for the last two hours. It's been a nightmare. While they were waiting for me, this detective and her assistant, they spoke to some of my neighbors. The neighbors heard arguing on Thursday night, Courtney yelling. As you know, she has a very distinctive voice. One of the neighbors reported hearing a loud splash shortly after midnight."

"My God," Anna murmured.

"While this detective was going through the living room, she found a drop of blood at the bottom of the bookcase. Now they want to go over the whole house for evidence. I have to move into a hotel tonight. Anyway, I'm packing right now. They sent for this cop, and he's here, waiting for me on the back deck. The detective in charge of the investigation is on her way over to see you. I didn't tell her about us. She didn't ask. But I think she might have put two and two together. Anyway, I just wanted to warn you."

Trying to take it all in, Anna hadn't moved from the corner in front of the store. She stared at the pay phone. The dangling handset had stopped swaying.

"Anna? Are you still there? The police should be at your place any minute now."

"I—I'm not home," she said. She started down the road—toward her dock. "But I'm headed there now. I was at Pete's Market. You—you said they found blood?"

"Yeah, they tagged it with a yellow Post-it. They tagged a bunch of other things. There must be a dozen of those yellow tags around the place."

Picking up the pace, Anna kept the phone close to her ear. From what Russ was saying, it sounded like the police were treating this more like a murder investigation than a runaway or missing person case.

"Another thing," Russ said. "I suddenly realized that Courtney's Best Debut Novel Award—or something like that—it's this heavy glass object, anyway, it's missing. It's usually on the bookcase where they found the drop of blood. I'm praying that the blood is old and that Courtney took the award with her. She was so proud of that stupid thing."

"Listen, Russ," Anna said—a bit breathless. She continued to walk at a brisk clip—and the grocery bag wasn't light. "On my way to the store, this car—a black Jetta—followed me. When I tried to take a picture of it, the car tore up the street like a bat out of hell. Then ten minutes later—it was right before you phoned—I got the strangest call. In this bizarre, creepy voice, he—or she, I couldn't tell—whoever it was called me a bitch and said, *'I saw you fucking kill her.'*"

"What?" he murmured. "Did they say anything else?"

"No, after that, they hung up." Anna glanced over her shoulder to make sure no one was following her. She didn't see anyone. "I think they may have even called from the pay phone outside the store. It must be the same creep who called me last night. But I don't know for sure.

The voice seemed different. Russ, does anyone else know besides the two of us that Courtney's missing?"

"Well, yeah, as of four hours ago, I told the police—"

"No, I mean, have you mentioned it to anyone else?" Anna pressed.

"No one," Russ said. "But—well, before the phone battery ran out, I told the police pretty much everything that happened on Thursday night. Do you think it's possible someone got it off a police scanner or the news went out on some kind of wire service? You're in the news business. Does it work like that?"

"Sometimes," Anna murmured.

"Do you suppose some nut got the news and decided to harass you?"

Anna wasn't listening. She was thinking about her stalker from last October—and last night's bizarre call, which had been before the police knew about Courtney.

"Anna?"

"Yes?"

"Let me know if you get any more calls like that. Listen, I need to go. I'm sure the cop downstairs is wondering what's taking me so long. They want to take me to the precinct and fingerprint me—"

"Fingerprint you?"

"It's just to eliminate all my fingerprints in the living room."

"Well, I was there on Tuesday and Wednesday, and so was George, my cameraman. They might want our prints, too. You might tell them that."

"Maybe you should tell the detective when you talk to her," Russ whispered. "Work it in somehow. I'd rather they not know we've been talking here. It might look bad."

"It's already looking bad, Russ," she said, feeling her insides tighten. "It's already looking pretty awful."

Anna passed her carport and noticed a young man standing at the dock gate. Tall, pale, and lanky, he wore dark trousers and a white, short-sleeve shirt with a tie. He seemed to be standing guard. Anna was pretty certain he'd already spotted her. She suddenly knew how Russ felt: talking with him on the phone seemed at the very least, suspicious. She almost wanted to hang up and hide the phone. But it was too late.

"Does the detective's assistant have blond hair and dress like a Mormon missionary?" Anna asked.

"Yeah," Russ said.

She waved to the young man. "He can see I'm on the phone," she whispered. "So I'm telling him we've talked— that you called to let me know the police were on their way over. I'm not going to lie to them about any of this, Russ. I won't volunteer anything, but I won't lie to them, either."

"Oh Jesus," he said, sighing. "Okay, yeah, you're right. I'll call you later."

"Gotta go," she said. Then she hung up.

As she approached the young detective, Anna once again found herself short of breath. "I'm Anna Malone," she called. She hated the little quaver in her voice. "Are you here to see me?"

CHAPTER NINE

Saturday, July 11—5:33 P.M.

Poised near the end of the dock, the woman was obviously trying to peek into Anna's living room window. Anna guessed she was about fifty. She had a pretty, slightly careworn face and crimped silver hair that fell down to her shoulders. Her tight-fitting blue blouse and khaki slacks showed off a buxom figure. She carried a notebook and murmured into a mini-recorder. Her police badge was pinned at her belt.

Anna couldn't take much offense to her snooping around. She'd done the exact same thing outside Russ and Courtney's floating home a few hours ago.

The officer waiting by the dock gate—the one who looked like a Mormon missionary—was in his early twenties. It looked like he'd cut his own hair—sandy blond mini-bangs. But he was still kind of cute in a nerdy way. A minute ago, he'd introduced himself as Officer Lloyd Bransky, and pointed out, rather bashfully, that he enjoyed her segments on the news.

"Well, thank you," Anna had said with a strained smile.

She'd slipped her phone into her purse. "I just got a call from Dr. Knoll. He said you were on your way. I'm sorry I wasn't here. I was at the store. I hope you weren't waiting long."

She'd figured this tack would give the impression of total transparency. But her voice still had that nervous tremor in it. For a TV journalist, it was maddeningly unprofessional. But she was still rattled over the news that they'd discovered some blood in Russ and Courtney's living room. All she could think about was the creepy voice on the phone, saying she'd killed Courtney. Of course it was a lie, but the part about Courtney being dead seemed more and more real.

The policewoman met her and the young cop by Anna's red front door. "Anna Malone? Hi, I'm Detective Kit Baumann." She slipped her recorder in her purse and shook Anna's hand. "I see you've met Officer Bransky."

The young officer whispered in Detective Baumann's ear for a few moments. He almost seemed like a kid telling his mom a secret. Baumann nodded patiently, but she rolled her eyes, too. "Okay, thanks," she said. Then she turned to Anna. "I understand that Dr. Knoll called you about our visit. So—that should save us some time. I just have a few questions."

Setting down her grocery bag, Anna took out her keys and unlocked her front door. "Yes, of course. Won't you come in?" She opened the door and let them go inside first. Then, brushing past them, she hurried into the kitchen and set the grocery bag on the table. "Can I get you something to drink? A soda or water or coffee?"

"No, thanks," Detective Baumann said, standing in the

kitchen doorway. "I understand you spent the better part of last week with Courtney."

Anna nodded a few more times than necessary. "Yes, I did a profile spot about her for the news. It aired on Friday."

"I know, I had another look at it on YouTube on our way here. Did you know Courtney very well?"

Anna was about to unload the grocery bag, but hesitated. "Well, we shot that segment for three days and one night. So—I guess you could say we sort of became fast friends. It's part of my job. When I do a profile piece on someone, I get to know a lot about them very quickly."

"You weren't friends with Courtney before?" the detective asked. "I got the impression you knew her."

"We ran into each other a few times before that, and then Courtney talked me into doing the profile about her. But I didn't know her all that well until we started working on the news story together." She glanced down at her bag. "Would you mind if I put some of this stuff in the refrigerator?"

Baumann smiled. "Go ahead. I didn't mean to hold you up." She glanced over her shoulder at the other officer.

Anna couldn't quite see the look that passed between them. She started to unload the groceries.

"During your time together with Courtney this past week, did she confide in you much?" the detective asked.

"I guess so," Anna allowed, setting a carton of milk on the table.

"Did she mention having any enemies, or if someone was stalking her, or threatening her?"

Anna stopped to consider the question. She shook her head. "No."

"Any guy friends she might have told you about?"

"No."

"I understand from her husband that Courtney had a lot to drink on Thursday night. Was that the first time you'd seen her intoxicated?"

"Yes. I'm afraid I had too much to drink that night, too. I don't remember much." She put the milk, a carton of orange juice, and a package of chicken breasts inside the refrigerator.

"I'll get to Thursday night in a minute. I'm trying to determine if Courtney has a drinking problem—or maybe even a drug problem."

"I didn't get that impression," Anna said, closing the refrigerator door. "Did you ask Dr. Knoll? He'd have a better idea about that than I would."

"Sometimes the husband is the last to know," Officer Bransky piped up from behind Baumann's shoulder.

"Well, I didn't get that impression," Anna repeated.

"What impression did you get?" the detective pressed. "I mean, how would you describe Courtney—in general?"

Anna shrugged. "I think she's—quite talented and ambitious. She never seems to let her disability slow her down. In fact—" Anna hesitated. She was about to say, *In fact, she uses it to her advantage,* but she thought better of it. "In fact, it hasn't slowed her down one bit. Courtney is assertive, very sure of what she wants. Her career is really important to her, and so is her image. I think she feels she's on the brink of becoming famous." She sighed. "I don't know what else to tell you about her." She grabbed a pint of gelato off the table and stashed it in the freezer.

Baumann gave her a sidelong glance. "You mentioned

earlier that Courtney talked you into doing the piece about her on the news. So it wasn't your idea?"

"Not originally," Anna answered. "But that's not unusual. Most of my news stories are assigned to me or someone persuades me to take on a certain subject." She nodded at her half-empty grocery bag. "I can put the rest of this away later. We might be more comfortable talking in the living room."

As Anna led the way, she got a waft of Baumann's patchouli perfume. She also noticed her flushed face and the beads of perspiration on her forehead. Anna figured she was probably having hot flashes. She was just about at that age.

Meanwhile, the young officer glanced around the living room in awe. "Nice," he murmured to his superior. "If I had a houseboat, I'd have one just like this."

He and Detective Baumann settled on the sofa while Anna sat down in an easy chair. "Let's get back to dinner at Canlis on Thursday night," Baumann said, all business. "You mentioned that both you and Courtney had a lot to drink. How many drinks would you say you had?"

"At least three cocktails, maybe four or five, I'm not certain," Anna answered. She got up, switched on the fan, and sat back down again. "Courtney kept reordering for me. And I'm not much of a drinker."

"How much would you say Courtney had to drink?"

"I'm pretty sure she'd had one or two cocktails before I got there. Lemon Drops, they were pretty strong. After that, she kept pace with me."

"So—she had at least four or five cocktails, maybe even more. How was her mood?"

Anna hesitated. She knew the detective had already

talked with Russ. Was she double-checking to see if their stories matched?

"Courtney was—argumentative," Anna answered carefully. "She kept picking at her husband, complaining how difficult it was being married to a doctor. It started out like she was teasing him, but then it seemed to grow abusive. And she was loud, partly because of being deaf. But she got even louder the more she drank. I was embarrassed."

Don't say any more, she thought. *If they think Russ has anything to do with Courtney's disappearance, this isn't helping. It's bad enough that they found blood in the living room.*

"Dr. Knoll seemed to take it in his stride," she added. "But I felt so tense that I just kept drinking. I remember getting through dinner, but I couldn't tell you when we left the restaurant."

"Dr. Knoll said that the three of you drove back to their floating home at around ten-thirty," Detective Baumann said. She brushed a bead of sweat from the side of her face. "What you say about Courtney's behavior jibes with what he told us. Apparently, she was even more argumentative when they got home."

"I'm sorry I don't remember," Anna said. "Then again, maybe it's a blessing I blacked that out."

"According to Dr. Knoll, you weren't feeling well, and he drove you home around eleven o'clock. You got sick, and he put you to bed. Do you remember any of that?"

"Vaguely," she replied. In truth, she didn't remember it at all, but she wanted to back up what Russ had said as much as she could. "It's all kind of a blur from the time we left the restaurant until I woke up Friday morning on the daybed in my study, horribly hungover. I was wearing a dressy pullover that Dr. Knoll must have mistaken for a T-shirt or a pajama top."

Anna thought this quirky little detail might bring some authenticity to the story— and show that Russ had the best of intentions. She also figured, being a woman, the detective might find this aspect of the story somewhat amusing.

But Kit Baumann barely cracked a smile. "Yes, he told us that he'd cleaned you up and helped you change into some nightclothes. That must have been embarrassing for you, a total stranger, practically . . ."

Here it comes, Anna thought. *Just how well do you know Dr. Knoll?*

"I felt so awful Friday morning," she said. "It didn't even dawn on me until later what exactly had happened. But then, I figure, he's a doctor, and I should be happy I didn't wake up in a puddle of my own vomit. He called me yesterday morning. In fact, his call woke me up. He wanted to know if I'd heard from Courtney. He told me that, after he left here, he went for a drive. When he came home around two in the morning, Courtney was gone—along with her overnight bag. We checked in with each other a couple of times last night. I left Courtney three messages, but didn't hear back. I figured Courtney must have switched off her phone and checked into a hotel or something. I thought maybe she was too embarrassed to talk to me, and she was giving her husband the silent treatment. But Russ—Dr. Knoll—he was genuinely worried about her."

Anna shifted in her chair. She couldn't believe she'd slipped up and used Russ's first name like that. Now she was starting to perspire, too. She told herself to keep talking.

"He said that if Courtney didn't show up to her book signing today, then he'd call the police."

"What do you mean by 'the silent treatment'?" the detective asked, leaning forward.

Anna shrugged. "Like—you know, when you're angry with someone and won't talk to them. I thought Courtney might have disappeared and become incommunicado to punish him or screw with his head."

"What gave you the impression Courtney would behave like that?"

Anna wasn't sure how to answer that question.

"During this last week with her," the detective pressed, "did Courtney confide in you about her marriage?"

"Not very much," Anna said. It wasn't really a lie. Courtney had told her all that garbage about Russ's infidelity nearly a month ago. "I know she was upset with Dr. Knoll because he couldn't attend her book signing at Elliott Bay Books on Wednesday evening. That's why she was giving him so much grief on Thursday night. I figured she might have taken the punishment even further by packing her bag and disappearing. But then, she didn't show up to that book signing, and now, I don't know what to think. Courtney wouldn't neglect her fans just because she's upset at her husband."

"You mentioned that Courtney's career and her image are very important to her," Detective Baumann said. "So perhaps that explains something very strange to me. It seems when Courtney packed her things, she left behind some night cream her husband says she uses every evening at bedtime. But apparently, she took with her a writing award of some kind. Does that make any sense to you?"

"Well, Courtney was pretty drunk on Thursday night," Anna said, wincing a bit. "Maybe she wasn't thinking clearly."

She knew the award that Detective Baumann was talking about, the same one Russ had said was missing from the bookcase. Anna had noticed it in the living room when they'd been shooting one of the segments at Russ and Courtney's floating home. It was a glass objet d'art in the shape of a writing quill—with a black base that was supposed to be an ink bottle. At least, the quill looked like it was glass. It might have been Lucite or crystal, Anna wasn't sure. The point of the quill was a tilted steel rod fixed to the inkwell base. The thing was about ten inches tall and looked heavy. The silver plate on the black base was inscribed: THE NORTHWEST LITERARY SOCIETY'S BEST FICTION DEBUT AWARD. Courtney had pointed it out to her and tried to dismiss the award as "tacky" and "phallic-looking," but Anna could tell she was secretly proud of it. The award was even mentioned in her website biography—and in most of her press releases. Maybe she had indeed taken it with her on Thursday night.

But Anna couldn't help thinking about how that bloodstain was on the same bookcase where Courtney had kept the award. And she couldn't help imagining a drunken Courtney saying something vile and horrible to Russ, pushing him to the breaking point. She could see him grabbing the first heavy thing within reach and smashing her skull with it.

Was the Northwest Literary Society Award with Courtney now? Or was it at the bottom of Lake Union with traces of blood and brain still clinging to it?

"What are you thinking about?"

Anna stared at Kit Baumann and blinked. "I'm sorry—"

Her phone rang.

Anna realized she'd left it in her purse on the kitchen table. She was about to get up, but hesitated.

"Maybe you should answer that," Detective Baumann said. She raised an eyebrow. "It might be Dr. Knoll."

Anna got to her feet. "Excuse me," she murmured. Hurrying into the kitchen, she reached into her purse and found the phone. She could still see the detective and the young officer on the sofa, watching her. The detective fanned herself. Officer Bransky leaned toward his superior and whispered something to her.

Anna glanced at the caller ID: *Unknown Caller*. Was it the same awful person with the raspy voice who had phoned before?

The ringing stopped. "It went to voice mail," Anna announced, stashing the phone back inside her purse. "Probably just a telemarketer."

She returned to the living room and sat down across from them again.

Someone else's phone rang. Anna wasn't sure if it was the detective's or her assistant's.

"Well, now it's my turn. Pardon me." Baumann reached into her satchel, took out her phone, and glanced at it. She tapped the screen. "Yes, Gary, what's going on?" she said.

Anna looked at the young officer. "Are you sure I can't get you anything to drink?" she whispered.

He quickly shook his head. "No, thanks," he said under his breath.

Anna was wondering about her own phone call, the anonymous one that had gone to voice mail.

"Well, that's fast work, thank you, Gary," Detective Baumann said. Putting down the phone, she frowned at Anna and sighed. "A couple of hours ago, I requested a check on Courtney's phone and credit cards. That was a colleague calling with the results. No activity at all since early Thursday evening."

"Oh God," Anna murmured under her breath. She was thinking about Russ's assumption that Courtney had called Uber or a taxi for a ride to wherever she was headed late Thursday night. This new revelation shot down that hypothesis.

Baumann turned to her colleague. "We've got to get forensics over there now," she muttered. "I want them to check the perimeter of the house and the dock before it rains again."

The two of them got to their feet. Baumann gave Anna a somber look. "Since you were in the house on Thursday night, we'll need to get your fingerprints so we can rule them out."

Anna stood up. She nodded. "Elimination prints, I understand. My videographer was filming the segment there with me on Thursday morning. Do you need his prints, too?"

"I sure do," the detective replied. "What's your colleague's name?"

"George Danziger," Anna said.

Her back to the other officer, Detective Baumann spoke over her shoulder to him. "You got that?" She started for the front door.

"I'm not sure how to spell it."

Anna spelled it out for him. She followed Baumann to the door and opened it for her.

The detective handed Anna a card with her contact information on it. "I realize it might be inconvenient, but could you and your colleague stop by the East Precinct within the next hour? The address is on the card. I probably won't be there, but they'll be expecting you. All they'll do is take your fingerprints and then you'll be on your merry way. I promise it won't take long."

"I'll call him right now," Anna said.

"You do that," Baumann said. "Thank you for all your help, Anna. We'll be in touch with you again, I'm sure."

"Thanks very much, ma'am," the young officer said, nodding at her. He followed the detective out the door.

Anna stood in the doorway and watched them walking down the dock. She figured Baumann was a woman of her word. She was sure to be in touch again.

Anna stepped back inside and closed the door.

She wanted to call Russ, but figured he was probably at the police station right now. She'd wait for him to call her.

Meanwhile, she'd have to phone George and give him the disconcerting news that the cops needed to fingerprint him. She hoped he was home. She'd offer to pick him up so that they could drive to the precinct together. She didn't want to go through it alone.

Anna returned to the kitchen and reached into her purse for her phone. Then she remembered she had a message from that Unknown Caller.

Taking a deep breath, Anna tapped the voice mail icon on her phone screen.

There were a couple of seconds of silence, and then that same raspy voice again, making her skin crawl: "Do the police know you've been fucking her husband?"

CHAPTER TEN

Sunday, July 12—10:22 A.M.

Driving north on Highway 99 toward the Aurora Bridge, Anna turned on to the spiraling, shady road that was a shortcut to the Queen Anne neighborhood. Traffic from the downtown Amazon campus made the route a veritable parking lot during rush hour on weekdays. But it was smooth sailing now, and the quickest way to George's house. Anna was alone in the car—with all the windows rolled down.

She'd taken this same road to George's place just fourteen hours ago—with him in the passenger seat. They'd been on their way back from the police station, their fingertips still slightly gray from the black fingerprint ink. Soap, water, and paper towels hadn't completely washed away the smudge marks.

George said the whole experience was surreal—and strangely intimate. "I feel like we just got initiated into a fraternity together." He glanced at his fingertips again. "It's like we're partners in crime."

Anna was thankful she'd had George to lean on throughout the ordeal. At the same time, it killed her that she couldn't tell him about her and Russ. George was her best friend, and she wanted to confide in him. But she also figured he'd be bitterly disappointed in her. So she held back. The story he'd gotten from her was the same one she'd given the police.

Pulling up in front of his place yesterday, they'd talked for a while. George had predicted that the news director would give her the Courtney story assignment— if Courtney was still missing today. It only made sense, since Anna had shot so much material on her for the profile piece. And she was one of the last people to have seen Courtney before she disappeared. "Plus, you know the husband and have been communicating with him, so they'll probably expect you to get an exclusive interview."

"God, I hope not," Anna murmured. She shuddered, imagining how such an interview would go viral and be analyzed to death if the word ever got out that the two of them were lovers.

"I have to admit," George said, "it still strikes me as weird that he took you home Thursday night and changed you out of your clothes. I know you'd just puked, and he's a doctor and all that. But you hardly know the guy. I find it creepy. And I still don't understand why you didn't tell me any of this on Friday."

"Because I knew you'd find it creepy," Anna replied, a hand on the steering wheel. "Plus I was embarrassed that I'd gotten so drunk. As for Courtney's husband, he was just being nice."

"Getting you undressed for bed is being nice," George

mumbled—almost to himself. He turned to her. "Okay, so why didn't you tell me on Friday morning about Courtney disappearing. You already knew, right?"

"Yes, but I didn't mention it because I—well, her disappearance seemed connected to a spat between the two of them. And I'm not one to gossip."

"Oh, c'mon, that's bullshit," he said with a chuckle. "You're always the first to tell me if you've heard about something going on with somebody in the newsroom. You live for gossip. It's one of the things I love about you." Eyes on the dashboard, he shook his head. "I don't get it, Anna. Working with Courtney last week, I have to say, you weren't yourself. I can't pin it down exactly, but you seemed so uncomfortable the whole time. I kept getting this weird vibe—like she had something on you, or you *owed* her." He turned to look at her. "So, you say the husband's nice? You don't think it's possible he bumped her off?"

"No, of course not," Anna said. "He's extremely nice. He's one of those Doctors Without Borders doctors. He's really a decent guy."

Anna fell silent as she noticed the front door of George's two-story, white stucco, Spanish-style house swing open. His wife, Beebe, stepped out on the front stoop. One hand on the doorknob and the other on her hip, she glared at them.

Anna nodded in Beebe's direction. "I've kept you long enough," she said. "I'm sorry. Please apologize to Beebe for me, too."

They said good-bye. She remembered George's gait as he headed toward his frowning spouse at their front door. *Dead man walking,* she thought. She felt sorry for him.

She waited until she got home to call Russ. It was around eight-thirty and starting to get dark out.

"Hey, I was just thinking of you," he said when he picked up.

"Is it a good time to talk?" Anna asked. She sank down on the sofa.

"Yeah, but I don't think we should chat for too long. I'm worried the police might be monitoring my calls, not exactly listening in —but keeping track of my phone records, who I'm talking to and for how long."

"My God," she murmured. She hated that he sounded like a guilty man. She squirmed on the sofa. "Should I— should I hang up?"

"No, it's okay," he said. "It makes sense you'd call me for an update on Courtney. They know we're communicating. I just don't think we should hang on the phone for more than a few minutes. Then again, I could be wrong about the cops having access to my phone records—"

"No, you're probably right. Why take a chance? Let's keep it brief. So, are you okay? Where are you?"

"I'm okay. No new developments with Courtney, at least, nothing that they've told me. I'm here at the Silver Cloud Inn until their forensics team finishes going over the house. It kills me, because I could start walking and be over at your place in ten minutes. But I don't think we should be seen together."

"Nor do I," she said. And that included being seen together on TV. She wasn't even going to ask him for an interview.

"So, what about you?" he asked. "What happened with the police?"

Anna told him about the talk with Detective Baumann.

"She didn't come right out and ask if you and I were having an affair, but I'm sure she knew. It's only a matter of time before they start to investigate just how well acquainted we are. And here's the scary part, Russ. Somebody already knows. I got another anonymous call while the police were at my place, the same raspy-voiced creep who'd phoned me earlier."

Anna had kept the voice mail recording, and she played it for him.

Russ asked to listen to it twice. He still thought the caller might be some nutcase who had picked up the details of Courtney's disappearance over the police radio. "I don't mean to downplay it, because this is really troubling," Russ concluded. "I think it might be some nut. I mean, it's happened to you before, one of the hazards of being on TV. Remember in March, that woman in Ballard who kept e-mailing you every day until you blocked her? I think this guy on the phone is just guessing about us. At least, it sounds like a guy to me. I suppose it could be a woman. It's not Courtney. I know her voice. Whoever it is, they don't really know anything. Last night, what he said to you was mostly gibberish. And in the call earlier today, didn't he say that he saw you kill Courtney? I think he's saying whatever might get a rise out of you."

"You're probably right." Anna sighed. From the sofa, she stared out the windows and the sliding glass door. She would close the curtains as soon as she got off the phone.

"Still, I'm worried about you over there all alone," Russ said. "Do you have anyone who could put you up for the night? Maybe your friend George? Didn't you once mention that he had a guesthouse over his garage or something?"

"Yes, but George's wife can't stand me. I'd rather take my chances here. I'll be okay. I'll be sure to lock all the windows and doors."

Before they hung up, Russ once again made her promise that she'd call him if she got scared. Anna remembered him telling her the same thing when that stalker had been tormenting her in October. But Anna didn't want him to have to lie to his wife about a phone call and why he was running out the door in the middle of the night. Russ had already lied enough to his wife because of her. She hadn't been comfortable putting him on the spot then, and she didn't want to put him on the spot now. This time, it wasn't his wife who would wonder about a late-night call; it was the police who might question it.

Anna had leftover Thai food for dinner. Then she started to wonder when the phone might ring again. She was so on edge. She must have moved the curtain and checked outside at least twenty times. Every little noise— inside and out—made her whole body tense up.

At 9:55, her phone rang, and Anna almost jumped out of her skin. She snatched it up and checked the phone screen: *Unknown Caller*.

After two rings, the phone went silent in her shaky hand. It didn't go to voice mail.

For the rest of the night, she'd waited for the phone to ring again— or for someone to start banging on her door or for a rock to fly through one of the windows. Still jumpy, she'd gone to bed at one in the morning and finally drifted off to sleep around three.

Then the phone had woken her at 8:50 this morning. It had been the news director, Josh Southworth, wanting her to cover Courtney's disappearance.

Half-asleep, Anna had argued that she would have a hard time keeping objective about it, since she was part of the story. Plus, she hardly ever did any hard news reporting. Couldn't they give the assignment to somebody else?

"Nonsense," Josh had said. "Your involvement is what makes it intriguing. Besides, there is no one else available. I don't think any of the other stations are covering this. It's a routine missing person case from what I can tell, but you profiled Courtney on Friday and that makes her news as far as KIXI's concerned. I want three minutes. Since you were one of the last people to see Courtney before her disappearance, we're counting on you to put a personal spin on the story. Could you possibly get an exclusive interview with the husband?"

"I don't think Dr. Knoll is talking to anybody except the police," Anna had told him.

Now she was on her way to pick up George so they could put a story together for the five o'clock news. Anna didn't see how she could report on this accurately without making Russ look guilty and making herself look ridiculous. After building Courtney up to be a saint in that profile piece on Friday, she would have to expose her as drunk and belligerent in the last moments that anyone had seen her.

She hoped George might have some ideas on how to approach the assignment. Anna's phone was in the holder bracketed on her dashboard. It hadn't rung since this morning's call from her news director. Taking her eyes off the road for a moment, Anna tapped the phone screen twice.

George answered after three rings: "I was just remembering that, yesterday, I predicted you'd have to cover this story. I forgot to mention it when you called me an hour ago. Don't you hate that I'm always right? Are you here?"

"I'm about five minutes away," Anna said, with her eyes on the road again. "And yes, I hate it when you're right. I don't have a clue how to approach this story. I texted Detective Baumann, who's in charge of the investigation. I asked if we could get a statement from her. I still haven't heard back. Other than that, I thought maybe I could do the segment intro and wrap-up from the dock in front of Courtney's house—that is, if the police don't have it sealed off."

"That's good. Maybe we could use some of the footage we shot from Courtney's book signing at Elliott Bay Books. You're not interviewing the husband, so we'll need to use the shots of him that we used in the profile. People will want to see what he looks like. Anyway, we'll hash it out when you get here. I'll be waiting out front for you."

"Sounds good, see you soon," she said. She tapped the phone screen to hang up.

As she drove down the residential street, Anna thought about how she could depend on George. Yet Russ was the one she loved, and she couldn't rely on him at all. They had no future together. If ever there were any doubts, the last couple of days had confirmed that for her. Maybe deep down, she'd known it from the start.

She pulled into George's driveway. Straight ahead,

past the white stucco house with the Spanish-tile roof, was a matching garage with steps up to a small apartment. Beebe's mother had stayed there when she'd been sick and dying last year. That was another reason Anna would never ask to use the apartment for a couple of nights: someone had died there.

She popped the trunk and left the motor running. Staring at the house and the slightly neglected, yellowing front lawn, she waited a couple of minutes.

Finally, the front door opened, but it was Beebe who hurried out. Her graying brown hair was a mess, and she wore an oversize T-shirt and cutoffs. Scowling, she continued at a brisk, determined clip—right up to Anna's car window.

Wide-eyed, Anna stared at her. "Beebe, is everything okay?"

"Well, I hope you're happy!" she screamed. Particles of saliva hit Anna in the face. Beebe looked like a crazy woman. "George and I are splitting up! That's what you've wanted all along, isn't it?"

"What are you talking about?" Anna asked, shrinking back from the window.

George's wife looked like she might reach inside the car and grab her by the throat. "You should know that I kicked him out of the house last night. Are you satisfied? The two of you can stop sneaking around now. You're free to fuck each other's brains out. I don't care anymore! I hope you have fun. That's quite an accomplishment, breaking up a marriage of sixteen years and ruining the lives of two children. How does it feel, Anna? You selfish, manipulative bitch."

"My God, Beebe, that's insane!" Anna shook her head. "George and I are friends. We've never . . . ever . . ."

"Beebe? What's going on?" George called.

Anna turned and saw him coming along the driveway — from the general direction of the garage. He was carrying his video equipment.

Beebe turned toward him. "I'm telling your whore that she's welcome to you!"

"Oh, for God's sake, Beebe, that's total lunacy," he wailed. George looked exasperated. Stopping in front of the car, he set down the bags. "Why are you doing this? You're embarrassing yourself. Anna doesn't deserve this—"

She glared at him. "Don't tell me I'm embarrassing myself, you son of a bitch."

"For the umpteenth time, listen to me," George said. Then he punched each word: "Anna . . . hasn't . . . done . . . anything!"

Beebe swiveled toward Anna again. "That's right," she snarled. "You haven't actually *done anything*. No, it's even worse than that, because he thinks he's in love with you. You've just been leading him on all this time. You've had him wrapped around your little finger. Did that make you feel superior or desirable or pretty? Was it good for your ego, Anna? You prick tease —"

"Jesus, Beebe, enough already! Leave her alone!" George pointed to the house. "Go inside! Stop making a fool out of yourself and go inside." He was talking to her like she was a bratty little girl.

Beebe marched over to him and said something under her breath.

His arms crossed in front of him, George whispered something back to his wife.

Dumbfounded, Anna sat at the wheel and watched the two of them standing in front of her car. It looked like Beebe might haul off and slap him. But she muttered something else, swiveled around, and flounced back toward the house.

Shaking his head, George opened the trunk to Anna's Mini Cooper and loaded his video equipment inside. He shut the trunk, opened the passenger door, and plopped down on the seat. "Just shoot me," he said, staring straight ahead. "No questions. Just put a bullet through my head and end this misery. On behalf of my deranged wife, I apologize."

"What the hell was that all about?" Anna asked—with her hand over her heart.

"Could you please just get us out of here *now*?" George asked. He nervously glanced toward the house. "I don't want her coming out again. I don't think I could take another round."

Anna shifted gears, backed out of the driveway, and then headed down the street. She didn't say anything.

She'd always thought Beebe was a flake. As for the kids, they had enough problems already. Their self-centered, phone-obsessed, fourteen-year-old daughter drove George crazy; and the eleven-year-old boy was being bullied at school and getting straight Ds. Beebe fancied herself an artist. She made clunky earth-tone plates, mugs, and vases that were scratchy to the touch, impractical, and butt-ugly. Last year, when the station had thrown Anna a surprise birthday party, Beebe had given her a couple of vases—atrocious even by Beebe's standards.

Anna had sent her a thank-you card. *I have the perfect place for these remarkable pieces,* she'd written. The eyesores were still stashed in the toolshed alongside the houseboat.

Anna always tried to be cordial to her. But during practically every encounter they had, Beebe would say something snide or catty to her. The last time, it had been at another work-related function the day after Anna's segment about a beloved teacher dying of cancer had aired. "Well, Anna, you sure know how to do *maudlin,* don't you?" Beebe said—with a little laugh. "Oh, how I wish George would get assigned to some *real* news stories."

George was always apologizing to her for his wife's bitchiness. "Beebe's just insecure—and jealous of you. She wants to be taken seriously as an artist, and she's still trying to find her way. Meanwhile, you're a local celebrity—with this glamorous job. You're talented and beautiful—and well, she knows how I feel about you. She knows our friendship is extremely important to me. And that drives her crazy. Anyway, it's my fault if she seems kind of cold and snippy around you."

That was as close to a declaration of love as George had ever given her.

Now Beebe had brought it out in the open. Hell, she'd screamed it.

Staring at the road ahead, Anna winced, "Beebe said she kicked you out of the house last night. So, are you staying in the apartment over your garage?"

"For the time being, until I find a place of my own," George replied. "That should be pretty soon, because the ghost of my mother-in-law is haunting me in that garage apartment. I apologize again. Beebe has completely lost it. She's delusional. But it's true that she and I are breaking up. I can't do this anymore. The kids have had it, too. It's an unhappy house. Something has to change."

"I'm so sorry, George. You poor guy."

"Well, I'm sorry you were swept up in it."

She tightened her grip on the steering wheel. "How do you think Beebe got such a crazy notion about the two of us? It's so utterly ridiculous."

"Well, thanks a lot."

"I didn't mean it that way."

"Beebe's accusations aren't totally out of left field," he confessed. "She's right to be jealous of you. But that's my problem, not yours. You never did anything. You're blameless. You never encouraged the situation. You wouldn't intentionally do anything to break up a marriage. You're not like that."

Anna swallowed hard and squirmed a bit in the driver's seat. She couldn't look at him. She felt awful. Would he still hold her in such high regard if he knew the truth?

She couldn't help thinking that Beebe was right. Knowing George had a little crush on her made her feel desirable—important. Plus he was safe. Anna had always figured nothing would ever happen with him—as long as he stayed married.

He'd just admitted he had feelings for her. Did he expect her to say something?

Her phone rang. His went off at the same time.

Anna kept her hands on the wheel. George took his phone out of his pocket and checked it. "It's a text from Josh—for both of us. He's asking again if you can get an interview with your friend Dr. Knoll. Looks like Josh got a tip from his pal in the police force. The luminol test they did in Dr. and Mrs. Knoll's living room—"

"Luminol, is that the glow-in-the-dark blood residue test?"

"Yeah, and their place lit up like a pinball machine. The cops found blood in the living room, the bathroom, and out on the back deck."

Suddenly Anna felt sick to her stomach.

George worked his thumbs over his phone as he responded to the news director's text. "Well," he said, sighing. "This just went from a missing person case to a murder investigation. It doesn't look very good for your doctor friend, does it?"

Eyes fixed on the road ahead, Anna tightened her grip on the steering wheel until her knuckles turned white. "No, I—I guess not," she heard herself say. She shook her head. "Tell Josh I tried, but—but Dr. Knoll isn't talking to anyone but the police."

CHAPTER ELEVEN

Sunday, July 12—11:47 A.M.

This close to lunch on a Sunday, the newsroom was deserted. So Anna used a phone on one of the empty desks to call Russ.

She could see George through the glass partition of Editing Bay C. He was at the computer, pulling up sound bites and unused bits from the profile piece on Courtney. That included photos of Courtney and Russ together. They'd use the material in the news story for tonight.

Anna had told him that she would give Dr. Knoll another try to see if he would agree to an interview. Now at least she had a legitimate excuse to get in touch with Russ. And if his calls were being monitored, the police would see that this call was from someone at KIXI News and not her private phone.

Sitting at the edge of the desk, Anna counted three rings. She wasn't sure Russ would pick up. His caller ID might show KIXI-TV, and if it did, would he realize it was her?

She heard a click. "Hello?" he asked, sounding guarded.

"It's me," Anna said. "I'm at the station. How are you?"

"I was going stir-crazy at the hotel," he said. "So now I'm walking around Chandler's Cove."

A marina on Lake Union, Chandler's Cove wasn't far from Anna's house. The hub used to have some popular restaurants and stores, most of which were closed now. Before Russ and Courtney moved into her neighborhood, Anna and Russ used to go for walks there. Holding hands, they'd look at the boats moored in the marina and take in the view of the lake and Gas Works Park. Those seemed like such sweet, simpler times.

"Well, you seem pretty calm," Anna said, fidgeting with the phone cord. She stole a glance at George, still at the computer with his back to her. "I'm in shock. I can't believe they found all that blood."

"What are you talking about?"

"The tests the police did."

"Which tests?"

"The tests that showed traces of blood in your living room and other parts of the house."

"Anna, I have no idea what you're talking about."

"You didn't know? I can't believe the police haven't told you yet! The police did a test and found evidence of blood—a lot of it, mostly in the living room. Apparently, it looked like someone had tried to clean it up. I found out about twenty minutes ago. Somebody on the force leaked it to our news director."

"Jesus," she heard him murmur. "I—I had no idea. I should have seen this coming when they found that drop of blood on the bookcase. This—this isn't happening. My God, Anna."

"I'm so sorry," she said. "I thought you knew."

"Then something happened to her in the house," he said—seemingly to himself. "That explains the missing towels."

"What towels?"

"Detective Baumann and I did a room-to-room search yesterday, and I noticed there weren't any bath towels in the linen closet. Baumann stuck one of her Post-its on the closet door. Courtney and her hotel-quality white towels— with her initials on them. Someone must have used them to wipe up the blood."

Anna swallowed hard. "The police probably think it was you—or me, or both of us."

"Jesus, I kept thinking there was a passable—*benign* explanation for all of this. But she's not coming back, is she? She's dead."

"Russ, you mentioned that you went for a drive after you left my place on Thursday night. Where did you go? Did anyone see you? Did you talk to anyone?"

"Baumann already asked me that—"

"Well, now I'm asking you. Where did you go?"

"I ended up driving over to that park off Magnolia Boulevard."

Ella Bailey Park. He'd taken her there a couple of times. It was one of Russ's favorite spots. The view of the city was phenomenal. But that was during the daytime. At night, the water and the mountains probably weren't visible.

"Did anyone see you there?" Anna asked.

"I— um, I didn't talk to anyone. I got out of the car and looked out at the city lights. Then some teenagers came along at around one-thirty in the morning. I don't think they even noticed me. They were loud and obnoxious. Then they started lighting off fireworks. So I left."

"Did you tell this to Baumann?"

"Yes, she said she'd check with the Magnolia Police."

"Well, that's good," Anna said. "If anyone called the cops about the fireworks, that'll prove you were there."

"I guess so," he murmured.

She could tell he was still trying to wrap his head around the news about the blood. "Russ, they want me to cover the story for tonight's five o'clock news. They want me to ask you for an interview. But I don't think it's a good idea." She once again glanced over toward George in the editing bay. "If I interview you on TV, and it gets out about us, then let's face it, that interview will be shown again and again and dissected to death. But I—I have to ask you, what was your reason for not going directly home after you left my place Thursday night?"

"You know why. Courtney was impossible—"

"Yes, I know. But I'm asking you as a reporter. People will want to know."

"Okay." There was a pause. "Courtney had too much to drink, and she was being very difficult. I thought if I drove around for a couple of hours, she'd be asleep by the time I got home. Instead, she was gone." There was another pause. "Is that a good answer?"

Anna grabbed a pen off the desk and scribbled it down on a notepad. "Yes, thank you. I'm sorry, Russ."

"I just can't believe she's dead. But if they found traces

of blood, there's no other explanation. Someone must have killed her, cleaned up the mess, and took her body away."

Anna put down the pen. "There's another possible explanation, Russ. Did Courtney ever read *Gone Girl*? Because that's what this whole thing reminds me of."

There was no response on the other end.

"I'm sorry," Anna said. "But how can you be sure Courtney didn't set up this whole thing just to make you suffer? Correction—not just to make *you* suffer, she's putting me through the wringer, too. What's more, think of all the media attention this will draw, all that publicity. Think of the book sales." Anna took a deep breath. "I'm sorry. Am I awful and terribly out of line to suggest this?"

She heard him sigh. "No, I've considered it, too—even before you told me about the blood. Courtney and I saw the movie when it first showed on Netflix. And I know she read the book."

"Do you think it's possible she's doing something like *Gone Girl*?"

"Well, it wouldn't be the first time Courtney copied another author's idea."

"What do you mean?"

"She stole the whole idea for *The Defective Squad* from someone in her old writers' group."

Anna heard a knock. She glanced over toward the editing bay, where George was standing on the other side of the glass partition. He stopped knocking on the glass, shrugged, and pointed to his wristwatch.

She nodded at him and quickly turned away. "Courtney stole that idea?" she said into the phone.

"Yeah, the group was pretty hostile toward her after

the first book came out. To hear Courtney tell it, the whole thing was just a misunderstanding. But no one from that group will have anything to do with her anymore."

"Listen, I'm getting the hurry-up signal from George here," Anna said. "It sounds crazy and warped, but I still hope Courtney's just screwing with us."

"You and me both," Russ said. "I guess I better call Detective Baumann and ask if there's anything else they're not telling me. I'll get in touch with you after your newscast, okay?"

"Okay," she said. She turned toward the editing bay and saw George was back at the computer. "I love you," she said under her breath.

"Love you, too," he replied.

Anna listened to the click on the other end. She hung up the phone and headed into the editing bay. George brought an image up on the computer screen. It was a photo of Russ and Courtney, looking beautiful and happy.

He glanced over his shoulder at her. "You and the doc were sure chatting up a storm. What did you do, interview him on the phone?"

"Something like that," Anna answered. She steered a chair on wheels over to the computer, and then she sat down beside George. Frowning, she watched the photo of Russ and Courtney dissolve into another shot of them together, and then another. "Did you create a montage?"

"Yeah, I figured that's how we'll show the husband. Why? Don't you like it?"

"No, it's good."

"You seem anxious," George said.

She shrugged. "I still don't have a clue how I'm going to handle this. I mean, I'm part of the story."

"If I were you, I'd leave myself out of it as much as possible. Look what I found in our archives." George typed on the keyboard.

On the screen appeared a video showing a sleek BMW driving up to the entrance of Canlis at night. For a moment, Anna felt as if she was back outside the midcentury modern restaurant, ready to walk in and meet Courtney for dinner.

"That's good," Anna managed to say, though her stomach took a turn. "Um, you can use that shot for about five seconds, when I mention that we met there for dinner. Then we'll cut to a shot of their floating home."

CHAPTER TWELVE

Sunday, July 12—5:08 P.M.

With yellow tape, the police had cordoned off the end of Russ and Courtney's dock. Anna stood as close as she could to the DO NOT CROSS line for the introduction of her live report for the five o'clock news.

Considering all the police activity at the end of the dock, Anna was amazed more reporters weren't on the scene. Except for her and George with his camera, only one other person with a camera was in the vicinity. A tall, skinny man with long black hair and a goatee stood about fifteen feet away on the dock, recording everything—including her. In fact, he seemed focused mostly on her. He didn't look like a cop or news reporter. But his video camera appeared to be professional grade. Anna tried not to let him distract her.

Three men——one of them in a police uniform—stood at the end of the dock, manipulating telescoping boat hooks in the water. A diver had just come up from under the lake's slightly choppy surface. He had on a gray diver's suit with a mask and an oxygen tank. He sat at the edge of the dock and took off his breathing apparatus for a moment. A police boat and two skiffs hovered nearby on the lake. Earlier, when Anna had been interviewing Detective Baumann, a police helicopter had loomed overhead for a while.

At first, Anna had wondered if the police had thought Courtney had drowned. But if they'd found traces of blood in the living room, bathroom, and on the back deck, then that ruled out drowning as Courtney's cause of death. The police must have figured that Courtney had been murdered in the house and then been taken outside and thrown into the water from the back deck.

But Anna had come up with that hypothesis on her own. Detective Baumann hadn't given her much to go on during the interview. For the press—or at least, for Anna—she was acting as if this was still a missing person case, not a murder investigation.

Perhaps that explained why, except for the lone, long-haired cameraman, no other news crews had come to this potential crime scene. The only reason KIXI-TV was interested was because Anna had profiled Courtney on KIXI-TV on Friday. And now they had this unconfirmed news leak about the blood in Russ and Courtney's home.

Working with George, Anna had used the editing equipment in the news van to put together the prerecorded portion of the news story. The van was parked about two blocks down from the entrance gate to Russ and Courtney's dock. Anna had also recorded her voice-over for the piece while in the van. She felt like a fish out of water. Hard news wasn't her specialty. And she was still worried that her crucial involvement in the story would make her reporting on it seem absurd. Plus, after building up Courtney as this noble, inspiring author in her profile on Friday, here she was, two days later, painting her as an argumentative drunk who may or may not have walked out on her husband.

Anna had swung by her place to pick up a pressed dark blue short-sleeve blouse and white slacks for the live TV introduction. She'd put on her makeup and fixed her hair in the news van. With Russ and Courtney's floating home in the background, Anna was poised in front of George's camera. She held a mic and waited for the cue from the newsroom to come through on her concealed earpiece.

At last, she heard the anchorman introduce her, and Anna started in: "Seattle author Courtney Knoll, whose young adult series, *The Defective Squad*, recently sold to Hollywood, has been reported missing since early Friday morning."

Then she got to relax for a couple of minutes while the TV viewers saw her narrated, prerecorded news story. It started with clips of Courtney autographing books and speaking or signing with customers at Elliott Bay Book Company on Wednesday night.

Anna's prerecorded voice-over came on: "Just thirty-two hours after celebrating the release of *Silent Rage*, the latest book in her popular Seattle-based series, Courtney Knoll disappeared. I was still editing an exclusive profile on the deaf author, whose writing has been an inspiration for disabled teens."

The next sequence was an interview outtake from the profile. Courtney looked beautiful and relaxed in her living room—the same living room where the police had unearthed traces of blood. Courtney was talking—and signing: "I've been writing stories ever since I was a kid. And even though the first *Defective Squad* book came out five years ago, I'm just starting to make a name for myself. I hope it doesn't sound conceited, but I feel like I'm on the brink of becoming famous."

The image on-screen switched to George's photo montage of Courtney and Russ looking so beautiful and happy together. "Courtney has been married to Seattle pediatrician Russell Knoll for six years," Anna's voice-over explained. "I met the couple for dinner at Canlis restaurant on Thursday night."

George's shot of the restaurant at night came up on the screen.

Next came the part of the story that Anna had struggled over until the very last minute. She still wasn't happy with it. "Courtney had too much to drink and became rather argumentative. Dr. Knoll drove us to their floating home on Lake Union . . ." George had gotten some good shots of the $2.5 million house. "But I wasn't feeling well, so Dr. Knoll took me home. Instead of returning to his house, he went for a drive. According to Dr. Knoll, he wanted to avoid going home until he thought Courtney would be asleep. But when he returned to their house at around two-thirty in the morning, his wife was gone."

There was another shot of the floating home—this time, George had pulled back to include the police boat, the helicopter, the diver, and the men searching the water with hooks on telescoping poles.

"I spoke with Seattle Police Detective Kit Baumann, in charge of the investigation."

Anna had interviewed the detective in front of the house about an hour ago. Obviously still battling her hot flashes, Baumann held a battery-operated, personal mini-fan in front of her face— right up until George was ready to shoot. She looked cool and collected in the interview. "Dr. Knoll noticed one of his wife's suitcases was missing along with some of her belongings," Baumann said. "He said he thought she might have packed up and left in the middle of the night. But he called several people on Friday, and they hadn't seen her. When Courtney didn't show up for a book signing on Bainbridge Island at noon on Saturday, Dr. Knoll notified us that his wife was missing. A check of Courtney Knoll's phone and credit cards has shown no activity since Thursday."

Before the interview had started, while Baumann had still been cooling herself with the fan, Anna had asked about the traces of blood they'd found in Russ and Courtney's house. "We won't be discussing that," the detective had growled. "I heard from Dr. Knoll about it. He wasn't supposed to know. The results of the luminol tests aren't conclusive yet. At this point, it could be old animal blood or urine or even bleach. If I find out who's responsible for leaking that little item to your boss, I'm kicking his ass from here to Walla Walla. If you ask me about that on camera, I'll end the interview."

For the piece, Anna had asked if there had been signs of a break-in or a struggle in the Knolls' home.

"There was no apparent sign of a break-in, but some items are missing from the house," the detective answered for the camera. "It's possible Courtney may have packed them. Our forensics team is still searching the house for clues that might help us determine Courtney's where-abouts."

"Have they eliminated the possibility of foul play?" Anna asked.

While they'd been editing the piece, George had made fun of her for the way she'd asked the question. He'd claimed, "I'm sorry, but it sounds so corny, like some-thing Brenda Starr would ask."

But Baumann hadn't found it amusing. "No, we haven't eliminated that as a possible cause for Ms. Knoll's disap-pearance," she answered glumly.

"Has Dr. Knoll been helpful with your investigation?" Anna couldn't help asking. She knew people would au-tomatically suspect him, and she wanted it on record that he was working with the police on this.

Detective Baumann nodded. "Yes, Dr. Knoll has been very cooperative. And if any of your viewers think they might help us locate Courtney, they can call our missing persons hotline: 1-800-MISSING."

While this prerecorded portion ran, Anna kept glanc-ing over at the long-haired man with the camera—aimed at her. The search crew continued to explore the water around the dock. But most distracting of all was what was happening near the dock's entrance gate. Three cars and two more news vans had shown up—all within the last couple of minutes. Reporters clustered at the dock gate. Anna wondered if the other reporters had just gotten the same unconfirmed story about the luminol test.

George waved at her, cuing her for the live wrap-up.

She quickly turned her focus on George and his camera. "That missing person hotline number is once again, 1-800-MISSING. And they'll be taking calls twenty-four hours a day. This is Anna Malone on Lake Union for KIXI-TV News. David . . ."

In her earpiece, she heard the anchorman, David Powers, thank her. "Anna Malone profiled Courtney on Friday's KIXI-TV News. You can view the segment online. Just go to KIXI-TV-News-dot-com."

George gave her the cut signal.

Switching off and lowering the mic, Anna squinted over toward the dock gate, which someone had just opened. The reporters charged down the dock toward her with their cameras and mics.

Anna turned to George. "What's going on?" Then she looked at the long-haired stranger, who took a few steps closer to her. "Excuse me, but who are you?" she asked.

Before the man or George could answer her, the reporters and cameramen descended on her. It was a small group—only eight people—but the aggressive way they rushed toward her was intimidating. A few called to her.

"Anna!" one woman yelled, louder than the others. Anna recognized the blonde from a rival news team. She wore a red sweater set and waved a handheld mic at her. "Anna, do you have any comment on the allegations Sally Justice made about you and Dr. Knoll?"

"Is it true?" a male reporter shouted over his colleague. "Are you having an affair with Courtney's husband?"

"Did you and Russell Knoll kill Courtney?" someone else yelled.

Stunned, Anna recoiled from all the mics shoved in

front of her face. The cameras were all aimed at her. She shook her head. "I have no idea what you're talking about."

Past the small mob of reporters, she saw the tall, long-haired man recording the scene with his camera. He was grinning.

CHAPTER THIRTEEN

Sunday, July 12—5:24 P.M.

The blonde reporter and her cameraman just wouldn't give up.

When that pack of pushy reporters on Russ and Courtney's dock descended on her, Anna decided to get the hell out of there. She'd bolted for the dock gate—just as another reporter had arrived. She'd headed for the news van. But the persistent duo had followed her for two blocks toward where George had parked the vehicle.

"C'mon, Anna!" the blonde called, trailing behind her. "Just give us a statement! Has Sally Justice been in touch with you about tomorrow's show? How long have you known Russell Knoll?"

Approaching the van, Anna reached into her purse for the key and realized George had it. She swiveled around and saw him, nearly a block away, hurrying to catch up.

The blonde thrust her mic in Anna's face, and the cameraman started recording. "Anna, any comment about tomorrow's *Sally Justice Show*?"

"I don't watch it," she said, out of breath. She shook

her head. "I'm not a fan. Now, give me a break, guys. I'm not the story." She nodded in the direction of Russ and Courtney's dock. "The story is about the missing woman who lives back there."

Lugging his camera equipment, George came up behind the blonde and her cameraman. "C'mon, get lost," he said to the two of them. Breathing hard and perspiring, he took the key fob out of his pocket and aimed it at the van.

Anna heard the vehicle beep. Then she quickly opened the door and climbed into the passenger side. Checking the side mirror, she watched the annoying reporter and her cameraman finally give up and head down the street—toward Courtney and Russ's place.

George loaded his camera in the back and then opened the driver's door and scooted behind the wheel.

"God, what took you so long?" Anna asked, frazzled.

He shut the driver's door. "I stuck around for a minute to find out what the hell was going on." He wiped the sweat off his forehead with his sleeve. "Some reporter you are. You're suddenly the focus of a news story, and you don't even bother to find out what it is. You just turn and run."

"Well, what did you expect me to do? That was insane. They were on the attack—like an angry mob. All that was missing were the torches and pitchforks."

"You know that tall hippie guy we noticed when we first got there?"

Anna nodded. "Yeah, he was really starting to get on my nerves."

"Well, I should have smelled a rat when I first saw him. It took me a while to recognize the guy. He's a freelancer,

Norbert Jobst. He does a lot of work for Sally Justice."
George took out his phone and started working on the
screen keyboard with his thumbs. "Apparently, tomorrow's *Sally Justice Show* is all about Courtney's disap
pearance. Sally claims you and Dr. Knoll aren't giving
everyone the full story—or some such bullshit."

"Oh God, no," Anna muttered.

"Sally started running promo pieces for the show
about a half hour ago. And . . aha . . . I think this is it."
He showed the phone screen to Anna and turned up the
volume.

A photo flashed on the screen of the Botoxed blonde,
sixtysomething Sally Justice—along with *The Sally Justice Show* in its familiar bold font. The half-hour show
ran five days a week on the 24/7 News Network.

"Tomorrow on *The Sally Justice Show*, the Courtney
Knoll case . . ," Sally announced in her slightly loud,
gravelly voice-over. Her narration here was accompanied
by pulsating background music that must have been the
soundtrack to an action thriller.

The onscreen image switched to a video clip of Courtney from an interview she'd done a year ago. Sally's
voice-over continued: "A beautiful, talented author, who
overcame her hearing loss to make the top of the best-
seller lists, has disappeared."

There was a shot that Norbert Jobst must have taken
earlier today—of the house and all the police activity
around it. "Is she missing—or murdered?" Sally asked in
voice-over.

The next clip showed a dark room with a tile floor
marred by some bluish, luminescent splatter marks.
"Seattle Police have uncovered the evidence at Courtney's

house—luminol tests that picked up traces of blood . . . blood left behind by a ruthless killer."

Then the soundtrack turned somewhat salacious as side-by-side photos of Russ and Anna appeared on the screen. Russ looked handsome, and in the unflattering shot of Anna, she had an uncharacteristic haughty pout. "This is the husband who waited *two whole days* before he reported his wife missing, and the local TV reporter he was with on the night his wife vanished . . . what they're *not* telling the police!"

The picture switched to a signature clip, which must have been a couple of years old: Sally in a black suit, turning toward the camera with her arms folded in front of her. "On the next *Sally Justice Show*!" she exclaimed. "It's what everyone's talking about!"

"Oh crap," George said, pausing the video.

Anna was speechless. She was thinking about Russ: Had he seen this? Had the press tracked him down at his hotel? Were they hounding him right now?

George patted her arm. "Listen, something like this was bound to happen, right? This is typical Sally Justice sensationalized garbage. People are going to see through the bullshit."

He started to replay the video.

"Tomorrow on *The Sally Justice Show*, the Courtney Knoll case . . ."

Anna nervously rubbed her forehead. "Oh please, not again."

"I want to check something out," he said, turning down the volume. He studied the phone screen. "Just what I thought, this shot of the luminol test. This wasn't taken in Courtney's house. That's not her floor. It must be a stock photo. Whoever leaked the news about the luminol test must have told a bunch of people." He shook his head. "And where did they dig up this picture of you? It's the worst." He laughed, but when he turned toward her, the smile ran away from his face.

Anna had automatically reached into her purse and taken out her phone. Now she realized George was staring at her. She hesitated.

"You were about to call him, weren't you?" he whispered.

"Who?" She wanted to stash the phone back into her purse, but it was too late.

"Knoll, Courtney's husband," he said, his eyes narrowed at her. He shook his head. "Jesus, it all starts to make sense now—the way you've been defending him. And that's why you were acting so weird around her all last week, like you owed her something. I kept thinking, *Did this woman blackmail Anna into doing this story about her?* It's so clear now. Why didn't I see it before? You've been sleeping with her husband. How long have you been seeing him, Anna?"

"About a year and a half," she murmured, unable to look at him. With tears in her eyes, she gazed at the dashboard. "I broke up with him for about three months last year. I was about to break up with him for good when all this happened."

"Did he kill his wife? Did you help him?"

Wiping her eyes, she finally looked at George and frowned. "How can you ask me that?"

"Because I thought I knew you, but obviously, I don't."

"Everything happened just as I told you. That's the

truth. The only thing I left out was that Russ and I have been involved—"

"*'Russ and I'*—Jesus, gag me," he muttered. He opened his door and climbed out of the van. He unloaded his video equipment from the back. Then he opened Anna's door and held out the key to the van. "Here, you can drive back to the base. I'll Uber home."

Anna sighed. "George, please, you're my best friend. I've wanted to tell you for so long. If you only knew."

"Save it. Call your married boyfriend. That's what you want to do right now. So call the SOB." He rattled the key fob. "Take the goddamn key."

She took it.

"I'm so disappointed in you," he whispered.

Anna started crying again as she watched him walk away with his video equipment cases. What killed her was that George knew her so well. He was right. All she could think about was calling Russ to make sure he was all right.

She stepped out of the van. "I'm sorry, George!" she called.

But he kept walking and turned the corner.

Anna shut her door, walked around the van, and climbed into the driver's seat. Reaching inside her purse, she took out her phone again—along with a travel packet of Kleenex. She wiped her eyes and blew her nose.

She was about to tap Russ's number on the phone screen, but hesitated. She wondered if the police were indeed monitoring his calls, but it didn't matter anymore. They knew. Everything was out in the open now. Hell, *strangers* knew about them.

With a sigh, she tapped the phone. It rang twice before he picked up.

"Hey," he said, sounding listless. "I was just watching you on the news."

"Did you hear about tomorrow's *Sally Justice Show*?" she asked.

"Yeah, that's why you're on the news —all the stations." His voice seemed flat.

"Have the reporters stormed your hotel yet?"

"I don't think they know where I am. Guess I'm lucky on that score."

"You sound horrible." She let out a sad laugh and wiped her eyes. "You sound like I feel. I just talked with George—about us. He didn't take it well. This whole thing—"

"I guess I should have expected something like this *Sally Justice* fiasco," he interrupted.

Anna paused. It wasn't like Russ to cut her off in the middle of a sentence. She wiped her eyes again. "Um, I know. George said pretty much the same thing about Sally—"

"But I was completely baffled by your news report. I didn't expect you to throw me under the bus the way you did."

"What?" She wasn't sure she'd heard him right.

"That's how it felt, Anna. Maybe you didn't mean for it to come out that way. But, God, did you have to talk about Courtney getting drunk and argumentative at the restaurant? And then, the two hours when I can't account for my actions—"

"But that's how it happened, Russ! People are going to find out eventually. Everyone around us at the restaurant saw what was going on. If something really happened to Courtney, people will come forward and talk about how drunk and loud she was that night."

"But did you have to go into it *now*? It was like you were telling viewers to connect the dots and figure out who the killer is. Anyone watching that report would think I'm as guilty as hell."

"I was doing my damnedest to make you seem innocent!" she cried. "That's why I pointed out the reason you went for the drive. I would've mentioned the park in Magnolia—and the fireworks that proved you were there—but I only had two minutes and twenty seconds. Didn't you see me with Baumann? I got her to talk about how much you were cooperating with the investigation. I wanted people to know you're a good guy." Her voice started cracking, and she felt tears in her eyes again.

"I'm sorry. I know you didn't mean to make me look bad—"

"I didn't even want to do the goddamn report!" she yelled. "And Russ, I didn't make you look bad. *You've made yourself look bad.* God, our whole relationship started out on a lie. You lied to me, and you've been lying to your wife all this time. You know, we haven't even discussed what Courtney said at dinner on Thursday. She pointed out, very clearly, that she was never leaving you. And that basically goes against everything you've told me about this *friendly separation* you were planning with her. God, who am I supposed to believe? Last week, working with her was sheer torture. How the hell did I let myself get talked into making that stupid profile piece on her anyway? Oh, wait a minute, I know! You kept telling me, *'Go ahead, do the piece . . . you'll never have to see her again!'* Goddamn it, I really wish I'd never met either one of you."

Anna stopped and took a few deep breaths. She heard silence on the other end of the line. "Say something," she muttered.

"I was listening," he said.

She rubbed her forehead. "I can't yell at you without feeling horrible about it."

Her phone clicked, and she saw another call had come in.

"The station manager's trying to get ahold of me." Anna sighed. She let the call go to voice mail. "I'm hearing directly from the top. They're not wasting any time. I'm sure he wants to tell me how my likability quotient will take a dive once people realize I'm an adultress involved in a possible murder case. I wonder if they'll fire me outright or leave me a shred of dignity and ask for my resignation."

"This is all my fault," he murmured.

"No, I probably deserve this. I mean, how selfish can I get? It looks like your wife may be dead, and all I can do is think about us and myself and my job."

"Well, it's not like you and Courtney were friends."

"She thought we were."

"No, she didn't. She was using you. And it's okay to worry about yourself and your job. I'm worried about mine—and my patients, all those kids who'll have to start with a new doctor. We're in the same boat, Anna. What parent in their right mind would want a confirmed adulterer and murder suspect looking after their child?"

"I know it seems far-fetched, but I still think Courtney might be alive. I think she could've orchestrated this whole thing. What better way to pay us back and screw with us?" Anna paused. "So—what are you going to do? You've got to do something to let people know you didn't kill her, maybe a press conference or something."

"No, I'll talk to my lawyer and the police. Then they can talk to the press if they want to. Meanwhile, Anna, you do whatever you need to do—make a formal announcement on your news program or give an interview. Whatever you do, I promise, I won't accuse you of throwing me under the bus. I was out of line with that."

"Well, I'm glad you seem to know what I should do about this, because I haven't a clue."

She heard a long sigh on the other end.

"What?" she asked.

"Anna, make a deal with the station manager. You give a prepared statement, a KIXI-TV News exclusive. You tell the truth about us and beat Sally Justice to the punch. Do it in exchange for a sabbatical or a leave of absence until this blows over. They'll hire you back."

What he said made perfect sense.

"And what about us?" she asked quietly.

There was a silence.

"Russ?"

"I think," he said, at last, "whether she's alive or dead, Courtney's won. I think we're finished, Anna."

Then she heard something she'd never heard him do before.

She heard Russ crying.

"It never would have happened if I hadn't had so much to drink. There was nothing premeditated about it. But I guess things had been building up for a while . . . That night, she was so nasty and abusive—first at dinner, and then when we came back to their place. I got so angry that I couldn't sleep. I had to go back there. I just wanted to tell her off. It wasn't supposed to happen the way it did. But she wouldn't shut up, and she was so goddamn mean. If she'd been able to hear herself, maybe she would have stopped barking all those insults at me. A part of me was so glad for the silence after I bashed in her skull."

—Excerpt: Session 3, audio recording
with Dr. G. Tolman, July 23

CHAPTER FOURTEEN

Monday, July 13—4:51 P.M.

Sally had ninety minutes until showtime. As usual, she'd arrived early at her studio to have her hair and makeup done. HDTV wasn't exactly made for sixty-nine-year-old celebrities. It didn't matter how many nip-and-tuck sessions, Botox treatments, and chemical peels she'd had—and that was well into the double digits—Sally still needed at least an hour in the makeup chair before every show. Hell, she didn't even leave her house—a five-bedroom estate in a gated community near Madison Park—without first putting on anti-aging serum, eye repair, foundation, concealer, rouge, eye shadow, mascara, lipstick, and one of her twelve ash-blond wigs.

Nine years ago, she'd made the mistake of leaving the house without her makeup and wig for a quick trip to the Red Apple Market. The idiot checkout girl had overcharged her, and Sally had merely raised her voice a little at the gum-snapping nincompoop. Who wouldn't? But some son of a bitch had recorded the whole episode on his cell phone, and "Sally Justice Has a Meltdown" had gone viral. The damn thing was still on the Internet—with six million hits and counting. But what had really irked Sally was how hideous she'd looked.

Three lifestyle changes had gone into effect after that incident. Sally never again left the house—even for a minute—without wearing makeup and one of her wigs, and she didn't shop or cook again. She now had a full-time housekeeper, a cook, and a chauffeur. That was three more people dependent on her—in addition to the twenty-nine employees working for *The Sally Justice Show*. They depended on her, too. That didn't even include her personal assistants, her agent, her attorneys, her publicist, her trainer, her masseur, and her twenty-seven-year-old daughter, Taylor. Sally supported them all.

And on top of that, she had to worry about her ratings and lawsuits and demographic shifts and algorithms or whatever the hell they used on the Internet to gauge her popularity.

Small wonder her back was constantly killing her.

Sally's studio was in the Ravenna neighborhood, not too far from University Village. The small, renovated warehouse used to have a billboard on top of it—with a photoshopped image of Sally, her arms crossed, her smile glistening, looking like a smart, savvy fortysomething attorney:

TAYLOR MADE PRODUCTION STUDIOS
Home of the 24/7 News Network's
THE SALLY JUSTICE SHOW
Over 20 Million Viewers Nationwide!

It was something of a local landmark and tourist attraction. But then, eight years ago, Sally had done a story on reverse discrimination that hadn't gone over well. She'd had pain-in-the-ass protestors picketing the place for days afterward. Someone had defaced the sign—with a crude rendition of what looked like a penis in front of her mouth. The culprit had also scrawled *IN-* in front of her last name—*how original and clever*. She'd had the sign taken down and never bothered to replace it. Since Sally was no stranger to controversy, her people had advised that it might be prudent not to advertise where her TV studio was located—what with all the nutcases out there. The whole billboard was dismantled months later.

Inside the studio, they had all the latest audio/video technology, a media library, recording booths, editing bays, dressing and makeup rooms, two greenrooms, a break room, and a kitchen.

The Sally Justice Show was broadcast live from six-thirty to seven in Seattle, nine-thirty until ten on the East Coast. For over a dozen years, the show was the crown jewel of the 24/7 News Network. Sally reported on injustice in many forms—whether it was the hardworking, single-mom waitress who had gotten stiffed by a movie star or the airline passenger who had gone ballistic on the person constantly kicking his seat back. Sally kept busy with this sort of stuff during dull news days. But she really made her mark with political scandals and high-profile crimes—including murder. These bigger stories often became the topic of several shows in a row. Sally usually reported the story from a mahogany desk with a nameplate front and center—just the kind of nameplate a judge might have. She talked directly to the camera and wasn't past smirking, rolling her eyes, or pounding on the desktop to drive home a point. Then she'd discuss the details with a victim, a witness, or a so-called expert. Sometimes the guest was in another locale, shown in split screen with Sally. And sometimes the guest was there in person with Sally, seated by her desk in what looked like a witness box. For the last ten minutes of the show, Sally took calls from viewers. And God help the poor fool who disagreed with Sally, because she could be brutal and sarcastic, and she often hung up as soon as a caller with an opposing opinion started to make a valid point. Viewers also got to vote online or over the phone about who was at fault for the latest reported injustice. Sally would read the results the following night, and she always got the last word in.

Social media always went abuzz with the voting results of *The Sally Justice Show*—especially with the high-profile cases. One Sally critic—and there were many—once pointed out: "Why bother having a civil or criminal trial when Sally Justice and her followers—with mounds of misinformation and sheer conjecture—have already determined months ahead of time if a defendant is innocent or guilty?"

Tonight's *Sally Justice Show* would focus on the disappearance of Courtney Knoll. Sally had already developed a theory about what had happened to the beautiful, young, deaf author, whose literary star had seemed on the rise.

"What exactly did Anna Malone's neighbor say?" she asked, seated in her makeup chair—in front of the lighted mirror. Sally had two makeup guys on her staff, both named Chad. What were the odds? Chad II was working today, applying her HD makeup. She liked Chad I better. Sally was addressing a third person in the room, a woman standing behind her.

On the corner of the makeup table was a small-screen TV, which was tuned to channel 8, KIXI-TV. Sally's people had discovered that Anna Malone was supposed to make some sort of statement on the news tonight regarding her part in Courtney Knoll's disappearance. Everyone was pretty certain that Sally's promo spots for tonight's show had forced Anna to come clean about her involvement with Courtney's husband. Any fool reading the police report could put together that something was going on between those two. It didn't matter if Anna's statement would be a full confession, a flat denial, or something in between, Sally didn't intend to miss a second. Her people would be recording Anna's announcement, and Sally had demanded fact-checks on everything. "I want to catch her on at least three lies tonight!" she'd decreed. She was pretty sure Anna's career wouldn't survive this.

"Are you listening to me, dear?" she asked, looking in the mirror at the full-figured, fortysomething brunette standing behind her. Despite a few too many pounds on her short frame, the woman was beautiful, with dark eyes and a gorgeous complexion. Her name was Brenda, and she was one of the private detectives Sally had on retainer.

Brenda glanced up from her phone. "Yes, the neighbor's name is Mrs. Britz. I showed her a photo of Dr. Knoll. She confirmed for me that she's seen him several times coming and going on the dock to Anna Malone's houseboat. Mrs. Britz has spotted them together at least twice, maybe more than that. She thinks he's been visiting her since last October, maybe before. The lady said Dr. Knoll was hard to miss, since he's so good-looking."

"Oh, I like that," Sally said, closing her eyes while Chad II worked on her lids. "'*Hard to miss*,' I'm going to have to use that on the show. You've gotten confirmation about his coming and going from only one neighbor? The other neighbors had nothing to say?"

"Nothing *you* want to hear," the detective replied. "They all love her. They said Anna's very considerate and sweet, does grocery runs for them when they're sick, looks after their mail when they're gone—"

"Stop, you're killing me," Sally said. "You're right. I don't want to hear it. Did one of these neighbors happen to notice any activity in or around Anna's *love boat* late Thursday night?"

"Nothing. I asked and asked again."

"Okay, fine." Sally sighed. "Are those two moron witnesses from the restaurant here?"

"One of them is here, the tall skinny woman with the mustache problem."

Sally opened one eye and looked at Chad II. "You're going to have to fix that with makeup or something. I want people listening to what she says—and not comparing her to David Niven."

"Who?" Chad asked.

"Never mind," Sally grumbled. "God, don't you millennials know anything?"

The two women she'd booked as "witnesses" for

tonight's show had been dining at Canlis on Thursday evening—just hours before Courtney had vanished. They'd been at a table near where Anna Malone and the Knolls had been seated. Brenda had tracked them down. The two women said they'd recognized Anna from the news. Apparently, both Anna and Courtney had been drunk. The mustached woman said she thought it odd, because, as the trio had left the place, "the man, who was clearly the deaf woman's husband, was sort of holding up Anna Malone. She was so drunk she could hardly walk." Far more damning, as far as Sally was concerned, was what the lady's friend had said. "I heard the deaf woman complaining about what it was like to be married to a doctor, all the disadvantages. I think everyone in the restaurant heard her. But she told her husband and Anna that it didn't matter, because she was never leaving him."

Then a few hours later, Courtney Knoll had disappeared. And the story Dr. Knoll had given the police was that he thought his wife had left him.

Tonight's guests were among the last people to see Courtney alive that night. Sally's assistant director had already videoed both women giving their testimonies earlier this afternoon—sort of a test run for each of them. Sally's people viewed the tests, and everyone felt both women lacked charisma and credibility.

Sally still had one eye open and watched Chad II working on the other. She focused on the detective. "Is my daughter here? Can you go get her?"

"Sure thing," Brenda replied, and she headed out of the room.

Sally glanced at her smartphone: 4:48. She still had

two more minutes until *KIXI-TV News at Five*. Courtney Knoll's disappearance was trending among the local and national news stories—thanks mostly to Sally's promo pieces for this show. Sally had checked the Amazon sales rank yesterday for Courtney's most recent book. It had been a bit over 41,000. Now Sally looked it up again, and *Silent Rage* was number 67. Courtney's other two books had rocketed up the sales charts as well.

The theme for the KIXI News show started up.

"I'm going to need you to close the other eye now, Sally," Chad II announced.

Staring at the TV, she held up her index finger. "You'll have to wait. I need both eyes to watch this. In fact, get lost for ten minutes. And if you see Taylor out there somewhere, tell her I want to see her now."

He let out a defeated sigh, noisily fussed with the cosmetics on the table, and then headed for the door.

"Tonight's top story on *KIXI-TV News at Five*," the anchorman announced. "A freight train derailment in Wenatchee has left two dead . . ."

"Oh, for God's sake!" Sally wailed. "Idiots! I can't believe that a train wreck trumped the Courtney Knoll story." She wondered when they were going to bring out Anna Malone to make her statement. Sally needed time to respond to it on tonight's show and make her out to be a liar.

On TV, a reporter stood in front of the smoldering train wreck, addressing the camera.

Sally grabbed the remote and turned down the volume. She checked herself in the makeup mirror. Behind her, she noticed the dressing room door open. Her daughter,

Taylor, came in the same way she always entered a room—inconspicuously.

Far less attractive women could turn heads with their style, panache, and magnetism—but these were all qualities that blue-eyed, brown-haired, mousy Taylor clearly lacked. Sally was always trying to get the Chads to do something to make her plain-looking daughter prettier and more appealing. Taylor had made about twenty appearances on *The Sally Justice Show* in the last two years. Sally brought her on as an "expert" because she had a BA degree in sociology, which wasn't very impressive, but to hear Sally talk, her daughter might as well have been Stephen Hawking. Test-market audiences found Taylor "smart," "sweet," and "dreary."

Sally spun around in the chair. "Honey, these two idiot women who are supposed to be my witnesses on tonight's show, I don't like them, nobody does. I might just run a brief clip of one of them talking about what she overheard at the restaurant. Then I'll bring you out to talk about Courtney, how close the two of you were and how brilliant she was—or *is*. Maybe you can even work in something about how worried you are about her right now."

Taylor slouched and rolled her eyes. "Mother, I've told you, I hardly know Courtney." She signed as she spoke. Her speaking voice wasn't always clear. When they polled a test audience about Taylor's appearance on the show, one audience member—obviously an asshole—wrote: "It's hard to understand her. She sounds like a dolphin that somebody trained to talk." Sally and the producer decided that, from then on, whenever Taylor appeared on the show, they'd automatically closed-caption her—as they did whenever Sally had a guest with a thick foreign accent.

Sally's only child had been deaf since birth. It was remarkable that she spoke as well as she did. One of Sally's critics once wrote: "Though Taylor Hofstad is drastically underqualified as an expert at anything, Sally insists on parading her deaf daughter onto the show in order to gain sympathy points."

The hard truth was, every time Taylor came on the show—and she and her mother spoke and signed with each other—Sally's likability rating went up with audiences.

Taylor leaned against the doorway frame. "I met Courtney three times—briefly. That's all. Each time was at some formal fund-raiser. You were there two of those times. *You* might as well talk about how much *you* miss her."

"It sounds better coming from you," Sally said. "Now, I'm in a bind here. Can't you help your dear old mother for just a few minutes? Please? Chad Two can make you up, and there are a bunch of gorgeous blouses and sweater sets in your size in the wardrobe closet."

"Mother, I'm sorry, but I don't feel right going on TV, pretending that Courtney and I were good friends. I'm sure the only reason she paid any attention to me at those parties was because I'm your daughter."

"Nonsense!" Sally said. Then she quickly glanced over her shoulder at the TV.

Courtney's photo was in a box above the handsome anchorman's shoulder.

"Mother, please—"

"Hush up, I need to see this!" Sally said, putting a hand

up to silence her daughter. She swiveled toward the TV, swiped the remote from the makeup table, and turned the volume back up. She turned on the closed-captioning for Taylor, though her daughter was quite proficient at reading lips.

". . . reported missing since early Friday morning," the anchorman was saying—over a shot of Courtney's floating home, cordoned off with yellow tape. The dock was buzzing with police activity. "Police still have no leads, but they have confirmed that traces of blood have been discovered—Courtney's blood type—in her living room. KIXI-TV reporter Anna Malone reported on Courtney Knoll's disappearance for Sunday's *KIXI-TV News at Five*."

The image on the screen switched back to the news desk with Anna Malone seated beside the anchorman. She was wearing a virginal white blouse—and Sally made a mental note to comment about it in a snarky way on tonight's show.

"Anna also spent three days last week with Courtney for a profile we ran on Friday's news. Anna . . ."

"Thank you, David," she said with a nod and a joyless smile. "Along with her husband, Dr. Russell Knoll, I was one of the last people to see Courtney Knoll before her disappearance sometime in the predawn hours early Friday morning. I've tried to be helpful to the police. And I tried to be as accurate as possible reporting about Courtney's disappearance here for KIXI News. I'd come to know and respect Courtney Knoll when we worked together on her profile piece that ran on Friday's news show. But originally, I didn't want the story assignment—for personal reasons. And for the same reasons, I didn't want to report on Courtney's disappearance. Today, I'm compelled to make those personal reasons public. I spoke to the Seattle Police this morning to clarify my role in the events that led up to Courtney's disappearance early Friday morning. My story hasn't changed much from what I'd already told the police and what I've reported to you. But I omitted one detail—which is that I've been in a relationship with Courtney's husband, Dr. Russell Knoll, for eighteen months."

Anna paused and took a deep breath. "I never would have pegged myself as the type of woman who would get involved with a married man. But at the time, I believed—we both believed—that Dr. Knoll and his wife would soon be separating. The last thing I wanted was for anyone to get hurt. Courtney's disappearance has completely devastated her husband—and it's also put an end to our relationship."

Her voice quavered ever so slightly, and Sally couldn't help wondering if it was an act. "So, now you understand that I wasn't completely forthcoming in yesterday's report on Courtney's disappearance," Anna went on. "I feel I've compromised my integrity as a journalist and my duty to our news team here at KIXI-TV. Most of all, I've failed you, our viewers. And because of this, I've asked for—and been granted—an indefinite leave of absence from KIXI-TV News. I plan to continue helping the authorities as much as I can in the search for Courtney Knoll. And I'm hoping for her safe return. Anyone with information that might be helpful in locating Courtney is urged to call 1-800-647-7464, that's 1-800-MISSING. Thank you."

"Thank you, Anna," the anchorman said solemnly. "We're all going to miss you here."

She merely nodded at him and gave a wistful smile—the kind of smile that said she was aching inside.

A new image appeared in the box over the anchor's shoulder as the camera closed in on him. It was a shot of a storefront with a broken window. "Seattle Police are investigating what's being described as a hate crime in the International District . . ."

"Goddamn it!" Sally bellowed, switching off the TV with the remote. "That bitch! She just ruined my show for tonight! I was going to expose her and her slimy doctor boyfriend. I was going to drop a bombshell, and now what do I have?"

"Well, people on the East Coast won't know," Taylor argued, signing to her mother. "It's just your Seattle audience who might have heard—"

"This show was mostly for my Seattle audience!" Sally shot back. "Don't you understand? People on the East Coast, in the Midwest, and anyone south of Portland aren't going to know who the hell Anna Malone is! I wanted to stick it to her here in Seattle—on our turf."

Wide-eyed, Taylor shook her head. She didn't speak, but she signed: "That's what all this is about, isn't it? You don't really care about Courtney." Then she spoke out loud: "You just want to stick it to Anna Malone because she made you look bad three years ago after that man in Spokane killed himself!"

"That wasn't my fault!" Sally argued. "I'm doing this story because it's important. It's news. And it's a travesty! I think Courtney's husband and Anna Malone killed her.

I'll bet you anything they planned it together. They had the motive and the opportunity. I can't believe the police haven't charged either one of them with anything yet. You just heard her admit on TV that she's a liar." Sally began to sign as she spoke. "I'm also doing this story for you, sweetie. Courtney was a—a beautiful, accomplished author—and a prominent member of the deaf community in Seattle—"

Taylor frowned. "Oh, Mother, save it for the TV audience."

"Okay, I'd like to destroy that bitch Anna Malone—if I can. But that's because I think she's guilty." Sally braced herself in the makeup chair and took a deep breath. "Now, go pick out a blouse for the show, nothing blue—I'm wearing blue. And nothing beige. You look washed out in beige. Start writing something about how close you were to Courtney and how much you miss your friend. I'll need to see it before the show. Meanwhile, send Arthur, Crystal, and Lauren in here. We have less than an hour to do some rewrites for the show tonight. And get Chad Two in here so he can finish me and then start in on you."

"Anything else?" Taylor asked, and then she folded her arms.

"You've read Courtney's books, haven't you?"

Her brow furrowed, Taylor nodded.

"Good. I'm going to have you on every night this week, talking about how talented Courtney is, how much of a difference she's made for the deaf community."

Taylor didn't respond. She just sighed and quietly slipped out the door.

Sally turned toward the mirror. "This is ratings gold—good for at least a week," she murmured to her reflection. "You just better hope what's-her-name doesn't show up alive anytime soon and ruin this."

CHAPTER FIFTEEN

Monday, July 13—6:03 P.M.

One voice shouted out louder than the others: "Anna, do you think your boyfriend murdered his wife?"

About a dozen reporters, videographers, and photographers had been waiting for her at the station's side door to the parking lot. They'd instantly swarmed around Anna, thrusting mics in front of her face. Holding a boxful of junk from her work desk, she headed toward her car.

She'd known they were out there waiting. The receptionist, Rosie, had warned her. They weren't just local news reporters. There were people from CNN, Fox, and 24/7 News, too.

So Anna had decided not to change her clothes or wash off her HDTV makeup. Besides, she was in a hurry to get home.

"No, I don't think Dr. Knoll murdered his wife," she answered, not breaking stride as she walked across the lot. "If you check with the police, it was Dr. Knoll who first alerted them to the fact that Mrs. Knoll was missing and that there were inconsistencies in the way certain items had been packed and certain items had been left behind—"

"How long have you been seeing Courtney's husband?" someone else yelled—practically cutting her off.

"As I said in my statement on the news earlier, we'd been involved for about eighteen months," Anna replied, staring straight ahead.

"Did the station want to fire you?"

"No, I offered to take a leave of absence without pay, and they accepted." She had her key fob in her fist—under the box of junk from her desk. She clicked it to pop open the trunk of her car. She'd already taken another boxload of personal items from her desk down to the car before her spot on tonight's news. This was the rest of her stuff: a fortune-telling 8-Ball, a stapler that looked like an alligator, a dictionary, a thesaurus, a scarf, and a Seattle Mariners coffee mug—among other things.

A few coworkers in the newsroom had asked if she'd like to go out for drinks at China Harbor with them, sort of an impromptu farewell party, but Anna had begged off.

"Anna, are you and Russ glad that Courtney's no longer in the picture?" the reporter from Fox News asked.

She frowned at him and shut the trunk of her car. "That's a terrible thing to say. How can I be *glad*? How could Dr. Knoll be *glad*? Our private relationship is now being held under public scrutiny—and it's finished. Dr. Knoll's career has been compromised. I just cleaned out my desk and am leaving a job I loved." Her voice cracked a tiny bit. "And not least of all, someone I never wanted to hurt is missing and may be dead." She opened the door on the driver's side. "So, in answer to your insensitive question, no, no one is *glad* about this."

She ducked into the car and closed the door, blocking out all other questions. A couple of the reporters knocked on her window, but Anna ignored them. She started up the car and pulled out of the lot.

As she merged into traffic on Westlake, she thanked God that she rarely had to do any of that kind of predatory *scoop* journalism, ambushing whoever was in the news, assaulting them with tactless questions. She realized, after this, she'd be lucky to get any kind of job in TV news. She hoped Russ was right. Maybe the station would hire her back after this blew over— if it ever blew over. Meanwhile, she figured she had enough to live comfortably for the next six to eight months. Certainly she could find a decent job before then—maybe not on TV or in journalism, but at least something to support herself.

Right now, all she wanted to do was go home, wash off her makeup, change her clothes, put her feet up, and call Russ.

But that wasn't going to happen.

The Sally Justice Show was on in a half hour. Obviously, Sally was out for blood tonight. Anna hoped her statement on the news just an hour ago might take some of the sting out of Sally's attacks. She couldn't hope to breathe easy until she'd watched the awful show, and Sally did her usual sign-off: "You get all the true talk on *The Sally Justice Show*!"

From the promotional ads for tonight's telecast, it appeared as if Sally planned to skewer Russ, too.

This afternoon, Anna had e-mailed Russ her statement

for tonight's news broadcast. She'd wanted to make sure she wouldn't say anything he might find inappropriate, embarrassing, or incriminating.

He'd e-mailed back:

This is fine, Anna.

I've been racking my brain for a way to tell you how much I love you and how sorry I am. But you already know that. Stay strong.

Love, R

Anna tried not to overanalyze the note. One thing was clear: he wasn't looking for a response. They'd both agreed last night that, unless it was an emergency, they were better off giving each other some space. Basically, it was over.

She'd texted George this morning, telling him that she was sorry and hoped things would work out with Beebe. And I also hope you won't stay mad at me forever, she'd added. Not seeing George would be the toughest part about leaving her job.

She still hadn't gotten a reply. Anna figured she'd better not hold her breath waiting for one.

This morning, she'd also talked to Detective Baumann, who had already gotten a "revised" statement from Russ last night. Apparently, Baumann had interviewed him at the precinct station for two hours. Russ's lawyer had been present.

Anna had waived her right to an attorney and spent only an hour correcting the omissions from her earlier testimony. As she'd pointed out on *KIXI-TV News at Five*, the fact that she and Russ were involved didn't really alter much of what she'd already told the police.

"I wanted you to hear it from us and not Sally Justice," Anna had told the detective in her tiny office, which had smelled like stale coffee. "You weren't the least bit surprised by this news, were you?"

"No, not really," Baumann had replied. "In fact, I was hoping you two would fess up about it soon, because I really want to believe your accounts about what happened Thursday night and Friday morning."

Anna had told her that, at no time, did she ever pressure Russ to divorce his wife. She'd never issued him any ultimatums. "I want you to know that—in case you think Russ might have gotten rid of Courtney so that we could be together. And you should know this, too: he rarely bad-mouthed Courtney. I don't think I would have liked it if he had. Then again, I wasn't very adept in this role as the other woman. I never wanted to be a homewrecker."

She'd wondered about Russ's alibi. She'd asked if there were any police reports about fireworks in the Magnolia neighborhood park around one or two in the morning on Friday as Russ had described.

"Yes, but it doesn't necessarily prove that Dr. Knoll was there at the time," Baumann had explained, leaning back in her desk chair. "He could have easily gotten the information off a police scanner or after the fact. Plus, for a week after July Fourth, there's always somebody setting off fireworks somewhere in the wee hours of the morning. He could have just thrown in that detail for a bit of authenticity."

"Well, if you think Dr. Knoll had anything to do with his wife's disappearance, just consider this," Anna had said. "You found all that blood in their living room and bathroom, and on the deck, right? If Russ knew about that, he'd have had two whole days to clean it up before he phoned you and reported Courtney missing. And he's a doctor. Cleanliness is a big part of his profession. I'm not saying you wouldn't have found any traces of blood at all, but from what I hear, your guys found a lot. And a doctor, if he was responsible for spilling that blood, he wouldn't have left so much evidence behind."

"Point taken," Baumann had replied. She'd cracked a tiny smile. "Y'know, any minute now, I expect you to break into a rendition of Tammy Wynette's 'Stand by Your Man.' Actually it's very sweet. And FYI, for now, you can relax. No one has charged Dr. Knoll with anything yet."

Anna had considered telling the detective about the harassing phone calls. But she'd decided to keep it to herself. No doubt, like Russ, she was a suspect—at the very least, *a person of interest*—in Courtney's disappearance. Why belabor the point by telling the detective about some anonymous caller who claimed to have seen her murder Courtney? Why even introduce that?

But Anna thought about it now, as she turned onto Eastlake and headed home. She heard some of the junk from her desk at work rattling in the car trunk.

Anna still couldn't remember anything from late Thursday night. Had her anonymous caller actually seen something? How could she be 100 percent sure she hadn't killed Courtney? She tried to imagine herself bashing Courtney over the head with that heavy glass award. She had no memory of ever picking it up. How did she even *know* it was heavy? She pictured Courtney's blood splattering on her jeans and her canvas sneakers. Or had that happened when she'd dragged Courtney's body out to the back deck and dumped it in the lake? The police still hadn't found a corpse in the water or amid the pilings by the house. Anna remembered how her skiff hadn't been properly tied to her deck on Friday afternoon. Was that because she'd taken the boat to Russ and Courtney's sometime after midnight—so none of the neighbors would see her on the dock? Had she placed Courtney's body in the skiff and then dumped her weighted corpse in the lake somewhere farther away? Maybe she'd bundled up her own bloodstained clothes and thrown them in the water as well.

The whole notion was completely ridiculous. She'd been so drunk on Thursday night she could barely stand up. Hell, she'd even puked. Russ had said that, when he'd left her, she'd been down for the count. She'd been in no condition to carry out a murder and cover it up. She hadn't even been able to climb the stairs up to her own bedroom that night.

Cruising down the narrow road that ran along Lake Union, Anna passed by her dock and noticed a news truck parked there. "Oh swell," she muttered.

She continued down for another block and a half to the carport. After pulling into her spot, Anna checked her watch. She had about ten minutes to get home, switch on the TV, and endure whatever Sally Justice dished out on tonight's show.

It was still light out, but under the moss-covered roof, the old carport was dark and shadowy. For a moment, Anna just sat in the car and watched the dashboard lights fade. She was in no hurry to watch herself get torn to pieces by Sally Justice.

With a sigh, she finally popped the trunk and stepped out of the car.

"Anna Malone?" The raspy whisper seemed to come from the darkest corner of the parking shed.

Gasping, Anna froze. For a moment, the voice sounded like the creep who had been making those menacing calls.

"Anna?"

She swiveled around and saw someone emerge from the shadows near the edge of the carport. Anna's hand went to her mouth.

"I'm sorry I scared you."

The woman's face was still swallowed up in the shadows. But Anna saw her signing as she spoke. For a crazy second, she thought the woman was Courtney. "Who's there? Who are you?" she asked, backing toward her car.

"I'm Taylor Hofstad," the woman said, spelling with her fingers. It was slightly difficult to understand her. Her speech was labored, similar to that of someone recovering from a stroke. "You don't know me. I'm Sally Justice's daughter."

She stepped forward, and Anna recognized the pale, slightly dowdy young woman. Though Anna rarely watched the show, she'd seen photos of Sally and Taylor together. She remembered Sally's daughter was deaf. "What—what are you doing here?" she asked, catching her breath. Her heart was still racing.

"Did you say something? I'm sorry, I can't tell."

Anna quickly took her hand away from her mouth. "I'm sorry. You startled me. What are you . . ." She trailed off and shook her head. "Why are you hiding in my carport?"

"I wanted to talk with you," she replied, signing again as she spoke. Taylor came a bit closer. "I'm sorry. I was going to wait by your dock. But some reporters are there, and I don't want it getting back to my mother that I spoke to you."

Anna squinted at her. "How do you know where I live? How do you know where I park my car?"

Taylor winced as if embarrassed. "I'm sorry. My mother has a couple of private investigators working for her. One of them had been checking you out since Sunday afternoon —as soon as my mother got wind of the police report on Courtney Knoll's disappearance. I read some of the investigator's notes. They included your houseboat address, the address of the carport, a description of your car, and the license number."

"Good God," Anna murmured, shaking her head. "Since Sunday afternoon?"

Taylor nodded.

"Does this private investigator drive a black Jetta?"

Taylor shrugged. "I really don't know what kind of car she drives."

"Was there anything in this investigator's notes about making phone calls to harass me?"

"I don't think so. At least, I didn't see anything like that."

Maybe it was the way she slouched, or how speaking clearly was an obvious challenge for her, but Taylor came across as so pitiful and defenseless. Still, she was Sally's daughter, and Anna was wary of her. She moved to her trunk and unloaded one of the boxes of work junk. "What did you want to talk to me about?" she asked, pausing to look directly at Taylor so she could read her lips.

"My mother, she's on the warpath. She's out to get you, Anna."

No shit, Anna wanted to say. But she nodded. "I know. I've seen the promos for tonight's show. And it's what half the reporters have been asking me about today." She glanced at her wristwatch. "The show starts in a minute. But thanks for the warning. Is that all?"

"I know you don't trust me, but I really want to help if I can. I thought your statement on the news tonight was really courageous."

"Thank you. I wonder what your mother thought."

"She was furious!" Taylor had a tough time saying *furious*. "You really pissed her off. So much of her show tonight was dedicated to exposing you and Dr. Knoll as lovers, and you ruined that for her."

Anna couldn't help smiling a bit. "Well, that's the first bit of good news I've heard all day."

"Sally even has a fact-checker investigating every word you said tonight. She wants to make you out to be a liar."

"A fact-checker? Well, that's ironic, considering how Sally has a habit of playing fast and loose with facts." Anna sighed. "I'm sorry. I shouldn't talk to you about your mother like that."

"It's okay. I love her, because she's my mother. But I don't like her very much."

Anna glanced at her watch again. "Apparently, you don't like her show very much, either. We're both missing it."

"They rerun it at eleven-thirty," Taylor said. "I'm sorry."

Anna let out a little laugh. "I should probably thank you."

"I've seen the script," Taylor said. "The first ten minutes are all about Courtney Knoll and what's happened. My mother will be talking about how I'm close friends with Courtney, which is a joke. I've met her only three times. After the intro, Sally—my mother—had planned to bring out a couple of witnesses who would say you and Courtney were both drunk at the Canlis restaurant Thursday night. Then Sally was going to accuse you and Dr. Knoll of having an affair. But as I said, you ruined that for her. So she's making her writers redo the whole second half of the show. They'll have to do a lot of rewriting, because I was supposed to be on tonight, talking about how Courtney was a pillar of the deaf community in Seattle. But I just couldn't do it. So I walked out. I had to warn you. My mother plans to spend the whole week on this. You know how on most of the shows, she has people phoning in and voting on something? Tomorrow, Sally will ask people if they believe the story you and Dr. Knoll gave the police about the night Courtney disappeared. She doesn't really care that much about Courtney—or her husband. This is all about destroying you—however she can."

Dumbstruck, Anna could only stare at her.

"My mother knows how to hold a grudge," Taylor said. "Do you remember the Ted Birch story you covered in Spokane about three and a half years ago?"

Anna nodded. "It was one of the things that really turned me off to your mother."

"You and me both," Taylor said. "Sally refused to be held accountable for that."

Anna remembered the case. Ted Birch was a redneck, good-old-boy petty thief who had been in and out of jail most of his life. He wasn't a very good husband to his long-suffering wife, Janelle, and he was a mostly absent father to his little boy, Teddy. But during his last stint in prison, he became determined to turn his life around. When he got out, Ted went straight and tried to make it up to his wife and son. Janelle got pregnant and had a baby girl, and things were looking up for them. Then one night in late October, when twelve-year-old Ted junior was sleeping at a friend's house, Ted and Janelle's neighbors heard arguing. Two hours later, the Birches' house went up in flames. The same neighbor who had heard the screaming saw Ted outside the house in his pajama bottoms, calmly watching the flames sweep through the house. His wife and baby daughter died in the inferno. One of Ted's prior offenses had been arson.

As part of her campaign to enforce a three-strikes policy for repeat offenders, Sally jumped on the case before she had all the facts. She campaigned for Ted Birch's immediate arrest. By the end of her second consecutive show dedicated to the Ted Birch case, Sally's audience voted him guilty of killing his wife and baby daughter.

In his defense, Ted told investigators that the screaming was just a joke—something he and his wife did when their baby was crying. Somehow, the competing noise always seemed to make the confused child quiet down. He also claimed to have a history of sleepwalking. One of his many early arrests had been for indecent exposure, when he'd unconsciously wandered down his block naked at two in the morning. Sally found all of this too far-fetched to believe and continued her campaign against him. Janelle's sister, who had always hated Ted, was a guest on Sally's show.

Police investigators determined that a faulty extension cord in the master bedroom had started the blaze and that Ted's story was accurate. But by then, Sally had moved on to another story. She never made any apologies or retractions. A lot of people never heard about Ted Birch's innocence; certainly none of Sally's followers did. Two weeks after the police had cleared him, Ted Birch borrowed a friend's hunting rifle. He waited until his son was in school the following morning; then he went into his backyard, put the barrel end of the rifle in his mouth, and blew his head off.

Sally's smear campaign had clearly played a part in Ted Birch's suicide. But she refused to see it that way and never discussed it publicly. Anna did a story for her Spokane station, focusing on Ted junior, who had chosen to live with a friend's family instead of his embittered aunt. The boy blamed his aunt and Sally Justice for contributing to his father's suicide. But his attitude was surprisingly optimistic. He talked about how grateful he was that his dad had made the most of his second chance to become a better person and a better father. They had two great years together. He said that he forgave his dad for all the bad times. When Anna asked the boy if he could ever forgive his aunt or Sally Justice, he just shrugged. "It's hard to forgive somebody when they're not really sorry, y'know?"

Anna's report was picked up by over thirty affiliate stations and went viral online.

Apparently, as far as Sally Justice was concerned, it had been a declaration of war.

"My mother took a lot of heat because of that story you did," Taylor explained, signing as she spoke.

"Your mother took a lot of heat because of *what she did*," Anna corrected her. "I didn't push an innocent man toward suicide. I have a theory about Sally. I think she knows she's a bullshit artist, but the trouble is, she believes her own bullshit, because her adoring public says she's right—no matter what."

"People will believe what they want to believe," Taylor said. "My mother blamed you because you blew the whistle on her. For a while, there was even a dartboard with your picture on it in the break room at my mother's studio. I took the picture down ages ago. But she's still mad at you."

"So this is all payback," Anna said, resting the boxful of work artifacts against the trunk.

Taylor nodded. "She's convinced that you and Dr. Knoll murdered Courtney. She won't even consider the possibility that someone else might have killed her." She touched Anna's arm. "What you did on the news tonight, it spoiled everything for her. If I can find out what my mother's planning for tomorrow night's show, I'll let you know. That way you can start planning on how to . . ." She momentarily stopped talking and gesturing.

"Head Sally off at the pass?" Anna said.

Taylor nodded eagerly. "You can be ready to discredit whatever she says."

"I appreciate this, Taylor, I mean it. But I have to ask. Why are you doing this for me?"

"I've stood by and watched my mother hurt a lot of

people who didn't deserve it, people like Ted Birch. I just can't stand by and watch anymore. I won't let her destroy you, Anna." Taylor patted her arm. "The private detective put your phone number in her report. I'll text you tonight or tomorrow—as soon as I find out what my mother has planned for tomorrow's show."

Anna nodded.

Sally's daughter turned and started to walk away.

"Thank you!" Anna called. But Taylor's back was to her, and Anna realized the thank you was in vain. She watched Sally's daughter turn the corner on the other side of the shed and disappear.

Hoisting up the box, Anna started down the block. She tried to process everything Taylor had just told her. So Sally Justice was convinced she and Russ had murdered Courtney. *"She won't even consider the possibility that someone else might have killed her,"* Taylor had said.

Anna realized her own thinking had been just as restricted. As much as she loved Russ and wanted to stand up for him, a part of her still suspected Russ of making Courtney disappear. But she didn't want to consider that as a possibility. It was easier to think Courtney had pulled a *Gone Girl* vanishing act to destroy the two of them and promote her book sales. Hell, Anna had even considered the ridiculous notion that she herself might have been the killer, sleepwalking through the whole thing like poor Ted Birch.

But she never seriously thought about the possibility that Courtney might have been murdered by *someone else*, a total stranger, or maybe somebody who hated Courtney. Anyone who used people the way Courtney did was bound to make enemies. Russ had once mentioned that, since they'd been married, Courtney had gone through several men. Anna couldn't help wondering if any of those discarded lovers were angry or bitter. And among them, had any dumped girlfriends or wives for Courtney? Anna had never been comfortable thinking of herself as a homewrecker. But Courtney probably had no problem taking on the role—as long as she got what she wanted and her public image remained unblemished.

The news van near the gate to her dock was from MSNBC. A good-looking reporter with silver hair was waiting by the gate with his videographer. He didn't lunge at her. "Can you answer a couple of questions, Ms. Malone?"

"Sure," she said, pausing. She shifted the box to one side so that it was balanced against her hip. "But let's do it right here."

"Right now, on her show, Sally Justice is saying that you and Dr. Russell Knoll should be considered suspects in his wife Courtney's disappearance. Do you have any comment on that?" He brought the handheld mic close to her face.

"Sally has a history of incorrectly rushing to judgment before she has all the facts. So I shouldn't be surprised. But I can assure you that I had nothing to do with Courtney's disappearance, and neither did her husband. I'm hoping for her safe return."

"Do you think *her safe return* is still possible considering the police found evidence of so much blood in the Knolls' floating home?"

"Yes, I'm hoping. As far as I know, this is still considered a missing person case. So I hope Courtney's okay."

He spoke into the mic again: "Would you set the record

straight? Were you fired from your job as a TV reporter because of your involvement with Courtney Knoll's husband?"

"No. I requested a leave of absence, and it was granted."

"Are you going to spend any of your new free time with Dr. Knoll?" he asked.

Anna shook her head. "No. I won't be seeing Dr. Knoll. I plan to spend my newfound free time doing everything I can to help the police determine what happened to Courtney Knoll." She shifted the box so that it was in front of her. "Now, this is getting heavy, so I need to move on."

"Thank you, Ms. Malone!"

As soon as she stepped into her house, Anna set down the box in the hallway, rushed into the living room, grabbed the remote, and switched on the TV. She changed channels to the 24/7 News Network. Like it or not, she figured she'd better catch the last few minutes of *The Sally Justice Show.*

A commercial for some diet pill was on.

Anna hurried into her study, where she had all three of Courtney's books by her desk. Carrying the books into the living room, she placed them on the coffee table and plopped down on the sofa. On TV, a slim woman and her boyfriend were walking along the beach, holding hands.

Anna gazed at the books in front of her—and the bold, stark graphics on the brightly colored covers. She'd remembered something Russ had told her about Courtney ripping off the idea for *The Defective Squad* from a former friend in her writers' group. "The group was pretty hostile toward her after the first book came out," he'd told her. "No one from that group will have anything to do with her anymore."

Sure enough, in the acknowledgments for *The Defective Squad*, Courtney had thanked the people in her writers' group:

> I'm grateful to my writers' group for helping me whip this manuscript into shape: Becky Arnett, Margaret Freeman, Sloane Lindquist, Sandy Myron, and Barb Riddle.

In her next two books, Courtney gave the usual thanks—to her editor, her agent, her mother, and Russ. Also she thanked someone named Gil, referring to him as *the forever helpful Gil* in all three book acknowledgments. But there was no mention of her writers' group in those two subsequent books.

On TV, they were listing the side effects of the diet pill.

Anna quickly pulled out her phone and texted Russ. She knew they'd said their good-byes yesterday. They'd made a necessary exception with their texts earlier today. She hadn't expected to be contacting him again for a while. He probably didn't expect to hear from her, either. But this was another exception:

> Sorry to bother you. I'm doing some investigating. Do you know who Gil is? He's mentioned in the acknowledgments of Courtney's 3 books. Thanks.

Anna figured this Gil person might know Courtney pretty well. She sent the text.

A few bars of the dramatic pulsating theme music from Sally's show came over the TV.

"I'm back!" Sally announced. She sat at her judge's desk, with a stern expression on her Botoxed face. Her ash-blond hair looked perfect, and her heavily made-up eyes stared down the camera. In the box over her left shoulder was a beautiful photo of Courtney—with the caption: *Courtney Knoll—3 Days Missing.* "I have a warning. The images you are about to see have graphic content and may be disturbing. And while you see these unsettling images from Courtney's living room, think about the fact that Seattle Police have not yet arrested anyone in connection with Courtney's disappearance. Think about the fact that the last two people to see Courtney alive were her philandering husband, Dr. Russell Knoll, and his mistress, the disgraced local TV reporter, Anna Malone. And the three of them were last seen at a restaurant, having a drunken, violent argument."

"Oh shit," Anna murmured.

On the TV screen, there was a photograph of Russ and Courtney's living room. A smeary luminescent substance covered parts of the hardwood floor by the bookcase.

"These are exclusive photos from the luminol test, part of the ongoing police investigation," Sally continued in voice-over. "This is Courtney Knoll's living room in her beautiful floating home on Seattle's Lake Union. Now it's a crime scene. The glowing blue-white spots indicate traces of blood. As you can see, there's quite a lot of it."

They showed a portion of the same photo—a close-up of the big bluish glow-in-the-dark splotch at the base of the bookcase, and then another portion of the same photo—with another luminescent constellation on the dark floor at the edge of a plush rug.

"Something happened in that living room shortly after midnight Friday—something Courtney's husband and his TV-reporter mistress aren't telling the police. What don't they want us to know?"

The image on TV went back to Sally at her desk. "On tomorrow's *Sally Justice Show,* I'm going to examine this duplicitous pair more closely. We'll look at their backgrounds and punch some holes in that tall tale they've told the police about the night Courtney vanished. And we'll hear from *you*—what some of *you* think about them. You won't want to miss it. You get all the true talk on *The Sally Justice Show!*"

The theme music started up.

Anna grabbed the remote and switched off the TV. If the rest of the show had been like this, Anna was glad she'd missed it. She probably wouldn't even bother setting her DVR for the eleven-thirty rerun—unless she was feeling masochistic.

She looked down at her copy of *The Defective Squad,* open to the acknowledgments page. She told herself that if she was looking for suspects in Courtney's disappearance, this was as good a place as any to start.

CHAPTER SIXTEEN

Tuesday, July 14 12:59 A.M.

Isn't this practically right next door 2 U? read the text from her friend Kristin.

Megan Jameson clicked on the attachment. It was a photo of a dimly lit room—or at least, a portion of a room—with a sleek designer chair, a plush shag rug, and a bookcase full of tasteful objets d'art. The *Architectural Digest*–like setting seemed to be illuminated in black light. The mass of bluish splotches on the dark wood floor gave off a strange glow.

A woman's voice came over the image. Megan quickly muted the TV and turned up the volume on her phone: "This is Courtney Knoll's living room in her beautiful floating home on Seattle's Lake Union. Now it's a crime scene."

"Oh, that skank," said Megan's friend Josie. Squeezed against Megan on the sofa, she was looking at the phone as well. "Kristin's totally trying to scare us. She's just mad you didn't invite her over tonight. Don't even reply!"

Megan recognized the photo and the voice on her phone from *The Sally Justice Show* earlier tonight.

She and Josie were both sixteen years old. Thin and pretty with shoulder-length brown hair, the two of them looked like twins—or so people said, except that Josie had braces.

Megan hardly ever watched Sally Justice—or the news. Everything that mattered to her and her friends came through social media on their phones. But tonight was different.

Megan's parents were in San Francisco, visiting her married sister, Kerry. They'd left on Friday and wouldn't be back until tomorrow afternoon. This was the first time Megan had been by herself for more than one night in their Lake Union floating home. Her folks had given her permission to have Josie over. So Josie had spent the night Friday. She'd also been there all night on Saturday for a slumber party, which Megan's parents hadn't known about—at least, not until four in the morning on Sunday, when one of the neighbors had called Mr. Jameson to complain about all the noise. Things had gotten out of hand with Megan's five friends—Kristin among them. Two guys had crashed the party, which had extended out to the back deck with swimming, diving, loud music, drinking, and laughing.

Megan's parents had gone ballistic on her. They'd said she was grounded for two weeks. The only reason they'd allowed her to have Josie sleep over tonight was because Megan was so nervous about the disappearance of Courtney Knoll, just one dock down from them. Throughout the day, Megan had been following the macabre story on the news. They'd said that Courtney Knoll might have been murdered in her living room. Sally Justice claimed that Courtney's doctor husband and his girlfriend were the main suspects.

Megan had seen a few of Anna Malone's videos on YouTube and always kind of liked her. But now that she knew Anna had been screwing this beautiful deaf author's husband, Megan thought she was a total sleaze. And Anna might have even killed the poor woman—to hear Sally Justice talk.

But there was also a chance the murderer was some drifter—or maybe a killer targeting the residents of floating homes and houseboats in the neighborhood. The police still hadn't found Courtney Knoll's body. Earlier in the day, Megan had stood at the end of her dock and watched the police search still in progress. A patrol boat was nearby while two men stood on the next dock down, working with a net and an extension pole.

Fortunately, Josie's parents were oblivious to the fact that Megan lived so close to the crime scene. And they had no idea about the party that had gotten out of hand on Saturday night. So they'd allowed Josie to sleep over again tonight. She'd come armed with pepper spray in her overnight bag. A lot of help that would be, Megan had pointed out: the expiration date stamped on the little canister was over a year ago.

But, Megan figured there was strength in numbers with the two of them there. Plus one advantage to having busybody neighbors was, if she and Josie started screaming, someone on the dock would probably call the cops.

They'd ordered pizza—for the third time in four nights—and watched a documentary about the Jonas Brothers on Prime. And, of course, they'd texted back and forth with their girlfriends most of the night. But nearly all of their pals had gone to bed about an hour ago. Kristin was the only one still up—at least, the only one they knew about.

They hadn't stepped out since it had gotten dark around nine-thirty. All the outside lights were on, illuminating the Jamesons' floating home. The doors and windows were shut and locked, and the air-conditioning was on. Every time the cooling system restarted, it would catch Megan and Josie off guard, and they'd momentarily panic at the sudden humming noise. A half hour ago, when it had started up again, Josie had shrieked and nearly given Megan a heart attack. Then they'd gotten a case of the giggles.

But it wasn't funny now. And Megan didn't appreciate the text from Kristin.

She decided to take Josie's advice and not reply.

But Kristin immediately followed up her text with another: *Look what I found . . . this day in history!* There was a link below the message.

"God, I hate her," Josie murmured. "Click on it."

Megan clicked on the link:

JULY 14, 1966—CHICAGO, ILL.—Eight student nurses were strangled and stabbed in their dormitory town house by Richard Speck in what was then called "The Crime of the Century."

"That's such a lie," Josie said.

"No, it isn't," Megan replied, frowning. "Kerry told me about it a while back. It really happened. There was an episode about it on that old show, *Mad Men*."

"I'm looking it up," Josie said, working her thumbs over the keyboard of her own phone.

"No, I don't want to look it up," Megan said. "It's just going to scare me even more. Please, let's just forget about it."

She fired off a quick text to Kristin: *U R not funny. Stop it.*

Tossing the phone on the sofa cushion, Megan got to her feet and headed into the bathroom. It was past one in the morning, and they still hadn't changed into their pajamas. She knew the two of them were too wired and too scared to sleep. Plus, Megan figured if they needed to run out of the house all of a sudden, they didn't want to do it in their pajamas.

It wasn't just the air conditioner restarting that unhinged them. Every little sound, every noise outside, every time they heard a splash in the water, it filled her and Josie with dread.

She'd left the TV muted. She would crank it up when she returned to the living room—if for nothing else than to drown out all those scary, incidental little noises.

She hoped Kristin was finished sending those stupid texts. Kristin was tight with Dan and John, who had crashed the slumber party on Saturday night. Megan kept thinking that her sometime friend might send the guys over to scare them. Both Dan and John were really cute, but at the moment, Megan didn't need somebody trying to spook her.

She secretly wished Josie would just calm down and stop thinking of tonight as this fun, scary adventure. Megan was genuinely terrified. Someone had been murdered in her floating home—just one dock away. And

Megan really didn't feel like talking about it—or about those horrible murders in Chicago fifty or sixty years ago.

She kept imagining the news tomorrow and people discussing how she and Josie had disappeared tonight. She could almost see the eerie photos of the sofa they'd just been sitting on—covered with all those glow-in-the-dark blue splotches.

Or would they be murdered in her bedroom? Megan figured she wouldn't sleep a wink tonight. She moved over to the sink to wash her hands.

"No . . . please!" Josie yelped.

Megan froze.

She heard a thud. Her friend let out a scream. But it was cut short.

With a shaky hand, Megan turned off the water at the sink. She heard footsteps, someone stomping toward the kitchen. Then all at once, the footsteps stopped, and there was just silence.

Megan felt her heart racing. She could hardly breathe. She hesitated and then opened the bathroom door. "Josie?" she called out, her voice quavering. "Josie, you're not funny."

She couldn't make herself walk out there. Instead, she stood in the bathroom doorway for a few moments. Megan kept thinking she'd hear her friend start to giggle—and then this would all be one big joke. But all she could hear was water lapping against the pilings outside.

"Josie? Quit clowning around, okay?"

She forced herself to creep toward the living room. The only light in the room was from the flickering, muted TV. The standing lamp that had been on when she'd gone to the bathroom a few minutes ago was now off —and lying on the living room floor, the shade askew.

"Oh my God," Megan murmured. Then she raised her voice: "I'm calling the police!"

If Josie had set this whole thing up, she'd come clean now. Her friend wouldn't let her call the cops. Josie wouldn't take the joke that far.

"I mean it!" Megan yelled. "I'm calling 911!"

She turned toward the sofa to grab her phone, but it wasn't there.

Megan froze. "JOSIE!" she screamed.

She thought about running out of the house and down the dock, where she'd pound on the neighbor's door. But she was paralyzed.

She heard a strange tapping noise. It seemed to come from the outside deck—off the living room. They'd shut the window blinds, but the blind slats were open on the tall window in the door onto the back deck. She couldn't see any movement out there. They'd locked the door earlier. Was it still locked?

The *tap, tap, tap* continued.

Megan swallowed hard and took a few steps toward the door. She had tears in her eyes, but she could see the dead bolt was still in place. Through the slats, she noticed her own reflection in the darkened glass.

A shadowy figure crept up behind her.

Megan swiveled around and screamed.

Startled, Josie shrieked back.

As soon as she realized Josie was all right, Megan punched her in the arm. "You're not funny!" she cried.

Josie recoiled. "Ouch! God, that hurt!" She rubbed her arm.

Megan couldn't help it. She broke down and started sobbing.

"God, Meg, I'm sorry!" Josie said, hovering near her. She touched her shoulder. "I thought you'd think it was funny."

Megan jerked away from her. "I hate you right now! It wasn't funny at all! Did I sound like I was having fun? Couldn't you hear how scared I was? And I swear, if you broke my mother's lamp, I'm going to kill you!"

"Relax! I just switched it off and laid it on its side."

"Where's my phone?"

"In the kitchen. Would you please stop snapping at me? God, can't you take a joke?"

"No, I can't, okay?" Megan shot back. She brushed past her, bent down, and set the lamp upright again. Switching it on, she marched into the kitchen, where she ripped off a square of paper towel and wiped her eyes and nose. She grabbed her phone off the counter, slipped it in the pocket of her summer shorts, and headed back into the living room.

Josie was at the windowed door, staring through the blind's slats at the deck. She turned to look at Megan. "Listen, I'm sorry, okay?" she said. "That was really dumb. I didn't realize you were so scared."

"You didn't realize . . ." Megan repeated, rolling her eyes. "You know I've been a nervous wreck all night . . ." She trailed off. She heard the tapping again. It was back.

"What is that?" Josie asked.

"I heard it earlier," Megan murmured. "I thought it was you."

Josie shook her head and turned toward the door again. She reached for the dead bolt.

"What are you doing?" Megan whispered. "Are you nuts? Somebody could be out there! It could be a trap."

Biting her lip, Josie hurried past her to the easy chair, where she'd left her purse. She sifted through it and pulled out the little canister of pepper spray.

All the while, the strange, intermittent tapping continued. Megan noticed the noise had a metallic resonance—and it definitely came from the deck area outside.

She didn't have much faith in Josie's pepper spray. So she headed into the kitchen and took a butcher knife from the drawer. She couldn't stop shaking. In the back of her mind, she wondered if Dan and John had come over and somehow snuck onto the deck; and now they were trying to lure them out there by making that noise. *Some joke.*

Then again, maybe someone else —a drifter or a serial killer—was the one trying to lure them out there.

Still trembling, Megan returned to the living room. She nodded at Josie, who stood by the door. Josie unlocked the dead bolt and cautiously opened the door. Megan stood behind her. After so many hours in the air-conditioned house, it was strange to feel the tepid night air creeping in through the doorway. She heard the water wash against the pilings— and that *tap, tap, tap.*

She didn't see anybody on the deck. The wicker patio furniture, her mother's potted plants, and the gas grill were just where they should be. Nothing was different from when Megan had cleaned out here on Sunday morning after the party. But she could still hear the tapping; the sound was very distinct now. It seemed to come from somewhere by the corner of the deck, near a potted Japanese maple.

With trepidation, she and Josie crept toward the corner

and peeked over the deck's edge. Megan reached into her pocket and took out her phone. She shined the flashlight beam into the dark water.

"What is that?" Josie muttered.

It took Megan a moment to make out the olive-colored hard-shell suitcase. It looked slightly bigger than a carry-on. Trapped amid the pilings by the deck, it floated on the lake's surface. With every ripple in the water, one of the suitcase's wheels tapped against a rusty cleat on the side of the deck.

"It's a suitcase," Josie said, answering her own question. "Oh my God, we've got to see what's inside! Maybe it's full of money."

"Yeah, right," Megan snorted. "It's probably empty—or it's full of rags that have lice or something. I'm sure a homeless person lost it."

Megan's hand was still shaking, and Josie helped her steady it—so the light beam was directed on the suitcase label. "Samsonite," Josie said. "It looks expensive. No homeless person lost this. Have you got something we can use to fish this out?"

With a sigh, Megan reluctantly nodded toward another corner of the deck, where a boat hook leaned against the house.

Shoving the pepper spray in her pocket, Josie fetched the pole. Then she returned to the edge of the deck and moved the hook end of the pole down to the water. Her mouth scrunched up in concentration as she tried to snag the suitcase handle.

Megan had a bad feeling about this. She nervously glanced around. She didn't see any activity out on the water. There was no one standing on any of the other docks nearby, no strange silhouettes. Yet she felt as if someone was watching them.

She heard splashing and turned toward her friend.

"Shit! This is heavy! Help me!" Josie struggled with the boat hook and staggered back a few steps. She was like an amateur fisherman trying to reel in a big game fish. She anxiously nodded toward the edge of the deck. "Grab it!"

The suitcase was half out of the water, bobbing up and down as Josie tugged at it with the boat hook. Megan moved toward the bag. But it banged against the edge of the deck, splashing her with water. Megan balked.

"Grab it!" Josie screamed. "I can't hold on! It weighs a ton!"

Megan reached out and took hold of the suitcase handle, avoiding the hook. The leather grip felt cold and slimy. She realized Josie wasn't kidding about how heavy it was. The suitcase might as well have been full of bricks.

Josie kept the hook lodged in the handle and backed up a few more steps. They hauled the case onto the deck and let it drop on its side. A pool of water bloomed beneath it on the deck.

Megan stopped to catch her breath. Josie dropped the pole, and it made a clatter that seemed to echo. They both stared at the wet suitcase in the moonlight.

Megan thought about Courtney Knoll, missing since early Friday morning. No way could anyone fit a body in that case. But maybe it was part of a body—perhaps a couple of arms, maybe the legs, or even her torso. The suitcase had certainly been heavy enough. This close to it, Megan detected a slightly putrid smell. She didn't want to get any closer. She didn't want to touch it again.

But Josie had no such qualms. Getting down on her knees, she started to struggle with the latches.

"Maybe it's locked," Megan said.

"No, just stuck," Josie replied, hovering over the bag.

Then Megan heard the latches snap.

Josie opened the case, and some water spilled over the sides. "Oh shit," she moaned. "It's just some old rust-stained pink towels."

Megan stared down at the wet towels crammed into the suitcase. She moved the flashlight beam over them. The water was pink, not the towels. They must have been white originally. And the stains weren't rust stains. That was blood.

With her finger and thumb, Josie pulled at the corner of one towel and started to pull it out.

That was when Megan saw the monogram: *CMK*.

"I know what they mean by deadweight. She looked so petite, but dragging that lifeless thing across the floor out to their dock was awkward and exhausting. I had the trash bags wrapped around her, but they started to tear, and blood leaked out . . . Like I said, I'd already loaded the suitcase in the dinghy. When I got her out there to the edge of the dock, I sort of rolled her into the boat. It almost tipped over. The goddamn suitcase fell into the lake. I saw it start to float away, but I couldn't get to it. By the time I cleaned and locked up the house, then got back into the boat, I couldn't find the suitcase anywhere on the water."

—Excerpt: Session 3, audio recording
with Dr. G. Tolman, July 23

CHAPTER SEVENTEEN

Tuesday, July 14—11:02 A.M.

Anna stood at the number 47 bus stop at Bellevue Avenue and Bellevue Place on Capitol Hill. She was near a little cluster of storefronts—a hip-hop bar called The Lookout, a jiujitsu studio, and the only spot among them open at this hour, a small mom-and-pop grocery store. The rest of the block was made up of apartment buildings. Nobody else was at the bus stop, which had a shelter— barely large enough for two strangers to keep a comfortable distance.

Right now, the shelter wasn't necessary. Anna could feel the sun on her face, and the thermometer was supposed to hit the mideighties today. She wore sunglasses— with a pretty, white summer blouse and khaki slacks. It was the kind of outfit she'd wear for one of her news reports—nice, but not flashy. She wanted to look the way she did on TV.

She was supposed to meet someone here at eleven o'- clock, someone who knew her only from her appearances on KIXI-TV News.

Anna had been anxious about the meeting and arrived ten minutes ago. She'd been a bit unclear if this woman was getting off the bus when it arrived or just meeting her at the stop. But there was no bus and no one else around, so Anna had been waiting.

With her phone in her hand, she reread Russ's text from last night:

Don't know who Gil is. I'm ashamed to admit I never read Courtney's book acknowledgments very closely. If I don't recognize a name, I just assume they're someone with the publisher. I watched Sally Justice last night. Sorry she was so rough on you. It's because of Courtney & me that you're going through all this misery. You deserve better. Forgive me. Love you.

It had been only two days since she'd last talked with Russ on Sunday, but it seemed like forever. Maybe that was because everything they'd said was so final. For the past couple of days, Anna kept having these little crying jags that sort of snuck up on her. She felt one coming on now and tried not to succumb to it.

She still hadn't heard from George and didn't really expect to.

George wasn't the only person she'd disappointed— far from it. Anna had made the mistake of opening her work mail this morning: 493 e-mails—practically all of them negative. She had Bible-thumpers claiming she was going to hell, loyal fans who were let down and disillusioned, and everyone in between. She hadn't read all of the e-mails yet and wasn't responding to any of the critics, most of whom just seemed to be venting. There was no point in engaging with them. She sent thank-you notes to the handful of people who had e-mailed their support and said they hoped to see her back on TV soon. In her brief replies, she didn't mention that she was pretty certain her television career was over. Instead, Anna kept things upbeat.

Last night, she'd Googled the names of the women in Courtney's writers' group. The only one with a working phone number from the online white pages had been Becky Arnett. She'd answered after three rings.

Anna had explained who she was—and that she had some questions about Courtney Knoll. She wanted to make sure she was the same Becky Arnett who had been in a writers' group with Courtney.

"Yeah, that's me," Becky had answered. "And I can see from the caller ID that you're Anna Malone. But I'm having a hard time believing you're the Anna Malone from TV. I'd have to meet you first before I start spilling my guts about Courtney. How about if we meet someplace late tomorrow morning—say at eleven o'clock? There's a bus stop by a bar called The Lookout . . ."

Anna now checked her wristwatch: 11:09. She looked up and spotted a thirtysomething brunette on the sidewalk, wandering toward her. The woman was totally focused on her phone. She stopped by the shelter, gave Anna the briefest of glances, and went back to her phone.

"Excuse me," Anna said. "You're not Becky, are you?"

Barely looking up, the brunette frowned, shook her head, and turned away.

"Thanks," Anna said to the woman's back. Sometimes she hated what cell phones had done to polite society.

With a sigh, she decided to go back to her own phone
and catch up on all those e-mails—and all the people who
thought she was sinful, selfish, and immoral. Anna cringed
as she read the subject headings to some of the latest
incoming messages. *You're Disgusting* got right to the
point; *So Disappointed in You* felt like a well-deserved kick
in the stomach; and *A Pig by Any Other Name* was immediately deleted.

Near the top of the current e-mails listed was one from
Taylor H. with the subject header: *Tonight's Sally Justice
Show.*

Anna opened it:

Dear Anna,

On tonight's show, my mother is talking mostly about you
and Dr. Knoll and your backgrounds. I couldn't get any
details, but she's going into your family history. She's
determined to make you look bad. She's interviewing
someone you worked with at the TV station. Unfortunately, I
don't have a name or any other information about who it is,
just someone work-related.

Since I refused to appear on last night's show by running
out on her, my mother's not sharing much with me. One
thing I know, she's zeroing in on your claim that you don't
remember anything from the night Courtney disappeared.
She thinks it's a big cover-up, and it's where she's going to
keep jabbing away at you on her show.

Anna, if you could remember, and go public with that, Sally
wouldn't have much to use against you. I think it might help
Dr. Knoll, too. Right now, remembering exactly what

happened Thursday night and Friday morning seems like your best defense. I know a hypnotherapist who might be able to help. She's had amazing success with people who have had blackouts or repressed memories and things like that. If you're interested, let me know.

If I'm overstepping here, please tell me and I'll back off.

I hope this is some help. I'll text you if I can get the name of that coworker my mother will interview on tonight's show.

Take Care.
Taylor

Anna wondered if Sally Justice had gotten to George. But she couldn't imagine that George would betray her— no matter how angry he was at her right now. She'd been on good terms with nearly everyone in the newsroom. So she wondered who else Sally had booked on her show tonight.

She dreaded what Sally would broadcast about her dead parents. But there was nothing she could do about that. She told herself she shouldn't care, *sticks and stones* and all that. But she had a career in TV, and it mattered what people thought of her.

She fired off a reply to Taylor:

Dear Taylor,

Thank you so much for your note and all your help.

If you can find out who your mother is interviewing tonight, maybe I can reach out to them ahead of time. I'm not certain what kind of negative stories any of my work associates might have about me. But if you can find out anything more I'd appreciate it.

Thanks also for the advice about jarring my memory of Thursday night. You're not overstepping at all This is very helpful. Maybe we can discuss it later.

The truth was, a part of her didn't want to remember.

Had it all happened just as Russ had described? Or had he lied to protect himself? Knowing Russ, he could have been lying to protect her.

But Anna knew she couldn't have murdered Courtney. It didn't matter how drunk or angry she'd been, she couldn't have killed her— at least, not deliberately. Why was she still haunted by the lie that creep had whispered to her on the phone Saturday afternoon?

She heard a rumbling down the street and saw the number 47 bus turn a corner and pull up toward the stop.

She quickly typed: *Thanks again! All my best, Anna.* Then she pressed send and put her phone away.

The bus rolled up to the stop, and the doors opened with a hiss.

Removing her sunglasses, Anna watched an older woman step down to the sidewalk. The gray-haired lady didn't look at her. She was followed by a man on his phone and a woman on her phone. The bus driver—a stout woman of fifty with short-cropped curly gray hair— stepped down to the bus door. "We leave in five minutes," she announced—for Anna and the woman still staring at her phone. "You're welcome to board and pay now, or wait out here. We leave promptly at eleven-twenty." She smiled at Anna. "Well, if it isn't Anna Malone, the genuine article. I'm Becky."

Before Anna could answer, Becky turned to the woman on her phone. "Hey!" she barked. "I was talking to you a second ago. Are you getting on the bus or waiting out here or what?"

The woman looked startled. "Um, I—I can wait."

Becky ducked back into the bus, and then reemerged with a satchel. She looked at Anna and nodded toward the small grocery store. "C'mon, let's talk over here."

Anna followed her, and they stopped in front of the store window. "Thanks for agreeing to talk to me," Anna said. "You said to meet you at the bus stop, but I didn't expect you to be driving the bus."

Becky dug into her purse. "I've published three books— all small press, but legitimate. I'd be homeless and starving to death if I wasn't driving this bus around the city thirty hours a week. That's the life of a struggling author— in a nutshell." She fished out a pack of Virginia Slims. "Mind if I light up?"

Anna shook her head.

"I was ninety-nine percent sure you were the real Anna Malone, but I wanted to meet you in person. Before I let you go, I want your autograph."

Anna smiled. "I'd be happy to give you one, but really, I'm just a local TV reporter. I'm not a celebrity."

Becky lit her cigarette and turned her head so that she didn't blow the smoke in Anna's face. "Are you kidding me? I watch trashy TV. I saw *The Sally Justice Show* last night. You're getting more and more famous every day. I have to confess: I may have gotten you here under false pretenses. I'm not sure what I can tell you about Courtney.

I haven't seen her in about three years. That's when she left our writers' group. Actually, we voted her out."

"I got the impression from Dr. Knoll that there were some hard feelings."

"That's putting it nicely. When Courtney sold that first book, *The Defective Squad*, we were all so excited for her. We thought we'd already read most of the book as a group. But no, Courtney went in an entirely different direction from the first draft we'd seen. And half of her ideas she stole from us. For example, I was writing a memoir four years ago, and I shared it with the group. My father was a security officer, an ex-cop, and an alcoholic. He used to beat me—and my mother, who, by the way, was half-Tlingit. Mom got the worst of it. One night, when I was eleven, Dad handcuffed me to the stove and beat my mother to death with his nightstick. Then he shot himself. I watched the whole thing. Sound familiar?"

Anna stared at her in wonder. "That's what happened to the mute girl in *The Defective Squad*," she murmured. It was Courtney's dramatic explanation for how the girl had become mute. The girl had screamed throughout the whole ordeal, and then didn't utter another word after that. The mute girl in the book had a Native American mother, too.

"She never asked me if she could use that story," Becky said. "She took my personal pain and exploited it. She stole from all of us."

"I understand from Dr. Knoll that the whole idea for *The Defective Squad* came from someone else in the group."

Puffing on her cigarette, Becky nodded. "Crazy Sandy, she's the one who first wrote about the team of disabled teenage superheroes. She got about four chapters into it and then gave up. That was typical of Sandy. She'd get a plot idea brewing, start a book, and abandon it after a couple of months. But Courtney never asked Sandy if she could use the idea. She totally ripped her off. After Courtney's book came out, Sandy went nuts and told Courtney that she was going to sue. Courtney claimed that Sandy had given her permission to use the idea—which was a bald-faced lie. She also claimed that Sandy would have never gotten the idea in the first place if it weren't for Courtney being in the writers' group and being deaf—which is maybe half-true, I guess. But it was still a raw deal for Sandy. She was all bent on hiring a lawyer and going after Courtney. But the group talked her out of it. Sandy was always kind of nuts, hence the nick-name Crazy Sandy. Of course, no one called her that to her face. Anyway, all a judge or jury would need is fifteen minutes of listening to Sandy rant and rave, and they'd throw the case out of court. We all figured what's the use? and moved on. But Sandy never got over it. I mean, she hated Courtney with a passion."

Becky dropped her cigarette on the sidewalk and stepped on it. "In fact, when you announced on the news Sunday night that Courtney was missing, and Sally Justice said she might even be dead, I thought, *Well, maybe at last, Crazy Sandy got her revenge.*"

Dumbfounded, Anna stared at her.

Becky glanced toward the bus, and Anna followed her gaze. A man was at the bus door, but he hesitated and looked at Becky expectantly.

"We leave in a minute!" she called. "Go ahead and board. Pay me when we're ready to take off!"

"Are you going to Nordstrom Rack?" he called.

"We stop right by it!" she called back. Then she turned to Anna again.

"Do you know how I can get ahold of this Sandy?" Anna asked.

Becky shrugged. "I have an e-mail address. I'm not sure if it's still good. The group broke up about two years ago. The rest of us have kept in touch. But Sandy kind of fell off the grid." She reached into her purse again and took out a spiral notebook and pen. "Sandy's phone number and e-mail are in my laptop at home. If you give me your e-mail—along with your autograph—I can send you Crazy Sandy's contact info, if it's still good." She handed the pen and notebook to Anna. "And for the autograph, Becky is with a *y*."

Anna scribbled down her e-mail and phone number. Then she wrote: *To Becky—Thanks for everything! All my best, Anna Malone.* She handed the notebook back to Becky. "By the way, there's someone named Gil in the acknowledgments of all three of Courtney's books. You don't happen to know who that is, do you?"

Shoving the notebook in her satchel, Becky laughed. "That's an inside joke. For a while, the girls in the group all lived vicariously through Courtney, because she was having more sex than the rest of us combined— most of it behind her husband's back, too. She used to complain about Russ never being around, so she had to go out and get her fun elsewhere. She was a regular love-'em-and-leave-'em girl. She once joked to me that when she wrote her acknowledgments, she'd have to thank all the guys she'd laid because they kept her from going insane while writing her book. *Gil* is code for 'Guys I've Laid.'"

Anna let out a surprised little laugh, "Seriously?"

Becky nodded. "Seriously."

"Do you know if any of her boyfriends resented being loved and left? Did any of them have wives who might have held a grudge?"

Becky gave her a shrewd half grin. "Are you looking for suspects?" She shook her head. "What a dumb question. Of course you are. Sally Justice is trying to pin Courtney's disappearance on you and your boyfriend."

With a sigh, Anna nodded glumly.

"Well, what Sally doesn't know is that Courtney must have a whole bunch of people who wouldn't mind seeing her dead. But the guys she was seeing three years ago? That's a long time for a guy to hold a grudge. Besides, I can't even begin to remember any of their names. She always referred to them as the Gym Guy or the Tennis Player or Mr. Light Rail. If you're looking for suspects, I still think you're better off tracking down Crazy Sandy. Now, she's the type who will hold on to a grudge until the Rapture."

Wide-eyed, Anna nodded. "Okay, thanks."

"Well, I've got passengers tapping their feet." Becky started to back away—toward the bus, where four people were now waiting to board. "I'll e-mail you Sandy's contact info."

"Thanks again!" Anna called.

She watched Becky Arnett board the bus, and then the passengers followed her in.

"Hey, Anna!" she heard Becky yell.

She came to the door of the bus.

Sitting at the wheel, Becky smiled at her. "I wanted to say, I really enjoyed meeting you. You're a nice person. And I think Sally Justice is full of shit."

"I needed to hear that," Anna said. "Thank you."

Becky nodded and reached for the door lever. The bus doors closed with a hiss.

Anna waved, and then she watched the number 47 bus pull away from the curb and head down the street.

CHAPTER EIGHTEEN

Tuesday, July 14—6:11 P.M.

The TV news kept showing that same footage of police searching the lake around Russ and Courtney's dock. They also showed—over and over—the same author photo of Courtney, looking intelligent and beautiful.

Early this morning, some teenagers had discovered Courtney's suitcase, the one Russ said she must have packed and taken with her when she'd disappeared. The case had been floating in the water by a neighboring dock north of Russ and Courtney's house. Inside the carry-on were two bloody bath towels and a hand towel—all monogrammed with Courtney's initials. Several more items were stashed in the suitcase, including Courtney's phone, her purse, and other articles Russ had noted as missing. Courtney's glass quill award wasn't among the items found.

Anna sat in her living room, watching the news coverage, clicking back and forth among the networks. It was national news now. Her phone was beside her on the sofa cushion. At least a dozen times, she'd picked it up to call Russ and then changed her mind and put it down again.

She hadn't heard back from Taylor yet—and *The Sally Justice Show* was on in nineteen minutes.

Anna had left a voice mail with George, asking if he knew about someone at the station appearing on Sally's program tonight. He hadn't phoned back. Anna couldn't believe he was still that angry at her.

There was no follow-up yet from Becky Arnett about Crazy Sandy. But Anna had hope that Sandy was just the tip of the iceberg of potential suspects in Courtney's disappearance. It couldn't be just Russ and her. According to the news reports, Russ hadn't been charged with anything yet. Only one station—a competitor of KIXI-TV—had mentioned her in today's coverage of the case, and for that, she was grateful.

The phone rang, and Anna grabbed it. The caller ID read: *Russell Knoll, MD*.

She muted the TV and tapped her phone screen. "How are you doing?"

"I've had better days. I know I shouldn't be calling—"

"I'm glad you did. In fact, I was hoping you would before I broke down and called you first. Are you watching the news?"

"Yes. The police had me come down and identify the contents of the suitcase at around noon today. On the plus side, all of the stuff in the suitcase was stuff I reported as missing when I first talked to the cops this past weekend. So they know I've been telling them the truth, at least, about that. But it's the only plus, the rest is just bad. I mean, this pretty much confirms that Courtney was murdered—as if the luminol test in the living room didn't already make that abundantly clear."

"What does your lawyer say?" Anna asked. It was odd to see Russ's photo flash up on the TV screen while she was talking to him—odd and troubling.

"He said I should prepare myself. Anytime now, the police could charge me with Courtney's murder."

"Oh God," she murmured. "But you've been cooperating with them! The fireworks in the park proved you were there when Courtney disappeared—"

"Anna, honey, the way they see it, they don't have a body or a time of death. I had all night to kill her and dump the body someplace. Proving I was in a park in Magnolia at one in the morning doesn't give me an airtight alibi for the night she disappeared."

"That's crazy. I mean, why aren't they looking for other potential suspects? I talked to someone from Courtney's writers' group today. Did you know Becky?"

"The name sounds familiar. But that was three years ago."

"Well, this Becky confirmed what you said about Courtney ripping off one of the other authors in the group. In fact, she stole from everyone, but she *really* burned Sandy. She was the one who had the original idea for *The Defective Squad*. According to Becky, Sandy was livid that Courtney used it—and Sandy's also pretty crazy. Becky told me she wouldn't be surprised if Sandy still held a grudge and maybe on Friday morning, she finally did something about it."

"Yeah, I remember Courtney got a lot of flak from her."

"Becky was supposed to e-mail me Sandy's contact information, but I haven't heard from her yet. You know, the police should also consider all the men Courtney's been with, all the hearts she broke. She was no saint—despite how I played her up in her profile on TV."

"The police know about her infidelities," Russ said soberly. "But of course, as far as they're concerned, that just gives me a stronger motive for killing her. But this Sandy person, I'll be sure to tell them about her. Thanks."

She heard him sigh on the other end. "Listen, Anna, the reason I'm calling is that I think you should contact a lawyer about this. If they come after me, I'm worried they'll try to implicate you, too."

"I haven't looked into a lawyer yet. I—I'll do that to-morrow, I promise."

"I'll talk to my guy and have him e-mail you a list. And don't worry about the cost. I'm going to pay for this. If it weren't for me, you wouldn't . . ."

"Please, stop it," she interrupted. "I knew what I was getting into when we got back together last year. I'm just as responsible as you are. You don't have to—"

A loud knock on the door interrupted her.

Startled, Anna got to her feet. "Someone's at the door," she murmured into the phone. "Just a sec." At the door, she checked the peephole. Through the slightly warped glass, she saw George standing outside. He looked like he was getting ready to knock again.

Anna unlocked the dead bolt and the lock and then flung open the door. "George . . ."

He seemed frazzled and out of breath. "Anna, I'm sorry."

She held the phone to her chest. "What's wrong? Are you okay?"

His eyes narrowed at her. "Are you on the phone with somebody?"

In response, Anna almost lied, but then she realized he knew about Russ. Everyone knew. "I'm talking to Russ."

He nodded. "Well, I need to talk to you, too. It's kind of important." He glanced at his wristwatch. "Do you want some privacy? Do you want me to wait out here or what?"

She opened the door wider. "I'm sorry, George. Please, come on in. Sit down. I'll be off the phone in a minute." She retreated to the kitchen. "Russ?" she whispered into the phone.

"I heard. Go talk to George. I was done anyway. I'll e-mail you that list of criminal attorneys."

"And I'll text you the contact information for Sandy as soon as I get it," she promised. She wanted to ask if he planned to call her again, but decided to leave it be. "I miss you," she whispered. "Take care, okay?"

"You, too," he said. Then he hung up.

Anna touched the phone screen to hang up, and then she took a deep breath. "Can I get you anything to drink?" she called.

"No, thanks," George answered.

She wiped her eyes and stepped into the living room.

His arms folded, George stood by the coffee table. "I thought that you and he were finished," he muttered. "Or was that just something you said on TV for the viewers at home?"

She frowned at him.

"I'm sorry. It's none of my business. I shouldn't have asked."

"We're finished. That's the first time we've talked in a

couple of days. He wants to send me a list of attorneys—just in case."

George nodded. "That's a good idea."

She plopped down on the easy chair and nodded toward the sofa. "Why don't you take a load off? You're making me nervous standing there."

With a sigh, George sank down on the sofa. "Listen, I got your voice mail. So this afternoon, I dropped by the station and started asking people what they'd heard about tonight's *Sally Justice Show*. And Janice, the camera operator, said someone in the newsroom told this troll from *The Sally Justice Show* that you and I were *awfully close*." George made air quotes and frowned. "Anyway, I need to apologize for what's about to happen."

Anna shrugged. "What are you talking about?"

"Sally Justice's people, they got to Beebe." He checked his wristwatch and cringed. "It's on right now—if you want to catch the shitshow."

Anna grabbed the remote off the coffee table and switched to the 24/7 News Channel. Sally's show was already in progress— rehashing the same footage of police searching the water around Russ and Courtney's dock.

"Bloody bath towels!" Sally exclaimed in voice-over. "That's what they found in Courtney Knoll's suitcase, the missing suitcase her husband claimed she must have packed herself the night she vanished without a trace. Does he expect us to believe that Courtney packed those bloodstained towels—along with her purse and her phone? Who packs their own phone and purse in a suitcase? And how did that suitcase end up in Lake Union? That's what I'd like to know."

There was a clip of Russ and Courtney looking happy,

beautiful, and glamorous together at some formal function. "Tonight, we're going to examine Dr. Russell Knoll. Who is this man, who waited two days before reporting his wife as missing? Who is this man that we now know cheated on his beautiful, talented, deaf spouse? And what do we really know about his mistress, the disgraced TV reporter Anna Malone? You might have watched her on the news every week, doing her sweet, cute stories. But obviously, we still don't know what she's capable of."

"I want to throw up," George muttered, hunched forward on the couch.

"She's repeating herself," Anna pointed out. "She called me *disgraced* in last night's show, too."

"As far as we know, Dr. Russell Knoll and Anna Malone were the last two people to see Courtney alive." Sally described their dinner Thursday evening at the Canlis restaurant as if it were a drunken brawl. Rolling her eyes and shaking her head, she recounted Russ's narrative of what happened later that night.

"Dr. Russell Knoll, who has been two-timing his poor wife for well over a year, has asked us and the police to believe this cockamamie story," Sally said—in a stare-down with the camera. "Just who is this man? Well, it's safe to say that Russell Knoll has gotten by on his looks and his money for most of his overprivileged life. He was born—silver spoon planted firmly in mouth—thirty-four years ago in Bellevue, Washington, a posh suburb of Seattle. His parents were very wealthy. Anything Russ wanted, Russ got. He was the golden boy."

While Sally described Russ's accomplishments in high school and college, a series of photos of the handsome young jock playing basketball and baseball, and in a tuxedo at his junior prom, appeared on the screen. There was also a yearbook portrait with a long list of honors and activities beside it; and video footage of him swimming in a friend's pool. Indeed, he came across as too good to be true. While all these wholesome images flashed across the TV screen, Sally's tone became more ironic, and the soundtrack took on a menacing quality.

"The stalker music in the background is a nice touch," George remarked.

"At the University of Washington, he joined a fraternity, of course, and then decided to become a doctor," Sally said, somehow making Russ sound like a spoiled, entitled, elitist brat. To hear her talk, his medical degree might as well have been dropped in his lap.

Anna noticed Sally skipped mentioning that Russ's parents had died in a plane crash while he'd been in medical school —probably because such a detail might have made Sally's audience feel some sympathy for him.

"When he met Courtney Matheson, Russell Knoll had a dream job as a doctor in a plush medical clinic. Courtney was a struggling author, eking out a living teaching sign language to deaf children and their parents. They were a beautiful couple."

A photo montage of Courtney and Russ together backed up Sally's statement.

"You may ask yourself, how could this man —this handsome doctor, this golden boy—be capable of deception, evil, and maybe even murder. And I have three words for you: *Dr. Jeffrey MacDonald.* He was an honors student, a dedicated doctor, and a Green Beret hero. On the surface, MacDonald seemed to be a perfect husband and father—until one rainy night in February of 1970, when he called the military police, claiming hippies had broken into his home and brutally murdered his wife and two little girls."

A handsome photo of Russ dissolved into a picture of Dr. Jeffrey MacDonald, convicted of murdering his family.

"Oh God, no," Anna muttered. On TV, they showed black-and-white photos from the 1970 murder case, including grisly shots of the crime scene: the children's bloodstained beds, the word *PIG* written in blood on the bed headboard in the master bedroom, and the bloody carpet at the foot of that rumpled bed, where Colette MacDonald's body was found.

"Clever," she murmured to George. "Except for that one photo of the luminol test, Sally doesn't have any pictures connected to Courtney's disappearance, so she's using these—from murders committed fifty years ago."

"Not very subtle, is it?" George said—over Sally, who was talking about how it came out in the trial that MacDonald had been unfaithful to his doomed wife.

On the TV screen, a photo of Dr. and Mrs. Jeffrey MacDonald dissolved into a shot of Dr. and Mrs. Russell Knoll. Then the camera went back to Sally. "When we return, just who is Anna Malone?" she said. A clip obviously bootlegged from Anna's profile of Courtney— showing Anna interviewing her—came up on the screen.

"Who is this woman some of us Seattleites have allowed into our living rooms at least once a week? It seemed to us that she was Courtney's friend. Courtney apparently thought so, too. What you don't know about local TV reporter Anna Malone will shock you! That's next on *The Sally Justice Show*! Stick around!"

A commercial for an allergy medication started up, and Anna pressed the mute button of the remote. "I'm going to need a glass of wine for this," she said, getting to her feet. "Are you sure I can't get you anything?"

"What the hell," George said with a shrug. He followed her into the kitchen. "Pour me a glass of whatever you're having."

Anna paused for a moment and just stared down at the kitchen counter.

"You're dying to call him right now, aren't you?" George asked.

She nodded. "I keep thinking of him, alone in his hotel room, watching her on TV as she makes him out to be a monster. But Russ and I had a talk on Sunday, and we agreed that it's over. Since then, we've already texted each other a couple of times— and then there was the call you just walked in on a few minutes ago. I can't keep calling him every time something like this comes up." She turned, opened the refrigerator door, and took out a bottle of chardonnay.

George had been to her place enough times that he knew where she kept the corkscrew. He opened her utensil drawer and took it out. "I'll bet he calls after Sally takes her potshots at you."

She handed him the wine bottle. "Maybe. Then again, he knows I'm with you."

"I'll get lost if he calls." George went to work on opening the bottle.

"No, please, don't, George. I'm glad you're here." She smiled at him.

He stopped to gaze at her—with just a trace of longing in his eyes.

Anna turned away and reached for the wineglasses from the cupboard. "Did Beebe give you any indication on just how she plans to skewer me live, coast to coast?"

"I haven't the foggiest." He went back to twisting the corkscrew. "As soon as I found out that Sally's people wanted to talk to Beebe, I called her—again and again. I must have left about six messages. I finally got ahold of my daughter, and April didn't know anything except that she and Lucas got dropped off at their aunt's house. So I talked to Beebe's sister, Cheryl, who now thinks I'm the Antichrist—"

"Is this the same one who wouldn't lift a finger to help with her sick mother?"

George popped open the cork. "That's our Cheryl. All she'd tell me was that she had the kids for the evening, and Beebe would be 'telling it like it is' on *The Sally Justice Show* tonight. That's all I know."

He poured the wine and handed her a glass. "Are you ready for another round of Sally's abuse?"

"I feel like I need a cigarette and a blindfold." Anna took a swallow of the chardonnay and nodded. "Okay," she said.

Then they headed into the living room together.

CHAPTER NINETEEN

Tuesday, July 14—6:38 P.M.

Leaning back in a swivel chair, Officer Ken Stoecker had four small TV monitors in front of him, all of which had split-screen images. They showed what the security cameras picked up at every exit of the Silver Cloud Inn—as well as the elevators and the two levels of the underground parking garage.

Ken was forty-four, slightly out of shape, and losing his hair. He felt he was too old and too experienced for this mindless assignment. Cushy as it was, the job seemed more appropriate for a know-nothing rookie. He and his thirty-year-old partner, Deshawn Bailey, were keeping tabs on murder suspect Dr. Russell Knoll, now temporarily residing in room 227 of the hotel.

Knoll hadn't been charged with his wife's murder yet. But that was expected to happen anytime now. Meanwhile, Sweaty Betty—Ken's nickname for Detective Kit Baumann—had decreed that a couple of cops needed to keep an eye on the doctor to make sure he didn't skip town or kill someone else. Ken and Deshawn got the assignment. Ken had it slightly better than Deshawn, who was now in the unmarked patrol car, parked in the garage's lower level, watching Knoll's BMW.

Though the hotel security office was tiny, windowless, and cramped, and the security guard was a blowhard who considered himself utterly fascinating, at least Ken could get up and stretch his legs every hour. He made it a point to walk by the front desk and chat with the cute clerk, named Jen, who was working tonight.

Despite all the TV monitors in front of him, Ken started to pay more attention to the movie he'd brought up on his phone, the 1980s comedy-drama *Nothing in Common*. He had his earbuds in and listened as Tom Hanks told his mom, Eva Marie Saint, that his diabetic dad, Jackie Gleason, required surgery and might lose his foot.

Ken was getting into the movie and lost track of the time. But he was pretty sure he'd checked the monitors just a few minutes ago. And certainly Deshawn would have called him if he'd seen Knoll get inside his BMW and drive away.

So Ken couldn't figure out why, on the monitor showing the lower level of the hotel's parking garage, it looked like Knoll's car was suddenly gone. Leaning forward, Ken squinted at the screen. He knew where the doctor's BMW should be—in the third parking space after the support beam on the far left side of the monitor. Right now, that spot was empty.

"Shit," he muttered, putting down his phone.

The security guard had shown him how to operate the monitors. Ken pressed the control to slow-rewind the security video for the garage's lower level. While he watched the video back up, Ken grabbed the two-way radio: "Hey, Deshawn. Can you hear me? Over."

His partner picked up: "What's going on?" He sounded confused.

"His car is gone," Ken said. "Were you asleep? Over."

"No."

"You're lying."

Ken could hear some movement, then a car door opening and shutting. "Fuck me!" Deshawn said. "It's gone."

"You better pray he just stepped out for a quickie with his newslady girlfriend," Ken said. "Haul ass up to the front desk and get a key card for two-twenty-seven. Call me as soon as you get there, and please, please, please, tell me his stuff is still there in the room. Otherwise, Sweaty Betty's going to bust our balls. Move it! Over!"

He clicked off. Then he grabbed his cell phone and switched off the Tom Hanks movie.

Something on the monitor for the garage caught his eye. Ken watched the grainy video, still playing in reverse. The BMW backed into the TV frame, stopped in front of the doctor's parking place, then it turned forward into the spot. Nothing happened for a few seconds. Then the driver's door opened, and a man in a dark hooded sweater climbed out of the car—back first. He seemed to reach inside and pull out a small duffel bag. Shutting the door, he started walking backward toward the edge of the monitor screen.

Ken stopped the video and played it forward. He tried to catch a glimpse of Knoll's face—just to verify it was him. Maybe someone had stolen the guy's car.

He slowed down the video and carefully watched it again, but he still couldn't see the face of the man in the hoodie. From the guy's build and height, he looked like Knoll. Ken figured they'd have to search for him on the security videos for the other exits and on the elevator to the garage.

Ken heard static on the two-way radio: "Hey, Stoecker, are you there? Over."

"Yeah, what is it?" he answered.

"I'm in his room. A suitcase and some clothes are here, and the TV's still on. But I've got a feeling he's packed some of his stuff."

"What do you mean?" Ken asked. But Deshawn must have still had his thumb on the talk button, because there was no response.

"What's here isn't enough to fill this suitcase," Deshawn continued. "Plus there's nothing in the bathroom— y'know, toothpaste, toothbrush, shaving shit. I have a feeling he packed another bag and split. Over."

Ken stared at the slightly blurry, frozen image on the TV monitor: the hooded man with a duffel bag—reaching for the car door.

He took a deep breath. "Okay, you call it in." He glanced at the date and time at the bottom of the TV monitor. "Suspect, Russell Knoll, last seen in a dark hoodie sweater, left the Silver Cloud Inn, on his own steam, at six thirty-seven p.m. He's driving a black BMW, license plate . . . whatever the hell his license plate number is. Do you have it written down?"

"I memorized it—K-K-C-four-oh-five. Washington plate."

"I'm going to keep looking for him on these security videos," Ken said, feeling sick to his stomach. "You call it in that the suspect's at large. Over."

CHAPTER TWENTY

Tuesday, July 14—6:40 P.M.

On TV, there was another commercial, this one for an auto insurance company—with some guy in a gorilla suit driving a car.

George returned to his spot on the sofa, and Anna was about to sit down beside him. But then she figured, in a couple of minutes, George's wife would be on national television, accusing the two of them of God knows what. So Anna sank down in the easy chair instead.

On TV, a few bars of *The Sally Justice Show* theme played, and Sally returned, once again perched behind her judge's desk. She had her trademark stern look. "Welcome back!" she said. "If you just joined us, we're examining the disappearance of bestselling author Courtney Knoll. I just got word during the break that Courtney's new *Defective Squad* adventure, *Silent Rage*, just went into a second printing. Along with her two previous books, *The Defective Squad* and *Blind Fury*, it's now one of the top sellers on Amazon and at Barnes & Noble."

Eyes on the screen, Anna sipped her wine. She still wondered if it was possible that Courtney had somehow orchestrated this whole thing for the publicity—and to stick it to Russ and her. But it was hard to hold on to that hypothesis now that the police had the carry-on filled with bloodstained towels, Courtney's purse, and her phone. Still, Anna couldn't figure out why anyone would kill Courtney and then go to so much trouble to make it appear as if she'd run away. It was the type of thing only a murderous husband might do, and Anna refused to be-lieve Russ was capable of that.

Sally finished her recap of Courtney's disappearance. Then an unflattering photo of Anna came up on the screen—beside a shot of Russ, who didn't seem capable of taking a bad picture. "Jesus-please-us, where does she get these terrible photos of you?" George asked. "You look drunk and pissed off."

Anna just shrugged and shook her head in resignation.

"By their own admission," Sally said, "Courtney's hus-band, Dr. Russell Knoll, and Seattle TV reporter Anna Malone have been carrying on an illicit affair for quite some time."

Another clip—with *Property of KIXI-TV News* embla-zoned across the bottom of it—came on the screen: Anna's announcement on Monday evening's news show. "I spoke to the Seattle Police this morning to clarify my role in the events that led up to Courtney's disappearance early Friday morning," Anna said from the news desk. "But I omitted one detail—which is that I've been in a re-lationship with Courtney's husband, Dr. Russell Knoll, for eighteen months."

Sally came back on the screen. She clicked her tongue and shook her head. "This bombshell hit us just forty-eight hours after Anna Malone had made what seemed like a video valentine about Courtney for her news program," Sally pointed out.

On the screen, they showed a muted scene from the KIXI-TV News puff piece with Anna talking to Courtney. "And just think about it," Sally narrated. "When this was airing on Friday night, Anna Malone already knew that Courtney had disappeared. She and Courtney's husband were still keeping it a secret. Look how chummy-chummy she is with her lover's wife! Butter wouldn't melt in her mouth."

"Oh brother," George murmured.

Anna took another swallow of wine.

"Just who is this Anna Malone?" Sally asked, as a more flattering photo of Anna appeared in a box over her shoulder. "It's stunning how much we don't know about the people we trust to bring us our news every night on TV. We know from her official KIXI-TV News biography online that Anna Malone is thirty-four years old—"

"Try thirty-one, Sally," Anna grumbled.

"She studied broadcasting in college," Sally went on. "Then she worked at a small TV station in Spokane before joining the KIXI-TV news team in Seattle two years ago. Here's what the official biography doesn't say."

Anna's least favorite childhood photo—eighth-grade graduation—came up on the screen. Even with the acne airbrushed out, it was terrible. She smiled awkwardly, her mouth closed to hide her braces, and her hair looked greasy from some product she'd put in it the night before to remove the frizz.

This dissolved to a photo of the big, impressive redbrick house in which she'd spent her childhood.

"Like her married lover, Anna also had a privileged childhood, growing up in this mansion on Bainbridge Island, Washington. But to say she came from a *dysfunctional* family would be putting it politely. *Criminal* would be a more accurate adjective. Her older brother, Stuart, was arrested several times before he ran away from home and completely disappeared at age eighteen."

They showed a slightly fuzzy snapshot of Stu, one Anna hadn't seen in a long time. Her heart ached to look at it now. She glanced back at George, who knew all about her family. He caught her eye and gave her a sympathetic look.

Turning back toward the TV, Anna saw another old photo fill the screen: her and her father at some silly high school daddy-daughter dinner dance. Then there was a studio portrait taken of him for his company newsletter— the same one used for his obituary. "When Anna was sixteen," Sally continued, "her financier father, Martin Malone, was arrested and convicted of insider trading. He hung himself in federal prison. Penniless, Anna and her mother moved into this houseboat on Seattle's Lake Union."

On TV, there was a shot of Anna's floating home.

"Oh, thank you for showing my house, Sally!" she moaned. "Why not give out the address so every nut and his brother will be stalking me?"

A photo of Anna's mother came up on the screen, one

Anna had never seen before. Her mom must have been about thirty when it was taken. She was holding a baby—Stuart, obviously. She looked so pretty and happy.

"Anna's mother, Jacqueline Malone, became an alcoholic," Sally said —as the sweet picture was replaced by a driver's license shot of Anna's mom in her later years. She looked haggard and wasn't smiling. Anna still remembered her mom practically crying when she'd gotten home from the DMV with the new license. But then they'd somehow ended up laughing about it.

"Four years after her husband committed suicide, Jackie Malone, driving while drunk, killed herself and a pedestrian."

Anna shook her head. "That's not how it happened," she said to George.

"Anna was in the car at the time," Sally went on. "And we don't know for sure if Anna wasn't actually driving the car that killed her mother and that unfortunate pedestrian—a young woman who was about to be married, by the way. All I can say is that it's possible, and Anna never proved that she wasn't behind the wheel."

"What?" Anna yelled. She got to her feet. "Where did she get that idea? God, that liar! I should sue her."

"It's no use," George said. "She's got a whole army of lawyers. Anyway, c'mon, consider the source."

"My mother wasn't drunk at the time," Anna said, rubbing her forehead. "There are medical records to back that up. Y'know, Sally can invent all the lies she wants to about me. But she's going after my dead mother, and that's something altogether different."

Anna was only half paying attention to Sally, who was

still sniping about something. On the screen was the clip of Anna interviewing Courtney for the KIXI profile piece that ran on Friday. It was probably the only image available showing her and Courtney together.

"Take another look at her, pretending to be Courtney's friend!" Sally said, once again on camera. She had a disgusted look on her face. "Well, that seems to be the way this homewrecker works. And I don't use that term lightly. My guest tonight is someone whose marriage was constantly undermined by Anna Malone."

The camera pulled back to reveal George's wife, Beebe, in the "witness box" beside Sally's judge-desk. She wore a navy blue dress and her brown hair fell around her shoulders. She must have had on the minimum of makeup for a television appearance. She looked like an overworked mom who had barely had time to put herself together for this TV appearance. Anna imagined that anyone who didn't know Beebe would instantly feel sympathy for her.

"I'd like you to meet Beebe Danziger, an artist, a mother of two, and married for fifteen years to George Danziger. Her husband has been Anna Malone's cameraman for nearly all of her news stories since she started working in Seattle. Thank you for being on the show, Beebe."

"Thank you for having me, Sally. I'm a really big fan."

"Well," George muttered, "already that's a lie. Beebe never watches this piece-of-shit show."

"First off, Beebe," Sally said, "tell us a little bit about your family."

"Well, my two children—April, who is fourteen, and Lucas, he's eleven—they're my touchstones." Beebe's voice quavered, and her eyes started to well with tears. A family photo of the Danzigers on vacation at the beach came up on the screen. "I sometimes feel like I'm a single mom. I've practically raised these kids on my own. Anna is so demanding of my husband's time. She has her pick of videographers for her stories, and she always insists on using my husband. It's been like that for the two years she's been working at KIXI-TV."

More family snapshots came up on the screen. Anna thought George looked cute in the photographs; Beebe, not so much.

"Jesus, my kids are going to be mortified," George murmured. "I need to go to them as soon as this is over."

Back on camera, Beebe wiped away a tear. "Anna has always been so controlling. George used to complain about her. Then, after a few months of them working together, I noticed the complaining stopped. I never thought of George as the type of husband who would stray. He told me that he and Anna were work friends, and I believed him. I even tried —very hard—to be Anna's friend. As I said, I'm an artist, and I spent hours and hours creating these two beautiful vases. I'm sure I could have sold them for at least a thousand dollars each. But I gave them to Anna for her birthday."

It took Anna a moment to realize that Beebe was talking about the two hideous eyesores she had stored in the toolshed outside.

"She never even thanked me," Beebe said.

"Well, that's bullshit," Anna said. "I sent her a card, remember?"

"I'm sorry," George whispered. "And for the record, I didn't complain about you."

"It's okay," Anna murmured.

"She pretended to be my friend," Beebe continued. "And all the while, she was trying to steal my husband away."

Frowning, Sally shook her head. "And she was carrying on with Courtney's husband at the very same time. It just makes me sick."

"I know how Courtney Knoll must have felt," Beebe said, a hand over her heart. "I've been victimized. And the thing is, my husband insists that he and Anna have never had sex. But she clearly seduced him, and he—he's fallen in love with her. He won't deny it. We've recently separated. It's been absolutely devastating for our kids."

Sally now had this pained, compassionate expression on her face. "Tell me, Beebe," she said, her voice dropping to a whisper. "If you could talk to Anna Malone right now, what would you say to her?"

Beebe sighed. "I'd ask her, *Why my husband?* Why did she pick the father of my children? She already had a lover. She certainly must have realized my husband was falling in love with her. I could tell months ago. So she must have seen it, too. Why did she keep insisting that he work with her? I think she enjoyed the attention—and having a man at her beck and call. It's been good for her ego as well as her career. Never mind about the children she's hurting. It's all just a game to her. It wasn't enough that she already stole one woman's husband. She had to go after mine."

Behind her, Anna heard George clear his throat. "I'm so, so sorry," he murmured.

"Beebe, do you believe Anna Malone and Russ Knoll

when they say that they had nothing to do with Courtney's disappearance?"

She slowly shook her head. "Not for a minute. And I guess I should feel lucky. I shudder when I think that what happened to Courtney could have easily happened to me."

"Thank you, Beebe. It was really brave of you to come here and share your story with us."

The camera zeroed in on Sally for a close-up as she turned to address her viewers. "So, what do you think? The disappearance of Courtney Knoll is no longer just a missing person case. This is clearly a murder without a body. Do you believe Dr. Russell Knoll and his mistress, Anna Malone, when they claim they don't know what happened to his brilliant, beautiful wife? I'll take a call or two after the break. You can go online to tell us what you think. Make your opinion count! Yes or no? Is this illicit couple telling the truth? Go to www-dot-vote-sally-justice-dot-com! We'll be right back."

With the remote, Anna switched off the TV. Then she took a final gulp of chardonnay, draining the glass.

"Well, that was humiliating for everyone involved," George said. He got to his feet.

Anna turned toward him.

Obviously, George couldn't look her in the eye. With the half-full glass of wine in his hand, he stared down at the floor. "All I can do is apologize again for Beebe. Do you— do you want any kind of explanation for what she said?"

"Not right now, George," she murmured. "There's so much going on. Maybe later."

Her phone chimed. She immediately thought of Russ.

She reached for the phone on the coffee table but hesitated and glanced at George.

"Go for it," he said. "I need to leave anyway. I want to go check on my kids and make sure they haven't died of mortification."

She snatched the phone off the coffee table and checked the caller ID. It was an incoming text from Taylor Hofstad.

"Is it him?" George asked quietly.

Anna shook her head. She knew the disappointment on her face must have killed him—if what Beebe had said about him loving her was true. And she knew it was. Even though it was supposed to be over between her and Russ, she still longed to hear his voice. She wanted him to re-assure her that they'd get through this.

George finally looked at her, and Anna worked up a smile. "It's a text from Sally's daughter, Taylor."

She'd already explained to him about Taylor earlier, when she'd left the message about someone from the office appearing on Sally's show tonight. George cleared his throat. "What does your spy in the enemy camp have to say?"

Anna tapped her phone screen and read the text aloud: "'*I'm sorry I couldn't get more accurate info ahead of time re Sally's guest tonight—*'"

"She calls her mother *Sally*?" George asked.

"Sometimes," Anna answered. She went back to reading the text out loud: "'*I'm also sorry for the shoddy, malicious treatment you got tonight. Tomorrow's show focuses on the fact that you claim not to remember anything from Thursday night. Sally will also look at famous movies and books with illicit couples plotting to kill a*" *spouse:* Body Heat, Postman Always Rings Twice, *and* Double Identity . . .' I think that's supposed to be *Double Indemnity*. Good old autocorrect."

Anna scrolled down the screen and continued reading: "'*Sally's scheduled guest is a shrink who will talk about why certain single women go after married men. All this could change if there are any new developments in the case tomorrow. I hope this is some help.*'" Anna looked up from the phone. "I sense a recurring theme here."

George nodded. "Yeah, Sally sure has a burr up her butt about you." He started toward the door. "Are you sure you can trust this Taylor?"

Walking alongside him, Anna shrugged. "Well, she says that she and her mama don't get along. I believe her on that score. If she hadn't warned me about tonight's show, I never would have alerted you—and you wouldn't be here right now." She touched his arm for a moment. "For that I'm grateful, George. Thank you for coming over tonight—and helping me get through this. It would have been unbearable to watch that without you."

He opened the door. "Well, if you need me, I'm here for you." He paused and let out a sad, little laugh. "What a thing to say when I'm running out the door, right?"

"You got me through the worst part," Anna said, managing a smile. She wanted to hug him, but couldn't. "Go to your kids. They need you right now."

George looked like he wanted to hug her, too. But he just nodded, turned, and headed down the dock.

Anna closed the door and double-locked it.

She stood in the front hallway for a few moments. She realized she was playing the self-sacrificing other woman role again—this time with George. *"Go to your kids. They need you right now."* Well, it was true. It only made sense that they were his first concern.

Then Anna had another realization. Back when her mother died, she'd lost the one person who considered her more important than anyone else.

She could sometimes fool herself into thinking Russ felt that way about her, but if that was truly the case, he would have left Courtney for her a long time ago.

Or was she so important to him that he'd killed for her?

The phone rang again. Anna hurried into the living room and grabbed it off the coffee table. The caller ID showed it was George. She tapped the screen. "Hey, are you okay?"

"Yeah, I just wanted to give you a heads-up. There's a patrol car parked near the gate to your dock. And just as I started down the street, I saw an ABC News van arrive. Sally's show must be bringing the press out. Either that or something happened."

"Well, if something happened, I think Russ or the police would have called me," Anna said. "Do you think anyone noticed you?"

"I know the police saw me, but I don't think anyone else did. At least, I hope not. Jesus, I can just imagine them getting video of me sneaking away from your place moments after Beebe's fifteen minutes of fame. I don't want to see that on *The Sally Justice Show* tomorrow."

Anna had yet another realization. If she hoped to lean on George during any of this, it would have to be in secret. After tonight, he couldn't afford to be seen with her.

The call-waiting signal sounded. "Just a second, George,

I have another call." She checked the caller ID: *Det. K. Baumann.*

"Oh God, it's the police detective in charge of the investigation," Anna whispered. "I better take this."

"Text me later, okay?"

"Okay," Anna said. Then she switched over to the incoming call before it went to voice mail. "Detective Baumann, is everything all right? Did something happen?"

"Have you heard from Dr. Knoll?"

"Yes, he called me about forty or forty-five minutes ago. Why?"

"May I ask what the two of you discussed?"

Anna hesitated. "We talked about people who might have been behind Courtney's disappearance, people who might want to see her dead. I learned today about a woman in her old writers' group—"

"Russ isn't there, is he, Anna?" the detective interrupted.

"No," she murmured, baffled.

"And he's not on his way there?"

"No—"

"Did he say anything to you about going anywhere tonight?"

"He's not in his hotel room?"

"He snuck out about a half hour ago. We have video of him in a dark sweater, leaving with a group of people through the hotel's front doors. He must have merged in with them. We think he waited until someone exited the garage before he slipped in to get his car. We have him on security video in the garage, wearing the same sweater, only with the hood up. He was carrying an overnight bag. You sure he didn't say anything to you?"

"Positive," Anna said, suddenly short of breath. "He wouldn't try to run away. It would be stupid. He knows how bad that would look. He's innocent. Do you think he's on his way here? Is that why there's a police car and a news van at the gate to my dock?"

"I can't speak for the news van," Detective Baumann answered. "We haven't shared any of this with the press. But yes, the patrol car is there in case Dr. Knoll decides to pay you a visit. Right now, he's considered a person of interest, and his whereabouts are important to us. And you're right. This doesn't look good for him. I'll ask you again, Anna. In this phone conversation tonight, are you sure Dr. Knoll didn't say anything to you about leaving the hotel for any reason?"

"No, all we talked about were other suspects the police should be considering," Anna said pointedly. "And Dr. Knoll also told me that I should look into getting myself a lawyer."

There was a pause on the other end.

"I'd say that was sound advice, Anna," the detective replied.

CHAPTER TWENTY-ONE

Wednesday, July 15—6:33 P.M.

The man in the hotel security video was unmistakably Russ. Wearing a dark sweater with the hood down, he blended in with a group of about a dozen people leaving the hotel lobby at the same time. They all seemed to know each other—except for Russ. Looking about rather suspiciously, he slipped though the double doors with the others.

In the video from the garage a few minutes later, he had on the same sweater, only with the hood up. There was little doubt it was the same person.

Anna had already watched both videos on the news twice. This time, Sally Justice was showing and analyzing them on her show.

"Talk about shifty-eyed, just look at him!" Sally said in voice-over as she showed the video a second time. "Well, Dr. Russell Knoll has been missing for twenty-four hours now."

Anna stood in front of the TV in her darkened living

room. All the blinds were down. She had the remote control in her hand.

The video ended, and Sally came up on the screen. Perched behind her judge's desk, she had a photo of Russ on display in a box over her shoulder. "Dr. Knoll has left his girlfriend, former TV reporter Anna Malone, in the lurch," Sally said—with a sneer. "If she knows anything about where he is, she's not talking. No surprise there! What surprises me—no, *enrages* me—is that this low-life quack has taken it on the lam, and he's so obviously guilty. Yet he still hasn't been charged with his wife's murder." Sally threw up her hands. "What do the police want—a signed confession? A map to where he's hidden her body?"

Anna muted it. She couldn't take any more.

Turning away, she went over to the window that looked out on her back deck. She peeked through the blinds. It was still light out. Three medium-size boats bobbed in the water near her dock. On each vessel, there was someone on deck with a camera ready—just waiting for her to emerge from her house or open the blinds. She felt like the groundhog on Groundhog Day.

An hour ago, she'd been up in her bedroom loft. From the east-facing window, Anna had a view of the other floating homes on her dock—along with the gate. Through the trees on the shoreline, she'd noticed the crowd of reporters and onlookers—along with a cluster of news vans parked on the street.

Anna hadn't talked to any of the reporters. She'd made a brief statement over the phone for her friends on the KIXI News team. "I have no idea where Dr. Knoll is," she'd told them. "I'm as surprised as anyone else about his disappearance. I know he's under a great deal of stress right now. I also know he's an innocent man. He's also been very transparent and cooperative with the police investigation. I'm hoping for his safe return."

As far as she knew, all those reporters and news vans were still there, waiting for her to step outside or for Russ to show up.

She wished he would show up. How could he be so stupid? For once, she had to agree with Sally. His running away was like an admission of guilt. Anna was scared to death for him. She'd left several voice mails and texts. She prayed he'd phone back. At the same time, she didn't want to be put in the position of knowing where he was—and not being able to tell the police. Didn't he realize that he was just making things worse for himself?

Every time her phone rang or chimed, Anna ran to it.

And it had rung and chimed plenty of times. There were two calls and two texts from her coworkers at KIXI-TV News. George had phoned to check in on her. He was still living above his garage. Beebe wasn't talking to him. And the kids, humiliated by their mother's appearance on *The Sally Justice Show*, weren't talking to her. *And it's all my fault*, Anna thought.

She'd also gotten a text from Becky about Crazy Sandy:

I tried to e-mail Sandy and it came back as undeliverable.
Her phone number isn't working, either. But Margaret
Freeman from the writers' group may have a lead.
She agrees that if anyone wanted to see Courtney dead,
it would be Sandy. Am waiting to hear from her. Great

meeting U yesterday. U got a raw deal on Sally J last night!
Screw her! Take care!

There was also an e-mail from Taylor:

Dear Anna,

New developments in the case (Dr. Knoll disappearing)
have forced Sally to change the focus of tonight's show. It's
mostly news-related now. But she will talk about you & the
fact that you can't remember much from Thursday night
(she says it's "awfully convenient" you have no memory of
what happened). The therapist who was supposed to
analyze the single-women/married-men situation is now out.
The new guest is someone named Eddie Vaughn, who
claims to know you. I'll try to find out more. Hope this is
some help.

Sincerely,
Taylor

PS: I had to get all this info about the show from one of my
mother's assistants. My mother is still mad at me for
deserting her yesterday & she's not talking to me.

Terrific, thought Anna, *more people not talking to each
other because of me.* She had no idea who Eddie Vaughn
was. She went online and didn't recognize any of the
Eddie Vaughns that came up on her Google and Facebook
searches. She even dug out her high school and college
yearbooks, but didn't find anyone named Eddie Vaughn.
    Now she was curious. If not for this Eddie Vaughn

person, she wouldn't be subjecting herself to another episode of *The Sally Justice Show*.

One of the three boats by her floating home, the nicest one —it looked like a small yacht—finally pulled up anchor and started to sail away. They were giving up. Anna hoped the other two boats would soon follow. She hated this. She wanted to open the blinds—if only just for a while. It felt so claustrophobic in her house, like she was living in a cocoon.

She glanced back at the TV and saw her official KIXI News portrait in a box over Sally's shoulder: her in a blue sleeveless dress, her smile and hair looking perfect. It was a bit too airbrushed for Anna's taste, but it was still a good shot. She was stunned that Sally was actually using a flattering photo of her for a change.

With the remote, Anna unmuted the TV and started toward the set.

". . . Our next guest probably knows Anna Malone better than anyone else," Sally was saying.

A gaunt, thirtysomething man with shaggy, dirty-looking grayish hair appeared on the screen. Sitting in front of some ugly lime-green curtains, he obviously wasn't in Sally's studio. He was talking to her remotely from somewhere else. Dark circles hung under his eyes, and he had a neck tattoo. He looked like a drug addict.

"Who is this creep?" Anna murmured to herself.

Squinting, Sally's seedy-looking guest scratched his head. It was obviously a nervous tic. He sort of winced, and the dimples showed on his unshaven face.

"My God," Anna whispered. She stopped dead in front of the TV. For a second, she couldn't breathe. She hadn't seen her brother in sixteen years.

Anna sank down on her knees and almost reached out toward the TV screen.

"You call yourself Eddie Vaughn, but that's not your real name, is it?" Sally asked him.

He shook his head and smiled shyly. His teeth looked awful—a sign of crystal meth use. "No, my real name is Stuart Malone. But I changed it about sixteen years ago when I ran away from home at age eighteen . . ."

The TV went to split screen—with Sally and Stuart in discussion.

Anna watched with tears in her eyes. Her once-handsome, sweet, funny brother looked emaciated and ravaged.

"You're Anna Malone's older brother," Sally said. "Isn't that right?"

Nodding, he scratched his head again. "Yeah, I'm three years older."

"Can you tell us where you are right now?"

"I'd rather not." He squirmed in his chair. "I can't explain, but it's just not a good idea to let on where I am."

"Fair enough," Sally said. "Can you tell us what your sister was like when you were growing up together?"

He smiled again—with those awful yellow-gray teeth. Anna thought about how he used to have such a winning smile. "Well," he said, "I used to call her Anna Banana. She was kind of spoiled, because she was younger and all that. She was like *daddy's little girl*."

"Your father was a very rich and powerful man. Would you say he favored Anna over you and doted on her?"

"Yeah, sure," he replied vaguely. Then he let out a little laugh. "When it came to the old man, she got away with a lot. I mean, for example, he used to bring his scotch and water to the dinner table before we sat down to eat. Then he'd always go wash his hands. He was like a clean freak. And sometimes, Anna would hide his drink—like in the breakfront or behind the curtains or someplace. The old man would return to the table, and then go back to the kitchen, looking for where he left his drink. And you could tell he thought he was losing his marbles."

Stu started to laugh, and for a few seconds, Anna saw her sweet brother again in that waste of a man. She'd forgotten about those dinners at home when Stu would egg her on to tease their dad.

"Then my father would realize Anna was messing with him," Stu continued. "And he'd laugh like he thought it was really cute. But the thing is, I couldn't have done that. If I ever tried to mess with him like that, he would have started yelling at me or maybe even smacked me in the face."

Wiping her eyes, Anna nodded at the screen. She realized Stu was probably right. For a moment, she felt like she was back in their family room, sitting on the floor in front of the TV—just as she was now.

"Like I said, she was his little princess. She could do whatever she pleased. Me, he was always jumping on my case about every little thing I did."

"You got into trouble a lot, didn't you?" Sally asked quietly— as if she were his therapist.

He frowned. "Yeah, I never caught a break."

"After you ran away from home, your father was imprisoned and committed suicide. Then your mother was killed in a car accident while driving drunk."

Anna shook her head. It bothered the hell out of her that Sally kept accusing her mother of driving while drunk when she'd died.

"All of this happened after you left home," Sally continued. "Do you sometimes feel that you shouldn't have left your parents alone with your spoiled little sister?"

"Oh, for Christ's sake," Anna muttered.

On the split TV screen, Stu just shrugged.

"You've had your share of struggles, haven't you, Stu?" Sally asked. "May I call you Stu? I know that's not the name you go by now, but . . ."

He squinted, scratched his head, and nodded.

"Tell us about your struggles."

"Well, after I ran away, I took on a lot of menial jobs to survive. I traveled a lot—all over. Mostly, I hitchhiked. I really liked New Mexico. I lived there for a while. But I always came back to Washington State."

"Your sister was a TV personality in Spokane for a few years before she became a reporter with a Seattle station. Were you following Anna's career?"

He nodded. "Yeah, I saw her on TV a lot."

"Did you ever try to contact her?"

"Yeah, about two years ago," he said. "I—I'd fallen in with this crowd, and they were all into drugs. It's because of them that I got hooked on crystal meth. And I had some scrapes with the law. Anyway, I was trying to quit meth. I needed help. I mean, I really needed help." As he spoke, something to one side of the camera seemed to catch his attention. "So I called my little sister. I figured, she was a big local TV star now. And she—she always did these sweet, heartwarming stories on the news, stuff about families and reunions and people helping each other. But when I reached out to Anna for help, she didn't want anything to do with me. I know I wasn't the best brother in the world, but you don't do that to your family. I called her several times and e-mailed . . ."

Anna could tell he was reading off a cue card.

"She e-mailed back and told me to leave her alone, so I did." Stu shrugged and shook his head.

"Didn't Anna understand that you were in trouble?" Sally asked.

"Yeah, I told her everything. I told her that she was the only one who could help me."

"And she turned you away." Sally's voice dropped to a whisper. "Do you still have a drug problem, Stu?"

With a forlorn look, he nodded.

"I'm assuming that's another reason you'd just as soon not reveal where you are," Sally remarked. "Stu, what would you say to your sister, Anna Malone, if she were listening right now?"

He looked up—obviously at the cue cards again. "Um, I don't hold any grudges, Anna. I—I always thought I was the unlucky one in our family. But I look at all the people around you, and what's happened to them. And maybe you're the one who isn't lucky. Or maybe you just bring bad luck to people when you don't really mean to. I know you're in trouble right now. And I'm praying for you, Anna Banana."

"Shit," Anna murmured. Tears streamed down her face. She figured Sally must have paid him for this. Poor Stu had to be desperate for money if he'd agreed to spout all those lies.

"Thank you for sharing your story with us, Stu," Sally said. "And I really hope you get some help soon."

Anna grabbed the remote off the floor and switched off the TV. Digging a Kleenex from the pocket of her shorts, she wiped her eyes and blew her nose. Then she crawled over to the coffee table, where she'd left her phone earlier. She started writing a text. But her hands were shaking, and she kept hitting the wrong letters. It seemed to take forever to compose a few lines:

> Someone from the show must know where my brother is and how I can reach him. Please find out for me as soon as possible. He never tried to contact me, and I really would like to see him and help him. Please do whatever you can. I'd appreciate it so much. Thank you.

Then she sent it to Sally's daughter, Taylor.

Just as she pressed send, the phone rang.

For just a second, Anna hoped it was Russ. But George's name came up on the caller ID, and she was so disappointed. Then she felt guilty for her disappointment.

She tapped the phone screen to pick up. "Hey . . ."

"Was that really your brother—or some actor on Sally's payroll?"

"That was Stu." She sighed. Anna had told George about Stu ages ago.

"He never reached out to you, did he?"

"Nope." Anna wiped her eyes again. Still on the floor, she rested an elbow on the coffee table.

"I'm so sorry, Anna. Are you going to be okay?"

"Eventually, I hope."

"Have you heard from—Dr. Knoll?"

"Nope."

"I can come over if you need some company."

"No, you can't. No one could get past the gate to my dock unnoticed. It's a regular convention of news reporters out there."

"Well, I can hang on the phone and talk with you—if you want."

"Thanks, George," she murmured. "Not to be too dramatic about it, but I think I just need to lie down on the couch and have a good cry. This is a pity party of one."

"I understand. I'm around if you need me. Just give me a call. Are you sure you're going to be okay alone?"

"I'll be all right. But thanks, you're sweet. Take care, George."

"G'night," he said. Then he hung up.

Anna tapped the screen to disconnect.

She was still sitting on the floor of her darkened living room. She didn't want to move. Right now, just getting up and walking over to the sofa for her crying session seemed like too much of an effort.

The phone rang in her hand.

Anna automatically touched the screen to pick up. "George, really, I'm fine."

There was no response on the other end. But somehow, it felt as if someone was listening. Anna glanced at the caller ID: *Unknown Caller.*

It dawned on her that Russ wouldn't use his own phone to call her. "Russ?" she said anxiously. "Is that you?"

"He's a fugitive because of you," said the raspy-voiced caller. "He's taking the rap for you, bitch. I know, because I saw you kill her."

Then the line went dead.

CHAPTER TWENTY-TWO

Thursday, July 16—3:27 A.M.
Tacoma, Washington

Transcript of the 911 call:

Operator: 911. What's your emergency?
Woman Caller: I just saw a guy jump off the bridge! The Tacoma Narrows Bridge. He—he was a ways in front of me in his car. He pulled over to the side and got out . . . then . . . then he climbed over the railing and jumped.
Operator: Do you have a description of the car?
Caller: It's a black BMW. License plate K-K-C something.
Operator: That's good. Do you know if he was the driver of the car?
Caller: I guess so. He got out on the driver's side. And the car's still there as far as I know.
Operator: As far as you know? Are you no longer at the scene?
Caller: No, I slowed down, but I—I didn't want to stop

on the bridge. There isn't much traffic right now. But I figured it was dangerous, and I was scared.

Operator: Can I get your name?

Caller: No, no, no. I don't want to get involved.

Operator: Please, I need your name and your phone number.

Caller: No, forget it. I've already had some trouble with the police, and I don't want any more. This is a burner phone I'm calling from, so don't bother trying to trace the number.

Operator: You're not in trouble. We're asking for your contact information in case we need to ask you for more details.

Caller: Listen, I'm trying to tell you that some guy just offed himself. I'm only trying to do the right thing, y'know?

Operator: I appreciate that. Are you still driving on the bridge now?

Caller: You're just trying to track me down, and I've already told you that I don't want to get involved. So just forget it. I'm hanging up. This is what I get for trying to help. You'll find the car in the westbound bridge near the halfway point. The guy was about six feet tall, and he was wearing a dark hoodie. I'm sure he's dead. A fall like that would kill anybody.

End Call.

Thursday, July 16—6:49 A.M.
Seattle

Her first instinct was to ignore the ringing phone.

Then Anna remembered that Russ had disappeared on

Tuesday evening. That was why she'd gone to sleep last night with the phone on her nightstand and the ringer volume turned up.

Anna sat up and reached for the phone. The caller ID was nameless—with a number she didn't recognize. She thought of the raspy-voiced caller from last night. There had been no second call. Was this the follow-up call? While Anna hesitated, the ringing stopped and the call went to voice mail.

The bedroom loft fan was on. Past the whirling white noise, she heard a commotion outside. The crowd of reporters had still been out by the dock gate when Anna had gone to bed at one in the morning. Obviously, they were still out there—and making a hell of a racket. Over the din, she heard a neighbor screaming at someone: "This dock is private property! You're trespassing! I'm calling the police!"

"The police are already out here, lady."

It sounded like they were just below her window.

Someone rang the doorbell and pounded on her door.

Anna jumped out of bed and grabbed her robe. Throwing it on, she scurried down the narrow staircase and headed for the door.

"Anna! Anna, do you have a comment?" some reporter yelled out. Then he started banging on the door again.

She checked the peephole and didn't recognize the guy. But he had a mic in his hand—and a videographer hovering behind him. Behind the videographer was Anna's sixtysomething neighbor, Mrs. Gettle, in a pale blue sweatsuit.

Disoriented, Anna smoothed back her hair and then suddenly realized she still had on her night guard. She took it out of her mouth and stashed it in the pocket of her robe. Unlocking the door, she opened it as far as the chain lock allowed. She was careful not to get too close to the opening, because she didn't want to see her unwashed, morning face on the news later today. Warily, she peered out at the reporter.

He was a short, impish-looking guy in his midthirties with messy brown hair. He wore a denim shirt and jeans. He was so aggressive that Anna thought he might try to push the door in. "Anna! Do you have any comment on Dr. Russell Knoll's suicide?"

He shoved the mic through the door opening.

"What?" she asked. She told herself she hadn't heard him right. "What are you talking about?"

Her phone upstairs started ringing again.

"Don't you know?" the pushy reporter asked. "Haven't the police contacted you yet? Russell Knoll jumped off the Tacoma Narrows Bridge early this morning. He's dead."

"God, a million different thoughts went through my mind when I stared down at her, sprawled across the floor with that gash in her head. Her eyes were open. She seemed to gaze back at me, accusing me . . . My first instinct was to get out of there. But then I realized I had to dispose of the body and clean up the blood. Otherwise, everyone would have blamed Russ. That was the last thing I wanted. So I got the idea to pack a suitcase—and make it look like she'd left him."

—Excerpt: Session 3, audio recording
with Dr. G. Tolman, July 23

CHAPTER TWENTY-THREE

Thursday, July 16—6:37 P.M.

"Did Dr. Russell Knoll really throw himself one hundred and eighty-eight feet from the Tacoma Narrows Bridge into the icy waters of Puget Sound?" Sally asked. Seated behind her judge's desk, she read off the teleprompter. Sally and her writers had composed the script ninety minutes before, and now she was reading it live on her show.

It reminded her of thirty-five years ago when she'd been a reporter and anchor at a TV station in Denver. Reporting and analyzing news events on the air just hours after they occurred had always given Sally an adrenaline rush.

In the green screen box over Sally's shoulder, they were showing several stock photos of the spectacular twin suspension bridges that spanned 5,400 feet, connecting Tacoma to the Kitsap Peninsula.

"Yes, the police found Knoll's abandoned car there, midway across the westbound bridge," Sally continued. "Yes, they discovered what seems to be a suicide note inside the car, and several people at Dr. Knoll's clinic have confirmed that the note is in his handwriting."

Then Sally frowned and slowly shook her head. "But there are simply too many questions about this alleged suicide. I mean, how murky can this whole thing be? First of all, the location of Dr. Knoll's BMW—it just happened to be in a *blind spot* for the cameras on the bridge. So we have no video of him getting out of his car and taking that deadly leap. No one actually saw it happen—except for one anonymous witness. This woman phoned 911 about the alleged incident from an untraceable *burner* phone. How convenient that she just happened to have this burner phone in her car when she was driving on the Tacoma Narrows Bridge at three in the morning! She refused to give her name because she said she'd been in trouble with the police. I ask you, is this a credible source? We're supposed to believe what this elusive, mystery woman is telling us? She managed to evade authorities last night. Pierce County and Tacoma Police are working together to locate the witness. They've been examining traffic cam videos from the bridge in hopes of tracking her down through her vehicle."

Sally let out a heavy sigh. "Well, people, who's to say this so-called *witness* didn't make the call from another location? We know she must have been in Pierce County or Tacoma, because her 911 call was routed to the police there. But she didn't necessarily have to be calling from the bridge. So when you get down to it, we have no idea where this *witness* really was when she called. And we don't know *who* she was."

A photo of Dr. Russell Knoll appeared in the box over Sally's shoulder. "Finally, we have no body," Sally announced. "The police have not yet found Dr. Knoll's corpse. We don't even know for certain if he's dead! So—we have an alleged suicide without a body or a credible witness. All we have, folks, is the abandoned car and a suicide note."

Though it was on the teleprompter, Sally had the text of the note typed—in a sixteen-point font— on a piece of paper in front of her. She read aloud from that, because, for the viewers at home, it created the illusion that everything else she said was off the cuff and this was something she actually needed to read. The text came up as if someone were typing it—superimposed over Russell Knoll's image in the box over Sally's shoulder:

"*I've come to an impasse. Right now this seems like the only way out. I apologize to Anna Malone, who never hurt anyone and never deserved the heartache I've brought upon her. To Anna, and all the other people who believed in me, I apologize for letting you down.*'"

Sally looked up at the camera and sighed. "Well, it was awfully noble of him to exonerate his girlfriend, Anna Malone. But is he to be believed? Dr. Knoll never really admits whether or not he killed his wife. I mean, as far as confessions or suicide notes go, it's awfully vague. I wonder how much Anna Malone has to do with this supposed suicide. Is she as innocent as her lover makes her out to be? She claims not to remember anything from the night Courtney Knoll disappeared. Well, I think that's bunk.

"When we come back, I'll talk to some callers about what *they* think. This so-called suicide of the fugitive Dr. Russell Knoll: Is it for real or is it a hoax? Tell us what you think! Go to www-dot-vote-sally-justice-dot-com! We'll be right back."

In her earpiece, Sally heard them cue up her theme music for the break. She kept looking at the camera and waited for the assistant director to give her the signal that she was no longer on the air. Out of the corner of her eye, she caught a glimpse of Taylor, standing behind the second cameraman.

At last, they gave her the signal.

"Chad! My forehead's shiny, I can feel it!" she screamed. She turned toward the people over in the sound booth. "Paulette, you better have some good calls for me!" Then she frowned at her daughter. "Why are you here? I didn't think you wanted to have anything to do with me."

Chad I rushed onto the set and started patting down Sally's forehead with pancake makeup.

Sally closed her eyes for a moment. When she opened them again, her daughter had stepped forward. She was signing—and not speaking. Whenever Sally and her daughter argued in front of other people, they bickered in sign language.

Back when Taylor had been diagnosed as deaf, Sally's husband, Boyd Hofstad, had started taking lessons in sign language right away. He'd become fluent. Sally had been busy building her career in television. She'd picked up bits and pieces, but fell way behind Boyd and Taylor in her sign language abilities. She often felt left out of their conversations.

After Boyd had been shot dead in a road rage incident, Sally went on the air about how the Denver Police seemed to be dragging their feet in the investigation. It took them two weeks to hunt down her husband's killer: an armed

twenty-two-year-old drunk driver who already had one
DUI. Sally took to the airwaves to criticize how the police
and prosecutors were handling the case.

That was how Sally Hofstad became Sally Justice.
And since Taylor was down to only one parent, Sally
buckled down and learned sign language—so her ten-
year-old deaf daughter would have someone to commu-
nicate with. Though she got by, Sally never became an
expert at signing. Her TV career had always come first.

Still, she'd made certain Taylor's nannies and teachers
were adept at sign language. She'd also sent her daughter
to the finest special schools. Under the circumstances,
Sally figured she'd done the best she could for her child.

So she couldn't help resenting it just a little whenever
Taylor flared up and gave her a lot of attitude. Her daughter seemed pretty hostile right now.

Taylor silently signed to her and mouthed the words:
"You really should stop attacking Dr. . . ." She spelled out
K-n-o-l-l. Sally caught Taylor's signal for *and*. Then her
daughter spelled out: A-n-n-a M-a-l-o-n-e. Taylor always
spelled so rapidly with her fingers that Sally sometimes
had difficulty following her. "What if he's really dead?"
Taylor continued. "You're going to look awful—if you
don't already look awful. This is just like T-e-d B-i-r-c-h
in S-p-o-k-a-n-e. You drove him to suicide, too!"

"Lovely to see you again, too, dear," Sally said out loud.
"I like your blouse." Then she signed, abruptly bringing
the little-finger side of her right hand down across her
open left palm, the sign for *stop*. "Okay, enough," she
silently mouthed to her daughter.

Chad I must have sensed her annoyance, because he

quickly finished touching up her forehead and backed away.

Taylor rolled her eyes at her. "People are going to get tired of your attacks on A-n-n-a M-a-l-o-n-e," she signed and silently mouthed. "Right now, they're probably starting to feel sorry for her. It's bad enough that you dragged her brother in front of the cameras to criticize her yesterday. Where did you find him anyway?"

"Down in Longview," Sally replied out loud, not bothering to sign. Her daughter could read her lips. "That new private investigator, Brenda, tracked him down. And we got him for cheap, too—thirty-five hundred dollars. It was quite the bargain considering he was ratings gold. Now, I have twenty seconds before I'm back on the air." Then Sally silently mouthed and signed: "Are we quite done here?"

"Yes, we're done, Mother," Taylor signed—and replied aloud. She had a sneer on her face. Then she turned and walked off the set.

Frowning, Sally watched her disappear in the darkness beyond the spotlights. She wondered if Taylor was right about her losing her audience. Were people going to get tired of her campaign to discredit Courtney's husband and that bitch who was his mistress? Sally felt like she was just getting started on Anna Malone. She really wanted to stick it to her. But it wasn't just about revenge.

Sally was convinced the illicit pair had indeed killed Courtney Knoll—and this whole suicide thing was a ruse. Someone had to speak out. And that was Sally's specialty. People had to be convinced.

But she wondered if all of this was worth it if she ended up alienating her daughter.

The assistant director gave her the cue and started counting backward from five.

In her earpiece, Sally heard a few bars of her theme music. She turned to the camera with her usual intense stare. The green light went on.

"We're back!" Sally said.

From: TaylorHofstad322@gmail.com
To: AnnaM@kixitvnews.com
Subject: Sally & Your Brother
Date: Fri, July 17 3:52 PM

Dear Anna,

I was so sorry to hear the news about Dr. Knoll.

I don't know if you watched my mother's show last night, but she spent most of it trying to convince her viewers that Dr. Knoll's suicide was a hoax and that he's really alive. I told her she's just being cruel—to his memory and to you.

Sally put it up for the usual online vote at the end of the show: Do you believe Dr. Russell Knoll really committed suicide? The results came in that 46% of the viewers believe he killed himself; 15% were undecided; and only 39% agreed with Sally. That's extremely low for her. I take this as a good sign. She may move on to other topics for the show if her audience continues to vote against her like this.

I'm sure all of this doesn't really matter much to you right now. But I just thought you should know. My mother also touched upon the fact that you don't remember what happened a week ago on the night Courtney disappeared.

She says that's "bunk." My offer to put you in touch with this hypnotherapist, Dr. Tolman, still stands. She isn't taking any new clients right now, but I'm sure she'll make an exception for me. Then again, defending yourself against Sally might not be a high priority right now. At the same time, you've just suffered a horrible loss, and if you need someone to talk to and don't have anyone, I can give you Tolman's number.

Your brother, Stuart, is down in Longview. The name Eddie Vaughn is a total fake that he used exclusively for the show. One of Sally's detectives, Brenda Melnick, tracked him down. They paid him to appear on the show. Sally's associate producer, Dan Lassiter, set him up for the interview in a motel down there. Dan said your brother was on crystal meth most of the time he was with him (I'm sorry, but I thought you should know).

Brenda has agreed to find your brother again and have him get in touch with me. Sally isn't in on this, and Brenda doesn't ask questions. I'm paying her separately. Please don't worry about paying me back. After all the pain my mother has caused you, this is the least I can do.

Once I hear from your brother, I'll let him know that you miss him and you want to see him. Does that sound ok?

Sorry about this long e-mail, Anna. My thoughts and prayers are with you.

Sincerely,
Taylor

CHAPTER TWENTY-FOUR

Monday, July 20—8:58 P.M.

From the Magnolia neighborhood's Ella Bailey Park, Anna had a spectacular view of Seattle. The bottom half of the Space Needle was obscured by Queen Anne Hill, but the slope of lush, green trees and the view of the city beyond it took her breath away. She could also see the grain elevators, the railroad yard, and Puget Sound—all bathed in the magic glow of summer twilight.

The park had a big playground and picnic tables. But this time of night, things were quiet for the most part, with only a few people around—perfect for Anna's melancholy mood.

This was one of Russ's favorite spots. Anna had come here hoping to connect with him somehow. Instead, she just felt very much alone.

She almost regretted making the trip here. It had been a hassle getting past all those reporters earlier. They'd been lying in wait for her on the street by her dock gate. But their numbers had dwindled a bit over the weekend.

Anna had counted them as she'd made a beeline to her car: two news vans, four reporters, and two videographers. She'd managed to count them without looking a single one in the eye.

She did a bit of tabulating now. It had been ten days since Courtney had disappeared and since Russ had come to this park for the last time. It had been four days since his apparent suicide. Neither Russ nor Courtney had been found yet. Every time the phone rang or Anna turned on the news, she expected to hear something about one of their bodies washing ashore someplace.

Detective Baumann had stopped by on Friday afternoon—Anna's only visitor since Russ's death. Baumann had come on behalf of the Tacoma and Pierce County Police Departments. They hadn't been able to track down the 911 caller who had reported Russ's suicide.

"We know it couldn't have been you," the detective had assured Anna as they'd talked in her living room. "The 911 call was automatically routed to the Tacoma Police Department. So you couldn't have phoned from your home. And you couldn't have left here early Thursday morning without getting spotted by all the reporters camped overnight here. So we know you weren't who called 911. Now, if this 911 call was part of a scam by Dr. Knoll to make it seem like he'd killed himself, he'd have needed this mystery woman to help him pull it off."

"You watch Sally Justice, too?" Anna asked.

"Yes, that seemed to be Sally's theory." Baumann nodded. "So here's the ten-thousand-dollar question, Anna. I know it's tactless, but I have to ask. Do you think it's possible Russ had another girlfriend—besides you?"

The question had hit her like a punch in the stomach. Anna let out a startled laugh and automatically shook her head.

Then she remembered Courtney's claim that Russ had been involved with a yoga instructor at one time. But that woman—if she even existed—was supposed to have moved to Pittsburgh two years ago.

Anna also briefly considered the possibility that Courtney was still alive, and that she'd been the 911 caller—as part of some sort of elaborate scheme to murder Russ. But it didn't make any sense. Besides, a standard burner phone wouldn't be equipped for a deaf woman to use—even on a 911 call.

Anna found herself once again telling Detective Baumann of her suspicions about Courtney's onetime fellow writers' group member Sandy Myron. Anna still thought Crazy Sandy might have been responsible for killing Courtney. Perhaps Sandy was somehow involved in Russ's death, too. "Maybe she wanted to make it look as if Russ had killed Courtney and then committed suicide," Anna suggested.

Nodding, Baumann took notes and said she would look into it. But Anna could tell the detective didn't take the Crazy Sandy theory very seriously.

"So you think it's possible Dr. Knoll isn't really dead?" Anna asked. "What do the Tacoma Police think happened?"

Baumann hesitated

Staring intently at her, Anna waited for an answer. Did they think Russ could have faked his own death and might still be alive? Or did they believe someone might have killed him and made it look like a suicide?

"They're examining every possible scenario right now," Baumann finally replied. "The circumstances of Dr. Knoll's apparent suicide might seem inconclusive. But it's not all that uncommon for someone to phone 911 to report an incident and want to remain anonymous. It happens quite a lot, as a matter of fact. So chances are this mystery caller was telling it like it is."

"Is that the general consensus among the police?" Anna asked.

"Don't quote me," Baumann said quietly. "But yes. For now, they think the 911 call was authentic. They believe Dr. Knoll jumped off the bridge—just as she said. And they believe that what he said about you in the note is true."

Anna sighed. "But they also believe he killed Courtney, don't they?"

Baumann nodded. "And that's all you're going to get out of me about what the police think."

Anna still considered Crazy Sandy a major suspect in Courtney's disappearance—even if the detective didn't agree.

Becky Arnett had texted her over the weekend. According to a third member of Courtney's writers' group, Sloane Lindquist, time hadn't healed any wounds as far as Sandy was concerned:

Sloane said she got an e-mail from Sandy several months back. Sandy moved to Florida. She asked about us and said she hoped that "bitch" Courtney was dead. She swore to get even with her—for about the 100th time. Sloane said

she'll try to hunt down the e-mail for me. She might have
deleted it. Stay tuned!

George had called a couple of times since Friday
morning -just to check on how she was doing. He'd offered to come over if she needed company. But with the
reporters keeping a vigil by her dock, Anna didn't think
his sneaking through their ranks to visit her was such a
terrific idea.

"I don't care how it looks," he'd told her at one point
Saturday night. "Beebe and I are finished. The atmos-
phere is toxic around here. I'm looking for an apartment."

"Well, I care how it looks," Anna had told him.

Besides, if George was infatuated with her, and he
certainly hadn't denied it, Anna didn't want to grieve for
her dead lover in front of him. That would have been insensitive. And she wanted to feel free to grieve without
worrying about someone else's feelings.

Anna's friend in Spokane, Christie, had offered to stay
with her for a few days. But Christie had a husband and
two kids. Anna didn't feel right dragging her away from
her family. Besides, she wanted to be alone.

She sat around her apartment like a zombie most of
the weekend, succumbing to crying jags whenever they
hit her. Though she'd been planning to break up with
Russ—hell, they'd agreed splitting up was for the best—
she was still devastated. She didn't want to believe he was
dead. She couldn't imagine never seeing him again. She
still had some saved messages he'd left on her phone, and
she must have played them back ten times. She knew
them by heart now.

She hated that there was no closure. Russ had left the

world with everyone believing he'd murdered his wife. Worst of all, Anna still couldn't be completely certain of his innocence.

"That's Anna Malone!" she heard someone exclaim.

This was followed by a chorus of giggles and someone shushing the others.

Anna spotted a trio of young women approaching her—all in T-shirts and shorts, each one with a phone in her hand. Anna couldn't tell if, age-wise, they were in late high school or their early college years. She'd noticed them earlier. They'd been hard to miss. They had that extra-loud-talking-and-laughing syndrome some girls acquired when in a group. Fortunately, they'd wandered out of earshot to another part of the park for a while. But Anna could hear them again now.

Obviously, she'd been spotted. They suddenly spoke in hushed tones—until one of them screeched and burst out laughing.

Anna decided to head for her car. She'd been practically hibernating on her houseboat since Sally had first gone on the attack a week ago. Though the press had been hounding her, this was her first brush with the general public since everything hit the fan.

Her head down, she started to loop around them to get to her car. She tried to keep her distance.

"Hey, Anna!" one of the girls called.

She glanced at them long enough for a brief nod and timid wave. Then she kept walking.

"Anna, can we take a selfie with you?" Brandishing a smartphone, one of them scampered toward her. Her two friends followed.

"I'm so sorry about your boyfriend!" another one of

them called. She almost sounded sincere. But then the third girl giggled.

All three young women hurried to catch up with her. It looked like one girl was taking a video of her. "C'mon, Anna! Just one group selfie."

Anna started walking a little faster. Shaking her head, she managed a polite smile. "Not now, thanks. Sorry."

All three young women stopped in their tracks. "God, what a bitch," one girl said.

Her head down, Anna continued toward her car. She still could hear them behind her.

"Fuck her," one of them said.

"What do you expect from a murdering skank?" her friend asked. "I'm sure she helped that guy kill his wife. That's what Sally Justice says. Did you get her picture?"

Anna finally reached her Mini Cooper and ducked inside. She wished she knew which car the three girls had come in. She'd ram into it—Kathy Bates *Fried Green Tomatoes* style. Let them take a video of that.

Yeah, right, that's all you need, she thought, *more publicity*.

Anna started the car and headed for home.

On the Magnolia Bridge, she thought about *The Sally Justice Show*. She'd purposely missed it tonight. She'd been feeling too vulnerable. Another battering from Sally would have pushed her over the edge. Apparently, tonight's episode had been bad enough. Taylor had sent another one of her postshow apology e-mails.

According to Taylor, among other things, her mother had replayed and then picked apart Anna's statement "outing herself" on *KIXI-TV News at Five* from a week ago. Sally had criticized everything from her sincerity to the "virginal white" blouse she'd worn. The question for Sally's voting viewers had been whether or not they thought Anna had been complicit in the disappearance of Courtney Knoll.

At least Taylor had included some fairly hopeful news in the e-mail:

> The private investigator, Brenda, was able to track down a friend of your brother's in Longview. All I got was a first name, Tony. I talked to Tony on Skype and told him that you'd really like to see your brother. I said that you aren't mad at him or anything. You just miss him. Tony said he'd pass it along to Stuart if he runs into him. I know it's not much, but it's something. Brenda isn't giving up there. She says she's determined to find Stuart for me.

Anna had e-mailed back that she was grateful—and she really was. Having an ally in Taylor took some of the sting out of Sally's on-air diatribes. Taylor hadn't mentioned her hypnotherapist contact in tonight's e-mail. But Anna was seriously starting to consider making an appointment with this Dr. Tolman—if for nothing else than an excuse to get out of the house for a couple of hours. She found positive write-ups on her in the Seattle Counselors Association and Western Washington Therapists Group, but there was no photo of her and no mention of hypnosis in either recommendation. Still, Anna needed someone to talk to. Besides—what if she could actually remember something that would prove Russ and she didn't have anything to do with Courtney's disappearance?

As for Stu, Anna tried not to get her hopes up for a

reunion anytime soon. He was probably afraid to face her—after lying about her the way he had on the air coast-to-coast.

One person she hadn't heard from over the weekend was her anonymous caller. There hadn't been any of those raspy-voiced calls since Russ had thrown himself off the Tacoma Narrows Bridge. Of course, Anna couldn't help wondering if her androgynous-sounding caller and the anonymous 911 caller weren't one and the same person.

Anna was only five minutes from home and about to start down Eastlake Avenue when the lights started flashing on the University Bridge. With a warning bell, the gate went down. It meant the bridge was going up, and she could add another ten minutes to her drive. Anna was in no hurry. She stopped and turned off her engine. She was second in line on the bridge.

She grabbed the phone off the bracket on her dashboard, leaned back, and started composing a text:

Thank you again for everything you're doing for me, Taylor. Could you please give me Dr. Tolman's contact information? I think you're right. She might be very helpful. Thank you!

Anna sent the text. She was just setting the phone back into the bracketed holder when it rang. Her first thought was *I shouldn't have wondered about my creepy anonymous caller*. But then she checked the Caller ID: *Rebecca Arnett*.

Anna tapped the phone screen. "Becky?"

"Hi, Anna," she said. "I know I usually text you, but I

believe bad news should be given in person—or something close to in person."

"What is it?" Anna asked, watching the grid sections of the four-lane bridge open up.

"Sandy Myron couldn't have anything to do with Courtney's disappearance—unless she hired a hit man to do the job for her. I just heard from Sloane, who got the lowdown from someone else who knows Sandy down in Florida. Sandy's been sick—cancer. For the last two months, she's been in a hospice in Orlando."

"Oh. Well, I—I'm so sorry for your friend," Anna said sympathetically.

"Yeah, it's sad, but to be honest, we weren't very close. I feel bad I steered you into thinking she might have had something to do with Courtney's disappearance."

"That's all right," Anna said, hiding her disappointment. "I appreciate your trying to help, Becky. I really do."

"Maybe I should get the address of this hospice and write a note to Sandy. I'll tell her what happened to Courtney. That ought to perk her up a bit."

Anna actually smiled for a moment. "Good idea."

"Listen, Anna, I'm sure there are plenty of people who couldn't stand Courtney, plenty of other suspects in this case besides Dr. Knoll and you—despite what Sally Justice says. You know, I met him once. You don't drive a bus for seven years without learning to read people. And he struck me as a good guy. I don't think he killed his wife. I don't believe you had anything to do with it, either. The police and everyone else will figure that out soon enough."

"Thank you, Becky," Anna said.

"I'm sorry I wasn't more help," she said. "Good luck, Anna."

After she hung up, Anna felt another crying jag coming on. She'd invested a lot of hope in the possibility that Sandy or someone like her had been responsible for Courtney's disappearance. She really thought this might lead to something. It was a crushing setback.

Anna listlessly watched the bridge go back down. She waited for the gate to go up and then restarted her car. The light turned green, and she drove on

It was dark by the time she pulled into the shadowy carport. But somehow, she wasn't scared. *You have to care what happens to you to be scared,* she thought, getting out of the car and locking it.

As she started toward her dock, she dreaded having to deal with the reporters waiting for her there. She could see the news vans in the distance. *Just walk fast,* she told herself, reaching into her purse for her keys. She noticed the cluster of reporters and onlookers stirring. She'd been spotted.

"Anna!" one of them called out. He waved to her.

Looking down at the pavement, Anna kept walking toward her dock.

"Anna, do you have any comment on tonight's *Sally Justice Show*?" another reporter yelled.

"Do you think Dr. Knoll is really dead? Did he fake his death?"

Eyes downcast, Anna threaded through the group. She tried to ignore the cameras and mics pushed in her path. They were all talking at her at once, a few louder than the others.

"Anna, what are your plans now?"

"What are the police telling you about Dr. Knoll?"

She made it to the gate. With a slightly shaky hand, she unlocked it. "Sorry, guys, no comment."

"Anna, is the TV station going to give you your job back?"

"Anna Banana?"

She stopped abruptly and anxiously searched the faces of the reporters, cameramen, and onlookers. And then, past the first row of them, she saw Stu, looking dissipated. His smile was tentative and hopeful. He broke through the ranks and approached her.

Astonished, Anna stared at him. Tears filled her eyes.

"Anna Banana, I'm so sorry," he said. He started to cry, too.

Anna couldn't talk. She threw herself into his arms.

He hugged her. Anna felt the stubble of his unshaven chin against her face. He didn't smell so great, but she didn't care. She kept holding on to him. He patted her back.

She was barely aware of the buzz among the reporters surrounding them. Then they started to shout questions at her.

"Who is this, Anna?"

"Do you have a new boyfriend already?" one tactlessly asked, talking over the rest.

Stu gently pulled away, but kept his arm around her. "Hey, I'm her brother, Stuart Malone," he announced, wiping a tear from his eye. He squinted and then scratched his head. "And I haven't seen Anna in sixteen years. So— I'm sorry if we're kind of emotional here."

Several photo flashes blinded them. Anna brushed away her tears as well. She tried to lead her brother away—toward the houseboat.

But Stu held his ground. He cleared his throat. "As

long as I have you members of the press here, I want to say something for the record. I was on *The Sally Justice Show* the other night. I really needed money, and they paid me to trash-talk my sister, Anna, here. So I told a bunch of lies on the show. I said what they told me to say. It was all on cue cards. I'm really sorry I did it." He nodded toward Anna. "See how sweet and forgiving my little sister is?"

She pulled him past the gate and then shut it. The photo flashes were still going off as she pulled Stu toward the end of the dock.

"I know what you're probably thinking," he whispered. "You saw the show. You heard I've had problems. But I want you to know, Anna Banana, I'm not doing any drugs. I've been clean for two days—two whole days."

Nodding, Anna unlocked the door and opened it for him. She patted Stu's shoulder as he stepped inside.

She wanted to believe him. She really wanted to believe him.

Anna walked in behind her brother and then double-locked the door.

CHAPTER TWENTY-FIVE

Monday, July 20—11:02 P.M.

"Oh my God, I'm having flashbacks to Crestview Road, Bainbridge Island," Stu said, leaning back in the breakfast booth. "I haven't tasted this in sixteen years. It's the same old recipe, too. I forgot how fucking great your homemade pizza is."

On the table in front of him, Anna had set four slices of reheated pizza on a plate along with a can of Coke.

"Well, if it ain't broke, don't change the recipe," Anna said. She sat on the other side of the little table with her glass of wine.

She hadn't wasted much time getting her brother to agree that he'd stay for a few days. He'd left some of his things in a locker at the Greyhound terminal. Anna and he would pick them up in the morning. Anna had also tactfully informed him that he smelled pretty ripe. She'd decided not to say anything about his awful neck tattoo or that he needed a haircut. It was too late to criticize the tattoo and too early to advocate a haircut.

She had some of Russ's clothes in her closet and figured Stu could wear them until his clothes were washed and dried. While Stu had showered, Anna had looked up online how to help someone withdrawing from crystal meth. The sites she visited suggested the patient get sleep, a lot of healthy food, a lot of liquids, sympathy, and professional rehab counseling

She'd changed the sheets on the daybed in the little study and decided to wait until tomorrow before she'd start talking about rehab places. She didn't want to scare Stu away on his first night. His coming here was a godsend, a dream come true after sixteen years And his timing was perfect. She needed the company. Plus she needed to get out of this self-pitying funk and focus on someone else.

Sitting across from Stu now, a flood of memories — bits and pieces of their life in the Bainbridge Island house — washed over Anna: their brother-sister lip-synching routine to "Bohemian Rhapsody"; the planks of wood across the branches of the backyard maple tree that had been Stu's tree house; all the solemn funerals they'd held for her various goldfish; the games of H-O-R-S-E using the basketball net above their garage door, which he'd always let her win. And when she was eleven, it was Stu who had managed to console her on 9/11. He alone had understood her panic and sorrow. He'd been the one to come to her rescue.

Now they were rescuing each other.

On his second slice of pizza, Stu looked like he was starting to choke. Tears came to his eyes, and he put down the pizza slice.

"Are you okay?" Anna asked, alarmed.

He wiped his eyes. "I'm just so fucked up," he sobbed. "I can't believe I went on that stupid show and told all those lies about you. It was such a betrayal. You didn't deserve it, Anna. It was just that I was so desperate. I owed these guys money. And somebody from *The Sally Justice Show* tracked me down and offered me thirty-five hundred bucks to come on TV and talk about you."

Anna took hold of his hand. "Hey, c'mon, let's forget about it. And not all of it was a lie. You were right. I got away with murder with Dad. And I forgot about all those dinners when I hid his drink."

He chuckled and then wiped his eyes again—using the sleeve of Russ's UW sweatshirt.

"Besides, you made it all right again and set the record straight when you gave your statement to the press," Anna went on. "You were very eloquent, by the way. Plus I think you may have given them just what they wanted. Maybe now they'll leave me alone. Earlier, when I was in Mom's room making the daybed for you, I looked out the window and noticed that most of them have left."

"I wouldn't have had the nerve to show up here tonight, only this guy I know, Tony, he said he talked online to some deaf girl who's a friend of yours. He said you wanted to see me and you weren't pissed off or anything." He picked up another slice of pizza and glanced around. "I can't believe you and Mom used to live here together and didn't drive each other crazy."

"Four whole years," Anna said, sipping her wine. "And believe me, we got on each other's nerves often enough."

"I remember the few times we spent the night here as a family, I thought the four of us would end up killing each other. I was so bored."

Anna remembered it differently. She recalled the family dinners on the deck and playing board games at this same kitchen table. Those nights for her had been fun family mini-vacations. But then, Stu had always been popular, and she'd been kind of a nerdy homebody. So he'd probably been focused on all the partying and carousing he'd been missing. She wondered if he'd already started messing around with drugs back then.

She wanted to ask, but didn't.

He grinned at her. "You don't know how many times I almost dropped in on you and Mom here." Then his smile faded. "But I was worried I might be an unwelcome surprise."

"You knew we were living here? You knew about Dad?"

He nodded. "I was in Alaska when that happened, and didn't hear about the old man until I got in touch with Jim Munchel about a year after the fact. You remember Jim from Bainbridge Island?"

Anna shook her head.

"Well, anyway, he told me about the old man getting thrown in the clink and offing himself. He said he'd heard that you and Mom had moved here. So whenever my travels took me back to Seattle, I'd swing by and check on you from one of the neighboring docks. I actually saw you guys a few times —coming and going, and once I saw you and Mom on the back deck. I came so close to rushing over here and banging on the door."

"Oh, Stu," Anna whispered. "Why didn't you? Mom would have given anything for that."

He shrugged. "I was afraid you guys would tell me to go to hell."

She shook her head. "No. You should have come by. I would have given anything for that, too."

He squinted down at the tabletop and scratched his head. "It wouldn't have worked out. I'd already started in on the meth. I'd turned a corner. I knew you and Mom would be disappointed in me."

"How are you feeling now, by the way?" she asked.

Stu took another bite of pizza and nodded. "I'm doing okay."

"I read up a little about what you're supposed to be experiencing as you go off crystal meth—headaches, paranoia, body aches, anxiety . . ."

"The first day was the worst. Today, mostly, I'm just tired. Don't be surprised if I sleep through the whole day tomorrow." He smiled, and his dimples emerged. "Thanks, by the way—for not lecturing me about the drugs."

She let out a tiny laugh. "Well, thanks for not lecturing me about my relationship with a married man. Mom and Dad raised a fine pair of kids, didn't they?"

"Y'know, I saw you guys together once—a few months back."

Anna sat up a little. "You saw us?"

"Yeah, I didn't stop watching you after Mom died. I checked up on you in Spokane a few times—when you were in college, and then later, when you lived in that duplex. I saw you on TV, and Googled you. Then when you moved back here, I peeked in on you a few times. One of those times, he was here and you guys were sitting out on the back deck, talking and watching the sunset. I was pretty far away, but still, it seemed to me like the two of you were good together."

Anna felt a little tightness in her throat, and her eyes teared up. But she managed to smile. "Thank you." She took a deep breath to compose herself. "I have to admit, knowing you've been watching me this long. I—I have mixed feelings about it. I'm not sure if I've had a guardian angel all this time or a stalker."

"Funny you should say that. A couple of times I've watched you come and go in the past year, I thought somebody else might be doing the exact same thing."

"What do you mean?"

"Well, once I was on the dock over there." He pointed out the kitchen window by the booth. "And while I was looking at you, I noticed this woman—at least, I think it was a woman—and she was on a boat, looking toward your place through a pair of binoculars. I remember thinking, *Well, that's some strange shit*. But then I figured, you're on TV a lot, and you probably have fans or weirdos following you around."

"When was this?" Anna asked.

Stu shrugged. "God, I don't remember exactly, last fall sometime."

"Last October?"

He nodded. "That sounds about right—"

"Did you get a good look at her?" Anna pressed. "You've seen Courtney Knoll's photo, haven't you? Do you think it's possible this woman on the boat could have been Courtney?"

"I was so far away. I could barely tell that it was a woman. It could have been anybody. Plus she had the binoculars in front of her face most of the time. But I'll tell you, it happened again a couple of months ago. I recognized the boat. I could see someone on deck, but it was night. Whoever it was, this person had on a dark windbreaker with a hood. I couldn't tell if they had binoculars or a phone or what. But they seemed to be watching you. And I'm like positive it was the same boat, a sports cruiser, about forty feet. I'd recognize it again in a second. It's just like Terry Adalist's boat. We took that baby out on the water practically every day my last summer on Bainbridge."

Anna glanced out the window—at the dark water and the city lights in the distance. She could almost hear that raspy voice on the phone: *"I saw you fucking kill her. I saw it."*

Stu chuckled. "Hey, I'm sorry, did I freak you out?" He took hold of her hand. "Don't worry, Anna Banana. I'm here to protect you."

Anna worked up a smile and nodded.

But she was still afraid.

CHAPTER TWENTY-SIX

Tuesday, July 21 —9:17 A.M.

The phone's chiming woke her up. Someone was sending her a text.

Anna didn't usually sleep in this late. But she and Stu had stayed up until two in the morning, talking and looking at old family albums. He'd said he would probably sleep all day, so she'd decided not to set her alarm. Picking up his stuff at the bus depot was the only thing they needed to do today.

Sitting up in bed, Anna grabbed the phone off her nightstand and squinted at the screen. The text was from Taylor:

Dr. Tolman is on vacation and having her office redecorated. But for me, she says she'll make an exception. She charges $230 per session, and sometimes it takes a few sessions to start getting results. Believe me, she's worth it. She says she has time this afternoon and

tomorrow afternoon. I can set it up for you. Just let me
know.

Two hundred and thirty bucks a session wasn't cheap—
especially for someone who wasn't currently employed.
Anna also wondered how much it would cost to get Stuart
into a decent rehabilitation center. But she figured the
sessions with Tolman would be worthwhile if she could
remember more about the night Courtney had disappeared.

Rubbing her eyes, Anna sat up straighter in bed and
started working her thumbs over the phone screen's keyboard:

> First off, thank you so much for bringing my brother back to
> me. He showed up at my place last night. Thanks to you, I
> feel like I'm part of a family again. I don't think I'll ever be
> able to repay you for your kindness, Taylor. We're both so
> grateful.
>
> Thanks also for volunteering to arrange things with Dr.
> Tolman. I'm free this afternoon and tomorrow afternoon.
> You said it will take multiple sessions. Maybe we should
> schedule both today and tomorrow? One glitch. My brother
> is staying with me, and it's close quarters, not much privacy.
> If Dr. Tolman's office isn't available, maybe I can meet her at
> her house. Could you give me her contact info? Then I can
> work it out with her. You've already done so much. Thanks
> again!

Anna pressed send.
She lingered in bed for a few minutes. When she got

up, she staggered over to the window. The blinds were lowered, and she pecked between the slats. She didn't see any news vans or people near the dock gate—at least not from here. Was it possible they were all gone?

Anna put on her robe and made her bed. She was about to head down the narrow stairs to the bathroom when the phone chimed again. She snatched it off the nightstand. It was another text from Taylor:

> Dr. Tolman can see you today and tomorrow at 3. Does that work for you? She'll meet you at my place. I'll step out and give you all the privacy you want. Not that I can overhear anything! ☺ I'm at 186 43rd East in Madison Park, Apartment 301. Does that work for you?

It struck Anna as a little strange that she would have her hypnotherapy sessions at Sally Justice's daughter's apartment. Taylor was just trying to be helpful and accommodating. But this seemed like too much. Then again, Anna couldn't have the sessions here, not with Stu in the next room, and Taylor had made it clear up front that Tolman's office wasn't available.

With a sigh, Anna texted back:

> That's great. But I hate to be an imposition on you. You've done so much already.

She sent it, and a text came back a minute later.

> The least I can do to make up for the fact that my mother has made your life hell. I'll step out while you have your session. See you here around 2:55!

Anna texted back: Thanks! See you!

But the moment she sent it, she had this strange feeling of dread in the pit of her stomach. She kept thinking that perhaps, deep down, she didn't want to remember what had happened that night. Maybe she didn't want to face some terrible truth about something she or Russ had done.

Anna quietly crept down the stairs to the main level. She was about to duck into the bathroom when she noticed the door to the study was open. She didn't want to wake Stu while she washed up. She tiptoed over to the study door to close it, but hesitated and peeked inside.

The daybed was rumpled—like he'd napped on top of it without getting under the sheets. Anna glanced over toward her desk. A couple of drawers were half-open. On the built-in bookcase above the desk, a few of her journalism awards—the expensive-looking ones—were missing.

"Oh no," she whispered. She hurried into the living room.

"Stu!" she called. But she already knew he was gone.

Swiveling around, she looked at the bookcase that held some of the family antiques. He'd taken their mother's silver pieces and some crystal.

"Goddamn it, Stu," she murmured as she headed into the kitchen. She'd left her purse on the bench of the breakfast booth. She searched through the bag. At least the car keys were still in there. He hadn't taken those. The credit cards were still in her wallet. But she'd have to cancel them. He could have copied down the numbers and expiration dates. All the money in her wallet—about ninety dollars—was gone.

Slump-shouldered, Anna returned to the small bedroom through the connecting door in the kitchen. In the mini-closet, she'd kept a wine carafe full of coins. He'd taken that. She couldn't help remembering how he'd stolen all of their dad's rare coins when he'd run away sixteen years ago.

Shaking her head, she sat down at the desk. At least he'd left her computer. She opened the bottom drawer and pulled out a purple spiral notebook. It was just where she'd left it—beneath two yellow legal pads. On the last page of the notebook, she'd jotted down all her passwords and user IDs. She was pretty certain he hadn't found it.

But then she checked the top drawer, where she kept her checkbook. It didn't take long for Anna to figure out that he'd stolen two blank checks.

Now she'd have to call the bank—along with the credit card companies.

She figured, for his own good, she probably should call the police, too. But she couldn't.

How could she be so stupid? She didn't know much about crystal meth addiction, but she certainly had been around long enough to realize that most meth addicts couldn't be trusted.

Anna moved over to the disheveled daybed and sat down.

It hit her that Stu had left wearing Russ's clothes. She'd probably never see them—or him—again.

Anna held her head in her hands and started to cry.

CHAPTER TWENTY-SEVEN

Tuesday, July 21—3:02 P.M.

"I'm picking up some apprehension, and you also seem a bit frazzled," Dr. Gloria Tolman said.

Sitting on the beige sofa in Taylor's living room, Anna let out a tiny laugh. "Well, you have some good radar there."

Dr. Tolman was about sixty. She had a kind, prematurely wizened face, and her frosted auburn hair was styled in a pageboy with bangs. She wore white slacks and a short-sleeve teal blouse that showed the crepe-paper skin on her thin, tanned arms. She sat across from Anna in a comfy-looking sage-colored chair.

Taylor's apartment building was sleek and new, with big windows that looked out at Lake Washington. When she'd arrived there ten minutes ago, Anna could see from the intercom by the front door that the building had twelve units. Taylor's second-floor apartment looked like something out of an old Pottery Barn catalog: semimodern, comfortable furniture in neutral tones. Anna was thinking of an old catalog, because the place seemed just slightly out of date and borderline bland. The only colors that popped in Taylor's living room were the red throw pillows on the sofa and a bouquet of red roses in a vase on the coffee table.

Despite her dreadful day so far, Anna had tried to put on a pleasant, relaxed demeanor when Taylor had greeted her at the door. Anna had become an expert at adapting this composed behavior for TV.

As Taylor had led Anna into the living room, signing and speaking, she'd asked Anna how things were with her and her brother.

"Oh, wonderful," Anna had lied. "Thank you again for everything you did to bring us back together." She'd decided not to say anything about Stuart ripping her off and running out on her.

Taylor had introduced Anna to Dr. Tolman and then announced that she had a few errands to run. Once she'd left, Anna and Dr. Tolman had settled in the living room. The surroundings were actually perfect for a therapy session—with those calm, neutral colors and the beautiful view of the lake out the huge picture window.

"Well, Anna," Dr. Tolman said. "I need you to relax if you're going to be receptive to hypnosis. So let's talk about why you're feeling a bit out of sorts."

"'A bit out of sorts' is a nice way of putting it," Anna replied. "Actually, I'm pretty haggard. I've just spent the last few hours on the phone with my bank and my credit card companies. My brother, Stuart—you know, the one Taylor mentioned? He ran away from home sixteen years ago, back when I was a kid. I haven't seen him in all that time. Well, last night, we had a lovely reunion—thanks to Taylor. She had a private investigator track him down.

Stuart has a drug problem, but last night we talked about how to get him some help. Then I woke up this morning, and he was gone—along with the money from my purse, a couple of checks from my checkbook, and some family heirlooms."

"But when Taylor asked you about him, I heard you say everything was wonderful."

Anna nodded glumly. "Well, Taylor went to a lot of trouble to help reunite us. I didn't want her to know it all went sour. That wasn't her fault."

"But she's going to find out eventually, isn't she?"

Anna considered it. "I suppose. But right now, she can be happy that she did me this kindness. In a few days, it won't seem as though she had anything to do with him robbing me and sneaking out early in the morning. If I told her now, she might think she's somehow responsible— and she isn't."

"That's very considerate of you. Are you always so careful about other people's feelings?"

Anna shrugged. "I guess so. You make it sound like a bad thing."

Dr. Tolman smiled. "I think it's a remarkably good thing, Anna. Tell me, if Taylor isn't responsible for what happened with your brother, who is?"

"Well, I should have taken some precautions. I mean, Stu surprised me when he showed up last night. But I had some time while he was in the shower. I could have hidden the valuables and been more careful where I'd left my purse. I knew he had a crystal meth problem, and a lot of drug addicts can't help themselves. I'm sure the temptation was too much."

"Are you always this quick to take the blame?" Dr. Tolman asked. "If you can't blame your brother, then blame the drugs. But it's not your fault, Anna. You know, you're allowed to be mad at him and be disappointed in him. He left you with a hell of a mess today, didn't he?"

Anna nodded. Then she thought of Russ. She was mad at him, too, and disappointed in him. And he, too, had left her with a hell of a mess.

Without much prodding from Dr. Tolman, Anna started talking about Russ—and how much she missed him. But she also talked about how she resented him—for lying to her originally, and then for stringing her along, for never putting her first, for suggesting she make the profile piece on Courtney, and for killing himself. "Of course, I feel horribly guilty for being mad at him," Anna pointed out. "This mess I'm in—Russ and I created it together. No one forced me to stay with him. I made a bad choice and then figured out a way to rationalize it and live with it. So I'm not guiltless here."

"Said the woman who is quick to take the blame," Dr. Tolman interjected. "Don't you ever cut yourself some slack?"

Anna sighed. "You can't be involved with a married man for eighteen months without cutting yourself some slack."

Dr. Tolman stared at her intently. "You say that, Anna. But something tells me you were hard on yourself that entire time. Don't you think it's time you gave yourself a break?"

Anna couldn't respond. It was comforting to hear a stranger tell her that. She wasn't sure why, but her eyes started to well with tears. She quickly shook her head. "I told myself I wasn't going to cry," she said, her voice a little shaky. "No, not this early in the session, I promise. I won't start blubbering."

"I have some news for you. It's not early in the session. We've been talking for over a half hour."

Wiping her eyes, Anna laughed. "You mean *I've* been talking."

"And that's good," Dr. Tolman said. "But I know you have a specific reason for being here. Taylor explained to me that you'd like to remember some things you might have repressed or blacked out."

Anna nodded. "Yes, from the night Courtney Knoll disappeared. I had too much to drink at this restaurant—"

"Canlis," Dr. Tolman interjected. She smiled reassuringly. "I haven't been living under a rock for the last two weeks. I'm familiar with the case. Plus, I read up on it again last night, so you can save some time explaining. You don't remember much from the time you ordered dinner at the restaurant until you woke up the next morning. Is that correct?"

Anna let out a long sigh and nodded.

"Do you recall what you ordered for dinner? Do you remember eating your meal?"

Frowning, she shook her head. "I have a vague recollection of sitting in the backseat of the car later—with Russ driving and Courtney in the front passenger seat."

"Canlis is on Aurora Avenue, isn't it? Do you recall what route Russ took home that night?"

"No, I'm sorry."

"It's okay. That's why I'm here. Let's just work on this."

Dr. Tolman reached into her bag beside the chair. She took out a digital recorder, switched it on, and set it on the coffee table between them. "I'm going to record you while you're under hypnosis. Is that all right?"

Anna nodded nervously.

"This is like a test run, Anna. Relax. The hardest part is over. You seem comfortable with me, and I'm going to guide you through this."

She spoke in such a soothing tone, Anna wondered if the doctor was already starting to hypnotize her with her voice.

"Do me a favor, Anna, focus on your breathing, and look out at the lake."

Anna turned toward the window and gazed at the water. *Breathe in, breathe out* . . .

"See how the ripples catch the sun. Isn't that pretty? Do you like the water?"

I live on a houseboat, I ought to, Anna thought. Or had she said it out loud?

"Now, close your eyes and relax and think about the beautiful water. You're floating, just floating . . . so content, peaceful . . ."

Dr. Tolman's voice was calm and comforting. It was like being read to sleep when she was a child.

Suddenly, Anna was with her mother and Stu— only he was a teenager. They were on the deck of a big yacht. *I'm dreaming*, she realized.

Yet, she could still hear Dr. Tolman talking to her in that quietly assertive voice.

A waitress was bringing Stu, her mother, and her their dinners, balancing the three plates. But now they were in the grand dining room of some luxury liner. For a moment, the waitress seemed confused, and Anna wanted to help her. "I'm having the salmon," she said.

But the waitress shook her head. She set the plates on the table, almost dropping them. Yet the plates didn't clatter or make any noise. The waitress looked upset, and she started to talk, but no words came out of her mouth. So she spoke in sign language. She seemed angry, but Anna couldn't understand her.

"Anna, you're aware of my voice," Dr. Tolman said in her tranquil tone. "You're safe. Whatever's been bothering you, it's gone now. Notice how relaxed and comfortable you feel right now. You're in your friend Taylor's living room. And you're safe, talking with me. You're waking up. You can open your eyes now, Anna . . ."

Anna kept her eyes shut. "Are you sure? I feel like I'm just going under."

"Go ahead and open your eyes," Dr. Tolman said.

Anna was obedient. She took a deep breath and sat up.

Dr. Tolman smiled at her. "You've been out for a half hour."

"You're kidding," Anna murmured. "Did I remember anything?"

"For dinner at Canlis, you had a salad, salmon, and wild rice. But you didn't eat much of it. When the bill came and Dr. Knoll paid, you noticed—"

"It was over eight hundred dollars," Anna said, sitting up. "I felt bad he paid so much for a meal I'd hardly touched. When we drove home, he went through Fremont, then looped around and took the University Bridge to Eastlake. I started to feel sick in the car, but didn't say anything."

Dr. Tolman nodded at the recorder on the coffee table between them. "It's all in there, But you don't need to listen, because you remember now. You might find yourself remembering more bits and pieces tonight. But don't try to force it. Tomorrow, we can pick up where we left off here."

Amazed, Anna slowly shook her head. "I can't believe this. I felt like I was just starting to drift off. And what happened at the restaurant, it's all so clear to me now."

A smile came to Dr. Tolman's careworn face. "So tomorrow at the same time?"

Reaching for her purse, Anna took out her checkbook. "That's perfect. In fact, let me pay you for tomorrow, too. That's a two-thirty a session. So I'll make this out for four hundred and sixty." She started writing the check.

She'd just paid a bank fee of $150 to stop payment on the two checks Stu had stolen. So she knew her account was safe for now.

She tore the check out of her checkbook and handed it to Dr. Tolman. "You know, with my brother no longer at my place, we can have tomorrow's session there—if that works for you. There's no reason to intrude on Taylor."

"Actually, this locale is more convenient for me," Dr. Tolman said, folding the check and slipping it into her purse—along with the recorder. "It's where we've established our comfort zone. I'd like to keep meeting here if that's all right with you, I know Taylor doesn't mind."

Anna heard the apartment door open and shut. She glanced at her watch: a quarter after four. She'd gone over her session time. She got to her feet. "Well, then, same time, same place," she said. "Thank you so much, Doctor."

"Gloria," she said—as they started moving toward the front hallway together.

Anna saw Taylor was back—with a bag of groceries that she set down on the floor. "Did you have a good meeting?" Taylor asked, signing as she spoke.

"Yes, excellent," Anna said. "At least, I thought so."

"Anna was asking that we meet at her place," Dr. Tolman said, talking a bit loudly and enunciating every word. "But I'd like to keep meeting here if that's okay with you, Taylor."

"That's fine!" Taylor replied and signed. "No problem at all."

"Well, I'm off to another appointment," Dr. Tolman said. "See you both tomorrow!" She gave Taylor the sign for *thank you*—along with a little wave. Then she headed out the door.

Taylor closed the door after her. "How did it *really* go? You can tell me. Are you happy with her?"

"I talked her ear off about my feelings and then—under hypnosis—remembered some details about that night—insignificant stuff, but still, I remembered. Anyway, in answer to your question, I think she's terrific. I feel good about this. Thank you, Taylor."

Anna impulsively hugged her and then immediately regretted it because she could feel Taylor's body become rigid. Anna pulled back and worked up a smile. She realized that, despite everything Taylor had done for her, they really didn't know each other very well, and maybe it was too soon to be hugging. Also—some people just weren't the hugging kind.

"Are you sure it's not inconvenient to have the session here tomorrow?" Anna asked. "I feel funny about imposing."

"It's no imposition," Taylor replied, signing as she spoke. "By the way, I texted with one of Sally's writers while I was out. Sally's giving you a break today. She's going after the police for their handling of the case. Her special guest is Courtney's mother, live from Florida."

"That ought to be interesting," Anna said. "According to Russ, Courtney and her mother hated each other." She glanced at the door. "Well, I should get going. Thanks again, Taylor."

"See you tomorrow," Taylor said, opening the door for her.

A young man was on the other side of it.

He took them both by surprise. Anna gasped and took a step back.

Looking startled, Taylor began speaking in rapid sign language to him, silently mouthing the words.

He looked just as surprised as the two of them. With a tiny grin on his face, he talked back to her in sign language.

Anna studied him. He seemed younger than Taylor, maybe twenty-five. Tall and lean, he had messy brown hair and a slightly dorky look. Anna wondered if he was Taylor's boyfriend, which, for some silly reason, made her feel better for her. She'd imagined Taylor as single, lonely, and a bit pathetic. But from the way the two of them were communicating, it looked like they knew each other pretty well.

He nodded at Taylor and touched her arm. Then, smiling at Anna, he headed into the living room.

"That's CJ," Taylor said, leading her out to the second-floor hallway. For a change, Taylor didn't sign as she spoke. "I'm sorry I didn't introduce you. But I'm pretty sure he didn't recognize you. And I wanted to keep it that way. He hangs out at the studio sometimes, and I don't want it getting back to Sally that you were here."

Anna stopped in front of the stairwell door. "Oh, I—I thought he might be your boyfriend or something."

"CJ?" Taylor quickly shook her head. "God, no! We're just friends. To tell you the truth, sometimes, I think he likes to hang around me mostly because I'm the daughter of a celebrity. I'm not interested in him that way. But he's fun—and it beats eating out alone."

Suddenly, Anna felt sorry for her again.

"Anna, can I hug you again?" Taylor asked, signing once more. "You surprised me earlier, and I wasn't ready, and it felt awkward."

Anna let out a little laugh. "Why, sure."

She held out her arms, and Taylor hugged her. Anna patted her on the back. It felt just as awkward as before, maybe even more so.

Taylor finally pulled back and smiled. "That was much better!"

"Much," Anna lied. She wondered if Taylor was lying, too.

"See you tomorrow!" Taylor said. Then she hurried back toward her apartment.

Anna started down the stairs. She thought about that uncomfortable hug. Maybe it was her own wariness at having Sally's daughter do so much for her.

Anna felt sorry for her. But Taylor was going out of her way to help her.

So—who was the pitiful one here?

Stepping out of the building, Anna headed toward her car. As she walked in the warm afternoon sun, it occurred to her that, just minutes ago, she'd been so enthusiastic about her therapy session. She'd felt good getting things off her chest—and hopeful about remembering what she'd blacked out from the night Courtney had disappeared.

Yet, in a matter of minutes, she was feeling bad again. Or maybe she just didn't want to get her hopes up because somewhere deep inside she knew this was all going to turn out horribly.

CHAPTER TWENTY-EIGHT

Tuesday, July 21—6:44 P.M.

"I'm still hoping against hope that my baby girl—to me, she's still my baby girl—I'm hoping she's all right and I can see her again soon. I know some people think I must be crazy. But I'm not ready to give up on her, not yet. I miss her!"

Courtney's mother, Sunny Matheson, started to cry—or at least, she feigned crying. Careful not to smear her makeup, she kept touching her cheeks to dab away tears that weren't there. Sunny was in her late fifties with a buxom figure and big, jet-black hair that must have been a wig. She looked as if she might have been pretty at one time, but her tan skin was sun-wrinkled and she wore too much makeup.

She was on the air, live, in a split-screen conversation with Sally on *The Sally Justice Show*. Sunny had on a pink dress for the interview. She was on a patio somewhere in Saint Petersburg, Florida. There were palm trees and a canal in the background.

Sally wasn't happy with her as a guest. Fifteen minutes before the show started, Sally had glimpsed the feed of the crew setting up the interview. Ensconced on the lawn chair, Courtney's mother had been smoking a cigarette while they'd adjusted her mic. She'd been complaining to Sally's production person about the fact that her daughter's attorneys wouldn't give her a straight answer about Courtney's will. "I mean, this is crazy," Sunny had grumbled before they went on the air. "Neither one of them have been declared dead yet. Meanwhile, where's the money going? Courtney had a one-million-dollar movie deal, and those goddamn lawyers won't tell me a thing. If he killed her—and it certainly looks that way—then he shouldn't have gotten a goddamn nickel of her money, right? But the lawyers won't say. I deserve to know. I'm her mother, her only living relation."

Sunny wasn't the type of grieving mother Sally had wanted for the show. She was no sweet, gray-haired old mom with the apple pie cooling on the windowsill. She came across as a floozy—and a big phony.

"Courtney had an older sister, Cassie," Sunny said for the TV audience. She dabbed at some more invisible tears. "And Cassie died of a drug overdose several years back. She was still just a teenager when she was taken from me. And now, Courtney, my baby, my special baby, who had such a tough time growing up deaf, she's been taken from me, too. A mother shouldn't outlive her children, y'know? It's just not right."

Putting on a pained look, Sally nodded for the camera. She had to give Courtney's mother snaps for that. It was pretty effective.

At the start of the interview, they'd already touched upon the fact that Dr. Russell Knoll was a handsome, too-good-to-be-true snake—and a terrible husband to the long-suffering Courtney. Sally still had a couple of questions, but decided to quit while they were ahead.

"From the bottom of my heart," she said in a quiet, reverent tone, "I'm so sorry for your loss. And I want to thank you, Sunny, for being our guest on tonight's show."

Courtney's mother nodded and brushed away another nonexistent tear.

Sally turned to the other camera for a medium shot showing her at her desk. "Just think about it, people, if the police had acted more quickly, arresting Dr. Russell Knoll and throwing him in jail, he'd be alive today—and perhaps we'd have some answers as to what happened to Sunny Matheson's special baby girl. A grieving mother's questions might be answered. Do you think the police botched this case? When we come back from the break, we'll hear from some of you viewers at home. It's right here on *The Sally Justice Show*. Stick around!"

In her earpiece, Sally heard them cue up the theme music for the break. Then the light on the camera switched from green to red, and Sally sat back. She glanced at the monitor and decided she looked all right. Then she eyed the production people in the booth to her right. "Gail, you better have some good callers. I'm dying here!"

From the booth, her producer gave her the thumbs-up sign.

Sally felt off her game. The show had been mediocre so far. Of course, it was no help that, last night, Anna Malone's brother had announced for several news services that he'd been paid to lie about his sister on *The Sally Justice Show*. The advice from execs at 24/7 News was that Sally not address this new development at all—especially if it was true. Sally's writers agreed, the rationale being, some people didn't know about Stuart Malone's statement. So why bring it to everyone's attention?

The overnight ratings for Monday's show weren't so hot. People must have started to lose interest in the Courtney Knoll case over the weekend. Unless something new and exciting happened, Sally would have to move on to another topic for tomorrow's show. The writers were advocating coverage of a dispute that grew violent between two women vying for a parking spot at a Walmart store in Omaha. They already had both women on standby for tomorrow's show.

"Sally?" One of her producers spoke in her earpiece. It was Gail in the control booth. "'*Sometimes you feel like a nut, sometimes you don't.*' We got one on line three. Are you up for it? I figure the show could use a boost tonight."

Sally was known for the way she handled crazy, disgruntled callers on her show. Sometimes she and her producers deliberately gave airtime to a nutjob calling in—just to shake things up. Sally was so sarcastic and unflappable that these exchanges often became newsworthy and went viral online. In fact, there were three different ten-minute video compilations of *Sally's Wackiest Calls* on YouTube, and each one had over six million hits.

Sally took a deep breath and braced herself. "Sure, why not?"

"It's Bud from Seattle. We'll do the five-second delay to please the censors—in case Bud's a potty mouth."

"You fucking well better," Sally joked. "Put him on first."

She heard another voice in her earpiece: "And we're back in five . . . four . . ."

Sally straightened up in her chair and watched the camera light turn green. "Welcome back!" she announced. "If you've just joined us, we're asking you, the viewers, what you think of the police investigation into Courtney Knoll's disappearance. It's been eleven days since the beautiful, deaf, bestselling author went missing—and a week since her suspect-husband's apparent suicide. And the police still haven't found either one of their bodies. What kind of performance rating would you give the police investigators here? We have Bud from Seattle on line three. Bud, what's your opinion?"

In response there was a long, asthmatic sigh.

"Go ahead, Bud, don't be shy," Sally said.

"I . . . saw . . . her . . . get . . . killed," he said in a raspy voice.

His creepy, teasing manner sent chills up Sally's spine.

It took her a second to recover. "You did, did you?" she asked. "Why didn't you report it to the police? As we now know, they certainly could have used the help."

"I . . . know . . . who . . . did . . . it."

"Well, Bud, don't keep us in suspense." Sally waited a beat for a reply. Then she continued—with a little smirk for the camera: "Was it Professor Plum with the candlestick in the conservatory?"

"Courtney Knoll was killed in her living room at twelve-fifty on Friday morning," the raspy-voiced caller said. The slow, teasing, singsong tone was gone. "I looked at my watch when she went down."

"You say you saw this?" Sally asked, still dubious. "And where were you at the time, Bud?"

"In a boat, not far from her home on Lake Union."

"Just what were you doing there at that particular time, Bud? Fishing?"

"I was watching her." He let out another sigh, which sounded more like a croak. "I . . . like . . . to . . . watch . . . deaf . . . girls."

Unnerved, Sally tried to keep a neutral expression on her face for the camera. The guy was obviously sick, but she wasn't going to let him get the upper hand while they were on the air. "Really?" she asked. "Why—why deaf women?"

"They . . . can't . . . hear . . . me . . . when . . . I'm . . . getting . . . close."

Sally thought of Taylor. Her finger hovered over the end call button. "Y'know, Bud, I don't think I want to listen to any more of this."

"Shut up and listen for a second. The three of them came back from the restaurant at a quarter after ten. Courtney was wearing a brown dress."

"How did you know that?" Sally asked.

She remembered those two women who had been dining at Canlis the night Courtney and her husband were there with Anna Malone. In the pre-interview, the woman with the mustache had mentioned that Courtney had been wearing a brown, sleeveless dress.

He didn't say anything on the other end. For a panic-stricken moment, Sally thought he'd hung up. "How do you know what Courtney was wearing?" she pressed.

"I . . . told . . . you," he said, using that mocking tone again. "I . . . saw . . . them."

"Were you at the restaurant?" Sally asked. "Is that how you know?"

"I was watching the house. Aren't . . . you . . . listening? I've been watching her and her husband for a long time. I probably knew before anyone else about him and the newslady. I've watched them, too. That night, Courtney's husband had on a black suit, but no tie. Anna Malone wore a red dress. The . . . lady . . . in . . . red. She weaved a little when she walked into their living room. I could see she was drunk."

My God, this guy's for real, Sally thought.

"So you were there that night?" she asked. "And you saw Courtney get killed? I'll ask you again, why didn't you call the police?"

"Because . . . I've . . . been . . . bad," he replied. "They'd want to know why I was watching the house."

"How can we be sure that you weren't just one of a hundred or so people at the restaurant that night? Or maybe you saw them in the restaurant parking lot."

"Courtney changed into this floor-length purple robe thing when she got home."

"You could just be making that up. No one would know."

"Anna Malone was there. She'd know. Anna Malone knows who killed her, too."

"Anna Malone conveniently can't remember anything from that night," Sally said. "How do we know you're telling the truth about what you saw?"

"When they find Courtney's body—and they will eventually—she'll be wearing that purple robe."

There was a click on the other end of the line.

CHAPTER TWENTY-NINE

Wednesday, July 22—3:29 P.M.

"**Y**ou're floating in the beautiful, cool water. See the ripples catching the sun, Anna? You have no worries. Just relax . . ."

Anna listened to Gloria Tolman's soothing voice. She kept taking controlled breaths in through her nose, holding, and then slowly breathing out through her mouth. She visualized the damn water and those stupid sun-kissed ripples. But it simply wasn't working today.

She opened her eyes and stared at Dr. Tolman. "I'm sorry, Gloria, I'm trying."

"That's just the trouble, Anna. You're trying too hard."

They were sitting in the same spots they'd sat in yesterday; Dr. Tolman in the easy chair; Anna on the sofa. Taylor had stepped out a half hour ago. Outside Taylor's living room picture window, Lake Washington looked beautifully serene.

But Anna couldn't put herself in a tranquil state.

"Too much is riding on this," she said. "How can I relax when it's absolutely essential that I get hypnotized and remember things today? Yesterday was just a test run. I wasn't under any pressure then. I'm sorry, but the sound of your voice and the visualization and the breathing— it's just not doing the job right now. Do you have any other methods we could try? Maybe a pocket watch you can dangle in front of me?"

Frowning, Dr. Tolman crossed her arms and shook her head. "Anna, you're just not receptive today. It happens sometimes. You can't force these things."

But Anna was desperate. Suddenly, it was imperative that she remember whether or not Courtney had put on a purple robe the night she'd disappeared.

The caller identified as "Bud" on *The Sally Justice Show* had dropped a bombshell.

It was covered on last night's late-evening news and all the network morning news shows. The call had been traced to a burner phone in the Seattle area. Everyone wanted to know if Bud was a crank caller, a credible witness, or perhaps Courtney's killer.

Sally had been the first one to speculate about her raspy-voiced caller—just moments after hanging up with him. "Well, people, Bud has admitted that he's obsessed with deaf women," she'd told her viewers. "And this immediately makes me wonder if he murdered Courtney Knoll. The police still haven't found a body. Is it possible that Bud murdered Courtney—and then kept her body as a trophy? That's one rather morbid speculation—probably because I've seen too many grisly murder cases. But if it's really what happened, why did Courtney's husband kill himself and defend his lover, Anna Malone, in his suicide note? I wouldn't be too quick to dismiss those two as our prime suspects. As distasteful as it was talking with him, I invite Bud to call me back tomorrow and tell us exactly what he saw at Courtney's floating home on the night of July ninth."

Detective Baumann had dropped in on Anna last night. She'd asked if she recalled Courtney donning a purple robe. According to Bud, Anna had been there when Courtney had changed out of her brown sleeveless dress. Anna had admitted to Baumann that she didn't remember. She'd told the detective about her plans to see a hypnotist the next day to help her recollect more clearly the events from that night.

Anna hadn't said anything to Baumann about Bud calling her several times in the past two weeks. His bizarre claim that she'd murdered Courtney still unnerved her. He'd been right about her and Russ *"fucking."* And he'd made that statement before anyone else had known. Maybe he was right about Russ *"taking the rap"* for her, too.

It had been a week since Bud had called her.

Now he was phoning in to *The Sally Justice Show*, live, on the air. Anna imagined him tonight, telling Sally and her audience that he'd seen *that bitch, Anna Malone*, murder Courtney.

It would be her word against that of a stalker. Nevertheless, Sally would be thrilled to have him in her corner.

Ironically, it was up to Anna to confirm the detail about the purple robe in order for anyone to take Bud seriously.

Anna couldn't help recalling Russ's warning the night after Courtney had vanished—that *I don't remember* wouldn't cut it with the police or the public. He'd been right. She couldn't keep saying that, not without people thinking she had something to hide.

With a sigh, Dr. Tolman collected her digital recorder and stashed it in her purse. "Why don't we cut our losses here and call it quits for the day?" She glanced at her wristwatch. "We'll meet same time tomorrow, and then you can pay me for half a session to make up for the early quit today."

Reluctantly, Anna nodded and got to her feet. "Thanks. I think that's a good idea."

Dr. Tolman stood up, too. "If you have any Valium, bring it tomorrow. It might take some of the edge off."

"I don't have any," Anna said, following her to Taylor's door.

"Well, I can't write you a prescription. But tell you what. Go to Bartell or Rite Aid and get yourself an over-the-counter stress supplement, something with L-theanine. It's not Valium, but it'll relax you a bit and help take your mind off things." She unlocked and opened the door, but then hesitated. "Oh, I just realized. Should one of us wait for Taylor to get back?"

Anna checked her watch. The session was supposed to go on for another twenty-five minutes. "I can wait here," she volunteered. "I don't have anything going on."

Once Dr. Tolman left, Anna returned to the living room and sat down. She took her phone out of her purse and switched it back on. She'd turned it off earlier for the session. She had seventeen new e-mails, five new texts, and two missed calls.

Bud had put the spotlight back on her. The news vans and reporters had returned to the narrow little access road to her dock this morning. The requests for interviews were pouring in. E-mails from former fans and strangers had become more supportive. The tide had changed after

Russ's suicide. Now that her lover was dead, people were ready to forgive her.

One of the missed calls was from George. Anna played it: "Hey, I can't remember what time you're getting your head shrunk. But good luck with the hypnosis. I hope you're able to recollect a lot of things. God, that guy sounded creepy on *The Sally Justice Show* last night. Nothing is new here. I hate working with these other reporters. They don't get my sense of humor. I moved some stuff into my new apartment. When things get back to normal for you, I'd love for you to come over and see it. Anyway, nothing else is new. I miss you. I'm babbling. Talk to you later."

Hearing his voice made Anna feel better—like things might really return to normal again.

She was about to call him back when she heard a key in Taylor's door. She checked the time on her phone: 3:53 p.m. Taylor was early.

Getting to her feet, Anna headed toward the door. "Taylor? Is that you?"

Then it hit her: *She can't hear you, stupid.*

Anna saw the door open, and she stopped dead.

Sally Justice paused in the doorway. She looked exactly like she did on TV. The makeup and ash-blond hair were perfect. She wore beige slacks and a black tunic. She didn't look surprised to see Anna there in her daughter's living room. She had that unflappable *Sally Justice* look. "Well, I heard you were here," Sally said, closing the door behind her. "But I had to come see for myself. Where's my daughter?"

"Taylor stepped out. She should be back soon." Anna stood there between the living room and the front hallway.

She folded her arms in front of her. For the last ten days, she'd thought of so many things she wanted to say to Sally Justice. But right now, she was at a loss for words.

Slowly shaking her head, Sally glared at her. "I don't know what you're up to, but I won't allow you to associate with Taylor in any way, shape, or form."

"Your daughter invited me here. And she's over twenty-one. She can do what she wants. And don't use that tone with me, Sally."

"Oh, really?" Sally asked haughtily.

"Yes, really," Anna whispered, glaring back at her.

After so many nights of Sally's on-air abuse, Anna could barely contain her rage. And she was convinced Sally's campaign against her and Russ had contributed to his suicide. Hell, Sally may as well have pushed him off the Tacoma Narrows Bridge. Now, here she was, in person, giving her this self-righteous look. More than anything right now, Anna wanted to slap that nasty old woman across her perfectly made-up face. She wanted to hurt her.

"You don't want to piss me off," Sally said calmly. "You think I've made things tough for you recently? I have a whole staff of people who work for me. I can delegate—and destroy you—with just a couple of phone calls. You're out of your league here, Anna. I've been a network star for over a dozen years. And you're just a second-rate local TV newswoman—a nobody."

Furious, Anna started shaking. "Don't push me, because it's all I can do to keep from punching in your Botoxed face. You can add assault and battery to the list of crimes you've accused me of on your putrid TV show. At this point, I have nothing to lose. I'm serious, Sally.

You're on the air in two and a half hours, and you'll have a tough time explaining a black eye to your viewers."

"All right, let's put our differences aside for just a minute," Sally said. "This is *my daughter* we're talking about."

"Said the woman who told malicious lies on the air about my dead mother, the same woman whose people paid my poor brother to lie about me." Anna shook her head. "Don't give me this shit about the sanctity of family, Sally, because it won't wash "

Anna fell silent at the sound of a key in the lock.

Sally stepped aside as the door opened.

A visibly stunned Taylor almost balked in the doorway. Then, after a second, she merely looked annoyed. She stepped in, closed the door, and set down her shopping bag. "Mother, what are you doing here?" she asked—and signed.

"I'm looking out for you," Sally shot back. "And obviously, you need looking after, *dear*." She pointed at Anna. "What's *she* doing here?"

"She's my friend. I invited her here. And I didn't invite you, Mother. Now, this is my place—"

"Which I paid for!" Sally yelled, signing clumsily. Then she seemed to lose her patience, because she stopped signing and kept talking. "That gives me the right to be here—that, and the fact that I'm your mother, and you've obviously lost your mind. This woman is not your friend, Taylor. She can't be trusted. When I heard she was here—"

"Who told you that Anna was here? Do you have people spying on me or something?"

Sally let out an exasperated sigh. "When that creep

called the show last night and he said he liked to follow deaf girls around, I got worried. So I asked one of my private investigators to watch your place. It's Jim Larson, you know him. He's just watching the place. That's all. I was concerned." She scowled at Anna for a moment. "Well, about an hour ago, he called me to say that *Anna Malone* had just gone into the building, and maybe I might be interested. I'd just as soon that Bud character was paying you a visit. You know how I feel about her. How can you betray me like this?"

"I already told you," Taylor said, signing. "I think what you're doing to Anna is unfair and vicious. She doesn't deserve it. You're just being vindictive—all because, a few years ago, she showed how you drove that innocent man in Spokane to commit suicide. And what happens? You did the exact same thing again with Dr. Knoll! How many lives will you destroy for the sake of your TV ratings?"

"Are you delusional, dear?" Sally asked, hands on hips. "You don't actually believe Courtney's husband was innocent, do you?" She nodded toward Anna. "And you think this one's your friend? Well, she was supposedly friends with Courtney, too—and with that Beebe woman I interviewed the other day. She's using you, honey. Mark my words. You want to hear something funny? This one . . ." She pointed to Anna again. "Just before you walked in, this one was talking to me about *family*. Isn't that a laugh? I don't need a lecture about *the sanctity of family* from a homewrecker."

Anna had enough. "Sally, you're so full of shit—"

"You're one to talk, Mother!" Taylor interrupted. "You think I don't know about all the affairs you've had, all the men you've slept with? And most of them were married— with families."

"Maybe, but none of them were *murderers*," Sally said. "And don't for a minute think your friend here wasn't somehow involved in killing that poor woman."

"That's a lie," Anna said. "Dr. Knoll didn't murder his wife. And I think you know it, too, Sally, just like you know I had nothing to do with whatever happened to Courtney. It's just what Taylor said. It's all about the fact that I made you take a good hard look at yourself a couple of years ago, and you blame me for what you saw."

Sally interrupted: "I didn't make that man blow his head off—"

"You're such a hypocrite, Sally," Anna cut in, talking over her. "You invite some creep who stalks deaf women to come back on your show—just to boost your ratings. Meanwhile, that just fuels his sense of self-importance. You're empowering him. And he's probably a murderer. He probably killed Courtney. But that's not your problem, right? After all, you can send a guard over to your daughter's apartment to watch over her. Well, what about all the other deaf girls out there, Sally? Who's going to guard them?"

Sally was still trying to get a word in when Taylor suddenly screeched: "Shut up!"

Both Anna and Sally stopped talking.

Taylor had tears in her eyes. "I don't know what either one of you are saying. I can't follow."

Anna took a deep breath and then touched Taylor's arm. "I'll go. I'm sorry, Taylor."

Pinching the bridge of her nose, Taylor nodded. "I'll

walk you out," she signed as she spoke. Then she opened the door for Anna.

Without giving Sally another glance, Anna headed out to the corridor. Taylor trailed after her and shut the door. "I'm so sorry, Anna," she said.

"No, I'm sorry," Anna whispered. "It was wrong of me to talk to your mother like that in front of you."

Taylor let out a little laugh. "It's okay," she said as they stopped in front of the stairway door. "I only caught about half of it. But the half I caught, I totally agreed with. I didn't get a chance to ask you. How did the session go? Did Gloria leave early?"

"We couldn't get liftoff. I was too wound up, and she couldn't put me in a hypnotic state. She said it happens sometimes. We're giving it another go tomorrow—if that's all right with you."

Taylor nodded. "It's fine. I'll try to get my mother to call off her spy. There's a back entrance you could use, too—just in case. I'll text you tomorrow."

"Thanks," Anna said.

Taylor hugged her. Again, it was slightly awkward.

Anna pushed open the door and started down the stairs. She thought about how nothing had been accomplished during this session.

All she'd done was piss off Sally Justice even more.

CHAPTER THIRTY

Wednesday, July 22—4:49 P.M.
Lake Bosworth, Washington

"I'm hot," Erin Donnelly announced, fanning her pretty, tanned, freckled face. "Aren't you guys hot?"

"I'm *totally* hot," replied Greg Zeigler, strolling alongside her on the sandy strip at the lake's edge. "I'm hot with two *t*'s."

Erin giggled and bumped her shoulder against his.

Walking behind the two of them, Rory Niefeld said nothing. He was tempted to shove Erin into the water. Maybe that would cool her off and shut her up.

The three of them were starting their sophomore year at Granite Falls High School in the fall. Erin was one of the most popular girls in their class. Rory thought she was pretty stuck-up. She'd always treated him like he was a disease.

Rory bagged groceries at the Granite Falls IGA. It was a great summer job. He got out at three in the afternoon on Wednesdays and Thursdays. His best friend, Greg, had called this morning and asked if he wanted to go to

Lake Bosworth when he got off work. Greg had found a little skiff in some woods by the lake earlier in the week, and maybe they could find it again and take it out on the water. Obviously, it hadn't occurred to Greg that the skiff—along with that stretch of land off the lake—was probably someone's private property.

For Rory, being Greg's pal was kind of like being friends with Ferris Bueller in that old movie. Greg was cool with a fun sense of adventure, but he could also be a selfish asshole at times. He got away with a lot, and Rory often felt like Ferris's friend Cameron, who was, rightfully, forever worried about getting in trouble.

The risk factor of this proposed adventure on the lake had seemed low compared to most of Greg's schemes, so Rory agreed to meet his friend after work. Greg's older brother had a cricket set, and Greg said he'd bring along a couple of cricket bats they could use as paddles if the little boat took to the water.

Greg had been held back a year in sixth grade. So he was a year older and already had his driver's license. When Greg had come by the IGA at three, Erin had been in the store. Greg had talked her into coming along with them this afternoon.

And that was how Rory had become the third wheel in this excursion. Actually, he was more like the fourth wheel—if he counted Erin's phone as another member of their party. She'd been texting practically nonstop since getting into Greg's mother's Toyota Highlander two hours ago.

For the past forty-five minutes, while they'd hunted for the boat, she'd complained about her cell reception in the woods. They'd never been able to find the skiff, further proof—as far as Rory was concerned—that the skiff, the woods, and that section of the lakefront were probably someone's private property.

Now the three of them were walking along the water. No one else was around. Somehow, Rory had gotten saddled with Greg's brother's cricket bats while Greg and Erin whispered, flirted, and giggled together a few paces in front of him. The two of them had on shorts and T-shirts, while Rory was in his work clothes: a white short-sleeve shirt and long black pants.

"Let's go swimming!" Greg suggested.

Still mostly focused on her phone, Erin bumped into him again. "That would be great if I'd brought along my swimsuit."

"There's nobody else around. And I'm not shy."

Oh shit, we're not going there, Rory thought, stopping in his tracks.

Erin stopped, too. "Are you trying to get me to swim naked? God, what a perv!"

"Hey, it's no big deal. Rory and I have swum here without suits. No one will see us."

Rory remembered. It had been a couple of years ago when they were in eighth grade. While it had been a fun, crazy, impulsive thing to do, the whole time, two things had weighed heavily on Rory's mind: that Greg already had pubic hair and he didn't, and that they'd get caught.

"No way!" Erin screamed. "You're not getting me naked. God, you really are a perv!"

But Greg pulled his T-shirt over his head. "Okay, so we swim in our underwear. C'mon, Rory."

If Erin hadn't been with them, he probably wouldn't have hesitated. He was hot and sweaty, and after a long day at work, he could have used a refreshing dip. Hell, they could have swum naked. He wasn't shy around his friend. But he didn't want to peel down to his underpants in front of Erin—and her phone.

Greg kicked off his sneakers and pulled down his shorts. Tan and trim, he wore gray briefs with a black elastic band. He probably didn't care if Erin took his picture or got him on video. Hell, he probably *wanted* her to take his picture or get him on video.

Meanwhile, Rory was pale and out of shape from working at the supermarket all summer. He wore white Jockey briefs under his long pants. Once he got in the water, the briefs would be transparent, and he was bound to have penile shrinkage. He could just hear Erin talking to her friends: *And it was like he had a peanut in his underpants.*

With a howl, Greg ran into the water and totally submerged himself. Amid a lot of splashing, he popped back up from beneath the lake's surface and let out another yell. "C'mon, you guys! The water's fucking fantastic!"

Erin captured the whole show on her phone's camera. After a minute or two, she kicked off her sandals and swiveled around to glare at Rory. "Don't look!" she commanded. Then she giggled and called out to Greg, more playfully: "Don't look! I'm serious."

Screw you, I'm looking, Rory thought.

She turned her back to the two of them and pulled her T-shirt up over her head. Her long brown hair fell back down over her shoulders. She was tan and slim—with no visible blemishes on her beautiful body. She wore a white bra. She carefully wrapped her T-shirt around her precious phone and set it down by a piece of driftwood.

Greg let go with another hoot as she stepped out of her shorts. She wore dark blue panties that showed off the top of her butt crack. With her arms crossed in front of her, she started into the lake and squealed: "Shit, it's cold!"

Greg splashed her, and she squealed again. Within a couple of minutes, the two of them were frolicking in the water. "C'mon, Rory!" Greg yelled. "What are you waiting for?"

He put down Greg's brother's cricket bats. They clattered as they hit the sand. He figured as long as Erin wasn't taking any photos of him, he was safe. He just had to remember to get out of the water and get dressed before she got to her phone again.

But as he unbuttoned his shirt, Rory had a weird premonition. Something was going to happen. He wasn't sure what it was. But this would end up badly. And it wasn't going to be one of those things he could laugh about later.

Then Erin called to him: "C'mon, Rory! Don't be a party pooper!"

He hastily took off his shoes, socks, and long black trousers. Then he ran into the water before she could get a good look at his pale, skinny body and his unsexy underwear. The cold lake was a shock at first, but Rory quickly got used to it. Greg and Erin kept splashing him, and he splashed them back.

After a while, they began to ignore him. Treading in deeper water, they whispered to each other and giggled. At one point, Rory felt his foot brush against something solid but spongy at the bottom of the lake. He panicked for a moment and swam away. He didn't want to think about what it might have been.

"Hey, Rory!" Greg called. "C'mon, I dare ya."

He turned to see his friend, in deeper water. His arm was up, and he held his wet, dripping underpants. The lake was clear enough that Rory could tell his friend was naked.

Erin was closer to him and seemed to appreciate the view. She kept giggling.

"Erin's not going to take off anything until you do!" Greg said. Then he spit some lake water out of his mouth. "You gotta do it, man! Take 'em off!"

"No way!" Rory declared.

"Don't be a chickenshit!"

"I won't look!" Erin promised. "I can't see anything from this far anyway."

Rory thought it over. He drifted toward shallower water. "You have two things to take off," he said to Erin. "You take off one thing, and I'll take off my underpants. Then you have to get totally naked, too."

Still waving around his soggy underpants, Greg gave a wolf whistle.

Rory figured his tactic was pretty brilliant, because she probably wasn't going to lose her bra or panties.

Erin started to swim away from both of them. Then she stopped and reached back for the clasp on the back of her bra.

Greg drifted closer to Rory. "Shit, I think she's going to do it, man," he whispered.

But Erin was so far away, they really couldn't see

anything. Plus she ducked into the water so that it was up to her neck. She seemed to wiggle under the surface, and after a moment, she raised her white bra in the air.

Greg let out a rousing cheer.

Rory figured if he couldn't see her, she couldn't see him. So he reached down and peeled off his briefs. He didn't want anyone calling him a chickenshit or a party pooper. He raised his arm out of the water, the underpants in his grasp.

Erin let out another scream.

All of a sudden, Greg lunged toward him. Rory didn't know what his friend was doing until Greg snatched his underpants out of his hand. Then Greg dove under the surface and started swimming away—toward the shore.

Stunned, Rory caught a glimpse of Erin putting her bra back on.

"Son of a bitch!" he yelled. Dog-paddling furiously, he started after his friend. But Greg was a better swimmer. He was already standing naked in shallow water, stepping into his wet gray underpants.

Rory struggled to catch up. He hit the shallower water just as Greg reached the shore. Laughing, his friend started to collect their clothes.

Emerging from the lake in her bra and panties, Erin ran along the sand to meet up with Greg. Rory realized the water was up to his waist now, and he couldn't come in any farther without exposing himself. "Goddamn it, you guys!" he bellowed, out of breath. "This isn't funny!"

But the two of them were howling with laughter as they quickly threw on their clothes.

Helpless, Rory covered his shrunken privates and

started out of the water. But then he saw Erin brushing the sand off her phone. He took a few steps back until the water came up to his waist again. "Okay, you guys, ha-ha, big joke, let's humiliate Rory!"

All he could think about was that half the school would see this on Instagram.

He was cold and shivering and filled with an awful sense of dread. If he wasn't so pissed off at Greg, he'd start to cry. This was so typical. His friend was trying to show off for this stupid girl. During the drive down from Granite Falls, Greg had sped most of the way—just to impress her. And now he was acting like an asshole because she'd think he was cool.

He watched Greg collect his work pants, shirt, socks, and shoes. Erin grabbed the cricket bats.

Waist-deep in the water, Rory stood there, freezing. He didn't say anything because it looked like Erin was recording his reaction, and he didn't want to give her the satisfaction. Still, he couldn't breathe right. If this was what a panic attack felt like, he was having one.

Greg took hold of Erin's arm and pulled her toward the woods. Rory saw them scurrying into the bushes and trees. Then they were gone—along with his clothes.

Rory's throat tightened up, and tears stung in his eyes. But he couldn't cry—and he couldn't move. Erin was probably hiding beyond the first cluster of trees, zooming in on him with her phone camera.

"You guys?" he called in a shaky voice. "Greg? Greg, please be careful with my pants, okay? My wallet's in there. It might fall out of the pocket. I don't want to lose it." He couldn't talk anymore, not without sobbing.

Rory imagined them making their way through the woods to where Greg had parked his mom's car and then taking off without him. It was over four miles back to Granite Falls. He shuddered and rubbed his wet, cold arms. "Hey, you guys?" he called. "Could you please, please, please give me a break here? I'm cold!"

He didn't hear a response—not even Erin's giggling. "Are you even there?" he cried.

Rory swallowed hard. He figured, if he ran out of the water, he could keep his hands in front of his private parts until he reached the trees. Then, once in the woods, he could snap off a tree branch and use that to cover himself.

Taking a deep, fortifying breath, he charged toward the shore with his hands clasped in front of himself. He ran naked across the sand and rocks until he reached the trees. Catching his breath, he tried to listen for Greg and Erin. He'd figured his nude sprint would have elicited a round of hoots and laughter. But he didn't hear anything.

Grabbing a leafy branch from a shrub, he snapped it off and used it to cover himself.

Suddenly, the woods turned dark. A cloud must have moved in front of the sun. Rory shivered, and his teeth started to chatter. Beneath his bare feet, the ground was cold, damp, and rough with twigs and rocks. He had an awful feeling that he was all alone in these woods. He couldn't even find a trail.

But then he saw a small patch of white—not too far away. It looked like a rag or something, draped over a shrub. As Rory got closer to it, he realized Greg had left his underpants there for him. Maybe his friend wasn't such an asshole after all.

Grabbing the briefs, Rory shook them out and then stepped into them. His muddy feet got the underpants dirty, but he didn't care.

"All right!" he yelled, straightening up. "I'm no longer naked! The joke's over! I'm cold, and I could really use the rest of my clothes, guys!"

No answer. But then he heard a twig snap somewhere nearby.

"Guys?" he called tentatively.

Rory continued deeper into the woods. He followed a rough path, winding around the bushes and trees. He stumbled across a small bald spot, where some black material caught his eye. It was bunched up by a mound of earth. Were those his work pants? It looked like Greg must have dragged them through the dirt and left them in a pile by that mound.

As Rory stepped closer, it looked to him like his pants were half-buried in the dirt. "Son of a bitch!" he grumbled. He reached for the material to give it a good tug.

He didn't realize until he'd already yanked at the black material that it was plastic. It felt like an old trash bag. It ripped apart in his grasp, and Rory fell back on his butt.

It knocked the wind out of him. He couldn't focus for a minute. When his vision righted itself, he saw that he'd pulled up something from that mound of dirt—something wrapped in a black plastic trash bag.

He stared at a woman's arm—sticking out from the crude grave. Her hand was gray, swollen, and decomposing. Ants were feasting on it. They crawled back and forth from her bloated fingertips—up into the purple sleeve of her garment.

Rory screamed and screamed.

And he prayed to God his friends would hear him and know the joke was over.

CHAPTER THIRTY-ONE

Wednesday, July 22—9:38 P.M.
Seattle

Anna stood in the shower, washing off the abysmal day. She'd had such high hopes for her second hypnotherapy session with Gloria Tolman this afternoon. She'd thought she would finally have some clarity about that night nearly two weeks ago. Instead, today's meeting with the doctor had been a bust, a huge disappointment. And it had been followed by that nasty confrontation with Sally. Since then, all Anna could think about were the things she *should have* said, potent zingers that would have left Sally speechless and full of self-loathing regret. Anything would have been better than: *"You'll have a tough time explaining a black eye to your viewers."* Did she really say that? Did she really threaten her with physical violence? How stupid was that?

Anna had gotten a small break on today's *Sally Justice Show*. She'd tuned in at six-thirty, expecting the worst. She'd figured Bud would phone in again, describing in his raspy voice how he'd seen her murder Courtney. She imagined him talking in that same menacing, singsong tone he'd used with her.

Sally had expected to hear from Bud, too. She'd devoted most of the show analyzing his call from yesterday's show, playing it over and over. Of course, she'd mentioned how Anna's "convenient memory loss" had made it impossible to confirm or deny Bud's statements. "What's she hiding?" Sally had asked her TV audience. "Maybe this man calling himself Bud will tell us if he calls in later."

But Sally had obviously counted on a phone call that never came. And she hadn't looked too happy about it. She'd ended up having her viewers vote on whether or not Bud was merely a crank caller or someone they should take seriously— as a witness or even a potential suspect.

Anna felt as if she'd gotten a stay of execution. She was all right for now, but there was always a chance that Bud would phone the show tomorrow with a detailed account of how she'd murdered Courtney Knoll.

For now, the shower seemed to wash away all the dirt and anxiety of her day. Eyes closed, she tilted her head back so that the warm water sprayed into her face and cascaded down her body. She remembered some of the showers she'd taken with Russ in this stall: soaping each other with expensive lavender body wash, or just standing there under the warm spray, holding each other.

But thinking about those shower sessions right now was too painful. Anna shut off the water, and the pipes let out a squeak. She grabbed a towel and started to dry herself off.

Her cell phone rang. She'd been keeping it within

reach for the last two weeks. It was on the sink counter now.

Wrapping the towel around her, Anna grabbed the phone and checked the caller ID: *Det. K. Baumann*.

She felt a little jolt in her gut. Her first thought was: *They've found his body*.

Lowering the toilet lid, she sat down and tapped her phone screen. "Hello?"

"Hi, Anna. Detective Baumann here."

Anna nodded, but said nothing.

"Are you there?" the detective asked. "I have some news."

"Yes, I'm sorry. Go ahead." She was still slightly wet and had started to shiver.

"Courtney's body was found this afternoon."

Stunned, Anna was speechless. Some small part of her had still clung to the idea that Courtney had orchestrated the whole disappearing act. But now, she knew. *Courtney's really dead.*

"They're flying her mother up from Florida to identify the body," Baumann explained. "But that's just a formality. They're certain it's her."

"Where?" Anna heard herself ask. "Where did they find her?"

"Lake Bosworth, it's near Granite Falls."

"I know it," she murmured. She'd done a story at Lake Bosworth last year—about an elderly couple who had gotten engaged by the lake and celebrated their sixty-fifth anniversary there. Lake Bosworth was about forty-five miles northeast of Seattle.

"Some kids found her, half-buried in the woods by the

lake," Baumann said. "The cause of death seems to be blunt-force trauma to the head."

"Was she—wearing a purple robe?"

"Yeah, that Bud creep from *The Sally Justice Show* was right about that. We wanted to keep it from the press and the general public. But the three kids who found the body are teenagers, and we figured keeping that detail under wraps was a lost cause."

"So the police are going to take this Bud person seriously now," Anna said glumly.

"At this point, we'd be fools to ignore him. We'd hoped to trace the call if Bud phoned Sally Justice tonight, at least try to pinpoint his location if he was using a burner phone again. But he didn't call. He's a major suspect, but he's also giving us details that are helpful to the investigation. Anyway, Anna, yesterday you mentioned you were going to a hypnotist to help you recall things about the night Courtney disappeared. Did you have any luck?"

"No," she hated to admit. "I'm sorry."

"Well, listen, I was hoping you could describe for me again the writing award Courtney had on display in her living room, the one that's missing. I haven't had much luck looking it up on Google. I've been searching for *glass quill award* and coming up with nothing. I thought you might remember."

Anna pushed her wet hair out of her face. "It's the— the Northwest Literary Society's Best Fiction Debut Award," she said. It was mentioned in Courtney's biography on her website. Anna wondered why the detective hadn't bothered to look there. "It's this bulky glass or Lucite thing that looked heavy," she explained. "The point of the quill is a metal piece that attaches it to the base.

You said Courtney died from a *'blunt-force trauma to the head.'* Do you think the award might be the murder weapon?"

"We're considering the possibility."

"Well, if you can't find a picture of it on Google, I know my videographer caught a shot of the award when we interviewed Courtney at her home the Wednesday before she disappeared. We never used the shot, but I'm sure George still has it along with the other outtakes. I can ask him to find the clip for me, make a copy, and send it to me. Then I can text it to you."

"That would be great. Thanks, Anna. Could you do that?"

"Certainly, I'll get right on it." Anna stood up and leaned against the sink counter. "Detective, how does all this look to you? I mean, with these new developments, do the police still think Dr. Knoll killed his wife?"

"It's too soon to say, Anna. If you could get that video clip to me as soon as possible, I'd appreciate it."

"Of course," she murmured.

After Anna hung up, she finished drying herself off.

She couldn't help thinking how strange it was that Courtney's body had ended up at this somewhat remote lake, where Anna had just happened to have shot a news story last year. It was also a bit odd that Baumann had asked her again about the award, when she could have easily consulted her notes and looked up the award online. It was almost as if Baumann had been trying to put her on the spot about the object possibly used to murder Courtney.

Anna figured she'd call George just as soon as she got

dressed. Then she'd ask him to try to get the video clip to her tonight—if that was possible.

She needed to show Detective Baumann and the rest of the police that she was helpful and cooperative. Still, she wasn't sure how much good it would do her. But she didn't have much choice.

She couldn't help thinking about Russ. He'd been cooperative with investigators, too—right up until the time he ran away and threw himself off the Tacoma Narrows Bridge.

CHAPTER THIRTY-TWO

Thursday, July 23—3:03 P.M.

"I hope you didn't spend too much money on the L-theanine, because I realized I have samples of something that's more effective." Dr. Tolman pulled an envelope from her purse.

That morning at Bartell Drugs Anna had purchased a supplement called *Stress Saver*, which contained L-theanine. "I got something, but it wasn't very expensive," she said, taking the envelope.

They were in their usual spots in Taylor's living room, and their host had once again made herself scarce. Taylor had set out two glasses of water—on coasters—on the coffee table for them. Anna tore open the envelope and shook out a white capsule. "What is it?" she asked. "Will I be safe driving home?"

"It's just a very mild sedative to make you more receptive to hypnosis," Dr. Tolman assured her. "It shouldn't impair your judgment. When I wake you up, you'll be alert."

Anna figured she needed all the help she could get to

relax. She didn't want another session like yesterday. And she had a lot on her mind since talking to Detective Baumann last night.

George had come through with a close-up shot of Courtney's Northwest Literary Society's Best Fiction Debut Award on the bookcase in her living room. Anna had texted the clip to Baumann later in the evening. She kept thinking that she should tell the detective—or somebody—about those unsettling calls Bud had made to her starting the night after Courtney had vanished. But then she'd have to mention the most disturbing of the calls: the one claiming she'd murdered Courtney.

Anna was afraid to bring it up until she knew for certain that Bud was lying. That was why this session was so important. She needed to remember everything she could about the night Courtney had disappeared.

Anna put the pill in her mouth and drank some water to wash it down.

Dr. Tolman set up the digital recorder. "So, did you have a lot of reporters waiting by your dock again today?" she asked.

Anna knew the drill by now. It was small talk to relax her. "Just two," she said, leaning back and getting more comfortable on the sofa. "They wanted my reaction to Courtney's death. I gave them a statement. I think the rest of my fellow members of the press were more interested in getting statements from the coroner or Courtney's mother."

As far as Anna could tell, neither one of the reporters had tried to follow her. She'd come to the back door of Taylor's building. She'd texted Taylor, who had met her and taken her up the gloomy back stairwell. Dr. Tolman had been waiting in the apartment.

Now, as she had for the last two afternoons, Gloria asked Anna to relax and look out at Lake Washington. The skies were overcast today, making the lake look choppy and gray. But the water still had a certain windswept, melancholy beauty. Gloria gave her instructions about her breathing. She spoke in that calm, comforting tone of hers. The drug must have worked fast, because Anna already felt herself slipping into unconsciousness.

She wasn't sure if Gloria was telling her to go back to that night two weeks ago—or if she was going there on her own. But Anna could clearly see herself on the dock to Russ and Courtney's floating home. It was a clear, balmy night. She remembered trying to walk straight and not stumble while Russ hovered at her side. He kept saying he could drive her home. But Courtney had mentioned something about making coffee, and that sounded like a good idea. Anna needed to sober up a little before she went home. She used to worry about her mom, alone and drinking too much. What if she tripped, hit her head, and bled to death before someone found her? Anna imagined that happening to her after all those Lemon Drops. She needed to sober up before she went home.

But once the three of them stepped inside the gorgeous floating home, Courtney threw her purse on a chair and headed into their sleek, modern kitchen. She pulled a bottle of chardonnay from the refrigerator and poured a glass.

"I thought we were going to have coffee," Russ said.

Courtney put down her wineglass long enough to sign

and reply to him: "You want coffee? You make it." Then she took her glass and herself into the living room.

Anna had a glass of water and used the bathroom while Russ made the coffee. She drank a cup and a half, but it didn't help any. In fact, she only felt worse. Maybe coffee didn't mix well with Lemon Drops. She was queasy and nauseous.

It didn't help her miseries that Courtney was still in a bitchy, snippy mood. Whenever she spoke to Russ, Courtney signed and angrily mouthed the words. Anna was grateful to be left out of the conversation, because Courtney really didn't have anything nice to say to either one of them. All she did was criticize them and pick fights over practically nothing.

At one point early on, Russ had put a Dinah Washington album on the stereo—just for some background music. Courtney must not have been paying attention, because the record had been playing for a while when she suddenly seemed to notice the light on the sound system control panel. Setting down her second glass of wine, she shot out of her chair and made a beeline over to the stereo. Her face pinched in anger, she dragged the needle over the vinyl record. Anna winced at the earsplitting screech as the stylus scratched the LP.

"You didn't tell me you and Anna were listening to music!" she barked, signing vehemently. "Was the music something romantic, Russ? Something for just the two of you?" She kept talking—but only to Russ. She mouthed her words and gestured wildly. She kept nodding in Anna's direction.

Anna could almost hear the accusations.

That was when she started to feel really sick.

"All right, that's enough, okay?" Russ finally yelled, signing as he spoke. It was the first time he'd gotten angry and raised his voice all night.

Courtney laughed, sat back down, and sipped her wine.

Anna cleared her throat and announced she wasn't feeling well. The room seemed to be spinning.

Russ said he'd drive her home. Out of politeness, Anna said he needn't bother. It was only about a ten- or fifteen-minute walk. But Russ insisted on taking her home. "It's almost eleven o'clock," she remembered him saying. "And that street along the lake is awfully dark. I'm driving you."

As the two of them headed for the door, Courtney remained slouched in her chair with her wine. She called out: "Don't forget to tuck her in, Russ!"

"She was still wearing her brown sleeveless dress," Anna heard herself say—as if narrating her own dream. "She hadn't changed her clothes. That's what she had on when I left."

She recalled Russ holding her arm as they walked up the dock. "I'm so sorry about the *Who's Afraid of Virginia Woolf?* show in there," he said.

"With pantomime," she added, covering her mouth. "I'm definitely the blond woman who threw up. What's her name, Sandy Dennis? I—I feel really sick, Russ."

He opened the car windows as he drove her home, and Anna felt better for a few minutes. But then she was wobbly and light-headed again as they headed down her dock to her house. Once inside, she ran to the bathroom and barely made it to the toilet before she fell to her knees and threw up.

Russ came into the bathroom and held her hair back and patted her shoulder until her stomach was empty. Then he helped get her undressed and cleaned her up. He made her gargle with mouthwash and gave her aspirin. "Let's put you to bed down here, close to the bathroom," he said, guiding her to the daybed in the study.

He gave her a T-shirt to put on. She was too out of it at the time to notice it was one of her best tees. But Anna remembered crawling into bed. Russ sat beside her, on the edge of the bed, stroking her hair and promising her that things would be different after this.

Anna remembered waking later. He'd left the living room light on and let himself out. She staggered into the bathroom to pee and then returned to bed. She fell asleep immediately.

The next thing she knew, the phone was ringing. It was after nine in the morning, and she was horribly hungover.

"There's more to it than that, Anna," she heard Gloria say with quiet authority. "Go deeper. It happened while you were sleeping."

Anna tried to remember. Suddenly, she was in the studio—at the TV station. They wanted her to anchor the news. She'd just woken up and knew she looked horrible. She was wearing the expensive J.Crew top Russ had mistaken for a pajama top the night before. She'd slept in it. She was totally unprepared to anchor the news, but took her seat at the news desk and tried to be professional. They had her reading everything off a teleprompter as the cameras rolled. All the while, she kept thinking that her career was going to be over because of this. Still, she kept reading the words—until the teleprompter went haywire. Everyone in the studio panicked. Then Anna noticed

Courtney, standing beside the broken teleprompter. Russ's wife started whispering and signing the news text to her. With uncertainty, Anna repeated the words for the camera. She started to perspire. It seemed to go on forever.

"Can I stop now, please?" she finally asked.

Then she heard Gloria's reassuring voice. "Everything's all right, Anna," she whispered. "You were feeling a little sick earlier, but you're fine now. You're good. We're in your friend Taylor's living room. You're listening to my voice, and you're waking up. You're opening your eyes, now."

Anna was obedient. She realized she was sitting on Taylor's sofa. In the easy chair across from her, Dr. Tolman slipped the digital recorder into her purse. "How are you feeling, Anna?" she asked—almost warily.

"Fine," Anna murmured, blinking. "I—I remember everything now. That night with Courtney, it was just as Russ—just as Dr. Knoll described. I left there around eleven o'clock, and she hadn't changed into a purple robe. She was still in the dress she'd worn at the restaurant. I didn't come back. Nothing happened."

Anna felt so utterly relieved, elated, and vindicated. In her euphoria, it took her a moment to realize that Dr. Tolman seemed guarded—as if it was too soon to celebrate. Clutching her purse in her lap, she looked anxious to leave.

"What's wrong?" Anna asked.

Dr. Tolman got to her feet. "Nothing," she said stiffly. "The session took longer than I expected, and I'm late for another appointment. But you—you seem like you're in a good place. I'm glad we were able to unlock some of those memories." She gave a perfunctory nod and headed toward the door.

Anna stood up—a bit too fast. She had a head rush and had to wait a moment for it to pass.

"Dr. Tolman?" she heard Taylor call. Then she heard the door open and shut.

Grabbing her purse, Anna started toward the door and almost ran into Taylor coming from the dining room, where she had her laptop on the dinner table.

"Is everything all right?" Taylor asked and signed. "Where was she going in such a hurry?"

"Um, she was late for another appointment," Anna said, puzzled. She checked her wristwatch: 5:10. She'd been under for over two hours.

"Was it a good session?" Taylor asked.

Numbly, Anna nodded. "I can't believe I was out that long," she murmured.

"I've been back for a little over an hour," Taylor remarked. "Did you remember anything? The purple robe?"

"Yes, I remembered everything," Anna said, smiling at the thought. She'd gotten over a huge hurdle, and she could say without any hesitation that she had nothing to do with Courtney's death. "When I left there that night, Courtney was fine, and she was still wearing the dress she had on from the restaurant. This Bud creep who called into your mother's show, he was wrong about when Courtney put on her robe. She must have had on the purple robe when he killed her."

"But didn't the police say there was no sign of a break-in?" Taylor asked, signing as she spoke. She shook her head. "Courtney wouldn't have let him in."

Anna considered it. Taylor was right. Courtney wouldn't

have opened her door to a stranger who came knocking after eleven o'clock at night—unless Courtney had already known this Bud guy.

"Are you seeing Dr. Tolman again or are you all finished?" Taylor asked.

Anna was stumped for a moment. "You know something, I'm not sure. She left in such a hurry, we didn't discuss it. In fact, I didn't pay her."

"I'll tell her to call you," Taylor said, moving toward the door and opening it.

Anna realized she'd probably overstayed her welcome. After all, Taylor had expected her to have finished her session over an hour ago. She started to leave, but stopped in the doorway. "You don't have to call her, Taylor. If you give me her number, I'll call her myself."

Taylor nodded. "I'll text the number to you. Let me walk you to the stairs. Do you mind going out the back way? One of my mother's private investigators is watching the front of the building, and I don't want him to know you're visiting me."

"No problem," Anna said as they headed down the hallway together. "And thank you so much for all your help and letting me have these sessions here."

"Before I forget," Taylor said. "I heard from my friend who's a writer on Sally's show. My mother hopes to provoke Bud into calling tonight. Her guest is a special consultant psychologist who's going to analyze his personality. As far as I could tell, Sally's leaving you alone."

"Well, that's a blessing," Anna said, stopping at the back stairwell door. "At least, a temporary one—I'm sure your mother's not finished with me yet."

Taylor touched her arm. "Anna, if you're not doing

anything tomorrow night, would you like to get together for dinner?"

Anna nodded and smiled. "Sure, that would be nice—as long as you'll let me pay. I owe you."

"You don't mind me taking you away from your brother for a night?" Taylor asked. "How is he, by the way?"

"He—he's just fine," Anna lied. "And I'm free tomorrow night, so dinner with you would be great."

"I'll text you," Taylor said. Then she gave Anna a hug. It was slightly less awkward than their last two good byes.

The back stairwell to Taylor's building had cement steps and gray cinder block walls. As Anna headed down the stairs, her footsteps echoed. She felt strange lying to Taylor about Stuart, but she didn't want to deal with it just now. She'd explain tomorrow night over dinner.

She thought about her session this afternoon—and how good it felt to remember everything from that night. But the way Dr. Tolman had practically run out of there was bewildering.

She recalled Dr. Tolman saying something to her in the middle of the session: *"There's more to it than that, Anna. Go deeper. It happened while you were sleeping."*

As Anna reached the exit door, it occurred to her that Tolman had taken the digital recorder with her.

Just when she thought she had remembered everything, Anna had to wonder: *What exactly was on that recording?*

CHAPTER THIRTY-THREE

Friday, July 24—10:22 A.M.

"**Y**ou've reached the offices of the Seattle Counselors Association. No one can answer your call right now. Please leave a message and one of our associates will get back to you. Your call is important to us. You can also reach us through our website: www-dot-Seattle-Counselors-dot-com."

Seated at her desk in her mother's old bedroom, Anna held her phone and waited for the beep. "Yes, hello, my name is Anna Malone," she said on cue. "I'm trying to get some contact information for one of the therapists listed on your website, Dr. Gloria Tolman. I'm not having any luck finding her phone number or e-mail address online, and it's imperative that I get ahold of her. So if you could get back to me as soon as possible, I'd really appreciate it. My phone number is area code two-oh-six, five-five-five-eight-three-four-nine." Anna repeated her phone number, thanked them, and hung up.

"Shit," she muttered, slumping in the swivel chair.

With a sigh, she set down the phone and pulled up her

e-mail account on her computer. Sitting straight again, she started to type on her keyboard:

Hi, Taylor,

I've sent you 3 texts (2 last night and one today) and I still haven't heard back from you yet. So I'm starting to worry. Please text or e-mail me as soon as you can, just so I know you're all right.

As I mentioned in my texts, I'd like to get ahold of Dr. Tolman. I can't find any contact information for her online. I need to talk to her about paying her and whether or not we should have another session. Finally, she has been recording our sessions and I'd like to listen to those recordings . . .

Anna stopped typing for a moment. Thanks to Dr. Tolman, she had a clear recollection of everything that had happened on the night she'd last seen Courtney. In real time— from when they'd arrived at Russ and Courtney's floating home until Russ had put her to bed here in this room—those events had unfolded in just over an hour. Yet, Anna had been under hypnosis for almost two hours. She couldn't have gone into that much detail describing what had happened. It didn't make sense.

She needed to listen to that recording and hear exactly what was on there.

But Anna didn't go into all this analysis in her e-mail to Taylor. She just needed to get Gloria's contact information and make sure Taylor was all right. She wrapped up the correspondence on a friendly note:

I'm still up for dinner if you are. Being a Friday night, we should make reservations. I was thinking of The Harvest Vine or Voila (both not far from you) or That's Amore (in Mount Baker). Do any of those strike your fancy? We can discuss it when you text me.

Hope to hear from you soon (please!). Thanks, Taylor!

Take Care,
Anna

Anna sent the e-mail.

She hadn't mentioned Taylor's mother in the note. But Anna had watched *The Sally Justice Show* last night. Bud hadn't called in. He'd been the topic of discussion for most of the program, which included—as Taylor had said—a "special consultant" psychologist who analyzed Bud based on the brief on-air phone conversation Sally had had with him on Tuesday night.

Sally had still managed to work some Anna-bashing into the show. It had been a small segue from the purple robe cloaking Courtney's corpse—a detail which meant Bud had to be taken seriously—to the spot where Courtney's body had been discovered. "I've lived in Seattle for sixteen years," Sally had announced, "and I've only *sort of* heard of Lake Bosworth. I certainly couldn't point it out on a map. But you know who could point it out? Anna Malone, that's who! She did one of her sweet little news stories from Lake Bosworth last year. I find it a strange coincidence that Courtney Knoll's body was discovered in this remote locale where her husband's mistress did one of her news stories. That's something to think about, folks. Now, getting back to Bud . . ."

Anna had wondered how long it would be before Sally

Justice saw that connection. But it wasn't as if Lake Bosworth was this totally obscure spot. It was only an hour away from Seattle. Still, Sally was probably right. It was a strange coincidence. Anna couldn't help thinking that whoever had murdered Courtney had set her up. How long before her missing old sneakers and jeans showed up with blood on them?

The computer chimed. Her e-mail inbox was still up on the screen. She could see a new e-mail at the top of the list.

TaylorHofstad322@gmail.com—Fri, 7/24 – Subject: Re: Where Are You?

Hunched close to the computer screen, Anna clicked on the e-mail and started reading:

Hi, Anna,

I'm sorry I haven't responded earlier. Something very disturbing has happened, and I didn't know how to explain it to you in a text.

Last night, Dr. Tolman came by again and gave me the digital recording from your session yesterday. She said it contained extremely sensitive data. She told me that I should have it since I arranged the sessions and I'm your friend. I didn't understand.

I told her you wanted to get in touch with her about paying her and scheduling possible future sessions. She said she doesn't want to be paid and would rather you not contact her again.

I'm sorry this is so harsh, but she was adamant about that.

I would never invade your privacy, but Dr. Tolman insisted that I listen to the recording, which she left with me (along with her recorder). I have a Live Transcribe app on my phone, so I was able to play the audio recording and read the text as it came up on my phone. Now that I've read the transcript of your session, I understand why Dr. Tolman was so upset. There's one section, which starts 51 minutes into the recording (according to the machine) that's most disturbing.

I'm not sure what to do, Anna. I consider you a friend. But this is so horrible. If you call me (regular phone, not text), I can play the section for you over the phone so you can hear for yourself.

Then maybe we can figure out together what to do. I repeat, I'm your friend and you're not alone in this. Call me as soon as you can.

Taylor

"Oh no," Anna whispered, feeling a sickly twinge in her gut.

She'd known yesterday that something was wrong from the way Gloria Tolman had practically run out of Taylor's apartment. Fifty-one minutes into the recording was probably after she'd described what she now recalled from that night. Whatever she'd said that was *so horrible* must have come up on the recording sometime after Dr. Tolman had prompted her: *"There's more to it than that, Anna. Go deeper. It happened while you were sleeping."*

Anna nervously reached for the phone and pulled up Taylor's number. Her hand was shaking.

It rang twice before someone picked up: "Hello, Anna," Taylor said. "When you speak to me, it'll go to text, so expect a tiny delay before I reply, okay?"

"Okay," Anna said. Her stomach was still in knots.

There was a second of silence. "So you got my e-mail," Taylor said. "I hope I'm doing the right thing here. This is the section of the recording I was talking about. If you can't hear, or if you want me to turn the volume up or down, just tell me. I'll see that you're talking. The text will show up on my phone screen. Okay, here it goes."

Biting her lip, Anna listened. It sounded like Dr. Tolman was talking, but the words were muted and muffled. "Taylor? Could you turn it up, please?"

After a moment, the volume increased, and Gloria's voice was much clearer: *"Go ahead, Anna"*

"It never would have happened if I hadn't had so much to drink," Anna heard herself say. She sounded tired, listless, and vague. *"There was nothing premeditated about it. But I guess things had been building up for a while . . . That night, she was so nasty and abusive—first at dinner, and then when we came back to their place. I got so angry that I couldn't sleep. I had to go back there. I just wanted to tell her off. It wasn't supposed to happen the way it did. But she wouldn't shut up, and she was so goddamn mean. If she'd been able to hear herself, maybe she would have stopped barking all those insults at me. A part of me was so glad for the silence after I bashed in her skull."*

Anna couldn't believe what she was hearing. Yet it was her voice. A hand to her throat, she sat hunched over the desk with the phone to her ear.

"Okay, Anna, back up a little bit," Dr. Tolman said. Her usual calm, collected voice sounded a little shaky. *"You told me earlier that Russ put you to bed."*

"That's right, but I woke up after a while," she said, sounding agitated. *"And I couldn't fall back asleep. So I got up and grabbed the first things I could from my closet—a sweatshirt, my jeans, and a pair of sneakers. I knew it was late, but I didn't care. I wanted it out in the open about Russ and me."* There was a pause, and then she seemed to have more poise in her voice. *"I never would have pegged myself as the type of woman who would get involved with a married man. For a long time, the last thing I wanted was for anyone to get hurt."* Then she groaned as if she'd lost her patience. *"But I was mad, and I didn't care anymore. I was going to have it out with Courtney. I got there and pounded on the door—"*

"Did you walk or drive?" Dr. Tolman asked.

"Neither, I took my little boat—right up to the end of her dock."

Anna remembered how she and Russ had discovered on Friday that the dinghy hadn't been tied properly. Now it made a weird kind of sense that the rope had been loose. But she still couldn't believe this was real. How could she have totally blocked it out?

"You said you pounded on the door," Dr. Tolman said. *"Did you forget that Courtney was deaf?"*

"I thought Russ was home. Anyway, I rang the bell, which blinks the lights so she knows someone's at the door. Courtney let me in. She was still up. She'd changed into this floor-length purple robe. I guess she was in the mood for a fight, too . . . She started right in on me, and I don't know what happened, I just snapped. I reached for

the first thing I could. She had this writing award on the bookshelf, a big, heavy glass object." There was another awkward pause, and then she continued: *"I grabbed it. I remember hitting her in the head with that thing. It's so clear to me now, I can almost hear the crack—and the strange, sickly warble that came out of her mouth. I was splattered with blood . . . It was all down the front of me— on my clothes and my sneakers. I felt the droplets on my face . . . A drop must have gotten in my mouth. It tasted like copper. When I went into the bathroom to get the towels to wrap around her head, I stopped and rinsed out my mouth at the sink. But I could still taste that little bit of blood—like an old penny."*

"Were you surprised at what you'd done?" Dr. Tolman asked.

"Oh God, yes . . . After it happened . . ." There was a pause, like she was drinking water or something. *"For a moment, I couldn't move. My heart was racing. I couldn't believe what I'd just done. But then something clicked, and I suddenly realized I had to clean up all the blood. I grabbed a towel out of the bathroom and wrapped it around her head."*

"What were you thinking about while you were doing this, Anna?" Dr. Tolman asked. *"Were you thinking about Russ?"*

"God, a million different thoughts went through my mind when I stared down at her, sprawled across the floor with that gash in her head. Her eyes were open. She seemed to gaze back at me, accusing me . . . My first instinct was to get out of there. But then I realized I had to dispose of the body and clean up the blood. Otherwise, everyone would have blamed Russ. That was the last

*thing I wanted. So I got the idea to pack a suitcase—and
make it look like she'd left him . . . So—yeah, I was thinking about Russ."*

"Go on, Anna," Dr. Tolman said. "*You cleaned up the
blood with some bath towels . . .*"

"*Yeah . . . I found some trash bags under the sink in
their kitchen. Large Heftys. I put one over her head and
used up a couple more to wrap up her body . . . Then I
packed some of her stuff in a suitcase with the bloody
towels—including her purse, her phone, and some of her
jewelry . . .*" Anna heard a long sigh on the recording.
"*I was able to get to my boat from their back deck, so I
loaded the suitcase onto the dinghy. Then I went to get
her body . . . God, I know what they mean by* dead *weight.
She looked so petite, but dragging that lifeless thing
across the floor out to their dock was awkward and exhausting. I had the trash bags wrapped around her, but
they started to tear, and blood leaked out . . . Like I said,
I'd already loaded the suitcase in the dinghy. When I got
her out there to the edge of the dock, I sort of rolled her
into the boat. It almost tipped over. The goddamn suitcase
fell into the lake. I saw it start to float away, but I couldn't
get to it. By the time I cleaned and locked up the house,
then got back into the boat, I couldn't find the suitcase
anywhere on the water.*"

Horrified, Anna listened. At times, there were awkward pauses in the middle of sentences—and between
sentences. It was as if she was hesitant about admitting
what she'd done. But how could it have actually happened? She couldn't have blacked out that much. Conscious or unconscious, she wasn't capable of murder.

"*All right, Anna, so you have Courtney's body on*

your little boat," Dr. Tolman said, her voice shaky again. *"Describe what—what happened then."*

"Well, there's this remote spot along Lake Union, down from my dock. The pier comes practically right up to the road. I took my dinghy there and went to fetch my car. By then, it was—like one-thirty in the morning, so no one was around . . . I transferred her body from my little boat to the trunk of my car. I drove back to my place and got a shovel and loaded that into the trunk. Then I walked back to where I'd left the dinghy and paddled back to my place."

"And while all this was happening, no one saw you?"

"Not that I could tell, at least not at the time," she answered. *"I'd done a story from Lake Bosworth, and I remembered the area has all these remote dirt roads and woods. That's where I buried her. I have to admit I was tired and didn't dig too deep a grave for her. I figured all the wood creatures would get to her before anyone found the grave. I got back around four-thirty in the morning. I cleaned myself up. Then I stashed my soiled, bloodstained clothes and shoes in the dumpster at the end of my dock."*

"What about the murder weapon, this—this glass thing you used to kill her?" Dr. Tolman asked. *"What happened to that?"*

"I really wasn't sure what to do with it," Anna heard herself admit in the recording. *"I didn't want to bury it with Courtney. So I hid it—on my houseboat. I washed the blood off, of course. There's a little crack in it now. Anyway, that's where Courtney's writing award is—for the time being. I'm pretty sure no one will ever find it."*

"Where on your houseboat did you hide it?"

"I'm . . . not . . . telling," she replied in a strange

singsong tone that reminded Anna of Bud. She shuddered.

"Okay, Anna, maybe you'll want to tell me later," Tolman said. *"So—you cleaned yourself up, threw your clothes in a dumpster . . ."*

"Yeah, and the city comes by to collect the garbage on Friday mornings—just hours later. So no one can connect those clothes to me."

"And after that, what did you do?"

"I had a little ice cream, and then I went to bed. It was starting to get light out."

Anna kept shaking her head over and over. She couldn't have done all of this. Yet she was hearing herself describe everything—often with little or no emotion. She didn't want to believe it, but she had to.

A part of her wondered if Dr. Tolman had hypnotized her into saying these things. But she could hear Gloria asking the questions and her answering. Besides, how would Dr. Tolman know that she ate ice cream when she couldn't sleep?

Anna heard a click.

"Anna?" Taylor said. "There's more, but what I played just now was the part I felt you should hear. Dr. Tolman said she isn't going to say anything to the police. As your therapist, I'm pretty sure she can't. I promise, I won't tell anyone a thing until you decide what to do. But maybe you should talk to a lawyer. I don't know much about this, but it sounds to me like, if you turned yourself in, you might plead manslaughter or temporary insanity. It certainly wasn't premeditated."

Anna was so flustered and upset. And Taylor kept talking and talking in her slightly impaired speech pattern. It was all Anna could do to keep from screaming. Here the poor, sweet woman was trying to help and protect her. But it was too soon for any discussion about how she intended to plea-bargain on murder charges. She couldn't have murdered Courtney.

"Taylor?" she said, a tremor in her voice. "I—I'm having a hard time believing any of this is true. I know it's my voice on the recording, but I don't remember any of this happening." She hesitated. "Are you picking up what I'm saying right now?"

There were a few moments of silence on the other end. "Taylor?"

"Yes, I see what you're saying. I'm reading it. Would you like to come over and pick up the recording?"

"Yes, please," she said. "I'd like to come over now if I can."

There was a pause. "All right," Taylor said. "Could you come to the back door again? Call me when you get here, and I'll come down to meet you."

"Taylor? Did you listen to—I mean, did you read the transcription of the entire recording?"

A few seconds passed. "Yes."

"Do I . . ." Anna's mouth had gone dry, and she tried to swallow. "Do I ever say on the recording where I hid Courtney's award?"

She waited.

"No," Taylor answered.

"I'm coming right over," she said. "I'm leaving now."

CHAPTER THIRTY-FOUR

Friday, July 24—11:39 A.M.

> Giving you another try. I'm still at the back door, waiting,
> and starting to worry about you. Hope you're just in the
> bathroom or something. I'll give you a few more minutes,
> then take my chances and try the front door.

Anna sent the text.

Traffic had been a nightmare—or maybe it had just seemed that way because Anna had been so anxious to get here. For the last ten minutes, she'd been waiting at the back door of Taylor's building. It was by an alley lined with dumpsters and recycle bins.

A narrow sidewalk ran alongside Taylor's building. Anna started to walk up it toward the front of the building—but then she turned around for the second time and went back to the door. She banged on it—on the off chance an inexplicably phoneless Taylor was waiting there in the back stairwell. Maybe she'd feel the vibration on the door.

No response. Anna wasn't surprised.

She desperately wanted to listen to that recording in

its entirety. Maybe there was some explanation for why she'd given this long, detailed, bizarre "confession." It couldn't be true. Different parts of the recording seemed vaguely familiar, like that part when she said, *"I never would have pegged myself as the type of woman who would get involved with a married man."* She remembered saying that to Dr. Tolman— or someone else— before. Or maybe the damn thing seemed familiar because she'd actually murdered Courtney, and yesterday, she'd relived it all while under hypnosis.

She needed to talk to Taylor about how well she knew Gloria Tolman. Who had recommended her to Taylor? Anna remembered, after the first session in which Dr. Tolman had so impressed her, she'd watched her talk to Taylor. She'd spoken loudly, overenunciating each word, like she'd never spoken to a deaf person before. Maybe Taylor didn't know her very well at all.

Anna wanted to kick herself for trusting a complete stranger. It was the story of her life. She'd put her faith in the wrong people: her father, her brother, Russ—and now this therapist. What had been in that pill Tolman had given her yesterday?

Anna banged on the back door again, more out of frustration than anything else. Once more, there was no answer.

Exasperated, she started up the narrow sidewalk. This time, she strode all the way to the front of Taylor's building. She checked out the lobby through the glass door, but it was empty.

Anna buzzed Taylor's intercom. She got a recorded greeting: *"Hi, this is Taylor. I can't answer your call right now. Please leave me a text message, and I'll get back to you. Thank you!"*

"How screwed up is this?" Anna muttered to herself.

Turning around, she looked at the cars parked across the street, in front of a playfield by the lake. A man sat in the driver's seat of a parked Honda Accord. His window was down. It looked like he was on his phone.

Anna marched across the street. As she got closer to the car, she could see the man more clearly: stocky, about fifty-five with a cocoa complexion, a graying goatee, and receding buzz-cut gray hair. He looked more like a private detective or a bodyguard rather than a creepy stalker.

He must have seen her approaching, because he put down his phone.

"Do you know who I am?" Anna asked him.

"Yes. You were here the other day."

"Did you just tell Sally that I'm back?"

He nodded. "Yes."

"You're Taylor's bodyguard, right?"

"Actually, I'm a private investigator. But yes, I happen to be guarding Taylor right now."

"Good. Have you seen her leave the building in the last hour? She's expecting me, and she's not answering my texts."

A look of concern flashed across his face. Then he quickly got out of the car.

Anna followed him as he hurried across the street. "So—I assume you haven't seen her leave the building," she said.

He shook his head.

"Do you have a key?" she asked.

He shook his head again. Reaching the front door, he pushed several intercom buttons. Anna stayed behind him.

"Yeah, who is it?" someone answered over the intercom.

"I have a package for three-oh-two, and there's no answer," Sally's man said. "If you buzz me in, I'll leave it by their door."

The front door buzzed. Anna grabbed the handle and pulled the door open. She wondered how he planned to get into Taylor's apartment. She didn't ask. She just followed the man up the stairs and down the hallway to Taylor's apartment. She saw the door and stopped dead.

It was open a few inches.

In front of her, the private investigator didn't hesitate to step into the unit. Though it was daylight, he reached inside and flicked the light switch on and off several times. Then he stomped his foot on the floor twice.

Anna almost called out to Taylor and realized Sally's man knew better. With the lights and the stomping, he was announcing his arrival. The phone in his hand, he moved into Taylor's hallway.

Anna followed him. As soon as she got through the door, she smelled something burning.

The private investigator peeked into the living room. But Anna headed toward the dining room and kitchen. One of the dining room chairs was tipped over. It was the chair closest to the kitchen entrance. "Hey!" Anna called to the man.

She turned around and realized he was right behind her.

"Don't touch anything," he said. Brushing past her, he moved around the corner into the kitchen. The sharp, burning smell came from there. Anna was almost afraid to follow him. She thought the worst. She imagined finding Taylor dead on the kitchen floor.

Covering her nose and mouth from the stench, she stepped around the corner. It was a modern kitchen with stainless steel appliances, granite countertops, and a subway-tile backsplash. After the smoke, the next thing Anna noticed was the dark red puddle on the black-and-white-tiled floor.

The private investigator stepped over to the stove and turned off one of the burners. A saucepan of tomato soup had tipped and spilled over onto the stovetop. It dripped down the oven door onto the floor. The burner was smoldering.

Above the counter, one of the cupboards was open. Below it, on the floor, was a box of saltine crackers and a broken soup bowl. It appeared as if someone had surprised Taylor when she'd been in the middle of making her lunch.

"I'll go check the bathroom and bedroom," Anna said.

Sally's man put his hand out to stop her. "No, don't go anywhere, and don't touch anything. Let me speak to Sally first, and then the police."

Anna was obedient. A hand still over her nose and mouth, she stood there and waited while the private investigator phoned Taylor's mother.

All Anna could think was that Bud had found himself another deaf girl.

CHAPTER THIRTY-FIVE

Friday, July 24—6:06 P.M.

"**R**ight now, I'm talking to the man who calls himself Bud. We all heard you when you phoned into this show on Tuesday night," Sally said, staring directly at the camera. She seemed to lock eyes with her viewers at home. But the usual, slightly arrogant, intimidating manner was gone.

Anna had never seen this side of Sally: she looked so subdued, maybe even scared. "I hope you're watching now, Bud," Sally said. "If you've got my daughter—or if you know what's happened to her, I'm asking that you call into the show again. Our lines are open. If you took my daughter, please, talk to her. She can read lips. You'll see she's a kind, giving, and beautiful girl. Taylor hasn't had an easy life. She was born deaf, and her father died— suddenly and violently—when she was just a child. She's endured a dozen different major surgeries to correct her hearing—the latest just a few months ago. None of them have been successful. But Taylor is still a cheery, generous, compassionate person. Taylor cares about other people. You'll see that she cares about *you*, Bud."

Anna sat in the greenroom at Sally's TV studio, Taylor-Made Productions, watching the show on a monitor. With the comfortable leather upholstered sofa, a desk and chair, and the stocked mini-fridge, the windowless waiting room was plusher than the bare-bones, slightly dumpy greenroom at the KIXI-TV News studio. On a side table, they even had a basket full of bottled waters and packaged snacks—both healthy and sugary.

Anna held on to her phone. She'd never heard back from the Seattle Counselors Association about Dr. Gloria Tolman. So she'd been looking up all the Tolmans in the online Seattle white pages. She'd found only three. None of them had seemed too promising, but she'd phoned each one to double-check. She'd gotten two *"There's no one named Gloria here"* and one automated *"The number you have dialed is no longer is in service."* Anna had been ready to check the online white pages for neighboring cities when Sally's televised plea had caught her attention.

She wondered if Bud would actually take the bait and phone in.

Was that why Sally had asked her to come here? Did Sally expect her to appear on the air and talk to Bud, too—should he call? If that was so, then surely Sally or someone in the studio would have told her that she might be appearing on the show. They'd have at least patted her down with a little HDTV makeup. Of course, knowing Sally, maybe she wanted Anna to look terrible for the telecast.

It was weird to be in the enemy camp. Everyone there

was nice enough, but it was strange nevertheless. At the moment, things at Sally's Taylor-Made Productions seemed pretty chaotic. Of course, Sally's daughter had been abducted today. And if that wasn't enough to throw the place into a tailspin, Sally's soundman for the last six years hadn't shown up for work. Apparently, no one could get ahold of him. Anna had overheard a crew member mention that the guy was an alcoholic with gambling debts. Everyone had scrambled around to find a last-minute replacement.

Most of Sally's production staff had seemed surprised when Anna had shown up at the studio about a half hour ago. Apparently, Sally hadn't briefed more than a couple of people about her arrival.

Anna had been answering questions at the police station with Sally's private investigator Jim Larson when Sally had called him and asked to talk with her. That had been around two o'clock this afternoon.

"Can we put our differences aside for a spell?" Sally had asked her over Larson's phone. "I'm on my way to the police station. But I think you'll be gone by the time I get there. Would it be possible for you to drop by my studio around airtime tonight so we can talk?"

Anna had reluctantly agreed.

She was reluctant because she didn't want to tell Sally about Gloria Tolman.

Anna had talked with the police for nearly two hours and hadn't said a thing to them about Dr. Tolman. Instead, she'd lied and said she'd come by Taylor's apartment because Taylor was tutoring her in sign language. She'd had to manufacture some excuse for being there four afternoons in a row. Anna had learned a bit of sign language in preparation for working with Courtney—not much, but a few basics that someone just starting out might know. She wasn't sure what explanation Taylor had given her mother for her presence in the apartment when Sally had walked in on them on Wednesday afternoon, but Anna figured she would find out soon enough.

She hated not being more transparent with the police—especially when Taylor was in apparent danger. But if she'd told them about Dr. Tolman, she may as well have told them about her recorded "confession." And Anna just wasn't ready to do that.

She needed to talk to Dr. Tolman before anyone else did.

She told herself that Tolman probably didn't have anything to do with Taylor's disappearance anyway. The creep calling himself Bud was almost certainly behind what had happened today.

But Anna couldn't deny there was a connection. Obviously, in order to get to her, Gloria Tolman had used Sally's naive daughter. With a combination of drugs and hypnosis, she'd coaxed Anna into making that bogus confession. Anna wondered if it was all part of some blackmail scheme. What if Taylor had been abducted because she'd discovered the recording was a phony?

If that was the case, wasn't it essential that the police and Sally know about Tolman? But Anna couldn't tell them, not without incriminating herself.

Earlier today, before the police had arrived at Taylor's apartment, she and Jim Larson had looked around the place. He'd been searching for clues. But Anna had found herself furtively looking for that damn digital recorder. She'd never found it.

They hadn't seen Taylor's phone or purse anyplace.

Larson had assumed Taylor's abductor had taken them. Anna figured the recorder must have been inside the purse.

She kept thinking about how Taylor had gone out of her way to help her. Now, when the poor young woman was in trouble, Anna could think only about saving her own skin. And that made her feel *too low for the snakes*, as her mom used to say.

She gazed up at the TV monitor bracketed to the wall. Sally was showing a photo of Taylor, looking sweet—but also a bit mousy. "Anyone with information regarding my daughter's whereabouts is urged to call into the show on our special hotline: 1-800-4TAYLOR," Sally said—and signed. Her eyes brimmed with tears. "We'll keep the lines open all night."

The Sally Justice Show theme music swelled up, and they cut to a commercial for cat food.

Anna looked at her phone again. There was an Andrew Tolman in Bellevue. She decided to try the number—in case he was related to Gloria. Maybe he'd have her address or a home phone number.

She was about to scribble down his number when her phone rang. Anna checked the caller ID: *Unknown Caller.*

She automatically tensed up, and then tapped the phone screen. "Hello?" she asked tentatively.

She heard a click—and then her own voice: *"I reached for the first thing I could. She had this writing award on the bookshelf, a big, heavy glass object. I grabbed it. I remember hitting her in the head with that thing. It's so clear to me now. I can almost hear the crack . . ."*

There was another click, and the line went dead.

For a few moments, Anna couldn't breathe.

Bud had found the recording.

And that *big, heavy glass object* was now hidden somewhere on her houseboat. If she'd actually killed Courtney, she'd hidden it. But if she was being set up, someone else had hidden it. Either way, Courtney's writing award—with a crack in it—was somewhere in her home.

"Anna? Are you okay? You look sick."

Startled, she looked over toward the greenroom door. She hadn't realized someone had stepped into the room. It was Sally.

Looking up at the TV, Anna did a double take. Sally was back up on the screen, too—only in a completely different outfit.

"We switched to *The Best of Sally Justice* for the rest of the show," Sally explained. She had a Kleenex in her hand and dabbed her nose. She took off her black jacket and hung it over the back of the desk chair with her purse. Anna noticed a little makeup smear on her white blouse. Sally fished her phone out of the bag. "I just don't have it in me to do a show tonight. Are you okay?"

Anna nodded. "Fine," she murmured. She glanced at Sally on TV again. As Sally talked to a caller, at the bottom of the screen, a notice ran: *YOU ARE WATCHING THE BEST OF SALLY JUSTICE FROM AN EARLIER BROADCAST . . . OUR HOTLINE IS OPEN 24 HOURS TO REPORT INFORMATION REGARDING THE WHEREABOUTS OF TAYLOR HOFSTAD . . . CALL 1-800-4TAYLOR . . .*

Sally stopped to glance at the basket of snacks and bottled water. She seemed to notice that she had the Kleenex and her phone in her hand. She turned to Anna and shrugged. "This is what I've been carrying around all day—ever since I got the call. Can I get you anything? There are sodas in the mini-fridge."

"No, thanks," Anna said. A part of her wanted so much to tell Sally about the call from Bud. But her survival instincts kicked in, and she couldn't say anything except, "I'm so sorry about Taylor."

Sally opened a bottled water and sat down beside her on the sofa. "Well, thanks for coming. After you left Taylor's place the other afternoon, she told me that she'd helped you and your brother reunite."

"That's right. I'm very grateful to her," Anna replied.

"Well, maybe you can help me reunite with my daughter by being completely honest with me." Sally took a swig of water. "According to Taylor, she originally contacted you and invited you over. Is that true? It's not the other way around? You didn't decide to get back at mean, old Sally Justice by going after her very vulnerable, fragile daughter—and maybe screwing with the girl's head?"

"No, Sally," she answered quietly. "Taylor was telling you the truth. And I like her. She's been very kind to me. I wouldn't do anything to hurt her."

"When I spoke with the police today, they said you'd been over at my daughter's apartment for the past four afternoons. They said that Taylor was tutoring you in sign language. I'm having a hard time buying that, Anna."

Anna thought a moment before answering. "You're right. That wasn't quite the truth. Listen, Sally, our afternoon get-togethers have nothing to do with Taylor's disappearance, I'm pretty certain of that. Taylor's been—well, Taylor and I have been helping each other out. I can't really talk about it without betraying a confidence. There's nothing fishy or salacious or illegal going on. It's just personal. I'm not trying to pit her against you or anything—if that's what you're worried about. You'll just have to take my word for it."

Sally slowly shook her head. "How can you expect me to hear that Mount Everest of shit and not wonder what the hell is going on between you and my daughter?"

"It has nothing to do with what happened today, I'm pretty sure of that."

Sally stared at her—that trademark, intimidating *Sally* stare. "Anna, you got to be fast friends with Courtney Knoll, and she suddenly disappeared. Then you got chummy-chummy with my daughter, and now she's vanished. What am I supposed to think? When you say these meetings with my daughter have nothing to do with what's happened today, I'm not buying it."

Anna squirmed beside her. "I told you, I like Taylor. She's a very sweet girl. I don't want any harm to come to her. I think it's obvious that this Bud must have taken her. You said so yourself just the other day. You were concerned about him going after Taylor."

It dawned on Anna that maybe Bud was working with Dr. Tolman. But then, what were the two of them after?

"What is it?" Sally asked. "What are you thinking?"

Anna shook her head. "Nothing, I'm trying to figure out why this is happening."

Sally took another swig of water and frowned. "In these deeply personal, private meetings with my daughter, did she ever mention any other friends or boyfriends?"

Anna shook her head. "I think Taylor's kind of lonely. She doesn't have any friends that I know of. But a guy stopped by just as I was leaving there on Tuesday. I forget his name. He was a tall, deaf guy with one of those initial names—like RJ or TJ."

Sally scowled. "You mean CJ? He's younger than Taylor—kind of pale and impish-looking?"

Anna nodded. "That's him. Taylor said he was more a friend than a boyfriend, and not even much of a friend at that."

"She told me a month ago that she'd stopped seeing him." Sally rolled her eyes and sighed. "She keeps attracting these loser con-artist types who are after her for her money—or because she's the daughter of a celebrity. She brought that CJ character here to the studio a couple of times. I was about to have him investigated when Taylor said she'd dropped him."

"Are you serious?" Anna asked. "You mean, if a guy shows interest in your daughter, you have him investigated?"

"I've had to," Sally replied. "Like I said, she's had her share of lowlifes who just want to take advantage of her. She's a naive, vulnerable girl."

"Did it occur to you that CJ—or one of these other guys—might be the one who abducted Taylor? Maybe one of them is Bud."

"What do you think I was talking to the police about for two hours today?" Sally answered.

A young woman with a headset stepped into the greenroom doorway. "Sally, FYI, the first TV news van just pulled up in front of the studio. I think we can expect more of the same soon. If you want to make a clean getaway tonight—"

"All right, all right, thanks!" she said, waving the woman away.

Anna took this as a cue to leave—before Sally grilled her again about her afternoon visits to Taylor's apartment. She was also thinking that Courtney's award might be hidden somewhere in her own home, and it gnawed at her.

She stood up. "I've pretty much had enough of my fellow journalists in the past week. I'd like to make a clean getaway myself."

Sally got to her feet. "You know, when I was going through Taylor's dating history with the police this afternoon, I didn't even consider CJ, probably because she'd told me they were kaput. Plus, he wasn't on the scene for very long. I had no idea she was still seeing him. I'll pass that along to the police—and my own people. You've been very helpful, Anna. Thank you."

Walking her out of the greenroom, Sally showed her to the side door of the studio. It led out to the parking lot. Through the window in the door, Anna didn't see any reporters. She turned to Sally. "Will you let me know if you hear anything?"

Sally nodded. "Of course. You know, Anna, I'm not through with you yet. This Courtney Knoll murder case is still a mystery. And I think there's still a lot you're not telling me about Taylor."

Sally opened the door for her. "The tidbit about CJ is helpful. So I'm going easy on you tonight—out of gratitude. But if my daughter is still missing tomorrow afternoon, I'll find out what you're hiding, Anna. And the gloves are coming off. Do we understand each other?"

Anna's eyes wrestled with hers, and she finally nodded. "I understand, Sally."

Then she headed out to the parking lot and hurried toward her car.

Saturday, July 25—2:27 A.M.

Anna's living room was a mess.

She'd cleared out the front closet, and everything had ended up in the living room. The sofa was piled with coats, jackets, and sweaters.

Courtney's Northwest Literary Society's Best Fiction Debut Award could have been hidden anywhere. Maybe it was tucked in a coat pocket and concealed inside a sleeve, or stashed in a boot. It might have been hidden among the cleaning supplies or in the rag bin. Maybe the incriminating objet d'art was in with the recycled grocery bags or among the twenty or so free tote bags she'd picked up over the years. Everything had to be examined. What had started out as a very organized search had turned into something desperate and muddled. Several times, she'd almost tripped over the junk scattered on her living room floor.

Anna had already been through her clothes closet and the little crawl space off her bedroom upstairs. Her bed was still covered with clothes, boxes full of holiday decorations, and stuff that had belonged to her mother. She'd even taken the fake Christmas tree out of its box— in case the murder weapon was hidden amid the collapsed tree sections. It would take hours to put everything back where it belonged.

While searching the bedroom closet, she'd made one important discovery. She'd figured out which sweater was missing—along with her comfy jeans and her sneakers.

It was a casual gray pullover from Banana Republic. Had the missing shoes and clothes really been tossed in the dumpster? Or would the police find them hidden somewhere near here—stained with Courtney's dried blood?

All it would take was a search warrant, and the police would discover Courtney's writing award, too—if Anna didn't find it first.

She hadn't even started a search of the kitchen, linen closet, study, or bathroom; then there were the toolshed and the dinghy outside.

Stepping over more junk in the living room, she lugged the stepladder from the kitchen to the front closet. On the top shelf were puzzles and old board games she hadn't touched since those rare overnights when her family had stayed here. But Anna couldn't bear throwing them away. She figured Courtney's award couldn't have fit inside any of those shallow boxes anyway.

But the glass quill easily could have been tucked away in one of three big Nordstrom boxes full of family mementos. Anna started up the stepladder, but when she reached for the first box, she banged the top of her head against the closet doorway frame. It hurt like hell. With one hand braced against the shelf, she stood there on the little ladder and tried not to fall apart. She was tired and at the end of her rope. She hadn't eaten anything all day. Her nerves were scraped raw, worrying about poor Taylor and that bizarre recorded confession. Her hands were filthy—and now her head was throbbing.

After a few deep breaths, Anna took the heavy boxes down from the shelf and carried them into the living room. She plopped down on the floor and opened the first box. It was full of photographs, old cards, and letters.

There, on the top, was a photo of her and Stu from when she was about eleven. It had been taken during a family day trip to Snoqualmie Falls. They were posed with the twin falls in the background, each of them bent forward with their mouths open so it looked like they were vomiting the waterfalls.

Gazing at it, Anna started laughing—but only for a moment.

She thought about Stu—and what had happened to him. He'd taken drugs as a way out; her mother had turned to alcohol; and her father and Russ had committed suicide when things became impossible for them. They'd all given up in one way or another.

There, amid the pile of junk on her living room floor, Anna started crying.

Like everyone who had ever really mattered in her life, she was ready to give up, too.

Sitting in a small rowboat in the middle of Lake Union, someone looked through a pair of binoculars at Anna. There was no way Anna could have seen the little skiff on the silvery-black water in the darkness of night. She was on her living room floor, surrounded by boxes and piles of clothes. It looked like she was crying. Obviously, she'd been searching for that heavy, glass quill award with the little crack at the top.

"You'll . . . never . . . find . . . it, Anna," her observer whispered in a raspy voice. "You're not even warm. You're . . . cold . . . cold . . . dead cold . . ."

CHAPTER THIRTY-SIX

He heard a woman scream.

The sound seemed to come from inside a house he'd never laid eyes on. Yet he knew the house was there, not too far away. He'd heard the screen door slam on occasion—and, rarely, the muffled sound of a TV or radio. Once, he was pretty sure he'd heard *The Sally Justice Show*. He knew he'd been taken to some remote location away from the city. The entire time he'd been here, he hadn't heard any people or traffic noise—just the crunch of gravel under tires as one car came and went. At night, there were sounds of woodland creatures.

"Shut up, dummy!" a man barked.

There was a clatter, like something had been knocked over.

"You want another?" he yelled.

The guy's voice was pretty clear. Obviously, the windows were open in his place.

Frustrated, Russ anxiously paced around the cramped bedroom of an old RV. The son of a bitch in the house was beating up a woman. And Russ couldn't do a damn thing about it.

He had no idea what time it was —just that night had fallen. The window above the queen-size bed was boarded up on the outside, and during the day, Russ could see a horizontal sliver of light between the wooden slats. If he knelt at the head of the bed and pressed his chin against the window, he could see some bushes nearby—and nothing else.

He'd been locked inside the bedroom for at least nine days now. That was how many times he'd watched it get dark out. Russ had the scruffy start to a beard, which he'd seen only when he caught his reflection in the glass of the boarded-up window. Connected to the bedroom was a bathroom. It looked like there had once been a mirror over the small sink, but someone had torn it out.

At least there was water and electricity. The water never got hot and tasted like bad well water, but it was drinkable. He could even shower in the tiny stall— as long as his body could stand the cold water. He'd washed out his clothes in the shower, too. His abductor had left him with a change of clothes: a Seattle Mariners T-shirt with the souvenir shop price tag still on it and a pair of sweat-pants. Russ had also been furnished with a towel, a washcloth, toilet paper, a toothbrush, a tube of Crest, and a bar of Irish Spring. The fresh soap smell was the only break he got from the stale, stagnant air in the room.

The air-conditioning went on only a few times during the day. The sweltering room cooled down a bit at night. There were sheets, a blanket, and one pillow on the queen bed—which took up about 80 percent of the room. Russ made the bed every morning—in an effort to keep up a routine and make the dumpy room habitable. Every stick of furniture had been removed; all that was left was the dirty blue wall-to-wall shag carpet and the built-in pressed-wood dresser. There were brackets on the wall for a TV set, which had been removed.

He'd been supplied with a deck of cards and about a dozen paperbacks. Russ figured the books couldn't have been selected with him in mind, since two were by Danielle Steel and one was a young adult novel.

His meals came to him through a slot near the bottom of the door, always 7-Eleven checkout-counter snacks or the kind of crap that came from vending machines: beef jerky; cheese and crackers packets; Rice Krispies Treats, small bags of Cheetos, Chips Ahoy! cookies, and potato chips; and warm sodas and bottled waters. One morning, he'd actually gotten an apple, packaged powdered mini-doughnuts, and a cold little container of orange juice. It had felt like Christmas.

There was just enough room on one side of the bed for him to run in place and do sit-ups, push-ups, and squats. It kept him from going crazy.

Russ had already checked every inch of the room for a way out. Three shiny new locks had been fitted into the bedroom door. The food slot had a cover that latched on the other side. There was also a reverse peephole in the door, so the guy who had abducted him could check up on him from time to time. The window was safety glass, and the escape hatch in the ceiling had a thick padlock on the latch.

Russ was certain whoever was holding him here must be responsible for Courtney's disappearance. She'd obviously lost a lot of blood during the attack. Was it possible she could still be alive?

Was Courtney the woman he'd heard screaming a few

moments ago? He knew her voice—and it had sort of sounded like her.

Or had it been Anna?

Ducking into the tiny bathroom, he stood under the small vent in the wall to listen for a minute. It was the best spot to hear sounds from outside. He couldn't hear anything—except an owl in the woods.

Anna had been on his mind constantly. His abductor must have been thinking of Anna, too—at least for a while.

Russ had seen the guy only briefly. He was tall and blond—with a dark handlebar mustache that looked fake.

Russ had been at the police station nine days ago to identify the contents of Courtney's suitcase. Then later, from his room in the Silver Cloud Inn, he'd phoned Anna, and they'd talked about hiring a good criminal attorney for her. He'd just hung up when someone knocked at the door. Russ had looked through the peephole. Its double layer of glass slightly distorted the view, but he could see a mustached man holding up a badge in a leather ID holder. "Dr. Knoll, it's Detective Avery," he'd called out. "I just have a couple of questions."

In the previous few days, Russ had had several cops come knocking on his door—first at home and then at the hotel. They'd all flashed badges at him. How was he to know that this one was a fake?

Once the man stepped inside, Russ noticed he was carrying a small duffel bag—and wearing surgical gloves. Before Russ could even say anything, the man set the bag on the bed and took a gun out of it. He pointed the semi-automatic at Russ. "Do what I say and quickly, or I'll shoot you in the head."

Russ backed up and bumped into the writing desk.
"Wait—"

"There's a sweater in this bag, Dr. Knoll. Put it on.
Now, quickly."

Russ nervously obeyed him. The sweater was a dark
blue zip-up cardigan with a hood.

"I want you to throw some of your things into the bag,
personal stuff, things you really need."

"What is this—"

"Just fucking do it!" the man growled. "No questions."

Russ followed all his instructions, which included
leaving the room with the guy and sticking close to him
as they walked to the lobby together. The man calling
himself Avery made it clear that if Russ didn't cooperate,
he'd shoot him and anyone else who got in his way. They
waited a couple of minutes—until a group came out of
the hotel's restaurant-bar area. As the group left the lobby,
Russ merged in with them—with Avery close beside him.
Once outside, Avery had him continue down the sidewalk
and around the corner to where a black Jetta was parked.

Russ remembered Anna telling him on Saturday that
a black Jetta had followed her down the road by Pete's
Supermarket.

The car's headlights blinked as the man unlocked it
with his key fob. "Okay, now, take off the sweater and
hand it to me. And don't fucking try anything."

Russ pulled off the sweater and gave it to him.

"Okay. Get in the backseat. Quickly."

Russ did what he was told.

"Now, bend forward and look at your feet. C'mon,
quickly, now."

Once again, Russ was obedient. He remembered thinking that *quickly* seemed to be the guy's favorite word.

That was the last thought he had before he'd felt the sickening blow to the back of his head.

Russ woke up in the galley kitchen of this old RV. All of the windows were painted over. He wasn't sure how much time had passed since he'd been knocked unconscious. It could have been hours or even a day. The back of his head was sore. Russ figured the guy must have hit him with the butt of his gun. He felt a lump and a cut back there, but the blood had dried. His arm was sore as well. He had bruises and three ugly puncture wounds—his abductor must have injected him with a sedative and had a hard time finding a vein.

He was still so groggy that he struggled to sit up in the galley booth where he'd been lying. It reminded him of the booth in Anna's kitchen—only this one was tacky and cheap. A pen and several sheets of paper were on the stained plastic laminate table in front of him.

Avery—or whatever his name was—wore a ski mask and stood near the mini-fridge, just far enough away so that Russ couldn't lunge at him and overpower him. Russ couldn't have budged anyway. Besides, the guy still had the gun, and it was pointed at him. In his other hand, he held a piece of paper "I want you to write something for me," he said, behind the ski mask.

In his dazed state, Russ realized he might make it out of this alive. Otherwise, why would the guy wear a ski mask? If Avery intended to kill him, there would be no need for the disguise or the mask.

"I know your handwriting, Dr. Knoll, and I want this to be *in your handwriting*. So keep that in mind as you jot this down. Are you ready? Pick up the fucking pen."

Russ grabbed the pen and leaned over the table to write.

The man dictated: "*I've come to an impasse. Right now this seems like the only way out. I apologize to Anna Malone, who never hurt anyone and never deserved the heartache I've brought upon her. To Anna, and all the other people who believed in me, I apologize for letting you down.*"

The guy made him write it several times. He kept saying, "That's too sloppy, do it again" or "I know your handwriting. It's got to match."

Russ kept at it, copying down the text from each previous attempt. When he had the opportunity, he looked around the galley for the duffel bag he'd packed.

"Okay, this will do," Avery finally said, glancing at the umpteenth draft.

"Where's my stuff?" Russ asked numbly. "What happened to that bag I packed?"

The man let out a little laugh. "You won't be seeing that again." He nodded toward the RV's bedroom. "Everything you'll need is in there. And you've earned a little rest. There's a nice bed all made up for you. C'mon."

Russ remembered staggering into the bedroom and collapsing on the bed.

The door shut behind him and the three locks clicked, one after another. That was the last time he'd seen the man who had called himself Detective Avery.

But now, he could hear him—and it was unmistakably him. "C'mon, get up, quickly, quickly," he yelled. "Don't waste my time. And don't pretend you can't understand me, dummy. I know you can read lips."

Russ listened to the screen door squeak open and then slam shut. He heard a woman sobbing. He thought it must be Courtney. Who else could it be?

His hands clenched into fists, he moved into the back of the bedroom. It was all he could do to keep from banging on the walls in protest at the abuse. As much as he'd despised Courtney at times, she was still his wife, and he couldn't stand knowing this son of a bitch was hurting her.

He thought they might have been on their way to the car. But then he heard a key in the door to the RV, and it creaked open. Russ crept over to the bedroom door and listened.

"C'mon, keep moving, stupid," the man said. "The doctor will take care of those bruises. Shit, I'm wasting my breath. You don't even know I'm talking. You've got your back to me."

He must have given her a shove, because she let out a startled cry—and from her footsteps, it sounded like she'd stumbled.

"Hey, Doc!" the guy called. He seemed to be on the other side of the door. "You've got company! You two are going to have a great time together. You know how to talk dummy talk, don't you? Now, do me a favor. See that little bell on the wall—near the window, on the wall by the bed?"

Standing by the door, poised to attack, Russ glanced over his shoulder at the little bell on a bracket attached to the wall. He'd been wondering what it was for. Like the locks in the door, the food slot, and the padlock on the ceiling escape hatch, it looked like something that had been installed especially for his incarceration here.

"Answer me, Doc! I can see you right by the door. I know you're listening! Or do you want me to slap this deaf bitch again?"

"All right, I'm looking at the bell," Russ replied irately. "What do you want me to do?"

"Go over there and ring it."

Russ reluctantly backed away from the door. As he got closer to the bell on the wall, he realized its purpose. It was extra insurance for the guy in case he had to stop looking through the peephole for a second. If Russ was on the other side of the room ringing the bell, he couldn't very well rush his abductor in the doorway. The small bell had a short piece of rope attached to it. Russ pulled at the rope, and the bell sounded.

It had dawned on him before, and this just confirmed it: no one else was nearby to hear the bell. And no one could have heard Russ's screams for help, either.

He stood there, ringing the bell and listening past the din as the three locks clicked. Suddenly, the bedroom door swung open. Russ caught only a glimpse of the guy—in his ski mask again—as he shoved the young woman into the room.

With a shriek, she fell onto the bed.

Russ stopped ringing the bell. He could see the girl wasn't Courtney.

The bedroom door slammed shut, and the three locks clicked, one after another.

Hurrying to the young woman on the bed, Russ gently took her by the shoulders and turned her over. Her face was bruised and tearstained. She had a black eye, and her lower lip had a fresh cut on one side. She looked slightly familiar, but Russ wasn't sure where he'd seen her before.

He looked over at the door. "Hey, are you still out there?" he called. "Hey."

"What?"

"Just hold on a second!"

Hovering over the young woman, he quickly checked for any broken bones or sprains.

She started to recoil from him.

"I'm a doctor," he whispered—and signed. From what he'd overheard the man saying, obviously the woman was deaf. She wore a short-sleeve beige pullover and olive slacks. Russ noticed a bruise on one of her arms. All of her other injuries seemed to be to her face.

"I'm going to need some ice!" he called. "Also, we could use some antiseptic, cotton balls, and aspirin or ibuprofen."

"Fuck you," the creep grumbled. "I'm not your scrub nurse. You've got cold water and a washcloth. You figure something out."

Russ heard him stomp toward the front of the RV. Then the door closed. After a few moments, he heard the screen door to the nearby house open and slam shut.

Russ turned to the young woman again.

Sitting up, she gazed at him in horror. She shook her head over and over.

"I'm a doctor," he said, signing again. "Are you okay? Do you feel dizzy or nauseated?"

"You're Courtney Knoll's husband," she said—and signed. Her hands were shaking. Her slightly impaired speech was characteristic of some people born completely deaf. "You're Dr. Knoll. You're supposed to be dead."

"What are you talking about?" he asked, signing. "I'm sorry. Who are you? You—you look familiar."

"I've met you and your wife a couple of times at parties," she replied, a bit calmer now. Her breathing seemed to slow down. "My name is Taylor Hofstad. I'm Sally Justice's daughter."

Russ shrank back a bit. As of nine days ago, Sally had been trying to crucify both Anna and him.

"I'm not my mother," Taylor assured him in her halting speech. "I think what she's been doing to you and Anna Malone is awful. I've been trying to help Anna. We've become friends."

Russ was confused, but he still nodded. "Okay, just a second," he said and signed. "Let me get something for your face."

He couldn't sit there and keep talking to Taylor with her face all battered. He hurried into the bathroom, rinsed the washcloth under the cold water, and squeezed it out. Now he remembered meeting Taylor at a charity function months ago. Courtney had mentioned at the time that Sally Justice's daughter might be a good connection to have—publicity-wise. *Typical Courtney*. But nothing ever came of it as far as he knew.

Returning to the bedroom, he sat down beside her and gently pressed the cold washcloth to the cut on her lower lip. It didn't look too serious. "So—I'm supposed to be dead?" he asked. He set the washcloth down for a second so he could sign for her.

"It's okay," Taylor said. "I can read lips." She stopped signing, took the washcloth from him, and dabbed her mouth. "Someone driving your car was seen on the Tacoma Narrows Bridge before dawn on Thursday. He stopped in the middle of the bridge, got out of the car, and jumped. Some anonymous woman called it in to 911." Taylor moved the cold washcloth to the corner of her eye. "My mother kept saying it all seemed pretty suspicious. But now, I think even she believes you're dead."

Russ realized that was what the cryptic note in his handwriting was all about. It was a suicide note, and in it, he'd exonerated Anna.

"What's happening with Anna?" he asked anxiously.

Taylor hesitated. She eyed him nervously and shrugged.

"What's going on? You said you were her friend."

"I am." She put down the washcloth. Then once again, she signed as she spoke. "I set her up with a hypnotist to help her remember what happened the night Courtney went missing. They recorded the sessions. The man   the one who abducted me—he knew about it. He knew I had the recording. I was saving it for Anna. I wanted to protect her. But he broke into my apartment and grabbed me. He was after the recording, he said so. He's got it now."

"Protect Anna from what?" Russ asked, his brow furrowed. "I don't understand."

"There are things on that recording no one should hear."

"I still don't understand."

Taylor frowned at him. "All this time, you haven't asked about your wife."

Russ realized she was right, and he felt horrible.

"They found Courtney's body on Wednesday, half-buried in some woods near Lake Bosworth." She spelled out *Bosworth*.

In shock, Russ just stared at her. He'd assumed that Courtney was dead, but somehow, hearing this blunt confirmation still managed to stun him. He slowly shook his head. "No . . ."

Taylor looked at him with pity and then caressed his arm. Then she took a deep breath and started signing. "On this recording Anna made with the hypnotherapist . . ." She spelled out *hypnotherapist*. "On this same recording, which that horrible man now has, Anna confessed that she'd bashed in Courtney's head and buried her in those woods."

CHAPTER THIRTY-SEVEN

Saturday, July 25—11:03 A.M.

Anna pulled up in front of the Craftsman bungalow on Shorecrest Drive. For a few moments, the sun peeked out from behind the clouds. A small rainbow appeared above the whirling sprinkler that watered the beautifully manicured lawn.

According to the online white pages for Lake Forest Park, this was the home address for Gloria Tolman, MD.

It had taken several tries before Anna had found the listing. She'd been tearing apart the houseboat, searching for the glass trophy used to kill Courtney. But every once in a while, when she'd gotten too tired and discouraged, she would take a break and search the Internet for Gloria Tolman's contact information. She'd figured Lake Forest Park was so close to Seattle that Tolman would have been included in the Seattle listings, but it hadn't been. Out of desperation, she'd Googled *Gloria Tolman, Lake Forest Park, WA,* and there it was. The white pages didn't give Dr. Tolman's telephone number, e-mail address, or website, just her home address.

Leaving her place in a shambles, Anna drove to Lake Forest Park to hunt down Dr. Tolman. Anna was going on about three hours of sleep. In the car's cup holder, she had her fourth cup of coffee of the day—this one from the Texaco mini-mart where she'd stopped for gas fifteen minutes ago.

Anna switched off the car's engine and gazed at the house. She took the Lexus parked in the driveway as a sign that someone was home.

She didn't have a solid game plan for dealing with Tolman. She just knew that the recording was a phony— something she'd been coerced into saying while under hypnosis. It was just so inconsistent. For example, how come she remembered all the events of that night until the time Russ had put her to bed, but had absolutely no recollection of killing Courtney and disposing of her body? She remembered, under hypnosis, telling Tolman about that first portion of the evening. But the rest was just a weird dream: her, without makeup, in front of a TV camera, reading the news off cue cards and repeating things Courtney fed to her.

Had she been dreaming that while speaking into the recorder, reading cues, and repeating whatever Dr. Tolman had told her?

Anna planned to confront Gloria Tolman and get her to admit that she'd set her up. Tolman probably had a duplicate recording there in the house.

Stepping out of the car, Anna realized Dr. Tolman wasn't about to admit to anything. Why would she suddenly crack under the pressure of a few direct questions? So what if Anna had tracked her down at her home? That wasn't going to make this woman cooperate. Anna wondered what she would do if Tolman stonewalled her. *Maybe bash her in the skull with the first hard object I can get my hands on.*

Anna stopped at the walkway to the house. She told herself once again that what she'd heard on the recording wasn't true. And she would make Gloria Tolman tell her it wasn't.

Anna stepped up to the wide front porch, which was supported by wooden pillars. Taking a deep breath, she rang the bell.

A dog started barking. Then there were footsteps.

Anna felt herself tense up as the door opened. A ruddy-faced, white-haired man in his late fifties stood on the other side of the threshold. He wore a polo shirt and shorts. A corgi was at his side, barking. "Okay, Enzo, that's enough," he said to the dog. Then he smiled at Anna. "Can I help you?"

"Does Gloria Tolman live here? Gloria Tolman, the therapist?" Anna asked.

The corgi started to get restless, and the man took hold of its collar. "Sorry. Um, I didn't catch your name."

"I'm Anna Malone. I was a client of Dr. Tolman's."

He grinned. "I thought I recognized you. Anna Malone from TV, of course! I had no idea you were consulting with my wife." The dog barked and tried to sniff Anna. "I'm sorry. Could you wait here? He's harmless. He doesn't bite, but he'll jump and slobber all over you." He led the dog toward the back of the house. "Honey?" he called. "Gloria, there's someone here to see you!"

Anna waited in the doorway. From what she could see of the house, it was neat and nicely furnished. She could hear the man murmuring to someone. The dog barked again.

A pretty, fiftysomething Asian American woman with gray-black hair and bangs came to the door. "Anna Malone?" she said with a cordial smile. "I'm Gloria Tolman. What can I do for you?"

Bewildered, Anna gaped at her for a moment. "Hi," she said finally. "I'm sorry to bother you. But are you the same Gloria Tolman who's listed in the Seattle Counselors Association?"

She nodded. "That's me. But that's from ages ago. Would you like to come in? I think my husband has our dog under control."

Anna numbly shook her head. "Are you by chance a hypnotherapist? I mean, do you sometimes hypnotize your patients?"

"No, I'm a psychiatrist. And I no longer see patients. I'm just doing consulting work now. What's this about?"

"I'm sorry, but do you know of another Gloria Tolman in the Seattle area? This one's a hypnotherapist—and she sees patients."

The woman shook her head. "I've never heard of another Gloria Tolman—here in Seattle or anywhere else. How did you find this hypnotherapist?"

"An acquaintance of mine, Taylor Hofstad, recommended her to me."

The woman's brow furrowed. "That name sounds familiar."

"Taylor Hofstad is Sally Justice's daughter."

The woman smiled and nodded. "Of course! That's where I've heard her name before. Are you sure you wouldn't like to come in, Anna?"

She shook her head. "Thank you. But I'm kind of in a hurry. So—you don't know Taylor?"

"I think I've seen her on TV once or twice, but I've never met her." She held up her index finger. "Could you wait for just a second, Anna?"

Anna watched her duck back into the house. The woman was gone for less than half a minute. When she returned, she handed Anna her business card. "Listen, Anna, if you're able to track down this other Gloria Tolman, will you let me know? You've got me very curious about this woman."

Anna took the card. "I'm very curious about her, too. Thank you, Dr. Tolman."

"Taylor-Made Productions, home of *The Sally Justice Show*. This is Barbara. How may I help you?"

Anna had been on hold for five minutes, waiting to talk to an operator. She hadn't wanted the real Dr. Tolman and her husband wondering why she was still parked in front of their house, so she'd driven two blocks and was now parked in front of a church.

"Hi, this is Anna Malone. I need to talk to Sally, please," she told the operator.

"Sally isn't available at the moment. Our message center is available twenty-four hours. Your call is important to us." It sounded like the brush-off.

"Barbara, this is Anna Malone," she interrupted. "I need to talk to Sally. This really is *important to you*. It's about Sally's daughter. If Sally's there at the studio, please put her on. If she isn't there, I need a phone number where I can reach her now. She'll want to talk to me."

There was a pause. "One minute, Ms. Malone."

"Thank you."

Anna restlessly drummed her fingers on the steering wheel. She thought she might be in for a long wait. But then, after about a minute, she heard a click.

"Hello . . . Anna?" The woman on the other end of the line didn't sound quite like Sally. She seemed distressed, even despairing, like she might have been weeping. Anna immediately thought about Taylor and wondered if she was dead.

"Sally?"

"Yes, have—have you heard something?"

"About Taylor?" Anna asked. "No, I don't have anything definite. Have you found out something? You sound upset."

"I just got some bad news here at the studio," Sally said, sniffling. "One of my production guys for several years, Gordy Savage, is dead. He shot his wife and then shot himself. A neighbor discovered them in their home this morning. I knew he had a lot of problems, but I had no idea it was that bad."

"I'm so sorry," Anna murmured.

Sally cleared her throat. "So, are you calling about Taylor?"

"Yes—"

"Is it about that CJ character?" Sally spoke over her. "Because my people and the police haven't had much luck tracking him down. You said he was over at Taylor's on Tuesday? Did Taylor ever say anything to you about him during one of your confidential talks?"

"She didn't say much," Anna answered. "Just what I told you last night. He was a friend and not a boyfriend.

Taylor didn't seem all that crazy about him. But he seemed pretty much at home at her place."

She heard Sally sigh on the other end of the line. Then it sounded like she blew her nose.

"Sally, did Taylor ever see a therapist or a counselor?"

"Well, she couldn't have spilled her guts to you very much during your afternoons together if you have to ask *that* question," Sally remarked. "Yes, Taylor has seen a bunch of therapists and counselors over the years. I should know, I paid for most of them. Why do you ask?"

"Do you know if, among them, there's a hypnotherapist calling herself Dr. Gloria Tolman?"

"A *hypnotherapist*?"

"Yes, and she's good at it, too, only I'm sure Gloria Tolman isn't her real name. In fact, I think she might have hoodwinked Taylor into trusting her."

"I don't remember writing a check to anyone named Tolman," Sally said. "And Taylor has seen her recently?"

"Very recently. I've met her. There's a Dr. Gloria Tolman in Lake Forest Park, but it's not her. That's why I think this hypnotherapist might be a phony."

"I'm going to look into this, Anna," Sally said, sounding determined. "Thanks. I'll call you as soon as I get something."

She hung up.

Anna was a bit startled at the way Sally suddenly finished the conversation. She tapped the phone screen to hang up.

She was about to start the car, but then Anna remembered something she'd observed between the fake Dr. Tolman and Taylor. The hypnotherapist had spoken to Taylor the way some people, who didn't know any better, often addressed deaf people. She'd talked loudly and overenunciated every word. Anna couldn't imagine her addressing Taylor that way for any sustained period of time. The two couldn't really have known each other very well.

If her guess was right, maybe this CJ person recommended Dr. Tolman to Taylor.

Something else hit her, and it put her stomach on edge. Now that Sally knew about the fake Dr. Tolman, she and the police might be a step closer to hearing that recording. Between the coerced confession and the murder weapon planted somewhere at her home, Anna knew she didn't stand a chance of proving her innocence.

With a nervous sigh, she leaned forward to clip her phone onto the holder on her dashboard. That was when she saw something in her rearview mirror—a man standing directly behind her car.

Anna gasped and dropped her phone.

She swiveled around in time to see it was a teenage boy—with a skateboard in one hand and a phone in the other. With a clatter, he tossed the skateboard onto the pavement, stepped on it, and sailed down the street with the phone to his ear.

Anna caught her breath and picked up her phone. It rang in her hand.

She was amazed Sally was calling back so fast. She touched the screen. "Sally?"

There was a click on the other end. Suddenly, Anna realized it wasn't Sally. She checked the caller ID: *Unknown Caller*.

She heard the bogus Dr. Tolman talking. It was from

the recording: *"What about the murder weapon, this—this glass thing you used to kill her? What happened to that?"*

Anna heard her own voice, responding: *"I really wasn't sure what to do with it . . . I didn't want to bury it with Courtney. So I hid it—on my houseboat. I washed the blood off, of course. There's a little crack in it now."*

Then the line went dead.

Anna stared at the phone for a few moments.

She wasn't scared. She was angry. She knew that Bud or CJ or the counterfeit Dr. Tolman was telling her, once again, that the murder weapon was hidden someplace in her home—as if she needed reminding.

But she also became more keenly aware of something she'd noticed when she'd first heard the recording yesterday morning. It was slightly choppy—with awkward pauses between the sentences. Had she really been answering the fake Dr. Tolman's questions—or merely been repeating things she'd been told to say? Had someone created this confession out of a bunch of sentences and phrases she'd been coerced into saying?

Anna clipped her phone onto the brackets on the dashboard and then started up her car. "I'm on to you," she whispered. "Whoever you are, I'm on to you, you son of a bitch."

CHAPTER THIRTY-EIGHT

Russ couldn't move.

Early this morning, before dawn, Taylor had told him about her ordeal with their captor, and she'd started crying. He'd held her for a few minutes until she'd calmed down. Then she'd asked if he could please keep holding her until she fell asleep.

Now, hours later, he was still fully dressed and sitting on the queen bed with his arm around Sally Justice's sleeping daughter. She rested her head between his chest and his shoulder. Russ was losing the circulation in his arm. But every time he tried to move, Taylor let out a distressed little moan. So he tried to keep still.

But he managed to twist around and check for daylight through the slats boarding up the window behind them. Taylor stirred for only a second and went right back to sleep. Russ guessed it was late morning or maybe even noon. The creep holding them captive hadn't pushed any food through the slot in the door yet. But that really wasn't an indication of the time of day. He slipped the food packets through the slot at random intervals. Sometimes Russ got three food deliveries a day, and sometimes only one.

A couple of hours ago, Russ had heard the house's screen door open and slam. A minute later, he heard the RV door open. With apprehension, he'd listened to the footsteps approaching the trailer's bedroom door. But the guy hadn't said a word. He must have been just checking in on them. He'd left after a minute. Then the RV door had shut and the screen door had slammed again.

Russ had managed to doze off a few times. He couldn't have slept much anyway, not after everything Taylor had told him.

She'd described how Bud had called in to her mother's show, claiming to have witnessed Courtney's murder. He'd admitted to being obsessed with deaf women—Courtney, in particular. But Taylor suspected he also had a fixation for Anna, too. "It's just a feeling I got from some of the things he's said to me and the questions he's asked about her," Taylor had explained.

On Sally's show, Bud wouldn't reveal who had killed Courtney. However, he'd mentioned that Courtney had been dressed in a purple robe when she'd died. Russ knew it well—a silk, floor-length number; Courtney looked gorgeous in it. According to the news reports, she'd been wearing that same robe when some teenagers found her corpse in a wooded area near Lake Bosworth. Russ knew of the place because Anna had done a story there last year.

Because Bud had been right about Courtney's robe, people took him seriously. Either he'd witnessed Courtney's murder or he'd committed it.

Taylor was convinced this Bud was the man who had abducted her. She'd never gotten a good look at him. He'd been wearing what had looked like a fake mustache when he'd broken into her place. Taylor had left the apartment door unlocked because she'd been expecting Anna.

Describing the abduction, Taylor had told Russ something he still couldn't wrap his head around: "It's funny, but when I felt someone sneaking up on me in the kitchen, at first, I thought it was Anna. For a second, I wondered why she hadn't blinked the lights on and off to let me know she'd let herself in. A half hour before, I'd told Anna about her confession on the recording. I'd been expecting her, and instead, this man creeps into my apartment, grabs me, and asks for this recording. How did he know about it?"

Taylor showed Russ the bump on her head where Bud had hit her and knocked her out. She'd regained consciousness in the trunk of his car: "It was so scary to wake up in total darkness. At first, I thought I was in a coffin. Then I felt the vibrations of the car and the bumps in the road."

Russ had asked her if the car was a black Jetta, and Taylor had confirmed that it was. She'd caught a glance of the vehicle after they'd arrived here. Bud had been wearing a ski mask when he'd let her out of the trunk yesterday afternoon. She'd noticed the old RV, hooked up to a power outlet along with a hose that stretched from the side of the dilapidated rambler-style house. She hadn't noticed any other homes in the immediate area—just a long gravel road through the trees.

Russ had asked if the guy had a partner. Taylor had said she'd never seen anyone else. Once the man had brought her inside the house, he'd tied her to a kitchen chair and left her there. She'd seen him on the phone once—when he'd come into the kitchen to get a beer out of the refrigerator. "So maybe he does have someone working with him," Taylor said—and signed. "The kitchen, by the way, was filthy. I saw mice, one dead in a trap, and another one scurrying around. I kept thinking it would crawl up my leg."

She said Bud had made himself a microwave fish dinner that smelled awful. He'd eaten it in another room. "I'm sure he took the ski mask off to eat," Taylor said. "But I never saw him without it on."

Then, after his meal, still stinking of fish, he'd started to molest her. She'd resisted, and he'd slapped her several times, trying to get her to submit. "I kept fighting," Taylor had said. "He couldn't do much to me while I was tied to that chair—except feel me up and hit me. So he gave up, left me alone for an hour or so, and then came back and tried again. Of course, I resisted, and he slapped me around some more. This went on all night. I guess he finally got fed up, because he untied me and dragged me outside. I thought he was going to kill me. But he threw me in here with you, thank God."

Russ figured it was worth a temporarily numb arm if he could help Taylor sleep off some of the trauma she'd experienced yesterday. The bruises on her face looked minor. Still, very soon, she'd wake up feeling pretty awful. If this Bud asshole had a humane bone in his body, he'd slip a few tablets of ibuprofen through the food slot in the door.

Russ could almost hear Courtney laughing at him for thinking that way—as if everyone, even the worst people out there, had a decent streak in them. She used to say he was a Pollyanna along those lines. Maybe he was.

He was hoping Bud had some sort of conscience. In fact, Russ was banking on it as he concocted a plan to escape from their dumpy little makeshift prison.

He'd figured out a way to lure Bud into the room. Once that happened, they could overpower the guy. After all, there were two of them now—and only one of him.

Or was that really true? Did he have a partner?

Taylor groaned and started to shift positions, knocking her knee into his leg. Suddenly, she sat up and stared at him. She seemed confused and startled.

"It's okay," Russ said—and signed. "I'm Russ Knoll." He spelled it out. "Do you know where you are?"

Nodding, she started to rub her bruised eye and winced in pain. "I'm sorry," she said. "How long was I asleep?"

"About five hours," he said and signed. "How are you feeling?"

"Horrible . . ." she mumbled, "and embarrassed. Excuse me." She crawled off the bed, ducked into the bathroom, and closed the door.

Russ got to his feet. Massaging his numb arm, he shuffled over to the other side of the bed where he usually did his exercises. When he'd first been locked in the bedroom, he'd noticed a loose piece of baseboard molding. The wooden board was the closest thing to a weapon he could find. He'd been kicking and tugging at it for several days. He was pretty certain he could pry the piece off the wall today—and then use it to knock their captor unconscious, or at least put the bastard out of commission for a short while.

But he still wasn't sure about a possible accomplice.

Though Taylor hadn't seen anyone else in the house, Russ figured the guy must have a partner.

Taylor had told him about the security camera footage of his "escape" from the Silver Cloud Inn. He'd been recorded leaving the lobby with a group of people, and minutes later, this Bud guy had been caught on camera in the underground parking lot. The guy was about Russ's height and build, and he'd been wearing the same hoodie Russ had had on for the walk through the lobby. The security video showed him ducking into Russ's car and driving away. So the police and everyone else thought the guy in the parking garage had been Russ.

But while all this had been happening, Russ had been unconscious in the backseat of the Jetta. So, Russ wondered, who had been looking after him and the other car? Bud couldn't have left the hotel in two cars.

Taylor had also told Russ all the details about his apparent suicide. He figured Bud had driven the BMW halfway across the Tacoma Narrows Bridge, and then someone must have picked him up—all within the bridge cameras' blind spot. After that, an anonymous woman had made the 911 call.

The guy must have had an accomplice. Most likely, it was the woman who had reported the bogus suicide. But odds were she wasn't in the house next door. Taylor hadn't seen anyone else there. And besides, what woman would stand by while a guy repeatedly beat and molested a defenseless deaf woman?

Again, Russ could almost hear Courtney laughing at him. There he was, thinking that even horrible people had their limits of evil.

This woman, whoever she was, could be a big obstacle

to his escape plan. Russ imagined luring Bud into the bedroom, overpowering him, and then finally emerging from the RV with Taylor—only to be met by some angry bitch with a gun.

But it was a chance they had to take.

Past the water running in the bathroom, Russ thought he heard the TV in the house next door. But then he recognized Anna's voice: *"I never would have pegged myself as the type of woman who would get involved with a married man. For a long time, the last thing I wanted was for anyone to get hurt . . . But I was mad, and I didn't care anymore. I was going to have it out with Courtney. I got there and pounded on the door—"*

At first, Russ had thought it was Anna talking on TV. But then he realized he was listening to the recorded confession Taylor had told him about.

"Did you walk or drive?" someone asked Anna.

"Neither, I took my little boat—right up to the end of her dock."

Russ recalled securing the rope to the dinghy for Anna that Friday afternoon. She hadn't been able to explain how it had gotten loose.

Taylor flushed the toilet in the bathroom. It was loud—and the rushing sound in the pipes as the tank refilled was just as noisy. It drowned out the recording for a minute or so.

Russ anxiously listened for Anna's voice. Finally the toilet finished refilling, and he heard Anna again.

"I guess she was in the mood for a fight, too . . . She started right in on me, and I don't know what happened, I just snapped. I reached for the first thing I could. She had this writing award on the bookshelf, a big, heavy glass

object . . . I grabbed it. I remember hitting her in the head with that thing. It's so clear to me now. I can almost hear the crack—and the strange, sickly warble that came out of her mouth. I was splattered with blood."

The bathroom door opened, and Taylor stepped out. "There's no mirror," she said and signed. "I must look horrible. I'm really—"

Russ put a finger to his lips to quiet her. "I'm listening to that recording you told me about—Anna's confession." Russ signed and silently mouthed the words. He pointed in the general direction of the house. "He's playing it next door."

But just then, the recording stopped.

He noticed Taylor, with her bruised face, staring at him. She looked frightened and concerned.

"I'm sorry," Russ signed and mouthed the words, "but from now on, I think we shouldn't talk out loud—in case this place is bugged or something. You and me, we need to break out of here today."

Now Taylor looked even more frightened. She shook her head and backed into the wall.

"We can't take any chances," Russ explained in sign language. "He's not finished with you. He's going to try again, maybe not tonight, but soon. Meanwhile, he and his partner—I'm convinced he has a partner—they're trying to set up Anna for Courtney's murder. That's the very least they're planning. I'm certain she's in danger. I just heard part of that recording. I don't know how they got her to say those things. I don't know how they set it up. But it's just not true."

"But I saw a transcript of the recording," Taylor signed

impatiently, mouthing only some of the words. "Wasn't it her voice on there? She told me it was her voice."

"I know. Yes, it was her voice. But I also know Anna, and she couldn't intentionally hurt anyone. She couldn't have murdered Courtney. She's been set up somehow. And like I said, God knows what else they intend to do to her. We can't just sit here while that happens."

Taking a deep breath, Russ moved over to Taylor, gently took her by the shoulders, and sat her down on the bed. "We need to break out of here today, tonight at the very latest," he silently explained. "I have a plan. It's kind of a half-assed plan, but maybe, between the two of us, we can iron out the kinks. We're going to lure that guy in here and then overpower him—a surprise attack."

Taylor was shaking her head. "I can't do it. I'm too scared," she signed, and then she grabbed hold of his hand.

Russ tactfully pulled his hand away so that he could sign to her. "We've got to try. I'm counting on you. This is going to depend on you. The thing is, if there's any kind of struggle, I'm pretty sure it's going to be him tangling with me. If that happens, you need to run. You can't wait around for me. You need to run and keep running until you can find some help. Don't wait around for me. Do you understand?"

She started to cry. She grabbed hold of his hand again and held it to her face. "I can't," she said out loud. "Please don't ask me. I'm too scared."

Russ pulled his hand away again so that he could sign. "You've got to. It's the only way. Please, promise me."

Taylor sprang to her feet. She ran into the bathroom and shut the door.

Russ sat down on the bed.

It sounded like she was getting sick in there.

CHAPTER THIRTY-NINE

Saturday, July 25—8:26 P.M.

Anna's study was a mess. She'd torn the place apart, continuing what seemed by now to be a pointless search for Courtney's award. She'd pulled things out of the study's closet she'd forgotten she had: an ugly umbrella stand, an antique lamp that had belonged to her mother, an old boom box, and from her physical-fitness phase last year, a bunch of weights, some latex resistance bands, a jump rope, and other exercise equipment.

Anna sat on the floor amid the rubble. She started to put things back into the closet. There was no point in having every room in the house look like a disaster area.

She still hadn't heard from Sally Justice about the woman calling herself Dr. Tolman. Anna kept her phone nearby. It was on the edge of her desk.

She started to gather up some papers that had fallen out of a work file box. She'd held on to all her notes and paperwork from her feature stories, in case of legal problems later. Notes from Anna's most recent broadcast were on top of the loose pile. She glanced at a hard copy of her "farewell speech" on KIXI-TV News from nearly two weeks ago. She ignored her scribbled annotations in the margins. One part of the text caught her eye:

> . . . My story hasn't changed much from what I'd already told the police and what I've reported to you. But I omitted one detail—which is that I've been in a relationship with Courtney's husband, Dr. Russell Knoll, for eighteen months. I never would have pegged myself as the type of woman who would get involved with a married man. But at the time, I believed—we both believed—that Dr. Knoll and his wife would soon be separating. The last thing I wanted was for anyone to get hurt.

"My God, that's on the recording," Anna murmured to herself. "*'I never would have pegged myself . . . the last thing I wanted . . .'* I knew that sounded familiar. I wrote it. I said it on the air."

The fake Dr. Tolman had blended bits of audio from that broadcast to help create the "confession." Anna wondered how many other sentences from other broadcasts had been used.

"So that's how they did it," she whispered.

It made sense now. Someone had taken snippets from her news stories and carefully combined them with phrases she'd been coerced into repeating while under hypnosis.

If she could just get her hands on that recording, she could prove it was a sham.

Her phone chimed.

Anna grabbed it off the desk and glanced at the screen. Sally Justice had sent a text. Anna clicked on it:

When U said "hypnotherapist" it rang a bell. Look at the woman on this link, and tell me if this is "Dr. Tolman." Go 4 minutes into it. Call U soon.
www.thesallyjusticeshow.com/archives/season9/episode37

Anna opened the link to an episode of *The Sally Justice Show*. She cued it to the four-minute mark. Just from looking at Sally, she could tell this episode was a few years old. Anna turned up the volume on her phone.

"Talk about sleazy!" Sally declared from behind her judge's desk. "This con artist—this *lowlife*—she ran ads like this to prey upon people in trouble, people with weight problems, sleep problems, addictions, you name it."

Up on the screen flashed an advertisement, which Sally read out loud—with dripping sarcasm:

FREE YOURSELF THROUGH HYPNOSIS!
Let Bianca Help Heal You!

Conquer Addictions, Lose Weight, Quit Smoking, Overcome Phobias & Build Your Self Esteem!

Your Better Tomorrow Starts Today!

DR. BIANCA DUNN, HYPNOTHERAPIST
Serving Seattle & Surrounding Areas,
REASONABLE RATES.

It looked like the ad had included a phone number, which was blocked out.

The advertisement on Anna's phone screen was replaced with a studio portrait of a smart-looking professional woman with a pleasant smile—the kind of picture a real estate agent might use on a billboard or business card.

The hair was darker and there were fewer wrinkles, but it was unmistakably the face of the woman pretending to be Dr. Gloria Tolman.

"This woman—who, by the way, is neither a real doctor nor a therapist—deceived hundreds of unfortunate people who reached out to her for help," Sally explained as her image filled the screen again. "Bianca Dunn wormed her way into their homes. They thought they'd be cured of their addictions and fears. They'd hoped to *free themselves through hypnosis*. They counted on Bianca Dunn to help them. Well, she *helped*, all right! While her trusting clients were under her hypnotic spell, Bianca helped herself to their wallets! But she was no dummy. She didn't actually steal anything—unless you count the two hundred dollars in cash per session she charged her clients while ripping them off. See, that's where Bianca was clever: she took down all their credit card information and asked her hypnotized subjects for their passwords, pin numbers, birthdays, and social security numbers. Then she turned around and sold the information to credit card scammers and identity thieves. It was a long while before some of Bianca Dunn's clients caught on to her scam. By that time, Bianca had amassed a small fortune. This quack hypnotherapist is currently in jail. But on tonight's show, we have her attorney, Gary McGoldrick, and one of Bianca's victims, Cecilia Kirk, whose identity was stolen from her. I think you'll—"

The phone rang in Anna's hand. She saw the call was from Sally. She tapped the phone icon. "Hello?" she answered, a bit breathless.

"Did you see the clip?" Sally asked. "Is she the hypnotherapist you met?"

"Yes, that's her," Anna admitted. Before she could stop

herself, she started spilling her guts: "Taylor recommended her to me. That's why I was going to Taylor's place every afternoon last week—for hypnosis sessions with this woman. Taylor thought it might help me remember exactly what happened the night Courtney vanished."

Then Anna hesitated. She still didn't trust Sally enough to tell her about the recording with the bogus confession. So she told a white lie: "I didn't want to say anything to you about it last night because Taylor was helping me build up a defense against all your accusations. I didn't think you'd like it."

"So, when you said these afternoon meetings had nothing to do with me—or with my daughter getting abducted—that was bullshit."

"I didn't know this woman had a connection to you and your show," Anna argued.

"I helped put Bianca Dunn away for five years. They were going to let her off easy until I went after her on my show. It's clear she decided to get even by going after my sweet, trusting daughter. I'm sure Bianca took up with some seedy underworld types while she was in the slammer, types who might be into kidnapping and extortion. Listen, why was Taylor seeing this quack? Did she say?"

"No. That's the thing I—"

"She probably thought this lowlife scum would help her hear," Sally interrupted. "*Healing through hypnosis*, my foot. We thought Taylor's last surgery was a miracle. They told us all the previous diagnoses were wrong. She wasn't completely deaf, and a new cochlear implant chip might help her. The surgery took seven hours, and afterward, my baby could finally hear—for about a day and a half, then nothing. Some stupid doctor who examined Taylor claimed her continuing deafness was psychosomatic or some such nonsense. Taylor must have actually believed that quack. She still has the chip. She still gets it recharged every day, just hoping it might suddenly start working again. I'm not surprised she tried hypnosis. Did she say how she found this woman?"

"No. That's what I started to say. I had a feeling they didn't know each other very well. I wonder if this CJ recommended her to Taylor."

"I wonder, too," Sally said. "In your sessions with this Bianca woman, were you able to remember anything?"

"Nothing significant," Anna answered steadily. "I wonder how long she's been out of jail."

"She's been out for eighteen months. My people have already gotten in touch with her probation officer for her current address."

"You're kidding. God, that's fast."

"Seventeen-twenty East Thomas, Apartment F, on Capitol Hill," Sally said. "I was just waiting for confirmation from you before I sent someone over to check it out."

Anna stood up and started searching for her shoes amid the wreckage on the floor. "Maybe I can meet your guy there first, and we can drop in on her together. I might be some help."

"And you might get yourself hurt. Worse, you might get Taylor hurt. No, you just stay put. I'll keep you posted."

"Okay, well, I'll be here," Anna lied. She swiped her shoes off the floor and hurried into the kitchen for her purse. "Thanks, Sally."

She tapped the phone to disconnect and then brought up Google Maps. She typed in: *1720 East Thomas, Seattle.*

The estimated travel time was eighteen minutes. Anna figured she'd make it there in a little over ten.

CHAPTER FORTY

Russ repeatedly rang the bell bracketed to the wall. He held the piece of the baseboard, which he'd finally pried off the wall a half hour before. It was about the size of a baseball bat, perfect for what he had in mind.

He gave the bell one last ring, then ran into the bathroom and yelled under the vent: "Hey! I need some help here! She's sick! She's seriously ill!"

Hurrying back into the bedroom, Russ pulled on the bell cord again.

Laid out on the bed, Taylor let out a shriek.

Finally, amid all the noise, Russ heard the screen door slam. He cued Taylor, and she started moaning and clutching her stomach. He continued to clang the bell until he heard the RV door open.

"What the fuck is going on in there?" the guy yelled.

Russ stopped and listened to the man's footsteps on the other side of the RV's bedroom door.

Standing under the bell, Russ stayed turned slightly toward the wall. He kept the baseboard piece close to his leg to hide it. He was pretty certain Bud was staring through the peephole by now.

"Are you out there?" Russ called, giving the cord another pull. "I need help! She's sick. She has abdominal pain. She's thrown up three times! I think it's her appendix."

There was no answer.

Taylor kept groaning.

"Are you there, for Christ's sake?" Russ yelled. He clanged the bell again. "I'm telling you, she's sick!"

"Well, don't come crying to me," he heard their captor mutter. "You're the goddamn doctor."

"I can't do anything for her here," Russ argued, clutching the concealed piece of wood even tighter. "She'll die if we don't get her to a hospital! Take a look at her yourself. Feel her forehead. She's burning up! Fever's one of the signs."

Taylor stayed curled up on the bed, wailing in agony. She was acting her little heart out. She'd been so apprehensive earlier—she must have gone to the bathroom four or five times. But she'd risen to the occasion, and was now quite convincing as the victim of an appendicitis attack.

"Shit," the man outside grumbled. "Okay, stay where you are and keep ringing the goddamn bell. If you try anything, I'll shoot her in the head. That'll shut her up. Do we understand each other?"

"I understand!" Russ answered. "Hurry, please!" He clanged the bell and kept the baseboard slat close to his leg with his other hand.

The bolts on the door unlocked, and the door slowly opened.

The man was wearing his ski mask again, and he brandished the gun. He remained in the doorway. "What the fuck do you expect me to do?"

"She'll die if she stays here," Russ said. "You need to get her to a hospital."

"I can't do that."

"Yes, you can. You—you could blindfold her, load her into the car, and drop her off in front of the closest hospital's urgent care facility. Then you can drive away. You have to do something! She can't stay here. She'll die."

Bud chuckled behind his mask.

"It's not funny!" Russ yelled. "Feel her forehead."

Taylor was doubled up on the bed, whimpering.

The man stepped inside the room and cautiously approached the side of the bed. He kept the gun pointed at Russ.

Russ didn't move. He still had one hand on the bell cord while the other clutched the concealed piece of wood.

The man bent slightly as he reached toward Taylor with his free hand.

She suddenly sat up and bit down on the hand holding the gun.

He howled in pain.

Russ hauled back and swung the makeshift club. But in a split second, the man twisted around, dragging Taylor with him. The baseboard slat hit him in the shoulder and then snapped in two. One piece flew across the room. The gun landed on the shag carpet.

Taylor fiercely clung to the guy. "Go!" she yelled at Russ. "Run!"

For a second, Russ glanced toward the open bedroom door. He had a clear shot at escaping, but he couldn't leave her. Frantic, he looked down for the gun on the shag carpet, but he didn't see it. He went to grab the man, who was still struggling with Taylor.

Suddenly, Bud shoved Taylor toward him. She let out a shriek as she plowed into Russ. He fell to the floor— with his back against the wall and Taylor on top of him.

Bud quickly readjusted his ski mask and swiped the gun from the floor.

Russ tried to disentangle himself from Taylor.

"Tell her to move into the corner," their captor said, catching his breath. He stood over them with the gun poised. "Tell her that in your dummy sign-talk or I'll blow her head off. You, I need. But her, I don't give a shit about."

Bud took a few steps back toward the door to clear the way for her.

Still pinned to the floor, Russ slid out from beneath Taylor. He moved her into the corner of the room so that he was between her and their captor. Hugging her knees and panting to get a breath, she remained in the corner.

Russ glanced up at the man.

"Get on your knees and put your hands behind your back," he commanded from behind the ski mask.

Russ glared at him, but did what he said.

"You stupid shit," the man muttered. Then he slammed the butt of the gun against Russ's head.

"Don't!" Taylor screamed.

It was the last thing Russ heard as he collapsed onto the floor.

CHAPTER FORTY-ONE

Saturday, July 25—9:12 P.M.

An old apartment complex from the '60s with ten individual cabins, 1720 East Thomas had an unkempt courtyard. The units had beige aluminum siding that was ugly and peeling. Though it was getting dark, only one unit had an outside light on.

It had taken Anna twenty minutes to get there, and half of that time had been spent looking for a parking spot. She'd finally found one two blocks away. Walking back to the apartment complex, Anna didn't see anyone sitting in a car nor on foot scoping out the place. She'd figured Sally's private investigator was still on his way.

Anna found Apartment F in the corner of the U-shaped compound. The drapes in the front window were half-closed, and a light was on. But Anna didn't see any sign of activity inside. She crept around outside the unit, checking the rest of the windows. On the west side of the apartment, no lights were on. The neighbors in Apartment E didn't seem to be home, either. The narrow sidewalk between the units was strewn with junk: stacks of empty flowerpots, a rake, an old bicycle missing a tire, and a section of chain-link fence leaning against the gas meter to Bianca's apartment. Around back, there was a garbage can and a tall recycling bin. The unit didn't have a backyard, just a small patch of crabgrass with hardly enough room for the rickety-looking lawn chair.

The screen door in the back was shut, but Anna noticed the kitchen door was open a crack. The narrow, dark gap revealed nothing. But Anna could hear music: Neil Diamond singing "He Ain't Heavy . . . He's My Brother." She didn't hear any other sounds inside. But would Bianca have stepped out, leaving the light and the radio on, and the back door open?

She had to be home.

Anna figured, whether she knocked or snuck into the apartment, there would be a confrontation either way. If she snuck in, at least she might get a quick look around the place and maybe even find a second digital recorder with her manufactured confession on it. She was convinced Bianca hadn't given her only copy of the recording to Taylor.

Whatever happened, Sally's guy was on his way. So Anna knew she'd have some help soon.

Biting her lip, she pulled open the screen door. It squeaked loudly.

Anna froze. She listened for a few moments to make sure the noise hadn't alerted anyone. She didn't hear anything, just Neil Diamond on the radio.

She held the screen door in place, half-open. Then she pushed at the inside door and squeezed through into the kitchen. The screen door squealed again as she slowly closed it behind her.

Though the kitchen window was open, the place was still muggy and smelled like sour milk. None of the lights were on, but Anna could still see everything pretty clearly by the last hint of twilight through the window. Looking over toward the small, banged-up dinette table, Anna noticed a purse sitting on one of the chairs. She recognized it from her sessions with "Dr. Tolman." It was where she kept her digital recorder. The purse's long strap hung over the seat back.

Anna told herself that Bianca wouldn't have stepped outside without her purse.

She tiptoed over to the kitchen table.

She almost jumped at the sound of another voice in the apartment. Then she realized it was just the radio: "You're listening to Seattle's favorite oldies station! And here's Lulu with 'To Sir With Love'!"

As the song began, Anna carefully looked through the contents of the purse. She didn't find a digital recorder. But she discovered that the woman had a burner phone. She was sure it was the fake Dr. Tolman's bag, but just to make certain, Anna opened the wallet. There wasn't any cash in it. But she found a nondriver's identity card with a current photo of parolee Bianca Ray Dunn. It was the same middle-aged woman who had pretended to be Dr. Tolman. The address on the card was this one.

Slipping the wallet back into Bianca's purse, Anna crept into the sparsely furnished living room. There was a ratty sofa, a standing lamp, a folding table and chair, and on the floor, an old TV. On the table were the remnants of a dinner: a can of Diet Coke, a carryout container, and a crumpled napkin. She wondered when Bianca had eaten that meal, because flies were buzzing around it.

A light was on in the bathroom, which, along with the bedroom, was off a little hallway. The music seemed to be coming from that part of the apartment. Anna poked her head into the bathroom. It was ugly with salmon-colored tiles. The counter was a mess. Towels were haphazardly draped over the shower curtain rod and the rack on the wall.

Anna moved toward the bedroom, but stopped dead in the doorway.

The music was clear now. It came from a clock radio on the nightstand.

Bianca Dunn was sprawled across the unmade full-size bed. She was dressed in jeans and a short-sleeve yellow top—only most of the top was stained with blood. It looked black in the dark. The sheets tangled beneath her body were bloodstained as well.

Anna noticed Bianca was wearing only one sandal. The other was on the floor near the foot of her bed.

Terrified, Anna thought she was going to be sick. But she forced herself to step closer to the bed. That was when she saw the box cutter in Bianca's hand—and the slash across her throat.

Bianca's eyes were open. She seemed to stare at the ceiling. A forlorn look was on her face.

For a moment, Anna was paralyzed.

"Eleanor Rigby" started to play on the radio.

Past the music, Anna was sure she heard the screen door squeak.

Panic-stricken, she turned and hurried back to the living room. She saw a light go on in the kitchen. A shadow swept over the kitchen doorway.

Anna ran for the front entrance and tried the doorknob.

It was locked. Her heart racing, she fumbled with the lock and flung open the door.

A tall man stood there, blocking the way. His face was in the shadows.

Anna let out a scream and shrank back.

A light went on behind her.

She turned around to see a buxom, fortysomething brunette standing beside the floor lamp. She wore a sleeveless top and jeans and carried a shoulder bag. She also had a gun—pointed at the floor.

Anna turned again toward the doorway. In the light, she recognized Jim Larson, the private investigator who had been guarding Taylor yesterday. He let out a little laugh and sighed.

"Well, that's five bucks I owe Sally," he said. "I told her you wouldn't be stupid enough to come here on your own. But Sally said you'd probably make it here before we did."

A hand over her heart, Anna stared at him and tried to catch her breath.

"I take it Bianca isn't home," he said.

"Her purse is in the kitchen, Jim," the woman said.

His brow wrinkled, he looked at Anna.

She nodded. "Bianca's home . . ."

CHAPTER FORTY-TWO

Without opening his eyes, Russ was aware of someone hovering over him on the bed. A damp washcloth soothed his aching head, but he still felt awful. For a few moments, he didn't want to move. He didn't want to think about anything. His escape attempt had failed miserably, and now he had no idea how he and Taylor would ever get out of there.

He remembered something Bud had said a moment before the guy had knocked him out: *"You, I need. But her, I don't give a shit about."* It didn't make any sense—especially coming from someone who was supposed to be obsessed with deaf women. Russ wondered why the guy considered him so essential and Sally Justice's daughter expendable. Why was he being kept alive?

Russ's eyes were still closed. He knew Taylor was at his side. She started to caress his cheek. It was sweet of her to comfort him this way. But it was also awkward as hell, since he barely knew her.

He felt her gently kiss his forehead. Her hand slid down to his neck and then to his chest. She unfastened the top button of his shirt and moved her hand over his chest.

"Hey . . ." Startled, Russ opened his eyes and sat up. The washcloth fell off his head.

Taylor pulled back. She looked flustered —and embarrassed. "I'm so sorry! I just wanted to make sure you were okay."

Russ nodded and touched the abrasion in the corner of his forehead. "Thanks, I think I'll be all right," he muttered, signing for her. "I'm sorry about everything. I really screwed up our *Great Escape* attempt."

"It doesn't matter," she said, smiling bravely. She picked up the damp washcloth and brought it to his forehead again. "You could have easily gotten away when he was struggling with me. You should have run when you had the chance. It's what you told me to do, remember?"

"Well, I couldn't desert you," he replied.

"I know. And if the tables were turned, I couldn't have deserted you, either. That's what I was trying to tell you before. We're in this together, Russ."

He took the washcloth from her and hung it over the headboard. "I guess you're right," he signed. "Thank you for looking after my war wound." He pointed to his forehead.

She blushed. "Isn't it funny how two people who hardly know each other are thrown together in a desperate situation, and they form this instant bond?"

Russ nodded and then signed: "Yeah, well, we'll get out of here. Don't worry. Between the two of us, we'll figure something out."

"You're so good at sign language," Taylor went on,

staring at him, dreamy-eyed. "I can imagine you and Courtney having all these intimate conversations in bed, signing to each other. You really were a beautiful couple."

He shrugged. "Well, thank you. That's kind of you to say. But Courtney and I had a lot of problems."

"Courtney was special. And maybe that's why she wasn't very easy to live with. Special people sometimes have their own special rules." She smiled. "Me, I'm just an ordinary, uncomplicated girl. But I guess you've figured that out by now."

She started to caress his arm.

Russ discreetly pulled away and repositioned himself on the bed. She was making him uncomfortable with her flirting. He wasn't even remotely interested in her that way. At the same time, he didn't want to hurt her feelings.

With her bruised face, she kept looking at him expectantly—like she was waiting for him to kiss her. "It means a lot to me that you couldn't leave without me," she said and signed. "I think we both feel—"

Outside, the screen door slammed. Taylor sat up on the bed.

Baffled, Russ looked at her. "How did you hear that?"

She shook her head. "I saw you react. You heard something. What was it?"

The door to the RV opened.

"He's coming back," Russ silently signed. He got to his feet and felt dizzy for a moment.

It sounded like the guy was approaching the bedroom door. "Hey, Doc, I'm taking your girlfriend off your hands! Let her know. Tell her to stand up—back to the door and hands behind her. Meanwhile, I want you to ring that bell. Understand?"

Taylor moved to the edge of the bed. "What's happening?"

"He's taking you out of here," Russ reluctantly explained. "He wants you to stand with your back to the door and your hands behind you."

Panic-stricken, Taylor shook her head. "No, I won't!"

Russ felt so powerless. "I'm sorry. You better do what he says." Then he silently mouthed and signed to her, "I'll figure out a way to get out of here and help you. For now, please, just do what he says."

"I can see you talking to her in your secret hand code," the man called, obviously at the peephole. "Tell her to get off her ass or she's a dead woman. I don't have all night. C'mon, quickly."

"He's going to kill you if you don't do what he says," Russ told her.

Tears in her eyes, Taylor sprang off the bed and threw herself into Russ's arms. She desperately clung to him. He felt her lips pressing against the side of his face.

He had to pry her away until he had her at arm's length. Russ stepped back—toward the bell on the wall. "You need to put your hands behind you so that he can see them."

He heard two of the three locks being unlatched. Then he reached for the little rope and clanged the bell. He could hardly look Taylor in the eye.

With a wounded look, she gazed at him and slowly shook her head over and over. She may as well have been standing in front of a firing squad.

Russ felt hopeless—and angry. He kept thinking there must be something he could do.

But then, past the bell resounding, he heard the last lock unlatch, and the door swung open. With a ski mask once again covering his head, the man stepped into the room. He held Russ at gunpoint. In one quick motion, he grabbed Taylor by her hair and pulled her toward the door.

She let out an earsplitting shriek as he dragged her out the doorway.

Russ rushed for the door. But it shut in his face.

He heard the locks click: one, two, and three.

He listened to Taylor crying—and the retreating footsteps. A few moments later, the RV door shut. Shortly after that, he heard the screen door bang.

"Shit," he muttered.

Frustrated, Russ started to pace in a U formation around the disheveled bed. As he passed the wall, he slammed it with his fist and dented the paneling. It hurt like hell, but he was too enraged to care. He kept thinking of poor Taylor, looking at him so dreamy-eyed just minutes ago— like he was her savior, her hero. *Some hero*, Russ thought. He hadn't been able to do a thing to help her. And that was the second time the door had been open today, his second opportunity for escape—and he'd blown it.

He took the cool, damp washcloth off the bed's head-board and wrapped it around his sore hand. Then he started pacing again.

What was that creep Bud planning to do tonight? Was he going to tie Taylor to that kitchen chair again? Would he succeed in raping her or would he end up killing her?

Russ was convinced this Bud scumbag had murdered

Courtney. One more dead deaf woman wouldn't make a difference to the son of a bitch.

He thought he heard the screen door squeak open.

Russ stopped and listened. It had been only about ten minutes since Taylor had been hauled out of the room.

Russ heard another door shut. Someone locked it, and then the screen door slammed.

He could hear murmuring, but couldn't make out what the guy was saying. Was Bud talking on his phone?

Russ moved into the bathroom and stood under the vent so that he could hear more clearly. He detected footsteps on gravel. Was it just one person or two? A car door opened and shut. The engine started. It sounded as if someone got out of the car for a moment and then climbed back inside. Russ heard the gravel snapping on the driveway as the car pulled away. Then there were just the sounds of the woods at night.

Russ anxiously glanced around the bedroom for a means of escape—as if he hadn't already considered every possibility. Still, he looked up at the escape hatch again. He'd already spent hours standing on the bed, trying to manipulate the padlock on the latch. All he'd gotten was a crick in his neck.

He swiped the broken piece of cheap baseboard off the carpet and banged it against the window. The glass didn't even crack. Still, he kept hitting the window. But it just made his aching hand sorer.

He massaged his sore hand as he paced around the room some more. He glanced at the dent he'd made in the wall. "That was brilliant, Russ," he muttered to himself.

Stepping into the bathroom, he set down the washcloth

and ran his hand under the cold water in the sink. It felt better. He kept waving his hand under the running water until his fingers turned numb. With his free hand, he pushed against the spot on the wall where the mirror had been torn out. The drywall seemed solid.

Crouching down, he opened the cabinet below the sink and examined the empty space. He could see the pipes for the sink faucet and drain. The wood panel at the back of the cabinet looked kind of shoddy, maybe even shoddier than the baseboard that had broken so easily.

Russ wondered what was on the other side of the wall. He couldn't remember the exact layout. But if he could smash through that back panel, maybe, with a bit of contorting, he'd be able to squeeze past the drainpipes and crawl into the main cabin of the RV.

Sitting down on the bathroom floor, Russ stuck his leg into the cabinet. He slammed his foot against the panel. He heard a couple of cans or bottles clanking in the next room. With his back against the wall, he stomped against the panel again. There was more rattling and a loud bang on the other side. It sounded like a shelf had fallen. Gritting his teeth, Russ stomped against the panel once more. He felt something give and heard a crack.

It was the crisp, beautiful sound of the wood splintering.

CHAPTER FORTY-THREE

Saturday, July 25—11:32 P.M.

"Thanks for the lift," Anna said. "And thank Sally for me, too."

She climbed out of the backseat of Jim Larson's car and shut the door. Sally's private investigator and his partner, Brenda Melnick, had driven Anna from the East Precinct back to where she'd parked her car on 16th Avenue East and East Harrison—a couple of blocks from Bianca Dunn's apartment. Anna had just spent the last two hours with them at the police station, answering questions about Bianca Dunn.

Detective Baumann hadn't been there. Anna had been interviewed in a hot, airless interrogation room by a pair of detectives she'd never met before. The two forty-something cops had been friendly enough. They'd provided her with a cup of stale coffee from a vending machine and turned a small desk fan in her direction during the questioning.

But Anna could tell they'd been dissatisfied with the interview. They'd caught her in a lie. She'd had to recant her story about visiting Taylor three afternoons in a row to get tutorials in sign language. She'd already admitted as much to Sally; so Sally's private investigators hadn't been at all surprised by this revelation.

But the police were understandably perturbed to learn that she hadn't been completely honest with them in her statement the day before.

Even as Anna revealed the real reason for her visiting Taylor, she couldn't be completely transparent with the police—or Sally's private investigators. She admitted that she'd seen Bianca Dunn at Taylor's apartment those three afternoons for hypnotherapy sessions to help her remember events from the night Courtney had vanished. Anna pointed out that, while Bianca had obviously duped Taylor and her into thinking she was Dr. Tolman, she'd still been a skilled hypnotist.

"With her help, I was able to remember a lot of details about that night," Anna told them. "But I'm sure none of it would be useful to your investigation. It was mostly things like what we ate at the restaurant and the route we drove home. The only detail of any significance I can now tell you is that Courtney was still wearing a brown sleeve-less dress when I left their place. She hadn't changed into the purple robe they talked about on Sally's show and on the news. I was glad to remember that detail. But maybe it's not significant to you at all."

Anna didn't mention a thing about the hypnosis sessions having been recorded.

But she gave them a blow-by-blow of how, earlier in the evening, she'd let herself into Bianca Dunn's apartment and then discovered her corpse in the bedroom.

The entire time she spoke to the police, she kept

thinking: *Why should they believe me? They've already caught me lying to them once. And they're not even getting the complete story now.* She was digging herself a deeper and deeper hole. But she wasn't ready to tell them about the recorded "confession" yet, not until she could prove it was fake.

Before the police detectives had let her go, one of them had told her that Detective Baumann would be in touch with several follow-up questions. He'd told her this with a sigh and a raised eyebrow, the kind of look no patient wanted to get from a doctor after a medical exam.

Anna figured she'd just made things worse for herself as far as the police were concerned.

Sally's private investigators had offered to give Anna a lift to her car. On the way, Brenda, in the front passenger seat, had been texting. When she'd finished, she'd asked Anna how things were going with her brother, Stuart. Anna had totally forgotten that this woman had helped Taylor track down Stu.

"Oh, he's fine, thanks," Anna had lied. "He's getting some help with his drug problem."

She hadn't felt like telling the woman that all her work had been in vain.

Now she took her key fob out of her purse and unlocked the Mini Cooper. The lights flashed. Opening the door, she cautiously peeked in the back and then climbed in behind the wheel. Anna waved at the two private investigators, and they drove away.

Just then, her phone rang, startling her.

She fished the phone out of her bag and checked the screen. Sally Justice was calling. Anna tapped the screen.

"Sally? Funny you should call. Your private investigators just dropped me off."

"I know. Brenda just texted. She gave me the lowdown on everything that was discussed at the police station. She said the police believe that Bianca Dunn has been dead for about twenty-four hours. And at first glance, it appears she might have killed herself. What's your opinion?"

"I'll tell you the same thing I told the police," Anna said. She glanced around as she spoke. She was on a tree-lined residential street, and it was awfully dark. She made sure the Mini Cooper's doors were locked. "It's damn suspicious. I mean, for starters, if I was going to commit suicide, I can think of less gruesome ways to do it than slashing my throat with a box cutter."

"I was thinking the exact same thing," Sally said. "As I mentioned earlier, I wonder if Bianca took up with some ruthless extortionists while she was in prison. Maybe with this kidnapping scheme she got in over her head—that is, if it wasn't a suicide."

"Sally, that's the second 'suicide' within twenty-four hours," Anna pointed out, "Bianca—and the man who worked on your show. I'm sorry, what was his name again?"

"Gordon Savage." Sally sighed. "He shot his wife and then himself—with his own gun. They were found in their house. He had a lot of problems—debts, depression, you name it. Are you saying that you don't think he committed suicide?"

"No, I just think it's strange, both happening on the same day. What was his job on the show?"

"Gordy was my soundman for years."

For a moment, Anna was speechless. It all made sense now.

"Anna? Are you there?"

"Yes. Did Taylor know him very well?"

"She knew him as well as she knows everyone else on the show. But it's not like Taylor's at my studio every day. Why do you ask? Do you think Gordy's death is somehow connected to Taylor's disappearance?"

"Maybe," Anna said. "Listen, Sally, can I call you back in a bit? Are you going to be up awhile longer?"

"You think I'd be able to sleep a wink until I know my baby's safe?" she asked. "If you can help me find Taylor, feel free to call me whenever you want."

"Thanks, Sally, bye," Anna said. She hung up and then started her car.

She still didn't trust Sally enough to think out loud on the phone with her.

As she drove home, it started to make sense. Bianca Dunn had hypnotized her and made her repeat certain phrases and sentences for the fake confession. More snippets of her talking were lifted from her various broadcasts. Then Sally's soundman, Gordon Savage, had edited everything into one seamless "session." But it was obviously a rush job, because Anna had noticed gaps and pauses in her dialogue.

Maybe Sally was right, Bianca might have gotten in "over her head" with some ruthless kidnappers. She and Gordon Savage had helped create the bogus confession, but they knew too much. Savage's wife was probably collateral damage in an effort to "clean house." And poor

Taylor must have figured out what was going on. Was she dead, too?

Tightening her grip on the wheel, Anna watched the road ahead.

She still had no idea why all this was happening. It didn't make any sense: Why was someone going to all this trouble to frame her for Courtney's murder?

Anna wondered if she'd survive long enough to find out the answer.

CHAPTER FORTY-FOUR

As he crawled through the debris on the other side of the opening, Russ heard his pant leg tear and felt something sharp scrape across his left calf.

"Shit!" he muttered.

He stopped and caught his breath. He was half in and half out of a broom closet, surrounded by old containers of cleaning supplies, a broom and a mop, several splintered pieces of paneling, and a dislodged shelf. He was filthy and sweaty. His shirt, soaked with perspiration, clung to him. And now, he could feel blood running down his leg.

It had taken about a half hour for Russ to kick apart the water-damaged panel at the back of the bathroom sink cabinet. His right foot ached from all the pounding. It had seemed to take forever for him to wriggle past the drainpipe, through the opening, and into the broom closet. Then he'd pushed open the closet door, which, fortunately, wasn't latched.

Throughout the ordeal, he'd listened for a car. But as far as he could tell, his captor hadn't returned. Russ didn't know if the guy had taken Taylor with him—or if she was, once again, tied to a chair in the kitchen.

Once he dragged himself through the opening, Russ was able to sit up. He sighed with relief. After close to ten days being cooped up, he'd managed to crawl out of his little prison.

With all the windows painted over, it was pitch-black in the RV's main cabin. Russ had to navigate the closet by the bathroom light that seeped through the opening. Staggering to his feet, he stumbled over the old cleaning supplies strewn on the floor as he felt his way toward the front of the cabin. He finally found the door and blindly groped for the handle. He prayed Bud hadn't installed an outside lock.

Russ pulled down on the door handle and pushed, but the door didn't budge.

He gave the door a kick, and it flew open. It had just been stuck.

Russ let out another grateful sigh.

The night air was incredible—so fresh and cool. He relished taking those first few breaths of freedom as he stepped outside. And he finally set eyes on the house—and that screen door he'd heard slam so many times.

Taylor's description of the house was pretty accurate. It was a dumpy little rambler in the middle of some woods. Russ didn't see any other houses or lights. The driveway snaked through the trees and then seemed to disappear in the darkness.

There was a light on in the window by the screen door. But an old bedsheet had been tacked over the window inside. Approaching the house, he figured this must be the back entrance. The door past the screen was windowless.

Russ pulled open the screen door and tried the doorknob. It was locked. He gave the door a push, but it didn't move.

Once again, he wondered if Taylor was on the other side of the door, tied to a kitchen chair.

He hurried around to the front of the house, which was just as decrepit and neglected as the back. But there was an outside light on by the front door —and the door had a window in it.

Russ jostled the handle. Locked.

Frustrated, he glanced around and spotted a brick border around a shabby patch of weeds and bushes. It must have been somebody's garden at one time. Grabbing one of the bricks, Russ threw it at the window. The glass shattered. He pushed out the remaining shards of glass until he could reach through the jagged opening and find the door lock. He unlocked the door and pushed it open.

Inside, he found a light switch and turned it on. The overhead in the living room was a naked bulb in the fixture. The furnishings were cheap and slapdash: an old sofa, and a desk with a stool on wheels. The threadbare beige carpet was littered with papers and food wrappers. Among the refuse, Russ noticed the discarded store packaging for a burner phone. There was also a paper bag from Pete's Supermarket, the store down the block from Anna's place.

Russ still had no idea where he was, but the house couldn't have been anywhere near their Lake Union neighborhood in Seattle.

He stopped for a moment and lifted his pant leg to

inspect the scrape on his calf. The blood dripped down to his sock.

He lowered his pant leg and headed into what looked like the kitchen. If Taylor was in there, she was being awfully quiet. She wouldn't have heard the window in the door shatter, but she'd have noticed the living room light go on.

He stepped into the kitchen. The room was practically barren except for an old avocado-colored stove, on which sat a microwave. Over against one wall was a mini-fridge, which was humming. The faded linoleum floor was littered with a few pieces of trash. But it wasn't quite the pigsty Taylor had made it out to be. There was no kitchen table.

And not a kitchen chair in sight.

CHAPTER FORTY-FIVE

Sunday, July 26—12:02 A.M.

As Anna pulled into the carport, she realized she'd have to tell Sally and the police about her recorded "confession." At this point, it could be connected to two "suicides," a murder, and most likely, Taylor's disappearance. The sooner the police and Sally knew about the bogus confession, the better chance they had of finding Taylor.

She should have told them about the recording as soon as Taylor had disappeared, but she'd been too worried about incriminating herself. Now Anna was ready to pay the price for that delay. She hoped it wasn't too late for Taylor.

She considered just restarting the car and driving back to the East Precinct. But she wanted to splash some water on her face and change her clothes for what would be a long night ahead in the police interrogation room.

Climbing out of the Mini Cooper, Anna locked it with the key fob. At a brisk clip, she headed down the dark, narrow street that ran alongside the lake. It was one of those nights when she hated the long walk from the carport to her home. And tonight, she had every reason to be on edge. Above her, the tree branches swayed in the gentle breeze, creating shadows that danced across the street pavement. Anna didn't see anyone else along the way, and she noticed only one boat out on the water—a sports cruiser, not far from her dock.

A bit breathless, Anna finally turned down the shadowy pathway that led to the dock gate. Sometimes, this was the scariest part of her journey home at night because, although she was so close to her destination, the spot was surrounded by bushes, and a tall elm tree nearby blocked out the moonlight. Anna never felt safe until she was able to lock the gate behind her. She already had the key in her hand.

She didn't see any lights on in her neighbors' floating homes. It was quiet—except for the sound of water lapping against the pilings.

"Anna?" whispered someone behind her.

She swiveled around. For a moment, she didn't see anyone.

Then Taylor emerged from the shadows.

Anna gasped at her bruised face. "My God, Taylor," she whispered. "You scared me! Are you okay? Everyone's been so worried."

"Just unlock the gate, okay?" she said under her breath.

Anna realized Taylor wasn't signing while she spoke. She also noticed the half-concealed gun in Taylor's hand. It was pointed at her.

Anna's heart was still racing, but she let out a baffled

little laugh and gestured at the gun. "What—what's that for?"

"Just in case," she replied. "Unlock the gate, Anna."

Still bewildered, Anna unlocked the gate and opened it. Then she turned to Taylor. "I don't understand. *Just in case* what?"

"I need you to do some things you won't want to do. I have the gun just in case you give me an argument." She nodded toward the dock. "Get moving."

Anna noticed Taylor's slightly impaired speech was almost completely gone. "I still don't understand any of this. What are you talking about?"

"I'm saying that I'm going to kill you, you stupid bitch."

Dumbfounded, Anna stared at her for a moment.

"Open the gate."

Anna tried not to panic. She immediately thought of the advantage she had over Taylor. Covering her mouth, she turned her head away from Taylor. "I need help!" she called out in a loud, shaky voice. "Can anyone hear me?"

"I hear you, Anna," Taylor said.

Stunned, Anna gaped at her. "You can hear?"

Taylor nodded. "Your neighbors can't help you, Anna. The Gettles and the Britzes aren't home tonight. That's one reason I decided to do this now. C'mon, move. I don't want to take any chances with people passing by. I can't afford to be seen out and about right now."

Anna started toward the house, but then hesitated and turned to speak to Taylor. "How do you know about my neighbors' schedules?"

"I have a helper," Taylor answered cryptically.

Anna gave a stunned little laugh. "I still can't believe any of this. You can hear me?"

"I've heard you this whole time, Anna," she said. "Keep walking."

Anna reluctantly continued on toward her front door. Taylor remained behind her.

"I had cochlear implant surgery several weeks ago," she heard Taylor explain in a voice which seemed so strange coming from her. "They gave me a new chip, no external hardware needed. I can hear noises, voices, music, though sometimes I still have to read lips to fully comprehend what people are saying. The surgery was a success. But then I decided: Wouldn't it be fun if people had no idea that I could hear them? I felt like one of those teenage superheroes in Courtney's books. The surgery has helped me to listen and learn to enunciate better, maybe not perfect, but better. I can talk in this voice, and no one recognizes the old Taylor. It's another one of my superpowers. I can eavesdrop on conversations—and still read the lips of people across a room. You should hear some of the awful things people say in front of you when they think you're deaf. My mother gets the prize for that."

"That's just crazy," Anna muttered.

"If I pretend I'm still deaf, it makes me more like Courtney."

Anna stopped at the door and turned to lock eyes with Taylor. "*You* killed her, didn't you?"

"We'll talk inside."

Anna unlocked the door and opened it. Taylor stepped in after her, and once inside, she was less furtive about the gun. She pointed it at the door. "Lock up."

Frowning, Anna followed her orders.

She'd left the hallway closet open, and still had some

junk scattered on the floor. Taylor seemed to take it all in. She cracked a smug smile. "Were you looking for something?"

"You killed Courtney and then tried to frame me for it," Anna said. "What did she do to you, Taylor? What did she do to make you hate her so much that you'd bash her head in?"

"I *loved* Courtney," Taylor said, still holding Anna at gunpoint. "She and Russ were the perfect couple, so beautiful together. Then you came along and fucked it all up. If Courtney was going to share her husband and her life with anyone, it should have been me. The three of us could have been like a family. Sure, it would have been unconventional, to say the least. But special people sometimes have their own special rules." She glared at Anna with disgust in her eyes. "Then Russ took up with you.' Talk about stupid, such a waste. The whole time I was watching you two, all those months, I kept thinking: *What in the world does he see in her?*"

Anna kept shaking her head. She couldn't believe what she was hearing.

"Well, Russ is falling in love with *me* now," Taylor said, gloating. "We've been hostages together for only a day, and already he's kissed me."

"Russ is alive?" Anna murmured.

Taylor nodded. "The suicide on the Tacoma Narrows Bridge was faked with a little assistance from my friend CJ. I'm the mysterious 911 lady. Isn't that perfect? No one would think a poor little deaf girl would be communicating so clearly on a cheap burner phone. It was pretty funny to watch my mother on her show talk about the *anonymous witness*. The last person she suspected was her sweet, innocent daughter."

"But Russ is alive," Anna repeated—almost to herself.

"All this time, he's been locked up in a trailer at a very remote spot near Edmonds. He thinks he's being held prisoner by someone who is obsessed with deaf women and you. Russ is just starting to get a taste of Bud's obsession with you. I think it's dawning on him that Bud is your self-appointed protector. Bud made him write that suicide note, exonerating you in Courtney's death. And he thinks Bud abducted me because I had the recorded confession you made. Russ has even heard part of it. I'm seeing to it that he slowly gets used to the idea that you killed Courtney. All of this will become very clear to Russ in the next couple of days while we share our little jail cell together—a jail cell with a big queen bed in it. I'll work on him. People who are thrown together in a crisis situation often fall in love. It's already happening to us. He's very gentle with me, Anna. You should have seen the loving way he tended to my bruises."

"I still don't understand any of this. Is Bud actually your friend CJ?"

Taylor grinned. "Congratulations. Go to the head of the class. You understand more than you think you do."

"Then CJ isn't really deaf, either," Anna said. "Tell me, what does he get out of this?"

"He gets to be a celebrity. Those fifteen minutes of fame on *The Sally Justice Show* were the thrill of a lifetime for him. And speaking of thrills, I see to it that his peculiar needs are satiated. You see, CJ gets his kicks in strange ways. For example, I know he secretly enjoyed beating me up."

"Did he enjoy killing your mother's soundman and his wife—and Bianca Dunn? He murdered them, didn't he? Or was that your handiwork?"

Taylor nodded. "That was CJ. I got what I needed from Gordy and Bianca. After that, they became a liability."

"You know, Taylor, the audio confession you worked so hard on, it might have rattled me at first. I'll admit that. But it'll never stand up under police scrutiny. A decent soundman would listen to a minute of it and know it's all edited together, I only heard snippets over the phone before I figured that out."

"The recording wasn't meant for the police," Taylor said. "I wanted Russ to hear part of it so that he'd think you killed Courtney. And I wanted you to hear it—to drive you a little insane and make you wonder whether or not you could have murdered her. Tell me the truth, Anna, it worked, didn't it? I had you worried." She glanced around at the mess Anna had made earlier. "You don't even have to tell me. I can see for myself."

"Was it really worth the lives of three people, Taylor?"

"Bianca was a con artist who ripped off dozens of suckers. As for Gordy Savage and his wife, they had so many addictions, debts, and problems, they're better off dead. So don't get sanctimonious with me, Anna." She took a deep breath. "Speaking of suicides, we need to get started on yours. Now, I need you to write a note." She pointed with the gun at the doorway to the second bedroom. "I believe the study is that way—if memory serves me correctly."

Anna didn't move. "You've been in here before."

She nodded. "Several times—since last October."

"So, you were the one behind all those little acts of sabotage."

Taylor chuckled. "I think my favorite was planting that dead seagull in the middle of your living room. I wish I had been around to see your reaction." Taylor's smirk faded, and she suddenly looked dead serious. "You never should have come between Russ and Courtney. It was a terrible, contemptible mistake, Anna." With the gun, she motioned to the second bedroom again. "Now, let's get started on that note. I want you to get out some paper and a pen."

Anna reluctantly headed into her mother's old bedroom. On her way to the desk, she stepped over the exercise equipment and other objects scattered on the floor. She opened the top desk drawer and took out a writing tablet and a pen.

"My God, these weights and the straps are perfect for what I have in mind," Taylor said—almost to herself. "Now, sit down at the desk and write what I tell you—in your handwriting. No block letters. I want that Catholic schoolgirl scribble of yours, Anna. Go ahead, sit down."

Anna sank into the chair and picked up the pen. She felt sick to her stomach. Her hand started shaking, and she wasn't sure she could write legibly.

"Okay, write this down," Taylor said, standing over her. "*I can't go on living with myself after what I've done . . .* period." She paused while Anna wrote. "*Russ had no idea about any of it . . .* period. *He's an innocent man . . .* period." She waited for another few moments until

Anna had jotted it down. "*I hated to see him take the blame . . .* period. *I miss him, and feel responsible for his watery suicide . . .* period. *I have decided to join him in eternity . . .* period."

Anna wrote it down. She figured anyone even remotely acquainted with her would know she'd never write corny stuff like *watery suicide* and *join him in eternity*. She handed the note to Taylor.

As Taylor looked over the letter, Anna saw it as an opportunity to catch her off guard and wrestle the gun away. But before Anna even made a move, Taylor looked over the top of the piece of paper.

"Perfect on the first try." She handed the note back to her. "Let's tape this on the glass door to your deck. I want people to see it before they step outside and notice the dinghy is missing."

Her stomach in knots, Anna got the Scotch tape out of her drawer and followed orders. As she taped the note onto the sliding door, she could see Taylor's reflection in the darkened glass. She was standing behind her with the gun drawn, watching her every move.

"See the sports cruiser out there?" Taylor asked. "That's CJ. He'll be accompanying us on our journey tonight."

Anna gazed out at the boat drifting on the water about a hundred feet from her dock. Only a cabin light was on. All its other lights were off. She couldn't see anyone on the boat.

"All right, time for a bit of heavy lifting," Taylor said. "You're going to load some of that exercise equipment onto your dinghy. Quickly now, we don't have all night."

As they returned to the study, Taylor said she just

needed the heavier barbells, the ropes, and the straps. It took two trips to load everything into the boat tied to Anna's dock. Anna kept stepping over and weaving around stacks of junk on the floor. On the second trip out to the dock, she had to ask: "So—where is it? Where did you hide the glass trophy you used to kill Courtney?"

Taylor followed her out to the dock. She watched Anna load the second batch of weights and straps into the dinghy. "Courtney's award," she said, laughing. "I was particularly proud of that little stroke of genius. I figured it would really drive you insane, believing that glass thing was somewhere around here. Shades of Lady Macbeth and 'Out, damned spot!' The thing had my fingerprints all over it—along with Courtney's blood." She glanced out toward the water. "I tossed it out there somewhere. It's at the bottom of the lake."

Standing in the boat, Anna stared up at her. "That 'confession' you and Bianca—or should I say *Dr. Tolman*— that confession you had me recite while I was under, that's pretty much how it happened when you killed Courtney, isn't it?"

A frown came to Taylor's bruised face. The light breeze tousled her brown hair. "Yes, that's pretty much how it happened," she said quietly.

"You didn't intend to kill her, but she pushed you over the edge, didn't she? What did she say to you, Taylor? What did she do?"

Taylor backed up to shut the sliding glass door— with Anna's suicide note taped to the other side. She gave a brief wave at her friend on the sports cruiser drifting nearby.

Anna glanced down at the weights and straps inside the little boat.

Join him in eternity . . . watery suicide . . .

It was suddenly clear to Anna what Taylor had planned for her.

"Sit down," Taylor said.

Obediently, Anna sat down in the boat—her back to the outboard motor.

Without taking her eyes—or the gun—off her, Taylor carefully stepped into the dinghy. "I'll tell you what happened that night," she said, "once we're out on the lake—in deeper water."

CHAPTER FORTY-SIX

At the end of the long, winding gravel driveway, Russ stopped to catch his breath. He braced a hand against a rickety, old, rural-style mailbox on the roadside. His right foot throbbed from having kicked out the panel beneath the bathroom sink earlier. And his left sock was soaked with blood from the cut along his calf.

When he'd started running up the driveway, Russ hadn't realized it was mostly uphill and about two city blocks long. The unlit gravel drive snaked through the pitch-dark woods. Russ had hoped he'd see a light through the trees somewhere—or maybe at the end of the driveway. But as he held on to the mailbox and finally started to get his breath, he glanced in one direction and then the other, and things looked decidedly bleak.

He'd reached a deserted two-lane road that cut through a huge wooded area. As far as Russ could see in both directions, there wasn't a light or a road sign.

He figured there had to be other driveways to other private residences off this lonely road. He simply couldn't see them from here. He'd find one of those homes and get help. He probably wouldn't even need to knock on the door. Anyone living in these woods would probably call 911 at the first glimpse of a stranger approaching their home—especially at this hour.

Back at that dilapidated little rambler, Russ had noticed that the clock on the microwave read 11:47. But he wasn't sure if that was right or not.

He'd gone through the house, hoping against hope to find the duffel bag with his phone in it. But he had a feeling the bag had been left inside his car parked on the Tacoma Narrows Bridge.

In his search through the house, Russ had also hoped to find some clue to help explain Taylor's involvement in whatever the hell was going on. Was her story about being molested and beaten while tied to a kitchen chair complete bullshit? Russ had seen her bruises. They were real. Had she let Bud beat her—merely to elicit Russ's sympathy and trust? It had sure worked. He'd been completely duped.

All those trips she'd taken to the bathroom before their escape attempt—had she been somehow communicating with the guy, telling him what to expect? She could have had a cell phone on her.

Russ now wondered if Taylor was even deaf. He remembered seeing her react when the screen door had slammed shortly before the guy had come to drag her out of the RV. Only a hearing person would have noticed that.

Russ had heard the car door open and shut twice when his captor had driven off a couple of hours ago. He was now convinced Taylor had left with him—of her own volition. But even if she'd been bullshitting him all this time, Russ still believed what Taylor had said about Bud having a fixation on Anna. Russ couldn't help thinking that they were going after her tonight. He had to warn her.

Once he got to a phone, he'd call Anna before he did anything else.

Russ hobbled into the middle of the seemingly endless road. He still had no idea where he was. He started to look for little breaks along the roadside that might indicate a driveway.

That was when he noticed a faint light in the distance where the highway came to a peak. The light grew brighter and brighter—until a pair of headlights appeared on the dark horizon.

"Thank you, God," he whispered.

But it suddenly dawned on him. What if it was Bud and Taylor returning?

For a moment, Russ wasn't sure what to do. Should he stand in the middle of the road waving his arms or go hide in the woods? It was still too far away to discern if the vehicle was a black Jetta. He'd have to wait until the car was much closer. In the meantime, he stood his ground.

It looked like a regular car, not a truck or a van.

Russ started waving his arms. He figured if it was the Jetta, he'd just make a run for it into the woods.

The vehicle hurtled down the hill toward him. Russ presumed the driver must have noticed him by now. He frantically waved and signaled for the driver to stop.

He could hear the humming engine and pebbles snapping beneath the tires. He yelled out over the noise: "Stop, please! Stop!"

The car zeroed in on him. For a moment, the whole section of road seemed to light up. Then the driver must have turned on the brights, because Russ was blinded. He heard the screeching tires. The sound was deafening.

Panicked, he leapt toward the shoulder of the road.

But he was too late.

Russ felt the car slam into him.

Along with the horrible thud, he could almost hear his own bones crack. He flew through the air, the breath knocked out of him. All he could see was white—blinding, harsh white. Then suddenly, he hit the ground on his side. It felt like he'd been dropped from twenty feet in the air. He heard more bones crunching. On impact, the gravel and dirt on the roadside seemed to shift beneath him.

But for a crazy second, he thought: *I'm okay, I'm not dead. I just broke a few bones.*

But he hadn't tried to move yet.

His vision came back. A red cloud of dust, reflecting the brake lights of the car, settled around him. The vehicle was idling just a few yards up the road.

Then he felt the searing pain.

He couldn't breathe right. It wasn't just a few broken bones.

Russ tried to move his legs. They were working, but the right one felt like a very bad break. It was bleeding, too. Still, he was pretty sure his spinal cord was okay. From the severe ache on the left side of his abdomen, he thought he might have a damaged spleen or a ruptured diaphragm.

The car was still there. But he couldn't see the driver.

"Call 911!" Russ yelled with what little breath he had.

God, please, don't drive off and leave me here, he thought. He was so afraid he'd pass out or die before anyone got to him. He had to tell someone that Anna was in danger. He imagined passing out, then waking up in a hospital two hours from now—only to find out that Anna was dead.

He heard a woman crying hysterically. "I've hit somebody with my car . . . He—he just came out of the middle of nowhere . . . I'm here all alone . . . I think he might be dead . . ."

Russ managed to lift his head, but couldn't see the woman. He figured she must be inside her car. He hoped she was talking to the police. But after a few moments, all he could hear was muted whimpering. He realized she must have raised her car window. It was the smart thing to do if she was alone. She was probably locking the car doors, too.

Please, be talking to the police, he thought. *Please . . .*

Russ wanted to yell out Anna's address and ask the woman to send the police there. But he knew she couldn't hear him. Still, the address went through his head like a mantra: *3221 Fairview Avenue, Dante-Patricia Moorage Number 3, on the Lake Union Loop.*

He had to tell someone.

His breathing was getting worse. He wondered if he had a lung injury. He knew he'd broken or cracked a few ribs. Maybe that accounted for the breathing problem. Russ figured, if he tried to diagnose himself, then that would help take his mind off the excruciating pain. He thought about the possibilities of internal bleeding and abdominal damage. One leg was definitely broken. One of his arms, too, he was pretty certain of that.

He felt himself getting colder.

Please, hurry, he thought.

The red brake lights of the woman's car were his reassurance that he wasn't alone. She hadn't driven off yet. She was waiting for help, too, God bless her. Nowadays, so many people would have driven off.

Everything started getting darker. *You're not dying*, he told himself. He was dizzy, probably about to pass out. The pain was making his body shut down. Still, as horrible as he felt, Russ tried to remain conscious. He kept struggling to breathe.

But for a few minutes, he must have blacked out, because suddenly he noticed the car had moved. The driver had backed up a bit and switched to her hazard lights. Russ couldn't hear the car engine anymore.

But he heard a siren in the distance.

He told himself to hang on and stay awake.

And if he had any breath left in him when the ambulance finally arrived, he'd tell the paramedic: *3221 Fairview Avenue, Dante-Patricia Moorage Number 3, the last house on the dock, the one with the red door* . . .

CHAPTER FORTY-SEVEN

Sunday, July 26—1:09 A.M.

Sitting across from Anna in the small boat, Taylor kept the gun pointed at her. "Knot it again. Give the cord a good tug."

Anna reluctantly tied the jump rope around the second ten-pound barbell, which was coated in a yellow rubbery material. Her hands shook as she tightened the knot.

Taylor intently watched her every move. She'd already admonished Anna for allowing some slack in the knot when she'd tied on the first barbell. "Shake the rope so I can see they're both on good and tight," she demanded.

Grimacing, Anna hoisted up the jump rope—with twenty pounds of weights attached to it. Her arm muscles strained and tightened as she wiggled the rope. Once Taylor gave a nod of approval, Anna lowered the cord. The weights hit the boat's floor with a thud.

Around each ankle, Anna had already tied an exercise strap with a baby blue eight-pound weight attached.

"Okay, fasten the jump rope around your waist—like a belt," Taylor said. "I want you to tie three knots."

With a sigh, Anna started to secure the weighted rope around her waist.

That made thirty-six pounds of deadweight she'd be carrying once she plunged into the deepest part of the lake.

Taylor would remain in the little boat until she was sure Anna had drowned. Then her friend CJ would pick her up.

Anna figured that, tomorrow, the search-and-rescue team would probably find the aimlessly drifting, empty dinghy long before they ever found her.

The sports cruiser had been trailing closely behind them since they'd pulled away from Anna's private deck. Anna hadn't gotten a good look at Taylor's friend, because the boat's lights remained off. But she remembered his dorky, impish face from their encounter at Taylor's.

Following Taylor's orders, she'd rowed out toward the middle of Lake Union—away from all the other floating homes and houseboats. Sweaty, scared, and exhausted, Anna had done what she'd been told to do, hoping it meant she could stay alive just a little longer.

Taylor's plan was clear to her now. Within the next day or two, everyone would know that the late Anna Malone had confessed to Courtney Knoll's murder. It was all there in a suicide note, taped to the sliding glass door in her houseboat. She'd written the note shortly before rowing out to the middle of Lake Union and drowning herself.

It would all be in the newspapers. CJ would slip a newspaper with the story through a slot in the door of the RV bedroom where Taylor and Russ were imprisoned.

"I'm sure Russ will feel bad when he reads about what happened," Taylor had explained while Anna had been rowing. "But by then, the news that you murdered Courtney won't be much of a surprise to him. I think Russ is already starting to accept it as fact. Still, I'm certain he'll be sad that you're dead. But don't worry, Anna. I'll be there to comfort him. And you know, Russ won't be the only one grieving for you. CJ has this whole routine worked out, a beautiful monologue Bud will give outside the RV for Russ to hear—a drunken rant about how devoted he's been to you ever since he first saw you on TV, and how he did all this to protect you, and how none of it matters anymore now that you're dead. And very soon after that, Russ and I will realize that Bud has left us. *Poof*. . . disappeared. I'll discover that he must have unlocked the door locks before clearing out in the middle of the night. He'll have taken all his things with him—including that recorded confession of yours. Then Russ and I will be free. He'll be so happy that he'll forget all about you, Anna. I'll see to it. He'll love me more than he ever loved you."

Silent, Anna had kept rowing the boat toward the center of the lake. She'd wanted so much to tell Taylor that she didn't stand a chance of pulling off her insane, cockamamie plan. What was to keep her friend CJ—or Bud or whatever he called himself—from turning on Taylor and killing her, too? Maybe she was protected because she was his cash cow. But he could still blackmail her. Taylor couldn't afford to have him out on the loose. As for Russ, even if he was gullible enough to swallow all the garbage she fed him—which he wasn't—there was no way he'd ever fall in love with her. Taylor was delusional to think they had a future together.

But Anna had held her tongue—until now.

Now she had nothing to lose. She was sitting in a boat in the middle of Lake Union with a crazy woman who had a gun on her. It was almost surreal. To the north, Anna could see the headlights from the traffic on the Aurora Bridge, which towered over the dark lake. East of the bridge was Gas Works Park—with lights twinkling on the old gas works plant. And in yet another direction, the sports cruiser was looming close by, waiting to pick up Taylor once her mission for the night had been accomplished.

"Taylor, do you really think you'll be happy with Russ?" she asked, looking her in the eye. "How can you expect to build a decent relationship with him when it's based entirely on lies and deceit? The whole time you're with him, you'd always be worried about Russ someday finding out that you murdered his wife—and me. And believe me, he will find out, Taylor. And when he does, he'll fucking hate you."

Taylor looked stunned. "No, he won't! Besides, he won't find out! And if he did, then Russ would love me even more because he'd realize that I'd killed for him." She took a deep breath to calm herself.

"Besides, I didn't set out to kill Courtney," Taylor said quietly. "That was an accident. It never should have happened. I loved Courtney. And I loved the two of them together."

"Then why did you do it?" Anna asked.

"It wasn't really my fault," Taylor answered, frowning

at her. "You're the one to blame, Anna. You came between the two of them and ruined everything. I knew about you before anyone else. I'd been watching Courtney—and Russ. I figured out that he was seeing someone else. You thought your affair was this big secret, but I've spied on you two countless times since last summer and fall." She smirked a bit. "Anna, if you're going to screw a married man you shouldn't live in a place with such big windows. See, I have a small boat like this one, though mine's nicer. From the water at night, I used to watch you and Russ. I told Courtney all about you two."

"When?" Anna asked.

"Last November. I lied when I told you that I barely knew Courtney. Yes, we met at a charity function. But then Courtney reached out to me. She was hoping I could introduce her to some of my mother's friends in TV and show business. I knew I was being used, but I didn't mind. Courtney was a beautiful, talented, important person. I was flattered she wanted my help. But the truth is, I'm not very well connected at all, and I couldn't help her. I sensed Courtney pulling away. So I made myself useful to her in another way. I told her about you and Russ. I was her spy. Like I told you, in my boat at night, I'd watch you two. With my binoculars, I could even read your lips sometimes, especially when you were both outside, talking on your deck. I told Courtney about some of your conversations. She took me into her confidence. We were very close."

Anna squirmed, and for a moment, the weights tied to her ankles dragged against the floor of the boat. Taylor was confirming what she'd suspected: Courtney had known about them for a long time.

"If you and Courtney were so close, why did you end up killing her?" Anna asked.

Taylor hesitated before answering. She looked down at her gun—and then at Anna. "That Thursday night," she finally said, "from my boat, I saw that you weren't home. Neither were Courtney and Russ. Imagine my surprise when I spotted the three of you together, coming down their dock. I could see how drunk you were. You could barely stand up. Later, when I spotted you and Russ leaving their house together, I started to follow you. But then, I decided to talk to Courtney instead." Her voice started to shake. "You see, I'd seen her with you for the last three days. I was angry—and maybe a little jealous. I hadn't been able to help her in the way you were helping her—with a TV spot and so much publicity. And all that time, she'd been ignoring me.

"Anyway, I was hurt, and I wanted her to know that. So I went to their door and rang. But she wasn't answering. I wondered if there was something wrong with the doorbell system. Maybe the lights weren't flashing. But finally Courtney came to the door. She'd changed into a gorgeous, floor-length purple robe. I tried to explain how upset I was at her, but she was drunk—so dismissive and nasty. I told her she wasn't acting like a good friend should. But she laughed and said we weren't friends. That's when I realized she'd just been using me. She was horrible to me that night, so mean . . ."

Taylor's eyes filled with tears and her voice quavered. "I know she was drunk. I shouldn't have taken her seriously, but she said, 'You're just a pest . . . a frumpy, little pest.' That really hurt me, and I desperately wanted to hurt her back." Taylor wiped her tears away. "So, I grabbed the first thing I saw and hit her. I bashed in her skull. The thing I grabbed was Courtney's writing award."

Anna stared at her—and at the gun in her hand. "So I was right earlier," she murmured. "Everything happened pretty much the way you had me describe it in the recording—only it was you."

Taylor nodded. "I dragged her body out to my boat, then rowed to my car and loaded her into the trunk. When I had Bianca make you say how difficult it was lugging around all that deadweight, believe me, it came from personal experience. I ended up burying her in those woods by Lake Bosworth. I remembered you did one of your stories from there. On the drive back, I got the idea about pinning the whole thing on you. So the next morning, while you were at work, I pulled out the skeleton key I've been using on your place and let myself in. I took some of your clothes, and I loosened the ropes to your boat . . ."

Anna wasn't listening anymore. She was trying to think of what to do. Though tempted to lunge at Taylor and snatch away the gun, she knew she'd only end up getting shot. She thought about tipping over the dinghy. But she had thirty-six extra pounds strapped to her. Once she hit the water, she'd immediately start sinking. She probably wouldn't have a chance to grab on to the side of the capsized little boat.

It seemed hopeless. Besides, even if she could surprise Taylor and overpower her, Taylor's friend was still watching over them. The sports cruiser drifted closer and closer. It was only a few feet away now.

"I never meant for Russ to be blamed," Taylor was saying. "That was the last thing I wanted."

Taylor fell silent as the little boat started to teeter in

the water. The sports cruiser came up alongside them. "CJ's getting impatient." She sighed. "And he's right. We've been out here too long. For someone who couldn't hear for most of her life, sometimes I talk too much."

With the other boat so close, Anna knew she didn't have a chance. She could almost reach out and touch the side of the sports cruiser. She glimpsed a shadowy figure on deck, but only for a second. He bent down, grabbed something, and then threw a rope ladder over the starboard side. The bottom wooden rung hit the water with a splash.

"It's time, Anna," Taylor said. "I want you to stand up—very slowly."

Trembling, Anna didn't budge.

From the other boat, Taylor's friend looked down at them. Anna could see him now. He wore a black T-shirt— and a ski mask.

Taylor gave him a brief glance and chuckled. "He wears that ski mask for Russ and me."

He climbed over the side. He was close enough to reach into the boat, but he perched there on the rope ladder for a moment, watching and waiting.

Anna knew she was doomed.

"C'mon, Anna, stand up." Taylor brandished the gun at her.

Suddenly, the man kicked the weapon out of Taylor's hand.

The gun flew into the water.

Before Anna knew what was happening, the man jumped down into the boat, almost capsizing it. Bracing herself, Anna clung to the dinghy's sides as water splashed all around them.

Taylor was screaming. "What are you doing? You stupid . . ."

Everything happened so fast. The boat violently rocked back and forth as the man stood between the two of them, with his back to Anna. He grabbed a weight from the boat's floor and then hauled back and hit Taylor in the face with it.

Anna heard a crack.

Taylor let out a frail gasp and collapsed.

The man in the ski mask was breathing hard as he stood over Taylor's crumpled form. Anna could see she was still alive—but completely incapacitated. Her face was bleeding. It looked like her jaw was broken.

He stood there for another few moments until the boat stopped teetering.

All Anna could think was that she'd been right about Taylor's friend CJ. He'd turned on her before they'd even finished their work together tonight.

She sat there, too stunned to move. She watched him push Taylor's near-lifeless body over to one side. Taylor let out a sickly groan.

Then he turned and sat down across from Anna.

She waited for him to start talking in that raspy singsong voice of his—to tell her that it was time for her to jump into the water.

Instead, he let out a sigh. "Hey, Anna Banana . . ."

That was when she noticed his neck tattoo.

Astonished, she watched as Stu pulled the ski mask from his head.

"I'm sorry I took so damn long," he said, still breathing hard. "I wasn't sure what the hell was going on. I was watching your place tonight and recognized the sports cruiser—just like Terry Adalist's boat back on Bainbridge. I saw it drifting near your place for a while. So— I figured, hell, I better go check this out . . ." Stu gasped for air. His face was flushed—and shiny with sweat. He looked so exhausted. "Anyway, I swam over and climbed aboard. Only this guy with a knife wasn't too welcoming . . ." Stu laughed and then coughed until he finally caught his breath again. "I knew he was either crazy or up to no good, because, here it is, a beautiful summer night, and he's wearing a ski mask."

Anna struggled to untie the weighted jump rope around her waist. "Stu, I can't believe you came back."

"I had to," he said, chuckling weakly. "I couldn't leave you thinking I was such a shit. And I was . . . I'm so sorry . . ." He closed his eyes for a second. It seemed like he was in pain. He did that nervous tic of his. Anna saw his dimples as he winced and scratched his head. "I've created a hell of a mess for you, Anna. That guy, I managed to take his knife away . . . but, I . . . I ended up using it on him. I—I stabbed him in the chest. The guy's dead."

Stu looked down toward his waist and pulled up the black T-shirt to reveal a bleeding slash across his stomach. "But he—he took a little chunk out of me first."

Anna gasped. "Oh my God, Stu."

He nodded. "Yeah, I know. I don't feel so hot."

"Hold on, Stu," she said. Unsteadily, Anna got to her feet. She tugged at the last knot to the weight-laden rope around her waist. It fell to the floor of the boat with a loud thump. Then she turned and switched on the outboard motor. She gave the cord a yank, and then another. The engine roared.

As the boat accelerated, Anna fell back onto the bench. She grabbed hold of the tiller and began to direct the boat back toward her dock. "Do you have a phone?" she anxiously called over the droning motor. "Stu? If you don't have a phone, pat her down to see if she has one."

Her big brother sat across from her as if in a stupor. He didn't seem to hear her.

"Stu, see if she has a phone and call 911! Tell them we need an ambulance to meet us at the dock. Stu . . ."

He started to sway and then flopped back against Taylor's listless body.

Anna let go of the tiller to reach for her brother. But the boat started to career out of control. All she could do was pull the bottom of his T-shirt over the crimson slash across his stomach. She figured the material might slow the bleeding a bit. She grabbed the tiller again and plopped back onto the bench. "Hang in there, Stu!" she called out breathlessly.

Water sprayed on either side of the boat as they sped toward her dock. Anna didn't know where else to go. She didn't know how long it would take to find a phone and call for help. She kept thinking her brother might bleed to death before she got ahold of the police.

She started crying. "Stu, don't give up on me, please!"

Still sprawled on top of Taylor, her brother was unresponsive. His eyes were open, but the color had drained from his face.

Anna reached over and held on to his leg.

They were approaching the floating homes and houseboats now. In the distance, she could see her dock. Someone had turned on the light to her back deck.

As the boat sped closer, Anna spotted a uniformed policeman on the little deck. Another policeman ran up the dock. He was waving at them and talking into his shoulder mic. The flashing red lights of patrol cars shone through the trees along the water's edge.

Someone had already called the police for her.

EPILOGUE

Russ had a private room at Swedish Hospital. Because of his many friends, associates, and patients—and all the people who thought he'd died—the room was full of cards, flowers, blooming plants, and balloons. Right now, the room was also full of interns and a couple of residents, reviewing Russ's post-op progress.

Anna had told Russ that she'd be by at three-thirty, and she was early. So she stood outside the room and waited for them to finish up. She already knew all about Russ's injuries, which included ruptures to his spleen and diaphragm, a punctured lung, three broken ribs, two fractured ribs, a broken arm, a broken leg, a dislocated shoulder, several sprains and bruises, and multiple cuts and lacerations that required a total of fifty-seven stitches. None of the stitches were on his handsome face, which had escaped injury. His two surgeries had been quite successful, and his recovery, so far, was exemplary. He'd just been moved out of the ICU the day before.

Anna listened to them talking in the next room. As they discussed Russ's case, the residents seemed to congratulate themselves. Russ was joking with them, charming everyone in the room.

Everyone loved him now that he'd come back from the dead an innocent man.

Anna loved him, too—for thinking of her while he'd been bleeding and broken on the side of Route 72 in Edmonds. He'd told the paramedics who arrived upon the scene to send the police to her address and make sure she was okay. For that, Anna would always be grateful.

She'd visited him every day. Anna had been there at the hospital while he'd undergone his surgeries. It was strange in the waiting room, meeting some of his other friends and associates for the first time. All of them had been cordial to her, but she'd still felt like the other woman, as if she'd been brazen just for showing up.

For the first couple of days of Russ's hospitalization, Anna had been met by the press as she'd come and gone from her houseboat and from Swedish Hospital. They'd asked her for updates on Russ's medical condition. To Anna, that had felt strange, too, because she wasn't his wife. Up until recently, she wasn't even supposed to know him. She'd been so accustomed to keeping their relationship a secret, that now, talking about him in public seemed completely reckless and shameful.

It was silly, and shouldn't have mattered, but Anna felt like everyone was judging her. Of course, it was no help that Courtney was still Saint Courtney as far as the media and general public were concerned. Courtney's book sales continued to soar. *Entertainment Weekly* had just published a profile on her—with a half-page sidebar speculating about which teenage superstars would be cast in the movie version of *The Defective Squad*. Courtney's publisher had just announced that a percentage of her book sale profits would be donated to the American Society for Deaf Children, a decision Courtney had nothing to do with, but which still made her seem beyond reproach.

Even Taylor Hofstad's confession—with a detailed account of the murder and its aftermath—had portrayed Courtney as an exceptional human being. According to Taylor, it had all been an accident, a misunderstanding, a "temporary insanity thing." Courtney never would have said those cruel things had she not been drunk. They'd been the best of friends.

Taylor had dictated her confession solely in sign language. Her broken jaw had been wired shut, and she wouldn't be able to talk for the next six weeks. She was currently residing in the King County jail infirmary, where she was under twenty-four-hour suicide watch.

Taylor's friend, Christian Jared (CJ) Holmes, had died from a stab wound to the chest while aboard a secondhand Monterey sports cruiser, which Taylor had purchased for him earlier in the year. If Sally Justice had had her daughter's friend investigated, she would have discovered that CJ had a list of prior offenses that included attempted criminal assault, aggravated kidnapping, reckless endangerment, burglary, and forgery. He'd also had several aliases, including the name Bud.

Fans of Sally Justice had been settling for *The Best of Sally Justice* on the 24/7 News Network for the last four nights. Anna wondered if Sally would retire or return to her show with its usual format. It seemed a bit incongruous for the mother of a confessed murderer to carry on as the beacon of righteousness five nights a week.

Sally hadn't made a public statement since the weekend debacle. She'd avoided the press, who had focused their unwanted attention on her more than they had on Russ and Anna. The number of reporters by Anna's dock gate and outside the entrance to Swedish Hospital had steadily diminished in the last few days. When Anna had left her place a half hour ago, there hadn't been a reporter in sight.

With her back against the wall of the hospital corridor, Anna tried to make herself invisible to the doctors filing out of Russ's room. She overheard two stragglers among the group, a couple of residents, talking as they headed down the hallway.

"Talk about a hunk," the redhead murmured. "I wouldn't mind helping him feel better."

"Yeah, well, wait in line behind several nurses and orderlies," her tall male cohort replied. "Besides, haven't you been paying attention to the news? He's been screwing that reporter from KIXI-TV for about a year now."

"You're kidding," she said, and then laughed. "Didn't his wife just get murdered or something?"

They continued down the hallway, and Anna couldn't hear them anymore.

She put on a smile and stepped into Russ's room.

In a hospital gown, Russ sat in bed with a cast on his arm and his bandaged leg elevated. He looked better than he had yesterday, even healthier and handsomer. One of those nurses or orderlies who had a crush on him must have washed his hair and given him a crisp, new gown this morning. He'd just picked up the latest Erik Larson book from his nightstand, but set it down again when he saw Anna. "Hey, you," he said, smiling.

She kissed him on the lips. "Hey, how are you feeling?"

"They're weaning me off the painkillers, so I'm sore, but a little less loopy. I see a nap in my future—probably within the hour."

"Well, I won't stay long," Anna said. She'd been ready to pull the chair over to his bedside, but now decided against it.

"That wasn't a hint or anything, babe," Russ said. He reached out and took her hand. "I've been looking forward to seeing you all day. I even got freshened up for you."

Anna let go of his hand to run her fingers through his hair. "Yeah, looks like someone washed your hair for you."

"Jesse. He used dry shampoo, which is basically like baby powder that he sprinkled in and brushed out. I've been dry-cleaned. How are you holding up?"

"I'm doing okay," she said, not very convincingly. "Have you had any other visitors today?"

"Heather Barclay was here just before the doctors came in for rounds."

"How come I don't know that name?" Anna asked.

"She's the woman who hit me with her car. She's about twenty-five, very pretty, and sweet. She was really nervous about meeting me, and all apologies. I thanked her for calling the ambulance and sticking around."

"Twenty-five, pretty, and sweet," Anna repeated, cracking a tiny smile. "If you two got married, think of the story you could tell people about how you met."

Russ grinned, but narrowed his eyes at her. "That's a weird thing to say."

"Yeah, I guess so." She shrugged. "I'm sorry, I was just kidding. Was she your only visitor?"

"No, Cliff came by this morning. He was singing your praises, by the way."

Anna worked up a smile. Cliff McKenna was one of the doctors at Russ's clinic. Anna had heard Russ talk about him for over a year. But she hadn't actually met Cliff until just a couple of days ago here in the hospital.

"He's a big fan of your news stories," Russ said. "He was talking about how great it was to meet you."

Anna sighed. "You don't have to say that, Russ."

"But it's the truth. I don't understand." He took hold of her hand again and gave her a look of concern. "What's wrong, honey? I noticed it yesterday, too. You've been acting like a stranger."

She shrugged again. "I feel like one."

"Well, what is it? Did one of my friends say anything to upset you?"

She shook her head. "No, they've all been perfectly nice."

"Listen," he said, squeezing her hand. "We're going to get over this hump, you know. We both just need some recovery time. I feel bad that I can't be there for you right now. But once I get out of this hospital bed and get my life back in order, I can focus more on you."

"The thing of it is, Russ, I'm not sure I want that," she heard herself say.

He carefully took his hand away.

"It sounds like—after more than a year—you're finally ready to fit me into a slot in your life."

He shook his head. "That's not what I meant. If it sounded that way, I'm sorry."

"I'm sorry, too, Russ. During the past two weeks, something that should have been painfully obvious to me for a long time finally hit me. If you really loved me, you would've left Courtney a long time ago."

"You never asked me to."

"I was afraid to ask. And I shouldn't have had to ask. You know, my friend George, he hasn't even kissed me. But he and his wife broke up because of me."

"I thought she left him, not the other way around."

Anna nodded. "Yeah, she left him because of me—to hear her tell it. The point I'm trying to make is that you weren't willing to change your life around for me. And I kind of feel like you still aren't willing to change. It's like you're going to get out of here, get on with your life, and the only difference is that I'll have replaced Courtney."

"No, the difference is you and I love each other," he pointed out.

"Yeah, but it's out of kilter. I made a lot of concessions for you. I was willing to give up a lot. I don't think you were ready to do that for me."

"I'm sorry," he murmured. "Are we breaking up?"

"Well, we kind of broke up on the phone about two weeks ago—before you died. Remember?"

He let out a stunned little laugh. "Yeah, I guess. That one was on me, wasn't it?"

Nodding, Anna placed her hand on the side rail to his hospital bed. "Do you hate me for doing this to you now? I know my timing seems terrible."

"You've obviously been thinking about this for a while," he said. "Why have you been coming here every day when, all along, in the back of your mind you must have thought . . ." He trailed off. Then he sighed and shook his head.

"I've come here every day because I care about you, stupid," she said. "I still care."

He turned and gazed out the window for a moment.

When he finally looked at her again, he had tears in his eyes.

Russ smiled reluctantly and rested his hand on top of hers. He didn't say anything.

Anna was grateful for that.

There was nothing he could have said.

On her way back from the hospital, Anna drove through Capitol Hill. She slowed down as she approached an old three-story brick apartment building on the corner behind the Harvard Market. Until three days ago, she'd never even noticed the place.

But on Tuesday morning, she'd gotten a call from a woman named Mackenzie who lived there. "Your brother, Stuart, has been staying with me off and on for the last few days, and some of his stuff is here," Mackenzie had explained. "Do you want it?"

Anna had driven there that afternoon. Though the building looked like a beautiful old classic from the outside, the inside was decayed and ratty. Mackenzie, a blonde in her late twenties, had looked rather the worse for wear herself. Anna guessed that the young woman and Stu must have had drugs in common—among other things.

Mackenzie had given Anna two paper bags full of

stuff—mostly clothes. But there was also a large, frayed manila envelope, which held old newspaper and magazine clippings about Anna—from the time she'd started doing stories for the TV station in Spokane up through a photo of her at a charity auction in *Seattle Met* magazine two months ago. He'd also held on to that awful grade-school graduation photo of her with bad hair and braces.

Anna had given Mackenzie a hundred dollars for her troubles. The young woman had counted the bills in front of her and looked slightly disappointed it wasn't more.

When she'd gotten home, Anna had found some pawn tickets in the pocket of a pair of jeans. On Wednesday, she'd tracked down the pawn shop. Two ticketed items had sold in the meantime. But for $600, she'd been able to buy back nearly all of the family heirlooms Stu had hocked.

It was strange to pass by that old brick apartment building now. The place suddenly meant something to her, because Stu had stayed there briefly.

He'd died in the ambulance on the way to the hospital.

Yesterday, Anna had purchased a burial plot for him— beside their mother's grave in Port Blakely Cemetery on Bainbridge Island. Anna knew Stu wouldn't have cared where he was buried, but their mom would have wanted him home again.

Anna had a good cry in the car on the way home.

While walking from the carport to her dock, she decided she'd drown her sorrows tonight with *Roman Holiday* on Prime and a pizza and salad from Pagliacci.

She turned down the pathway toward her dock and

found George waiting there by the gate with a bouquet of mixed flowers. "Don't you just hate people who drop by without any advance word whatsoever?" he asked.

Anna laughed. "Not when the person is you." She wanted to hug him but, instead, just patted him on the arm. "Have you been waiting long?"

"Not very," he said. "Listen, I have good news. They want you back at work."

She glanced at the flowers. "Oh, are those from them?"

"No, they're from me, you silly goose. I've missed you. I feel bad that we haven't seen each other these last few days."

"I've missed you, too, George," she said. "I really have."

"Like I told you on the phone, I'm really sorry about your brother."

"Thanks," Anna murmured. She unlocked the gate and took the flowers from him. "Would you like to come in?"

He nodded and smiled. Then they started walking down the dock together. The sun was shining, and the lake buzzed with activity. Several boats were out on the water. Kids screamed and laughed on a neighboring pier.

George bumped his shoulder against hers. "Hey, did you hear that Sally Justice announced her retirement today?"

"You're kidding," Anna said, surprised

"Nope, no more new shows. You'd think she'd go before the cameras just one more time to apologize to you and the good doctor for all the pain she's inflicted on you guys. But I guess that's expecting too much from her. People don't change."

"Some people can," Anna said. "That goes for Sally, too. Maybe her retiring is apology enough."

"So, are you coming back to the station?" George asked. "I want to start working with you again."

"I don't know, George. Do you think it would be too much for us to be working together and dating at the same time?"

He stopped abruptly. "Are you serious? Do you really want to give it a try? You're not worried we might screw up our friendship or some such bullshit?"

"Yes, I'm serious," Anna said.

"What about the good doctor?"

"He'll be okay. He has a line of interns, nurses, and orderlies just waiting to help him feel better."

"So you guys broke up?"

She nodded and started walking again. "About forty-five minutes ago. It was very amicable."

"Yeah, well, there's always time for bitterness and regret later. Are you sure it's over?"

Anna laughed and nodded. "Positive."

"So, am I going to be your rebound guy? Because I'm fine with that."

"We can wait awhile, if you want." She stopped at her front door.

He shook his head. "No, I don't want to wait. I've waited too long already."

She kissed him on the cheek and then handed him the flowers so that she could unlock the door.

"I can't believe you've finally come around, Anna Malone," he said with a triumphant smile.

She opened her door. "Like I said, George, some people can change."